DANGER IN A KISS

She touched the corner of his mouth with her tongue, wanting more than this simple taste of him. He opened to her.

The darkness of need set her heart pounding and her blood thrumming in a hot stream. His hand cupped the side of her knee, scorched her with so small a gesture. If they were ever naked, the conflagration would sear them both.

Something held her back, kept her teetering on the rim, but not falling over into that abyss.

That electricity wrapping them, soldering a molten connection between them. The power within him, power she'd felt before, but never so immense. Such a dark flame.

She tensed, and abruptly he pulled back. They stared at each other, drawing in gulps of air.

"The cops are nearly here," he said, without looking at the street.

She nodded, and silently they shifted, facing the street and the black-and-white pulling into the parking lot.

"You're powerful, Ram," she said in a low voice. "That kind of power changes things. Changes people. It's dangerous."

Other books by Kathleen Nance:

JIGSAW
DAY OF FIRE
SPELLBOUND
ENCHANTMENT
THE SEEKER
THE WARRIOR
THE TRICKSTER
PARADISE (Anthology)
MORE THAN MAGIC
THE MAGIC OF CHRISTMAS (Anthology)
WISHES COME TRUE
CELEBRATIONS

KATHLEEN NANCE

PHOENIX UNRISEN

LOVE SPELL NEW YORK CITY

*This book is dedicated to the people of New Orleans,
a city of my heart.*

*With many thanks to Sue and Val and Julie.
Your support is incalculable and much treasured.*

And, thanks, Val, for letting me co-opt your name.

LOVE SPELL®

October 2007

Published by

Dorchester Publishing Co., Inc.
200 Madison Avenue
New York, NY 10016

ISBN-10: 0-505-52703-0
ISBN-13: 978-0-505-52703-5

The name "Love Spell" and its logo are trademarks of Dorchester
Publishing Co., Inc.

Printed in the United States of America.

Visit us on the web at www.dorchesterpub.com.

A NOTE FROM THE AUTHOR:

When I first wrote the proposal for this book, the hurricane season of 2005 was still an unrealized future. Then, shortly before the book sold, came the devastating reality of Katrina. I questioned what to do with a book that could be set nowhere else but New Orleans. Eventually, I chose to set the story a short time in the future and to speculate what will be changed forever and what will endure. And to believe in the city's resilient spirit.

PHOENIX UNRISEN

Chapter One

Face down a crazed hermit with a shotgun? No problem. Sneak in—and safely out—of a satanic cult ritual? Been there, took the video. Get wrapped in a voodoo priestess's boa constrictor? Loved the feel.

Natalie Severin thrived on her work's strange challenges. Except one. Foggy nights. For sheer terror, nothing struck as raw a nerve as fog.

Simply put, Natalie hated fog. The loathing had been birthed when she was six and locked out of her foster home on a foggy night. It solidified when her twin routinely scared the crap out of her with his cower-beneath-the-covers tales. The way he spun it, fog always concealed something nasty. Fog meant the hunger of a heat-sucking alien or the looming face of a disembodied demon.

New Orleans fog was the worst. Born of the stifling humidity, condensed by the dark waters that entrapped the city, Big Easy fog was a clammy touch on sweaty skin and a distorting silent veil that reeked of rotting vegetation.

So, why was it always a foggy night when her editor sent her on one of these crackbrained stories? Check it out, Natalie. Lights in the bayou outside the city? Could be an alien infestation.

This world contained a lot of weirdness, but she'd never found a lick of evidence that any of it was caused by aliens.

She hitched her hobo bag more firmly across her sweat-soaked shoulder. The only things infesting this muck were underage dopers, gators, and swamp gas. She slapped at her bare neck. And mosquitoes.

Thick fog deadened each footfall as the bald spot of a parking lot vanished behind her and she picked her way deeper into the bayou. Tree trunks and saplings surrounded the narrow path in a dense, wet forest, while vines and hanging moss trapped her in the damp vapor. One false step and she'd be knee-deep—or worse—in the black, stagnant waters.

Mist eddied about her boots, covering her ill-defined route. Disoriented, she stopped.

Dampness sucked at her. She tucked a wayward strand of her red hair under her Saints cap and then un- did the silk scarf knotted at her waist. Draped over her neck, it offered a thin protection against the ravenous mosquitoes. Pulling her black T-shirt away from her sticky body, she fanned her belly with the hem. Where was her path?

The capricious fog shifted, and a few yards ahead, she spied her target—the cypress tree split by lightning. Ben- nie had said he'd meet her there ASAP, lead her to where the lights were moving. She closed the gap, then, risking the light, she hit the Indiglo button on her watch. 11:02 P.M. Where was Bennie? He said he'd be waiting.

She glanced around, but the infernal fog played its deceptive games, smudging gnarled cypress trees to eerie shadows, hiding movement with its own undulations. Her breath rasped against her teeth, too harsh for the ephemeral, vaporous night. She pressed her lips together, trying to swallow her irrational fear.

Sweat gathered along her spine as she waited beside the damaged tree. There were other routes—waterways accessible by pirogue, treacherous paths revealed only to those who knew the swampy lands. She was not one of those people. Her forte was the streets, not here. She had to wait for Bennie.

To be honest, she wasn't even sure she could find her way back to the parking lot. Anxiety crawled up her spine.

Too quiet. Not even the normal sounds of night insects and nocturnal predators, more at home than man in the undomesticated wilds. Beyond the faint drip of fog condensing on leaves and the pulse of blood in her ears, only silence existed, as confining as a casket.

White tendrils of mist wrapped her like frayed tendons. She shifted her feet, trying to break up the hated fog. Alternately concealing, then revealing as it curled along the bayou, it was a lie, a promise of beauty that hid evil.

She thought of the foggy night she'd found her estranged husband's incinerated remains.

Something cold brushed her arm. She spun, heart knocking against her ribs, and a bone-white hand slid from the fog. Out of her nightmares, it reached for her.

A yelp escaped her control. She flinched, and then shook her head to erase her momentary weakness. The hand was not a disembodied demon. It was attached to a moving shadow, physical enough to stir eddies of fog.

She braced her hand on the cypress, settling back into sweaty-palm edginess, while the shadow solidified into a skinny body. A man. When cavernous cheeks and greedy eyes formed on the ashy face, she let out a breath.

"Bennie! I was beginning to think you'd stood me up."

"Keep your voice down. I saw something." His nasal tones grated on her.

"The source of the lights?"

"Nope. A man, p'haps, but he weren't sticking around long enough for me to be sure."

Her terror of the fog was buried beneath the scent of a story. "You gonna take me to those lights?"

He glanced around, his hands in his pockets jingling coins.

"Backing out?" she challenged.

"You got the money?"

She pulled an envelope from her hobo bag and handed it to him. He took a quick look inside before shoving it in his back pocket. After another furtive glance around, he motioned for her to follow. "No talking."

Natalie followed. As they picked their way across the sodden ground, she was glad she'd worn boots and jeans despite the heat. Wet branches scraped against her denim-clad legs, and she gave a few more useless swats against the mosquito horde.

Just about the time she was beginning to think Bennie was as lost as she was, he drew up and motioned her to stop. He turned and laid a finger to his lips, an emphatic gesture for her to be quiet. She slid closer, her nose wrinkling as Bennie's rancid odor reached her nostrils. Rotting vegetation was a perfume compared to him.

She peered forward, and then bit back a muffled curse. Dratted fog covered too much. She edged closer to the tiny clearing formed where a couple of trees had fallen.

From the clearing, a beam of white light, strong enough to pierce the fog, blinked twice. Her heart battered against her ribs. Not E.T.'s ship—that was a flashlight. If there were monsters out tonight, they were the human kind.

As if waiting for that signal, the fog parted, at last giving her a clear view.

Two skinheads waited, giggling and sneering at something by their feet, and paying no attention to their surroundings, thank you, Jesus. Dawglip and Kracker were their street names. If those two sorry pieces of humanity were here, their headman, AX, couldn't be far away, and AX was the worst of a real bad bunch.

No fear of the unknown here. The sour taste on her tongue was the fear of the known. The fear of soulless cruelty.

Her fingers tightened around her bag strap, and before the punks saw her, she shifted further behind a tree. Not aliens, not ghosts, not demons. This crew was vicious, crude, and undisciplined, and they didn't give a donkey's ass about the supernatural. If AX was involved, then she was looking at something fricking illegal.

Hoohah, but she had story here! Excitement bubbled like seltzer. Nothing supernatural, but still something real and potent.

What exactly were the skinheads waiting for? She strained forward, trying to see more. Chances were AX wasn't the brains of whatever was going on. A trickle of breeze moved the fog, and she saw something else—poster-storage–sized tubes stacked at the edge of the black water, where an airboat hulked.

Weird containers for drugs.

A shadow on the far side of the clearing caught her eye. A man, gliding between the cypresses as easily as the fog. She caught enough of a glimpse to identify him before he disappeared again into the night.

Ramses Montgomery? He was a veterinarian, not a reporter or a cop. Hell and damnation, what was he doing here? And dressed in all black like her—for protection and stealth.

As though Ram ever went about unnoticed—

Dawglip and Kracker excepted. Even the deceptive fog hadn't blurred that hard, masculine body or softened the blackness of his hair. She caught another glimpse of him as he angled past a patch of fog. Nor did the stifling air blunt his crackling aura of determination. Suddenly her skin felt too tight to contain the rapid flush of blood.

He was one finely put-together man, a fact recognized by all of her double-X chromosomes.

Not that she planned on doing anything about it. Her skimpy supply of cautious instincts warned her to stay far away from Ram Montgomery.

For a lot of reasons.

"People shouldn't oughta treat a dog like that," Bennie muttered, drawing her attention back. "Even a stray."

The skinheads shifted, and Natalie saw what Bennie meant. Her stomach churned on the pizza she'd had for dinner, burning her throat with cheesy acid.

A dog was tied in place by a ragged rope. A street mutt of no determinable parentage, it stood its ground against the human beasts tossing sticks at it and occasionally striking out with a boot. The beleaguered dog snarled and snapped at its tormentors, but the blood matting the fur, the mangled ear, the heaving chest told a different tale. The dog was losing the fight.

Natalie lunged forward, furious.

Bennie hauled her back, his scrawny arm stronger than she would have thought. His fingers bit into her cheeks, holding her head still, while his other arm snaked around her shoulders. His knife tip pierced the silk scarf at her throat.

She stilled, even as she saw Ram appear at the far side of the clearing.

"I took a risk bringing you," Bennie hissed. "You wanted to know what caused those lights. Now you do. You ain't gonna finger me. We'll stand here real quiet-like, watching, until they leave. Montgomery's on his own. His funeral."

One veterinarian against two amoral toughs? With AX likely joining them real soon? Not favorable odds for the dog's rescue. Or Mongomery's health. She might have some personal issues with Ram Montgomery, but he didn't deserve to be skewered.

She waited for Bennie's knife to waver.

Ram thrust his body between the skinheads and the dog. Kracker let fly with another sharp stick and hit Ram on the cheek. A dark, thin line welled up. Blood.

She flinched in sympathy, her cheek stinging. Ram didn't acknowledge the hit.

The dog pressed its head against Ram's jeans-clad leg, instinctively turning to the human's protection. With his eyes on the punk duo, Ram reached down and, avoiding the injured ear, scratched the dog's head. *Hang on, pal.* She could almost hear the vet's reassurance.

"Leave the dog alone," he commanded, his voice a low rumble of anger.

Somehow, she didn't think the two would heed the warning. She waited, sweat dripping between her breasts, and drew in a breath of thick, hot air. As he watched the drama unfold, Bennie's knife tip relaxed from her throat. Slowly, she cupped her hands together, then slid them up her chest, shifting energy, drawing power into her arms and legs.

Ram's glance flicked toward her. Had he seen her? His cheek twitched, the line of blood shifting its slow trickle. "Go," he said.

Was he talking to her or the skinheads?

"Looks to me like there's two of us and one of you," sneered Dawglip.

"Take your boat. Leave the dog. And your merchandise."

Dawglip jerked his head to his pal, Kracker. "Bonus tonight. Someone's gonna get hurt."

"Unfortunately," Ram agreed. He gave the dog another pat, and then straightened.

Her heart thumped against her ribs, an echo to the dog's tail against the tangled weeds. Ever so slightly, she tilted back against Bennie, holding her breath against the stench, and put her throat further from his blade. Her toes dug deep in her boots.

Ram gave a nearly imperceptible shake of his head. Though he didn't look at her, something deep in her gut told her he'd seen her and knew what she was about. He was telling her to stay put.

Arrogant, macho—

Ram struck in an unreal blur, so fast she couldn't see the motion. Only heard the results. The thud of flesh. The crunch of bone. The curses. The raw scream.

She'd barely blinked and the moment had passed.

Kracker cradled his arm. "My hand!"

"That's for the paw." Ram stepped back, breathing controlled, untouched except for the blood on his cheek. Masculine power, leashed, but ready. Retribution in the flesh. He threw their confiscated knives— how in the name of sanity had he gotten those?—into the water, saying to Dawglip, who was moaning and holding the side of his head. "That's for the ear. Go, and don't make me repeat myself."

Dawglip and Kracker scrambled away, slipping on the fog-damp weeds and tripping on knobs of cypress knees.

Behind her, Bennie mumbled a fervent prayer.

Tension knotted in Natalie's stomach. Okay, maybe arrogant and macho were justified adjectives, but that didn't answer the break-all-barriers question: How the *hell* had he done that? Maybe it was a martial arts technique she'd never seen—and she'd studied several—but that wasn't what electrified the hairs at the back of her neck. Even the ex-SEAL who'd taught her last women's self-defense class hadn't moved that fast. Nobody had those kind of reflexes.

Nobody, apparently, except a Big Easy veterinarian.

Reporter's instincts kicked into overload, throwing each leaf, each drip of water, each labored breath into stark relief. She had uncovered something strange here, the tip of a very odd iceberg.

Despite the excitement, her mouth puckered around a taste of queasiness. A jumble of fears—the fog, the skinheads—snuck in like maggots in an abandoned pantry, sly and malodorous.

She must have been tricked by the deceptive fog.

Time to start doing what she did best—prying.

First things first—the dog, the knife at her throat, the—oh effing hell! Natalie's jaw froze. AX slid between the trees, gun cradled in his hand. His cronies, courage revived, circled to rejoin him. Ram, crouched beside the injured dog, his hands beginning an expert evalua-tion, was paying them no mind. He'd no notion of the stalking danger.

Bennie leaned over and breathed in her ear. "Move out quietly." His grasp on her relaxed.

Natalie gripped her hands together, tight, and thrust upward and outward, breaking his hold, shoving the knife away from her throat. She jabbed her elbow back, straight into Bennie's abs. Letting her go, he staggered back with a gasped "oof."

"Ram! To your left!" she shouted, sprinting forward.

AX spun toward her voice. She swerved; fortunately, his shot missed.

She'd given Ram the seconds he needed. In his hands, a loose branch became a missile. Fired straight at AX's gun hand.

AX cursed as the weapon spun from his grasp.

Natalie lunged forward and scrambled up with the gun before AX could reclaim it.

Dimly she heard Bennie mutter, "This ain't no good," as he faded away. Like she'd figured, Bennie was into self-preservation.

"Stop!" She trained the gun on AX, arresting his dive. Kracker and Dawglip edged back away.

AX was surprisingly handsome, if you were into smooth, and he gave her a practiced, knowing smile. One that had likely charmed numerous women into ignoring his reputation for rough sex.

She smiled right back, keeping the weapon steady.

"That's a man's gun," he told her condescendingly. "Not something a little thing like you wants to be experimenting with."

A little thing like her? Oh, please. She was five-eight and weighed one forty. "It's a .40 caliber Glock M-27 pistol. Nine rounds in the magazine. Minus the one you shot leaves me with eight. Grip's a bit big for my hand, but I'll manage."

AX's eyes narrowed. Without taking his gaze off her, he commanded. "Kracker, Dawglip, get your sorry asses back here."

"Stay where you are." She gave her own command.

"Damn, but I hate guns," Ram muttered.

"Fortunately, I don't, and, AX, mine's aimed straight at your family jewels. Anything makes me nervous, and you'll have one second to be a man." Mentally she played back her defense class. Two hands. Steady. Oh, dear Lord, keep my hands steady. She refused to swallow against the powder mouth, preferring to keep a steady eye on the target.

Kracker whined. "Let's go, AX, before this turns worse."

AX clenched his fists, biceps flexing, and the mouth

of his croc tattoo opened wider. Apparently, though, he had survival instincts too, especially when disarmed. His head tilted; then, glance shifting between her and Ram, he slowly backed away. "C'mon, boys. This ain't over. 'Til later. I know who you are, bitch."

Running into the bayou, the trio disappeared into the fog. Natalie started forward.

"Don't." Ram's quiet command stopped her. "He's still dangerous. And I need your help."

She was going to chase through the fog after three thugs? Not. She joined Ram and sat cross-legged at the dog's side. The animal lay quiet as Ram ran expert, assessing hands across its matted fur. "How is he?"

"She." Ram braced his palms on his thighs. A muscle twitched in his cheek. "Cut up. She's lost a lot of blood. I need to get her back to my office. IV fluids. X-rays—" He bit off the list, then leaned forward and probed at a lump. The dog whined.

"What is it? What's wrong?"

"She's still bleeding." His voice cracked, but he affectionately scratched behind the dog's ear. Trying to keep the dog calm, she realized.

"Bad?"

"Real bad."

After the effort of a whine, the dog lay limp and motionless. Natalie's jaw tightened. Dammit, they would not lose this innocent dog. She yanked off her silk scarf and thrust it at him. "You can use this to bind her."

He shook his head, not looking at her. "The bleeding's internal."

"Do something!"

With a determined move, he laid one of his hands against the bump, while the other grasped a raw pink gem attached to a steel-link neck chain. "Give her a name."

"What?"

"A name!" he snapped.

"Val. For a valiant heart."

"Okay, Val, we're going to try something different." His mesmerizing voice softened until she heard nothing but an indistinct chant.

She started to protest. They had to leave, had to do something. The dog could not wait.

"I know what I'm doing, Natalie," he warned, not looking at her. "Keep petting her for me."

Her mouth snapped shut. She hated feeling helpless, but he was definitely the one in charge when it came to healing animals. Laying the gun on the ground, she petted the dog's head.

Her world narrowed to the rise and fall of Val's chest, to the silkiness of the fur beneath the crusted blood. Val's dark eyes fixed on her, as their brave light faded.

Tears ran down Natalie's cheeks with salty heat. She blinked them back, swallowing a sob. "We're losing her."

Ram's only answer was a quick shake of his head.

He was wasting time! The need to act scorched across her muscles, but something in Ram's steady confidence held her in place. Dampness seeped through her jeans, and a cypress knot jabbed her knee, but she stayed at her job. The urgency inside her found release only in petting and soothing Val.

Whatever Ram was doing had better work.

"Put one of your hands on mine," he ordered, not looking at her.

"Why?"

"Just do it!"

She complied, one hand atop his, one hand stroking Val. The dog felt clammy. The man's strong hand was hot.

Abruptly, the fog thickened, gathering and pulsing around the locus of their hands. The hairs along her arm stood on end, as though electrified. Dense with humidity, the fog condensed when it touched her fevered skin.

Droplets of water slid down her arms, dripping onto Val's fur one by one.

They were encased, bound in wet white. She could see nothing except a gleam of golden fur and a shimmer of pink at Ram's throat. The muscles of his arms and legs, the black of his shirt stretched across his chest, the untidy dark hair, the strong neck as he bent and focused.

His voice—low, mesmerizing, inexplicable in meaning, undeniable in power—drew the fog in a bandaging shroud. Without explanation, he placed Natalie's palm on the dog's withers and let go of the gem. His hands painted fog across Val's fur. With one pass, he brushed across Natalie's knuckles. Not an erotic touch, not at this moment, yet the touch was as compelling, as deep-down familiar, as the caress of a treasured lover.

Her heart raced, and her breath came in gulps. Reaction to the man? Hatred of the encompassing fog? Fear for the beaten Val? She couldn't tell; the strands intertwined, inseparable and inevitable. Only her worry over Val kept her from fleeing the power of the fog and the man.

"Just a little longer, girl," Ram murmured. "Be strong."

The encompassing fog began to undulate. Gradually it picked up speed until it flowed across Natalie's hands like a river. Hot and cold, energizing, soothing. Moisture penetrated her skin, reaching deep into sinew and cell. It washed away the cramp in her fingers and the ache in her arm.

What the hell?

A faint vibration tickled beneath her knees. A gator passing in the nearby waters? An airboat carrying hunters? The vibration grew, from the heart of the earth, shaking her teeth with its rumbling power. She clamped her jaw together, fighting, until it peaked, then faded. As if waiting for that cue, the fog broke apart, moving off them and thinning to wisps.

Val gave a weak bark and licked Natalie's hand with a

rough tongue. Natalie jerked back, the uncertain ground shifting beneath her. Her gaze fixed on Ram. He stared not at the dog, but at her, his hands outstretched. In supplication? Pain? Power?

In warning?

Thin threads of horror wrapped around her throat like a garrote. If only the simple act of silence could vanquish the impossible.

The dog got up and gave a tentative shake, then another, stronger, bark.

Val's fur was still blood-caked, but the mangled ear was straight. The lump had settled.

Gone was the specter of death.

The dog was healed.

Chapter Two

Ram rocked back on his heels, a marrow-sucking ache pounding clear to his elbows. His muscles shook as if they'd sucked up every bit of energy and left him in a hypoglycemic attack.

He'd hoped to stabilize Val for the trip to the clinic; for five years, he hadn't been able to heal an animal who'd been so badly injured. Drained, he'd been on the edge of stopping, when his power surged a quantum leap.

How? What had replenished him? Recharging needed ritual and the interaction of Mages.

Whatever, the aftereffects were damn uncomfortable. He was experiencing an incredible acuity. The swish of a mosquito roared across his eardrums. A leaf swaying from a dragonfly's takeoff set up a current of air that felt like a gale on his forearms. He heard each drip of water, smelled a thousand separate odors. The very air tasted green.

Hyperaware, some might say.

Hyperaroused, parts of him might say.

Then, so abruptly that for a second he thought he'd

gone deaf, the sensation high vanished, and he was back to normal. Still feeling the simmering energy of the bayou, but not overwhelmed.

And all of it witnessed by Natalie Severin. Rubbing his thumb against the ring on his right hand, he eyed her reaction.

"Magic," she breathed.

Her mouth puckered as though the word left a sour taste, and she speared him with a look that defied him to deny what had happened. Her scorn rubbed across his skin like rough wool. *Magic*. One word, packed with familiarity and with distaste.

So, the whispers about her dead husband—that Charles Severin had been deep into the occult when he'd died—had truth to them.

Damage control and distraction. "You don't seem surprised," he challenged.

"New Orleans New Eyes reporter here. We at NONE specialize in the stories no one else believes." She paraphrased their motto with a touch of self-mockery.

"What's your story tonight?"

"I could ask you the same thing. Or are you just out for a midnight stroll?"

What to answer? Telling her to butt out would only make her dig deeper. Reporters could be annoying as gnats—all that prying—but he knew better than to antagonize one.

She could expose him. Them.

Ram lifted his hands to his mouth, warming his fingers with his breath, for the spell had left them icy. Natalie's scent—faint, exotic, spicy—clung to his skin and lodged in his memory. He inhaled again, not for air, but for the perfume of her, taking in a shot of oxygen and a shot of arousal.

He eyed her over his fingers and hungrily drank in

the sight of her: sleek jeans and long legs and a nicely tight T-shirt. Firm lips and eyes that took in everything. She'd taken off the ugly cap, baring her shaggy, very red hair. Last time he'd seen her, she'd been a blonde. And the time before that, white as a polar bear.

One look, and there he was, fricking hard against his jeans. Another problem with Natalie, besides her nosy tenacity. A one-sided problem.

From the first moment he'd seen Natalie, her effect on him was potent. She was intriguing, disturbing, infuriating, and arousing.

He'd heard a lot about her secondhand, but met her only twice. The first time she'd been married—strictly off limits—and the second time she'd been drunk, pissed, and still mourning.

While he'd been sober, pissed, and an in-her-face ass.

Before tonight, he'd touched her only twice, only briefly, and each time experienced a jolt of red heat. Crudely put, from the first moment he'd seen her, he'd wanted to take her to bed.

His lips twisted in rueful amusement as he shook out his hands. He had about as much chance of getting that need fulfilled as he did of being nominated Hunter of the Year. Because, by the look she was spearing him with, her interest in him had nothing to do with sex.

And he couldn't risk her prying too deep into his affairs.

He flexed the last vestiges of ice from his hands. Avoided reaching for her.

Val gave a soft woof, bringing his attention back to the dog, although the need for Natalie still lingered. He felt along Val's ribs, crooning softly, laughing as she licked his cheek with her rough tongue. Gut instinct told him she was hale, but utterly weary.

Natalie was still waiting for his answer. The woman

was a good enough interviewer to know not to fill the silences with revealing babble.

So did he. Get her focused somewhere else. He got to his feet and then swayed, kicked by the spell's aftermath. A headache careened from his eyes to his skull. Fog and pain blurred his vision.

Natalie grabbed his arm, steadying him. "You okay?"

There went that jolt of heat. "Just got up too suddenly."

She looked like she didn't believe the ready explanation, but she didn't challenge him. Only gave him another of those damned speculative looks.

"I'm out here because of the tubes," he told her grimly, removing his arm from her grip, and leaving behind a brief chill.

Natalie jerked her head to look, as if she'd forgotten about them. "You know what's in them?"

"I've got my suspicions."

"Then let's open them." She hurried to the tubes. He and Val followed a bit more slowly, conserving their energy.

Kneeling beside the tubes, they pried off the ends, and then gently slid out the contents. His stomach curdled.

Birds. Just as he'd suspected. Sedated and crammed into the dark, stuffy tubes for the long voyage north. Some with breastbones broken to keep them from squawking. His fingers dug into the ground, squeezing a clump of earth.

"Parrots. Macaws." Natalie picked up a tiny one, no bigger than her palm. "What's this?"

"A heron hatchling."

Stony-faced, she rubbed a finger across the downy feathers. "Some *monster* took a baby and shoved it in one of those tubes?"

"Yes."

Her jaw clenched, and his gaze followed the ripple down her throat, settling on the small hollow at the base.

What would she taste like if he touched his tongue just there? Rage found a companion in lust.

"Are they alive?"

Alive. Her question kicked him back into the bayou. Slowly, he opened his cramped fingers, loosening the hard ball of earth. What was the matter with him tonight? His emotions were more out of control than those of a sixteen-year-old driven by spurts of testosterone.

Focus. Normally a function at which he excelled. He brushed off his hands, and then picked up the birds one by one, smoothing their feathers. So fragile, so beautiful. The acid in his gut built with each innocent creature he examined, even as training kicked in. His throat tightened around the answers. "Most of them are sedated. Two suffocated."

"Can you—"

"No." He broke her off. "I can't change death."

"I was going to ask if you could set their broken bones," she said mildly.

"Oh. I'd rather wait until I can X-ray them. Make sure the bones are set at the proper angle." Right now, he didn't have the reserve to heal a hangnail.

"Why would someone shove sedated birds into tubes? And why would they be out here?"

"Wildlife smuggling. It's a twenty-billion-a-year business, behind only drugs." He surveyed the birds again, taking refuge in knowledge. "This haul is small as far as contraband goes, but the smugglers were select." He pointed to one. "That Lear's macaw alone is worth sixty K on the black market."

"Sixty thousand for a bird?"

"There's a fad for exotic imports." His jaw set. People shouldn't choose wild pets never intended for domestication, ones they had no clue how to care for. In his clinic, he saw too many of the broken results. "It's criminal. And cruel."

"But lucrative, apparently, and New Orleans offers a prime port of entry."

"True." Even five years past Katrina, there were still unrestored neighborhoods. Places that had become havens of dilapidated buildings and abandoned cars and empty streets, where smugglers could slip their goods in without being noticed. "Odd, the three heron hatchlings aren't that rare."

"Can you take care of them at your clinic?" Natalie asked.

"I can meet their immediate medical needs, but I'll have to find someplace to house them permanently." The zoo would want the Lear's macaw and maybe a couple of the others, but what about the hatchlings? He did a lot of work with the Audubon Institute; maybe he could pull in a favor or three. He eyed the array of animals. "That's a lot to carry."

She gave him a stern look. "We're not putting them back into those tubes."

"Did I say we were? Are you parked at the boat launch?"

"Yes." She glanced around, grimacing. "If I can figure out where it is. Bennie guided me here."

"I can get you there; my car's there, too. Between us, we should be able to carry the birds."

"We could make slings. Your jacket, my scarf."

"It'll ruin the silk."

Her lips made a so-what twist.

Nodding, he stripped off his jacket, while she laid out her scarf. Gently they transferred the birds into the makeshift carriers. "Be careful; a couple of them have injured wings."

They made quick work of prepping the birds for the short trip. Natalie stopped him, however, when he was ready to leave. "I want to check out that airboat, run my flashlight around the clearing here."

"What do you hope to find?"

"Won't know until I find it. You do realize AX was ordered away?"

He frowned. "What makes you say that?"

She pointed to her ear. "He had a small microphone. Otherwise, he would have been back by now, with a bigger gun in hand."

"Why was he ordered away?"

She tilted her head. "Now that's a right smart question."

One they wouldn't answer tonight. He checked out the far side of the clearing, while she examined the boat and the closer edges. "Find anything?"

"Nope," she answered quickly, her hands in her pockets. "Let's get those birds to safety."

He and Natalie each took a sling, and then he addressed Val. "Can you walk?"

He'd carry Val if he had to, but she was a hefty load of dog. Val's answer was a slow trot away from him, then a pause as if to say, "Coming?" He and Natalie trailed Val, and he kept an eye on the dog, looking for signs of lingering injury.

"How did you heal Val?" Natalie's question came like a shot.

"Heal her? She looks fine to me."

"You trying to convince me she wasn't hurt? Pull the other one."

He didn't answer.

"Nothing more to say? Nothing along the lines of: 'Drop it, Natalie, it's not a part of your story'? With that implied 'or else' threat tacked at the end?"

He winced as she threw back his own words, spat out a few months ago. Words, it seemed, that they both remembered too clearly. Apparently she hadn't been as drunk as he'd thought.

"No threats." He was gambling, but he didn't think she'd write about his actions tonight. At least not yet, and that gave him some time to counter her.

"Why?"

"Unlike some of your coworkers, you don't do specu-
lation and innuendo."

"How'd you come to that conclusion?"

"I read your articles."

"And you won't corroborate what happened tonight."
For once, it wasn't a question.

He cocked his finger at her, indicating she'd hit the nail.

Natalie studied him a moment, deciding. A man who
practiced magic was a man of secrets. Ones he
wouldn't give up easily.

Did she really want to pursue that story again, to
delve into that murky, dangerous world? Last time she
had, she'd lost everything, and the resulting pain had
barely formed scabs.

"How did you learn about the smuggling?" she asked
instead.

Apparently that was a safer question for them both.
He didn't hesitate. "There's been a sharp increase in the
number of abandoned exotics our clinic has been
called to treat. Last month, when the police found a
cache of dead tortoises, I knew there had to be an organized ring operating."

"Tortoises are smuggled?"

"In some circles, their meat is considered a delicacy.
And sea turtle eggs are reputed aphrodisiacs because
the animals copulate for four hours."

"Why not let the police handle it?"

"Because they're more concerned with dead humans
than deceased turtles. So, I nosed around a bit."

"What did you find?"

"Exactly nothing." His ground-out disgust held a familiar ring. She'd made those same pissed-off grunts a
few times she'd hit brick walls. "Until Bennie directed
me here."

"That son of a bitch! I paid him for exclusivity!"

Ram threw her an amused look. "I probably paid better."

Her lips twisted. "Ah, what the Montgomery family power can buy."

His amusement turned to irritation. "Your blind spot's showing, Natalie. Again. Money, influence, power, can all be used wisely."

"Yeah, right. Like when your family's influence protected my last lead?"

"My sister-in-law was not involved in that sordid mess."

The scab ripped off. "Not like my husband and my twin, you mean."

"No, I didn't—" He sucked in a breath. "God, I'm sorry—"

"Don't," she ground out. "Don't apologize. Bald facts. My husband, Charles, was there. My brother, Nathaniel, has disappeared."

After all, the papers had reveled in the story, the common consensus being that said missing brother had murdered said husband.

"Have you heard from Nathaniel?"

She shook her head, not trusting her voice with the truth. That the ripped-out part of her heart still hurt like hell. That the not-knowing—if he was alive, if he was near, if he was hurt, if he was guilty—was an acid that etched each day she breathed.

"I am sorry," he repeated, more gently. "My sister disappeared once. Turned out she'd gone off with the guy she married, but until we knew that, we were frantic. She was gone only three weeks. I can't imagine months of not knowing."

Eight months since Nathaniel had disappeared and her husband was buried. She drew in a torn breath. Ram's voice had a strange, hypnotic quality, the same tone he'd crooned to calm Val, and it seemed to work, soothing the raw emotional wounds. Or maybe she was just getting better at mental Band-Aids.

"Let's just keep the past where it belongs. In the past. Okay? We've got birds and smugglers to worry about."

"Agreed."

As they walked, Natalie hugged the birds close to her chest, imagining her warmth kept their tiny hearts beating. With the thinning fog, the trip back was better than the nightmare in, but she couldn't erase the uneasy sensation that the fog still hid a watching malevolence.

Annoyed with the childhood fear, she cast a glance at Ram and Val. Thick silence hung between them, broken only by the uneasy, unidentifiable rustles of the night.

Was the jeopardy she felt walking right beside her? Much as he denied it, she knew what she had seen, and experience warned that any man with that much power was dangerous.

How did Ram fit in with this story? As a vet or as a magician?

At last, she began to recognize landmarks; the lot wasn't far from that split cypress. She released a pent-up breath she hadn't even realized she was holding.

With the resumed sound of her breathing, she realized that the background of night sounds, even the whisper of leaves, had vanished. A cold stream of air wrapped around her neck, as thin as a noose. The unnatural chill, the smothering silence, shoved a tremor down her spine.

At the edge of the tiny parking lot, Val halted, her legs piston-stiff. Her throat rumbled with a warning growl and her ears lay back against her head. The fur at her rope collar rose; the hairs on the back of Natalie's neck stood up.

"What is it, girl?" Damn the crack in her voice.

She and Ram shone their flashlights across the stygian lot. The remnants of fog and the unyielding night swallowed her light. The yellow beam of Ram's light seemed to grow brighter. Glistening against prismatic water droplets as though light molecules became diamonds, the pure beam cut through the concealing mists.

Some fresh, strange power of Ram's? Or simply a trick of the eye?

A shadow swirled across the light and a raucous caw stabbed her eardrums, coming from nowhere and from everywhere. She jerked back; her light swung a wild swath through the night. A great blue heron rose from the waters, crossed the beam, and then vanished.

Cicadas sounded again, first a tentative buzz, then a braver, louder chorus. Slowly the electrified hairs at her nape relaxed. Whatever danger was out there had left.

Or maybe it was all in her screaming imagination. Her arms quivered with the burden of the birds. Damn, she hadn't been this rattled over nothing since her brother had used a fog machine one Halloween.

"Do you know what was out there?" she asked Ram, who was still peering into the dark distance.

"No."

"Did you feel something?"

He didn't answer. Obviously the man had decided to go laconic on her. She noticed, however, that he hadn't denied the eerie incident. She swung her light back onto the lot. Two cars remained, one being her Mustang convertible with the top up, red paint leeched out by the remaining swirls of gray fog. Focusing her beam on the other car, a beater with a flat, she raised her brows at Ram.

"Yours, Montgomery?"

The look he shot her was priceless disgust. "Apparently, Bennie hot-wired my truck."

"Guess you should have paid him even more. I'll give the birds a ride back to town." She gave him a sideways grin. "You're welcome to tag along."

"Thanks."

They stowed the birds in the back seat along with Val, who took no interest in their still forms. While Ram circled to the passenger side, Natalie opened the driver's door. That chill ran back down her spine. Resting on her seat was a feather. A feather like none she'd ever seen.

She picked it up as she slid into her seat, her heart thumping against her ribs, and a faint smell wafted to her. Black licorice.

Her throat tightened around wrenching memory. Nathaniel had loved licorice. Was some sick bastard playing a trick on her?

"Ram." Her eyes met his across the width of the car, and she held up the feather. It was about six inches long, a deep purple-brown, the color of a rainy twilight, with edges of gleaming, burnished old gold. "Do you know what species has this kind of feather?"

He took the feather, leaning forward into the car light to study it, and then his glance flicked back to her. "None."

Chapter Three

Ram leaned against the headrest as they drove back into the city. At last. Quiet. The pervasive hum of connections had muted. His power thrummed with a sweet vibration when he was outdoors. As refreshing and necessary as that connection was, sometimes he needed these moments of relative isolation.

Except, he wasn't alone. Even with his eyes closed, he knew he was in Natalie's car and that she sat but an arm-stretch away. The faint scent of her rich perfume was ingrained into the sporty interior. He heard the rustle of her cotton shirt against leather and the steady whish of her warm breath. She drove fast, but with control. The car engine hummed an in-tune pitch, the ride it gave as unhesitating and smooth as Natalie's walk.

Val, in the back seat, her face stuck out the partially opened window, gave a sigh of contentment. He knew how she felt. The heated breeze from outside carried enough energy to cool where it wafted across his sweaty neck.

Ah, the pleasure of a single moment. All he lacked was a glass of twenty-year-old bourbon.

He opened his eyes to watch Natalie ruffle the short hair at the back of her head. The breeze was no match for his feverish rush as he speculated which of the hair colors she'd sported was natural—from her coloring, he'd guess blond.

Ruthlessly he ignored the heat. "Thanks for the ride to the clinic. On the Mississippi River Bridge take the Magazine Street exit—"

"I know the way," she returned.

Interesting, since she'd never been there as far as he knew. The reporter had done her homework. He sprawled in the seat, twisting a bit to watch her, his arm stretched across the seat back, his fingertips resting near her shoulder. "What's your next step?"

"I've got a few leads to follow."

"We could work together."

She gave him one of those get-the-message looks, in this case the message being not-on-your-bloody-life. "So, you'll tell me if any of your clients have brought in a shiny, new, smuggled-species pet?"

He shook his head. "I couldn't give you names."

"Working together is not sounding too probable, then."

"Doctor-patient confidentiality."

"That holds for vets?"

"It does for me."

"I can be discreet. Tactful and pleasant, my middle names."

He gave a snort. She'd been a badger with his sister-in-law, Leila. "Pleasant, my ass. I've seen you in action."

"Yes, I know," she responded, stiller than stone as she crossed the lanes of traffic to exit at Magazine Street.

Her quiet answer nipped him with a bite of guilt. Their last meeting hadn't been pretty on either side. A freshly widowed, freshly inebriated—although he hadn't realized it at first—Natalie had confronted Leila very publicly, at a Restore New Orleans benefit. The accusations the reporter had thrown were ugly: ties to the occult, hiding information Natalie needed to find her missing brother.

The devil of it was, though Leila had no part in the sinister underworld of magic Natalie was pursuing, she *was* a strong practitioner. A fact she wisely kept hidden. So, he'd stepped in to protect her secret.

Not one of his more sensitive moments. But when he'd first cupped Natalie's elbow to guide her quietly out and she'd flung him off as though scalded, he'd been stunned by the wrenching power of that rejection. So, with a mere gesture, he'd ordered Natalie evicted from the fund-raiser, adding a few choice words.

"I could have handled that with more discretion," he admitted aloud.

"Yes. 'Wallow in your paranoia in private' wasn't precisely subtle." She waited a heartbeat. "I was . . . sorry afterward. That night, I wasn't myself."

"It's Leila who deserves to hear that."

Natalie cut down one of the side streets. At this hour of the night, away from the bustle of Canal Street and the French Quarter, these streets were quiet and brooding. Only rare beams of light from a car or a closed shop cut the remnants of fog, which wisped around the hulking warehouses and scraggly trees in the best ghostly tradition of New Orleans.

"She has. I apologized to her. Later."

Surprise took a bite from his indignation. That he hadn't known. His apology, it seemed, was the belated one. "I'm sorry," he said quietly, "I shouldn't have said what I did."

"You were protecting family."

They'd reached a more populous area, one of renovation and renewal. The streets here were also hushed, but it was a genteel quiet, not the desperate silence of abandonment. Even the fog seemed thinner here, less ominous. She pulled her car into the small parking lot at his Uptown clinic. The building was darkened, the lot empty, unlike during his busy office hours.

He made a step to bridge the gap between them. "My partner saw a woman with a new leopard kitten. I'll let you know what she says about where she got it."

She threw him half a grin, accepting the offer. "Does that mean you'll call me when you know something?"

"Yeah, it does." He knew it was worthless to ask her to do the same thing, yet he couldn't deny being glad they'd stopped ignoring the blot between them. "Can you help me get the birds into the clinic?"

"Sure."

Their arms were loaded with the birds, and Natalie was closing the Mustang door with a swing of her hip, when the warning slammed his body. Ugly, sour energy tainted the darkness.

Predators. Lurking too near.

Tiny missiles cut the night, sliced through his shields as delicately as a scalpel. One second. He had one second before the needle jammed into his shoulder. With a tiny white flare, the dart exploded and released its poison into his blood.

His heart galloped as the reviving power swirling inside him lost focus and containment and spun. He was as useless as a drunk.

Natalie? Blessed saints, she'd been hit, too. She stared, wide-eyed, as a red-tipped dart dropped from her bicep.

"Run," he slurred. Couldn't risk bringing anyone else out to be hit.

The command got through. Hunching protectively over her burden, she stumbled toward the clinic, her feet tangling against each other. Ram followed. Clinging to a tendril of his power, he swung it in a whirlwind.

There were too many for a lone drugged Mage to defeat. Keep one purpose. Expand shields. Protect Natalie, Val, his patients.

The drug spread quickly. Did they have long enough to get inside?

No. His arms and legs went numb, lost the ability to support. He dropped to the concrete, his knee absorbing the blow. Had he shattered a patella? Pain ramrodded through his leg, one brief stab of reality before the drug held him immobile. His protective shields snapped back. Surrounded him thanks to endless hours of practice.

Beside him, Natalie sprawled on her back, the birds she'd carried in a heap beside her. Her face contorted as her fingers strained, curled.

She couldn't escape either. Neither could Val, shaking with muffled whimpers. He struggled to expand the power. Protect. Focus against the whirlpool of colored incoherence.

Streetlights extinguished in a series of popcorn pops, blinding him. A misty veil obscured the remaining lights of the clinic. Not fog, that had dissipated with the city's concrete heat. No this was—

Something evil. The hairs on his arm, the only pieces of him able to move, stood straight up.

Four shadows, dressed in black, detached themselves from the darkness, moving as easily as smoke. He tried to sense something—an aura, a hitch in their walk, a sound of their breath, something to latch onto, to connect to, something to identify them—but they were black holes surrounded by streaks of color. Empty space working in efficient, absolute silence.

Four of them. Or was it six? They were cloaked in obscurity.

He couldn't sense Natalie. All connections dissolved. Only a meager residual power within. His mind floated, weightless above his unfeeling body.

Dissociative psychosis. He retained enough sanity to realize he was hallucinating. Not enough strength to do anything about it.

The attackers collected the birds, and then two of them faded into the night. He followed their track as deep as he could, uselessly seeking something to grab onto. A whimper from Natalie dragged back his mind. He heard, then felt the sound and the tiny connection sparked inside him, connected him to her. Tears ran silently down her cheeks and he saw where she was staring.

Two remained. One stood over Val, a gun pointing at the dog's chest.

No! With the force of will, he slid his hand across the hard concrete, until his fingers tangled with Natalie's. That surge of heat jolted him, ignited a reserve of strength. Her fingers spasmed at the tug of invisible threads.

Fuel the shields. A headache burst against his eyes as the drug fought him. Inner blackness mushroomed.

Shove out the shields. Force all mustered power into one thin layer of protection over Val and Natalie. Just as a silenced shot pounded vibrations against his ear-drums. Just as one shadow knocked the arm of the other with a vicious swipe.

The bullet skittered to the side and lodged in a wooden fence. The second figure's angry words slammed against Ram's mind, more than his ears.

We have what we came for. The drug will be wearing off soon.

The two vanished into the night, and the insanity won.

A Mack truck had rammed her body.

An insane tailor was stitching her palm to the ground.

Rain scraped like sandpaper and smelled like dog breath.

Natalie's body, when it finally reunited with her mind, was not a pleasant place to be.

She pulled open her eyes to find Val standing over her, panting and drooling. Scowling, she flopped a hand against the animal's furry side to shove the dog away and struggled to sit.

With a peep, the insane tailor abandoned his quest. She squinted, pressing her lips together against the wracking combination of exhaustion, nausea, and cotton mouth, barely able to see the mauve ball of fluff in her hand. A heron hatchling. The only one she'd been able to save. It had been pecking at her palm.

Nausea almost won. She sprawled back onto the concrete. Don't sit up; it'll go away. Good thing she was lying down. Phase two set in, as trembling racked her until her muscles ached.

At least by the time the spell passed, her vision had gotten a shade less fuzzy. She was now alert enough to realize that Ram had scooted to her side while she convulsed in his parking lot. She pressed her cheek against the rough concrete. "Do you know what they hit us with?"

"At a guess, ketamine or a derivative."

He held out a hand. Gingerly, she took it and he hoisted her to a sitting position. She swallowed hard, not wanting to add retching to her list of reactions. Stomach and muscles held.

"So that's tripping with Special K? Definitely not my drug of choice." She picked up the hatchling and rested it in her palm, where it proceeded to pick at her watch-band. "I only saved this little fellow. Did they get your birds, too?"

"All but the dead ones."

She tilted her head, not willing to let him see the pain

that slid into her gut. "That must have been some valuable shipment."

"Apparently more than I realized." He touched her hand, a small gesture, but somehow a calming one. "How are you feeling?"

"Nauseated and body slammed, but I'm not going to toss. How about you?"

"Likewise." Grimacing, he pressed a palm against his chest, as if his heart hurt. "We need to notify the police."

"I suppose so." When neither of them moved to go inside, she pulled her cell from her bag and punched her speed dial to the nearest station. After she'd given the basics, and mentioned the Montgomery name, they promised a squad car. "Wait inside?" she asked.

"Feel free, but I'd rather stay out here."

They moved to a wrought-iron bench beside the clinic door. Val stretched at their feet, and Natalie set the hatchling amongst the bushes. "Avoiding questions or watching for the bad guys?"

"I don't think our assailants will return." He lifted one shoulder. "I like being outside. I like hot nights."

Bless her stars, but the unintended double entendre, the fact that his muscle-carved shoulder rested a hairbreadth from touching her and his radiating heat blanketed that side of her body, threw seeds to her fertile imagination. Hot nights, the touch of hotter bared flesh, the pressure of muscled arms around hers. A movie short, starring Ram in full color and passion, began to unreel.

Ruthlessly she forced the images back into the cavern of her subconscious. Distractions needed. Check voice mail. Yuck, her mouth tasted like dead tuna. While she listened, she fished out a pack of breath-freshener strips, put one in her mouth, and then soundlessly held the pack out to Ram.

"Thanks."

Nothing exciting in the voice mails. Somebody wanting permission to bird watch on her property—*sure, soon as I can ice skate in hell.* An invitation from a friend to go to the movies tomorrow. When had she last been to a movie, not including the Internet shorts she played on her phone? Last October—that B horror movie retrospective. Since then, she'd been desperately working every spare minute, taking any job NONE threw out at her to fund the search for her twin.

A text message beeped across her screen. Bennie? The message was blank, just his phone number.

Stop wasting my min, she texted back.

Info on $ trail.

Better B good.

Meet u Tu. 10p. StL cem-tary.

Mugger City? No.

Dark Phoenix Wax. Same time.

K.

"Tell him to bring my truck," Ram said drily.

"Not nice to read over a lady's shoulder." She closed the phone with a snap, and then turned to look at him. "What did you do, Ram? Protection spell? Shield? Bending bullets? Turning ammo to rubber? That attacker aimed straight at Val, and he shot."

"The other one hit his arm, spoiled his aim."

She shook her head. "I know a magic spell."

"You really think magical powers exist?" His voice held a touch of scorn. "Can you conjure up something for us to eat?"

Good acting, Ram. "I don't discount the existence of anything—excepting aliens—until I prove it false. As for me doing any conjuring . . ." She got a protein bar out of her bag and twisted it in two. She offered him the bigger half. "Here's the closest I get."

After she'd finished her two-bite portion, she continued, "Magic is a very, very real power. That sensation is
unmistakable, like a faint electric charge."

He tilted his head just a little, so that their gazes met,
and she got the impression she'd startled him. "You feel
magic?"

"Sometimes, if it directly touches me."

Ram was sitting with an easy grace on the bench, not
exactly sprawled, but with a loose-limbed command of
his space. One arm was stretched across the top of the
bench, his fingers hooked into the scrollwork, while the
other rested upon his knee. He didn't move, yet she was
aware of the tension that had seized him.

"Don't bring your magic into this, Ram," she warned.

"I won't hurt you."

"That's what Charles said. And Nathaniel." Damn,
but that hurt still tinted her voice, and Ram, natch,
picked it up.

"What did they do to you?" The hand at his knee
clenched, unclenched.

"Nothing that matters now."

"I can't promise that I won't do whatever it takes to
protect you."

"Do not feel responsible for me."

"Not an option, and not because I doubt your abilities."

"Then why—"

"This." He closed the small space between them and
captured her lips with his.

Talk about an electric charge. Energy, the confirma-
tion that she was alive, swelled inside her. Not magic,
except the sweet conjuring of desire. Oh, and it felt so
very good.

Only their lips touched, so briefly, and then he slowly
pulled away.

She could have let him go. Should have let him go.
She didn't.

Instead she leaned forward, touched her lips to his, and dove into the maelstrom swirling around the eye of the kiss.

Without lifting, he gave a small murmur of approval. His lips were firm in their command of her mouth, soft in the feel of his skin. She touched the corner of his mouth with her tongue, wanting more than this simple taste of him. He opened to her.

The darkness of need set her heart pounding and her blood thrumming in a hot stream. His hand cupped the side of her knee, scorched her with so small a gesture. If they were ever naked, the conflagration would sear them both.

Something held her back, kept her teetering on the rim, but not falling over into that abyss. Not the public bench. Not her exhaustion.

That electricity wrapping them, soldering a molten connection between them. The power within him, power she'd felt before, but never so immense. Such a dark flame.

She tensed, and abruptly he pulled back. They stared at each either, drawing in gulps of air.

"The cops are nearly here," he said, without looking at the street.

She nodded and silently they shifted, facing the street and the black-and-white pulling into the parking lot.

"You're powerful, Ram," she said in a low voice. "That kind of power changes things. Changes people. It's dangerous."

"Power can be used for good."

"Even for good, it can be abused. The margins separating good and evil are so very slight." Neither Charles nor Nathaniel had been able to resist crossing the boundary.

Chapter Four

Ram ruffled the fur on Val's nape. "You look healthy. X-ray's clear." Now that he saw her in the light and freshly washed, he could see a touch of cocker spaniel in the floppy ears and a touch of retriever in the thick fur. Most noticeable, however, were the wiriness and lean ribs of a street mutt. "You're a survivor, aren't you?"

Val gave a woof of agreement.

Marisa, one of the night shift vet techs, joined them. "We're almost full tonight, but her pen'll be ready in a few minutes, Dr. Montgomery." She scratched Val behind the ear. "With those bright eyes, you'll be adopted in no time, sweetie."

Adopted. His chest gave a little lurch. He hadn't thought much about the next step for Val, although he knew the drill well enough. He stuck his hands in the pockets of his lab coat. Val would find a home with someone special, he'd make sure of that, and she could stay here at the clinic until he was positive they'd found a good match.

Marisa gave him a sideways glance. "You feeling

okay, Dr. Montgomery? After that excitement with the police and all?"

"I'm fine. Just tired." The effects of the drug had mostly worn off while he and Natalie had talked with the police, leaving him with only a sore shoulder and the traces of a headache.

As soon as they'd made their statements and been given warnings about letting the police handle the hunt for the attackers—warnings he figured Natalie planned to ignore just as he did—Natalie had declared herself fit enough to drive. Despite his protests, she'd left. He'd watched her car disappear, then come in to examine Val.

While Marisa readied the pen, Ram checked on his other patients. Val followed close at his feet. At first he tried to shoo her away, not wanting her to disturb the other animals, but she was stubborn. Since she stayed quiet, he let her come with him.

The usual assortment of cases—some routine, some challenging, some heartbreaking—filled the clinic. The little heron hatchling Natalie had saved tonight was sleeping after a bird-chow snack. He stopped to check a kitten who'd been hit by a car. Another twelve hours of monitoring and she'd be past critical. Then, Val still with him, he went into the area for the more exotic species. Normally they had a boarder and a couple more animals receiving treatment, tops. Tonight the cages were full, and they had been for the past month. He took stock of the menagerie.

Two cockatoos imported illegally and abandoned when they were found to be sick. A three-foot iguana, discovered in the bayou by a hysterical homeowner who thought his cats were being attacked by a gator. Three tortoises with broken legs. Anger flicked in his belly as he checked their bandages and fed them a lettuce treat. He might be able to save these, with luck, but they were the only survivors of an illegal shipment of three hundred. All because someone fancied a meal of tortoise meat or the ingredients for a fake love spell.

These were the victims that had driven him into the bayou tonight, following Bennie's last-minute tip. The ones that weren't cute and cuddly; the ones police and federal agencies were stretched too thin to care about. He wasn't an investigator, he'd admitted that, but he'd thought if he could get some real evidence, he might interest Fish and Wildlife or Customs.

Unfortunately, he still had nothing concrete, but he had a contact at F&W. His report about what he'd seen might be enough to get her sniffing around. He believed in using all resources, but he couldn't simply turn everything over to F&W. Or Natalie.

Marisa poked her head into the room. "All set for Val."

He gave a low whistle for Val to follow. She trotted eagerly after him until she saw the kennel; then she drew to a full stop. She pressed against him and looked up, her eyes wide and accusing.

"Maybe if you leave, Dr. Montgomery," Marisa suggested in a low voice, "she'll settle down. She seems attached to you."

"Yes." He took a step backward, and Val gave a soulful whine. "I'll be back tomorrow," he assured the dog as he took another step.

Hollow words for his own benefit, since she wouldn't understand them.

Val planted one paw on his foot, laid her head against his thigh, and looked up, beseeching.

"Looks like a case of puppy love," cracked Marisa. She reached out to coax Val. "C'mon, girl. There's food and water and a nice, soft bed."

Val gave a low growl and shifted between his legs, her paws covering his feet.

Abruptly he made a choice. "I'll take her home with me."

"What?" Marisa's eyebrows flew up. "You don't keep pets. You told me so yourself."

"Val isn't a pet. She's—" He broke off, unable to explain to himself, much less to Marisa, how Val seemed entwined with the entire night.

"Aren't you the man who told me when I fell in love with that cat, and I quote, 'Don't take the animals home, Marisa. There are too many, and you'll get so you can't help any of them.' End quote."

He rubbed a hand against the back of his neck. "As I remember, you took the cat home anyway."

"And the next day she scratched my hand and peed on my favorite comforter."

"You still have her," he pointed out.

"She's improved." Marisa's eyes softened. "Val's a lucky dog."

He scratched the stubborn dog behind the ear, much as he had done earlier. "Maybe I'm the lucky one. C'mon." He jerked his head toward the door.

With a joyous bark, Val raced to the exit, where she stood, quivering and waiting for him to join her. He grabbed a bag of food from the shelves, and then got one of the going-off-duty techs to give them a ride home.

The tech dropped them off at the end of his one-way street. Giving a wave of thanks, Ram walked with Val to the middle of the block. His missing truck was parked at the curb in front of his Uptown shotgun house. "Good decision, Bennie," he murmured.

As soon as he stepped from the sidewalk onto the stone path to his doorstep, he felt another warning. Faint vibrations brushed his soles. The alert spell around his home, a precaution all Mages took, had been activated.

Val's low growl rumbled in her throat. A quick gesture of his hand motioned her to keep silent. The sound stopped, but her ears still lay back, and her tail twitched.

He glided forward, soundless, as much a part of the night as the humidity. The hot air eddied around him, disturbed by the dark figure lounging on his porch.

He'd recovered enough to fortify his protective shields and include Val in their cloaking. By the time he reached the first step, though, he recognized the dark skin, sculpted face, and sharp clothes of his shadowy intruder.

LaMarr Washington.

"Your aura looks like mud," LaMarr volunteered without getting up, "and rumor has it you've had a bitch of a night."

Fifty-fifty as to whether LaMarr had learned that because he was one of the Custos Magi or because he was the gossip-magnet owner of the Haven Grill, favorite hangout of every cop in the city.

"Getting smacked with ketamine has that effect." Ram leaned a hip against the porch rail.

"I told you not to pursue those smugglers."

"Old argument. I'm not going to abandon the hunt, even if they have no connection to our purpose."

LaMarr leaned forward, the streetlights finally catching the whites of his eyes. "You were one of our strongest, once. A legendary Tracker, a linchpin. You've gotten back only a fraction of that power, and if you don't focus, you'll stay there, nothing but a fireball flinger."

"No, I won't," Ram said softly. Without moving, he touched the older man's shoulder with power, sliding easily through his shields. Using precise control, he undid the clasp of one of LaMarr's gold chains. The chain fell, and Ram's hand shot out, catching the jewelry on the tip of his finger. A tiny lift, and the chain was again fastened around LaMarr's neck.

Not a dramatic or useful demonstration, but the power, though still weakened, was tangibly potent. And damn if it didn't feel good to wield it. With Natalie around, in the aftermath of the drug, he hadn't allowed himself to fully savor what this meant.

He was a Mage again.

LaMarr grabbed Ram's hand with both of his, a huge smile creasing his face. "Glory be, you're back?"

Ram returned the grin, nodding to Val. "Before I healed her tonight, that dog was near death."

"How did you do it? Without ritual or reinforcement?"

"Maybe the time was right." Ram basked in pleasure. God, he had missed his magic.

"This is wonderful news." LaMarr let go and paced the porch in excitement. "The Magi will be delighted; you've been sorely missed. Are you ready to resume your duties? There's evidence in Wales of a dragon—"

"Whoa, wait a minute. I need to make sure the surge tonight was real, permanent. I'm still drained."

"A circle to replenish, Tracker, then you can return to the Central Council."

"Don't call me that." He hadn't earned back the title. "Not yet. No, I'm staying here. I need some time. Alone."

"Don't delay too long," LaMarr warned. "You'll weaken without us. Our magic is created by human-to-human interaction."

"Not entirely true," Ram replied. He also drew power from nature, a rare talent among the Magi. Laying a hand on Val's head, he added, "I have other responsibilities to consider."

"You're keeping the dog?" LaMarr sounded aghast, before asking sarcastically, "Can I trouble you when Magic Man resurfaces or will you be going after candy-ass smugglers?"

Ram pressed his thumb against the ring on his finger, his headache flaring. He didn't need to hear this; the tenets had been hammered into him: Power isn't limitless; magic has a cost and a responsibility; you can't split your loyalties. He'd lived those words, taught those words. Until now, he'd never questioned them. "I know where my responsibilities lie. I don't need lectures."

LaMarr acknowledged this with a tilt of his head. "You've pledged an oath; that's a bond not easily broken."

"I have no intention of breaking my word. I'll be there when you need me."

As LaMarr left, Ram absently scratched behind Val's ear. His thoughts swirled around a single pivot.

Natalie.

She was an experienced investigator who could expose the smugglers. Or him. She recognized his power for what it was, and she wouldn't stop digging until she found more. He should stay far from her.

Except, she had touched him. Threads of his power, as delicate as a spiderweb, had reached for Natalie.

Maybe it was the simple connection of a man desiring a woman, no magic but the power of hormones. That definitely was a factor, but no explanation for the full surge of power he'd felt in her presence. He knew the difference between magic and lust.

The conclusion he'd come to over the past hours was inescapable. In using Natalie for the healing ritual, he'd forged a tendril of connection to her. A tendril that impossibly fueled his power to a quantum level higher.

By all knowledge and experience, that shouldn't have happened. Natalie wasn't a practitioner; she wasn't one of the Magi. In fact, she actively loathed the concept of magic. Yet undeniably, the connection had formed.

The deeper question was why? He needed to prove

that the return of his talent was not dependent upon her; that it wouldn't fade come morning and separation.

The haze of marijuana smoke smudged the bar's decor, giving an Impressionistic feel to the muraled walls. At least until you noticed the predominant themes of bones, chains, and blood. Natalie paid little attention to either decor or weed as she slid onto the barstool and motioned to the bartender.

After giving the police her statement and leaving Ram, she'd found she couldn't face the long drive home. The fog would be intense north of the lake, and she was exhausted. She'd run through several excuses before she admitted she simply didn't want to be alone until dawn.

So, she'd detoured into the French Quarter and the Dark Phoenix, a club Nathaniel had once owned. The haunt of New Orleans denizens who prowled the night, the bar would just be getting lively.

The bartender, sporting the requisite black and two arms of tattoos, spied her. He came around the end of the bar and grabbed her in a bear hug. His exuberance was at odds with his slight appearance, for the embrace lifted her from the barstool before he released her.

"Natalie, been too long."

"Phones go both ways, John."

"A poor substitute for seeing your charming face, and you know better where to find me, oh elusive one." He hesitated, and she braced herself for the inevitable question. "Have you heard from Nathaniel?"

"No. You?"

"Ditto." The exchange was an empty ritual—if either had heard a whisper, the other would be the first to know—but necessary, an acknowledgment of the sting of loss.

He looked away, wringing the towel he carried. "Have you given up? Moved on?"

The new question shot a bolt up her spine. She leaned forward, palms flat on the bar. "Never," she snarled. "I will never give up!"

"Then you've got a new lead?"

She shook her head, his eagerness an accusation. Eight months at a dead end. Eight months without a shred of progress. Eight months of rehashing each clue, revisiting each contact, trying to think of some place she hadn't looked.

All she'd come up with was a single line in a newspaper article she'd found among Nathaniel's things. A mention of a village in Nepal, birthplace to a guardian cult of magic. The line hadn't been highlighted, there was nothing to indicate that Nathaniel had taken particular note of that offhand fact.

But the desperate lived on slivers of hope, and as soon as she got enough cash, she would be on a plane to Nepal.

He leaned back and studied her. "You look like something I stepped into on Bourbon Street."

"Gee, thanks."

"Said in all affection."

"I know." John Smythe—she suspected the name was not his own—had been her brother's closest friend. "It's been a disturbing night."

"What can I do for you?"

"A drink."

"That's all?" He tilted her chin up and gave her a kiss on the lips, a kiss a shade past friendship, a kiss of easy sexuality that said "I'm here if you're in need." His heavy aftershave filled the air. When she took the kiss no further, he released her without pressure.

"That's all," she confirmed, with a minor touch of regret. There was something to be said for being held by a warm, friendly body on a night like this. For sex with no strings, just comforting release.

You might have had Ram, she taunted herself. *Yeah, but there would have been nothing of easy comfort in his explosive touch.*

"Just a drink," she finished.

John reclaimed his place behind the bar. "What are you drinking?"

"My special."

His smile erased. "Not just the cola?"

"Nope."

"Must have been a shitty night." Without further editorial, he busied himself making her drinks. "Need a place to crash? My place is closer than NONE."

"Thanks. I can be gone before you get off work, if you're bringing home entertainment."

"I did have my eye on the DJ, and I think she's looking back."

"Swinging female these days, then?"

"That's the preferred gender." He set two glasses filled with ice and cola in front of her and pointed to the one at her left hand. "This has the rum." He dug in his pocket and laid a key on the bar. "Take this; I've got a spare. You don't have to leave early. Even if Delia comes home with me."

"I appreciate this."

"Anytime." He left to handle the demands of the bar.

She pocketed the key, and stared at the two glasses. Behind her, the trance music restarted with a whining drone. The mesmerizing beat held at bay too many outside stimuli. She was wrapped in the pain of her own thoughts and memories.

Picking up the rum and Coke, she lifted it to her nose and sniffed the sweet siren alcohol. Tempted her brain cells, the ones that wanted oblivion.

Her hand trembled as muscle memory urged the glass to her mouth. Her lips touched the rim. Her tongue wet her lips, a poor substitute.

Nathaniel was her twin, with her since conception. As adults, they'd established separate lives, but for so many years, they'd only had each other. With an unknown father and a mother dead from cocaine, they'd been thrust into an indifferent foster care system at the age of four. He was her only blood. Missing Nathaniel was like missing a part of her heart. The ache never went away.

She'd tried drowning her pain once before and the temptation still lingered.

Face the demon, Natalie, and beat it. The advice from Nathaniel may have been about a video game, but it worked here, too. With an effort, she forced the glass out in a mock toast. "To finding you, Nathaniel."

She thunked the full glass on the counter, lifted the other one, and then sucked down half the glass of straight cola.

Sometimes you had to face the demon. Stare down temptation and best it. After she'd hit dead end and bounced along at rock bottom, the booze had become a false friend. Never again. But sometimes she had to test herself to remember that fact.

She finished the cola in another gulp and set it beside the untouched rum. Victory.

Seeing the empty glass, John rejoined her. "Another?"

"Please." She pushed the rum and Coke toward him. "And get rid of this."

He nodded in approval, and then brought her the requested drink. She sipped it slowly, appreciating the sweet chill, before she faced a new truth.

Ramses Montgomery was a temptation far worse—and far better—than rum.

He'd awakened something in her tonight, a sweet thrill of arousal, of life, that had been absent for too long. She'd become numb well before Charles had died, she admitted, and she hadn't chosen to face how much she had missed desire.

Well, it had slapped her upside the head tonight and demanded, "Feed me!"

Devil of it was, in addition to that slam of desire, she admired Ram, at least from afar and when he wasn't turning on her with his righteous wrath. The work he'd done with animal rescue post-Katrina, the way he'd stayed to help put the city back together, she valued that dedication.

But he was a man of magic. Much as he denied it, he wielded a strange power. She'd felt the secondary touch of magic before. First that tickle along her skin, then the electricity at her nape.

Bile burned her throat. Later, had come worse. Sweet, supportive Charles practicing on her. Nathaniel drawn deeper into the hunt for power. And Ram was stronger than either of them.

Yes, Ram used his power for good. So had Charles, mostly, until the need for more had gripped him. Even Nathaniel was headed down that path before he disappeared.

So, keep away from the fire, the temptation. Scratch *that* itch somewhere else, even if not with John. Focus on the nice normal job—well, as normal as being a freelancer for NONE allowed. Let a simple story of greed be her grail—a solid, reputation-repairing work that would open new opportunities she could mine for Nepal airline dollars.

"Speaking of stories . . ." She dug in her pockets and pulled out the two objects she'd found on the airboat. With Ram there, she hadn't had time to examine them.

The bar was too dark to see well, so she fished out her tiny penlight and shone it on them. One was a receipt she'd found stuck to the wet sides of a beer can.

She peered at the faint header. They'd bought the brews at a New Orleans liquor store on the fringes of an area still Katrina-shattered. Not a place to visit at night, at least not as a lone white female, but in the day, before the predators came out, she might get a lead on AX's doings.

The other . . . what was it? The thumbnail-size disk had a drilled hole at the top and a tiny hinge on the side. A broken-off charm? She turned it over and shone the light on the decorative side. The disk was black, maybe made of obsidian, and the silver lines glinted in contrast. Some stylized design, one that nagged with familiarity. A flame? A feather? Where had she seen it before?

Don't think, don't force it. She leaned back in her chair, sipping her cola and staring at the piece on the bar. Her head bobbed to the rhythmic beat of the music, and she hummed along with the simple tune. The drive of the music hypnotized her. Mind wandering. Sway a little, body relaxed. Let the haze work. Her gaze drifted to the bar, to the mirror, to—

Discovery hit so hard, so fast, she gasped and jerked. Stiffly, she set her soda glass on the counter before she dropped it. Sweet Jesus in heaven, she *had* seen that design before.

It was right here in front of her face. Literally. Her gaze flicked from the mirror to the disk, and then she spun around on the stool to look at the reflected scene.

Chills chased heat from her trembling hands. The design was incorporated into the painted frame of the wall mural. Nathaniel had designed the decor.

Nathaniel had painted that same design.

Her story, her smugglers, might be the fresh lead she'd struggled for, the lead to her missing twin.

Chapter Five

Her exhausting night was wrapped up with a stellar finish when John and his paramour came home, kissing and stripping their way into the bedroom, where they embarked on a vigorous—and noisy—mattress dance. Natalie squinted one eye at her watch. Five effing A.M. She deserved a sleep-in. Pulling the blanket over her face to muffle the shouts of pleasure, she went back to sleep.

To an erotic dream, fueled by external sounds. A very pleasant, extremely erotic dream in which she mounted her own active rendition of that moaning dance.

With Ram. His mesmerizing voice slid across her nerves like soft flannel on fine glass. Telling her of his devotion, of his excitement and need. Smooth promises that made her heart yearn for lost dreams, until she wrapped her arms around him and pulled him to her. He covered her body with his; she felt the play of his hard muscles and the sensual slide of his hand on her thigh.

He was gentle, this man who could master an ailing

tiger. He was demanding, this man who could mend a tiny kitten.

Oh, his mouth. Even more enchanting. One by one, he took her nipples deep inside his darkness, sucked them to tiny points of prickly need. Their moans joined.

His hand moved from her thigh to between her legs, and she opened wide for him. He was a magician, knew just where to touch her for the most pleasure. Almost before she was aware of the need, he was there, meeting it. Circling a thumb against her nub. Slowly inserting a finger, then two. Caressing her breast with his palm, just so with the friction. She opened her mouth, inviting his kiss.

"Do you want to join us?" a woman asked.

"Delia, she's asleep," a man answered.

John? When did John—? With a jerk, Natalie opened her eyes. John and a woman with waist-length black hair and sex-mussed lipstick—Delia the DJ, Natalie assumed—were standing beside the couch staring down at her.

Natalie realized where her own hands were—breast, between her thighs, no wonder her dream Ram had known where and how to touch—and slowly shifted them to her sides. She would *not* be embarrassed. Or maybe that was em-bare-assed, she thought, catching a glimpse of Delia beneath an oversized T-shirt.

"She's not asleep anymore." Delia nibbled off the rim of a Pop-Tart.

"We were hungry and came out for a nosh." An amused smile played over John's lips.

"You don't need to stop." Delia jerked her head toward the bedroom. "Join us? We're open to a threesome."

"Thanks, but, ah, no." Natalie sat up and swung her feet to the floor, glad she'd left on her tank top and worn boxer briefs instead of a thong.

"She swings pretty straight," John said. "A regular non-judgmental prude."

"Pity." Delia gave her one more glance before John put an arm over the DJ's shoulder and turned her to the bedroom.

Just before they vanished into the bedroom, John turned and mouthed: I so gotcha.

Beast. Natalie stuck her tongue out at him, then gestured she'd be leaving.

He laughed and disappeared into the bedroom.

Running her hands down her thighs, she tried to erase the still-tingling feel of her dream lover's tempting touch. Damn her awakened libido. Work called, and she didn't need the tempting distraction of Dr. Montgomery, as a dream or as a reality. She scrubbed her hands over her scalp, finishing the wake-up process, and then made short work of getting out of there.

Natalie struck out at the liquor store where AX had bought the beers—too many anonymous customers passing through. Similarly the few souls awake at this hour were too wary or surly to give up any useful information. She was soon headed back toward town.

The neighborhood she drove through never failed to elicit a warm glow of hope. Every time she came here, there was something else alive and fresh—a patch of flowers newly planted, a tilting porch propped up and painted brilliant white, a school with children running in the refurbished playground. These people had been devastated by the effects of Katrina five years ago. These streets had been abandoned to the water, then to the mold and the weeds.

Yet, gradually, they had come back and rebuilt their homes. Fighting turtle-paced government agencies and tightfisted insurance companies, they reclaimed their shattered lives, bit by scraggly bit.

A few blocks away, where AX probably lurked, was a place of still abandoned streets and half-razed houses.

A community populated by the seedier elements—
squatters, dopers, criminals, and anyone with a need to
disappear—it served as a striking reminder of how
much still remained to be done, how much would
never be done, and how many things had irretrievably
changed.

But, here, these streets were an undeniable promise
of hope.

She turned off the car's air-conditioning and opened
her window. Yeah, it was hot and humid; in a few minutes she'd be sweat-soaked and scrambling for the cool
air. For these minutes, though, she cherished that sauna
heat. Children in the playground were shouting and
laughing, and Natalie smiled. The laughter of children
was a sound that had been missing for too long in her
city. It was good to have it back, and she never took it
for granted.

Soon, she was parked and walking toward her destination, a pet shop on Esplanade. She'd once written a
story on the owner, Kenzie. He'd garnered a following
by claiming he was a miracle-performing guru, until
she'd exposed the "miracles" as a product of hallucino-
genic cane toad poisons.

"If you want a puppy, go find a bitch," read the sign in
the window. Natalie pushed open the door, her arrival
announced not by a bell, but by the call of a howler
monkey. The air inside was thick with the scents of saw-
dust and lizard chow.

Definitely no puppies or gerbils here. Iguanas, snakes,
toads, and giant spiders, yes, but the only kin to cuteness
was fuzzy litter of ferret kits. She strolled around examining the animals; they all looked well cared for. Kenzie
might have had a few brushes with the underside of the
law, but he did love his merchandise. For that alone, Natalie gave him points.

She'd reached the cage of a colorful king vulture

Laveau, held court these days in a refurbished home donated by her devotees. The move had taken place when Odette's home became one of those beneath the eight feet of water in the news photos.

Three mutts and enough children to populate a kindergarten played like charged electrons in the brown-baked yard while a fat ginger cat lolled in a sunbeam and watched with lazy majesty. Ram left Val to join the fun; neither mutts nor kids had trouble accepting a new playmate.

Carrying a bouquet of snapdragons, Odette's favorite flower, he knocked on the front door, then pushed it open when a voice inside called, "Come in." After the bright sunshine, his eyes took a moment to adjust. The blinds had been drawn, bringing shadows indoors. Ceiling fans circulated air thick with the scents of perfume and cayenne pepper. West African music with an enticing beat played softly in the background.

A woman seated in the front room, rocking and mending a dress, directed Ram. "Odette's out back in the kitchen."

Odette was cooking, the simmering pot smelling like a rich gumbo. She didn't look like a voodoo priestess with her graying hair drawn into a tight bun and wearing polyester slacks and a purple sweatshirt. But Ram was convinced that beneath the flash and the theater and the astute reading of her fellow human beings, this was a woman with a true gift.

He handed her the flowers. "Thanks for agreeing to see me."

"You thought I might refuse because we clashed about Randy?" Smiling, she put the flowers in water.

"It occurred to me."

Odette made a fatalistic gesture. "We disagree on certain subjects. Not the same as dislike or disrespect. Now, sit and take a taste of my gumbo filé."

Ten o'clock in the morning. Not his ideal time for scarfing spicy gumbo, but one didn't say "no" to Odette, especially when she added, "It'll help that ache in your head."

How did Odette know about the lingering headache? The logical would say she saw some symptom like dark circles under his eyes. The faithful would say Odette had "the sight." Ram took it as a mix: good observation and sharp intuition, with a little lagniappe mystery thrown in. He glanced around. "I'm not going to sit on Randy?"

"Randy's enjoying his sunshine." She nodded to the window.

Sure enough, there was Randy, draped over the sill and coiling down across the countertop. The most pampered eight-foot boa constrictor Ram had ever known. Randy lay on a silk runner, his three diamond-studded rings gleaming in the sun.

"Do you want another?" Odette cooed.

He almost asked, "Another what?" before he realized Odette wasn't talking to him, the major clue being the fact that Odette held a squirming mouse. *Please don't put that in the gumbo.*

To his relief, Odette delicately fed the meal to her pet. Randy's scales undulated while the wriggling lump made its slow, lethal descent down his throat.

Odette turned back to the stove and ladled up a bowl of gumbo. She set it on the table, then sat in the chair opposite. "Eat. You can ask what you need until Randy finishes eating. Then I've got to give him his massage."

Ram took a spoonful of the gumbo. "This is good."

"So, what are you needing? And remember, you can't fool the third eye." She tapped her forehead.

"You know anything about a street thug with the handle AX?"

"Bad. Hangs out deeper in New Orleans East."

"You know who he's working for these days?"

"Same old. Drugs." Odette rattled off a couple of known dealers. Too small-time and unimaginative to be the person he sought.

"Anyone else?"

"Like what you thinking?"

"Animal smuggling."

Odette sucked in a breath. "I'd heard rumors. Hadn't found out if they amounted to much yet. If I hear anything I'll let you know."

From the set of her lips, Ram figured Odette would be as tenacious as Randy with a rabbit in squeezing out any information to be found. As if thinking about him had prodded the snake, Randy began to move, rippling sinuously off the windowsill.

"Any thoughts on where we could look next?"

"We?"

How had that slipped out? Still, he knew better than to lie to Odette. "Natalie Severin."

"Now there's one fine woman. She did a piece on me. Respectful it was, and restrained enough not to interest the crazies. She helped clear my Walter of a bogus fraud charge, too."

Walter was Odette's grandson and her pride, next to Randy. "How's he doing?"

"He's gonna graduate from LSU next May. With honors in chemistry."

"Tell him congratulations." Ram had always liked the smiling young man.

Odette gave Ram a speculative look. "You sleeping with Natalie?"

"None of your business, Odette."

"Ah, but you will."

Damn third eye.

Randy was now curling up the table leg. Ram ignored the boa, calling on standard behaviors in snake handling. Stay still. Breathe steady and deep. "Know anyone who might give up AX? A rival?"

"Raoul. Don't know his last name. One of them new-comer Spanish moving in on our jobs, our territory."

"Where might I find him?" Randy began wrapping his legs.

Odette shrugged. "Wherever employers go to recruit. Don't go looking before Friday. I'll talk to the *orisa*, see if they'll intervene and encourage him to spill, but these things take time."

"Thanks." With one eye on the snake, whose eye remained intent on him, Ram began softly crooning. He scratched the top of Randy's head, relaxing the snake before it started giving him a hug. "Odette, where did you get Randy?"

Odette pulled Randy off him, allowing the massive snake to wind around her body. Her face lost all humor, all friendliness, all warmth. A line had been drawn in the sand, and Ram was no longer welcome past it.

"Don't you go confusing him with your voodoo," she said coldly. "I think it time you was leaving."

The offices of New Orleans New Eyes, NONE to the initiated, were housed in a peeling-paint cottage in Algiers, a ferry ride across the river from the Quarter. This particular section of the neighborhood had yet to be bitten by the restoration bug, so it had one great advantage to NONE's owner: The rent came cheap.

Natalie grimaced when she pulled up. Zolton's boat of a car—a perfectly maintained 1979 Rolls Royce Silver Shadow—was taking up the driveway. She'd planned a quick freshen-up and change of clothes, maybe some food or a can of something highly caffeinated.

Also in the plan was a few more hours' reprieve before having to match wits with her boss. Adam Zolton was a creature of nighttime. She'd have considered him a candidate for vampirism, except she'd seen him in daylight. He never came in before two, never left until after midnight. Why'd he have to be prompt today?

Parking where she hoped she'd still have her tires when she got back, she trudged through the June heat into the house. She avoided the route that would take her within eyesight of Zolton's office, skirting the main hall for a side porch that led to the back kitchen and what was once a maid's room, now her office.

She wasn't an employee of NONE. Like all the paper's reporters, she freelanced—a technicality that allowed the paper to avoid niceties like benefits. Still, Zolton kept her working on a regular basis, paid well enough— including expenses—to meet her property taxes and eat, and allowed her to nest at the office when necessary because her home was so far out of town.

All in all, not a bad gig, especially since she liked the stories she covered for NONE. She'd always opted to cover the offbeat before she'd been fired from the *Times-Picayune* for her miserable lapse of professional judgment.

She'd created the one fly in her proverbial professional ointment. After the scandal attached to Charles's death and her crash-and-burn run-in with the Montgomerys, her reputation was sour with any of the legitimate press. She didn't appreciate being considered a hack by her colleagues. Weird tastes? A nut for the bizarre? Those labels she didn't mind. Those labels she'd earned. Incompetent? That's the one that hurt.

Well, that was about to change.

She rummaged around her work space, but found only one clean outfit: a fuzzy pink top and white capris. She'd have to shower and change her hair color before she wore pink. Time for a visit to the homestead and a reload.

Mitch, a fresh-faced young-un reporter with the empathy of an iguana, poked his head into her space. "What an ugly outfit, Nat."

"I happen to be partial to pink. And don't call me Nat."

"Wear that and you'll look like a lunatic Barbie."

"Play with many of them, do you?"

"Har-har. Zolton wants to see you. Pronto." He disappeared.

Well, blast and bother. Couldn't prolong this one. She ambled over to Adam Zolton's office. Her boss—managing editor and new owner of NONE—looked up as she came in, his black unrevealing eyes slanted and his blacker hair tied back in a ponytail. Again she was struck by his resemblance to something dark and wild.

"Hey, Zolton. And before you ask, no, it wasn't aliens."

"Well, shit," he said mildly, the English accent making the expletive seem almost dignified. "I'll find them one day."

"You're chasing an illusion." She sprawled into the chair opposite his desk and picked up a delicate, cut-glass figure of a dragonfly. "Aliens don't exist."

"How can you believe in ghosts, vampires, and selkies, and deny aliens?"

"Because I am one, and I'm trying to throw you off the scent." She turned the dragonfly over in her hands. How had the artist gotten that gossamer look to the wings? And the eyes to glisten?

He snorted. "Pull the other one."

"Because I'm xenophobic and the idea would drive me mad."

This got her a sigh. "If it wasn't aliens, what did you find last night?"

"Animal smugglers." She held up the winsome glass figurine. "This is exquisite. Where'd you get it?"

"This is expensive, and how it came into my possession is none of your business." Carefully, he plucked the glass from her hands and set it on his immaculate desk, positioning it exactly as it had been. "Animal smugglers are nothing to interest our readers," he said dismissively. "I've got a report of a fortune-telling gourd in Missouri. We'll pay expenses to the Ozarks."

"I fell for that expense trip ploy once—flea bags and Mickey D's were all that fit my budget."

"I'll up it 20 percent. Add a bonus for mileage."

"Let's talk about those smugglers instead."

"There's more?" His voice got sharp.

"Possibly." She set his desktop Newton's cradle in motion—two balls, click, two balls on the other side, click. How much to tell him? "I found something, a disk." She laid it on the desk.

He stopped the Newton's cradle motion before he picked up the disk. "Odd design."

"You've seen it before?"

"Never."

"Neither has anyone I've talked to." Not even her best sources: the curator at the voodoo museum, supernatural author Feydor Blaze, and a street mime named Valparaiso, gender unknown.

"So? It's a random design."

She rubbed a finger along the edge of his desk, not looking at him. Her stomach ached like a marathon trotter, knowing she was about to damage her cause. "The same figure is part of the decor at Dark Phoenix, a design of Nathaniel's."

"Ah, so this is about finding Nathaniel?"

"No. Not entirely. Well, yes."

He leaned back, steepling his fingers. "Why are you telling me this? Admitting you're going after an obsession isn't a good ploy for gaining approval."

"Because I don't repeat mistakes. Before, I didn't tell my editor there was a tie to Nathaniel in the story I was pursuing."

"That personal involvement and your public melt-down got you fired."

She winced from the dry observation, then wiped her sweaty palms against her wrinkled jeans and looked at him. Direct and sober. "I'm not proud of that moment. I deserved what I got. Yeah, I'm emotionally involved," she admitted, her voice as cracked as dried mud. "Yeah, I'm obsessed. But, I've learned, and I won't let either fact get in the way of the story."

"It's still not enough to interest our readers," he said flatly.

"Nathaniel was enmeshed in the occult. If the smugglers are connected to him, maybe there's an angle."

"House of straws, Natalie. You're pulling connections out of coincidence."

"There's more, I can feel it. The smugglers were too determined to get their contraband. Enough that they drugged me and Ram Montgomery."

"Ramses Montgomery? He was there?" The sharp edge of his voice slashed across her ears.

"Yeah." Damn, but he perked up at the mention of Ram. Now that was interesting, how his fingertips were pressed together so hard the nails had turned white.

"What exactly happened last night?" he asked.

Shoving curiosity aside for the moment, she gave him a quick summary, leaving out only the fact of Val's healing. Why, when Ram was the supernatural angle their readers devoured, she couldn't say. The need for more proof? Doubting her eyes? The narrow glitter of Zolton's gaze rousing wary suspicion?

Or did something more intimate lie beneath her reluctance? Something more protective of Ram's secret?

"Why are you interested in Ram?" she asked.

"Did you know"—Zolton loosened his hands—"he disappeared for five years? He wasn't here. There's nothing in the newspapers about him. No record of conference attendance. No mention of where he was. He simply vanished, then returned, right before Katrina struck."

"No, I didn't. You want me to investigate Ram Montgomery? Why?" The mere question left behind an ashy taste of betrayal.

Zolton lifted one shoulder in a gesture more Gallic than Anglican. "A story about him would skyrocket circulation. You're my best reporter, Natalie. I'll green-light your smuggler story. But you might find Ramses Montgomery a valuable ally."

"You want me to partner with him?" She filed away the fact that Zolton was still avoiding the "why."

"Best way to bring me back a story I can use. Something stellar."

"And if I don't?"

"You'll go to Missouri?"

"Hell, no. Give it to Mitch. He'd probably love the chance to detour to Branson."

"A story, Natalie. That's all I ask. Reporters who work for me always come through."

She heard the implied threat. Bring back something he could use or she was out of work again. She nodded, accepting his terms, her chest feeling as cold as fog.

As she turned to leave, he added in a low voice, "You might consider, Natalie, that eight months ago, you were pursuing the wrong Montgomery in connection with your brother's disappearance."

Chapter Six

The second floor of Dark Phoenix contained an oddity known mostly to the patrons—a macabre wax museum paying homage to late twentieth-century horror movies, an obsession of the man who'd bought the bar from Nathaniel. The bar had since passed to other owners, but the wax displays endured.

Natalie paid her minimal fee to the bartender, not John tonight, and got her keypad code for admittance. The wax museum was dark, AC-cool, and nearly empty, ten being early for the Phoenix clientele. Three reasons Bennie had likely picked it for their meeting.

Her eyes adjusted to the switch from dark to darker as she looked around. No sign of Bennie, but that wasn't surprising. She hitched her bag a little more firmly to her back and thumbed her phone to vibrate. Best to stroll through, and let Bennie pick his time and place.

She paused at the first panorama: the venerable Jason, Freddy Krueger, and Michael Myers, complete with hockey mask and razor fingers. The figures were eerily lifelike, except their waxy hue signaled they weren't quite human. The near approximation of reality gave her an off-kilter feel.

"Eerie."

"Ram!" Natalie spun at the familiar voice. Her heart gave a tiny lurch. How had he gotten so close without her hearing? She was so intently aware of the heat of him, the strength of him.

Still as a cat on a hunt, he returned her momentary stare. Only his dark eyes moved, flicking like a tail, as though he was absorbing the sight of her, too. *Wishful, dangerous thinking, Natalie.* But, damn, he looked good in khakis, an unbuttoned linen shirt, and a navy Polo. His dark hair gleamed and he had a hint of five-o'clock shadow.

"You changed your hair color," he observed.

"Ash blond goes better with pink."

He brushed a hand across the strands of her fuzzy top, his hand skimming half an inch above her sleeve. "Soft."

Heat, and he wasn't even touching her. She gathered her errant thoughts. "Here to see the sights?"

"Not unless you are."

"I don't remember Bennie texting you to this meeting."

He ignored her jab and glanced around, rubbing a hand down his arm. "This place gives me the creeps. The displays are so good, I keep expecting to feel life in them."

She was a bit surprised to hear him admit the vulnerability, especially when it matched her own misgivings. "I'll protect you if a mannequin attacks."

"I'd appreciate that." He threw her an amused glance, the corners of his lips barely upturned. How could he flip all her senses with such a small gesture?

Knowing it was worthless to suggest he leave, and frankly glad of the company, Natalie nodded toward the displays. "Shall we go find Bennie?"

Slow enough for Bennie to meet them where he

wanted, they strolled past noted characters in modern horror cinema.

"I told Fish and Wildlife about the smuggling ring." Ram broke their easy silence.

Natalie gave him a disgusted look. "Not bad enough that NOPD had to be told about the ketamine and the smugglers? Now the Feds are mucking about in my story?" Hell, she might as well send out neon invites.

"Althea Robinson's a decent agent. She'll have sources we don't."

"She's going to share all the information she gets?"

"I think she will."

"In whose fairy tale?"

"Same fairy tale that persuaded a woman with an illegally imported jaguar kitten to tell me about the Internet broker who calls himself, or herself, 2Wyld. That's the number two and W-Y-L-D."

You were pursuing the wrong Montgomery. "How did you persuade her? Or know that Althea will share info?" she asked, numbed by a wash of suspicion.

He stopped, forcing her to stop, too, and look at him. His eyes narrowed, and suddenly she was aware of the brush of his anger, aware that they were alone in a gore-celebrating museum, the surrounding dark lit only by spotlights on faux humans. "I used a truth spell," he said in a low voice. "I forced them, against their will, to reveal whatever I wanted them to reveal."

She swallowed hard, hammered again with how gorgeous he was, how tempting, and dangerous. "So you admit to using magic?"

He leaned closer; she refused to back up or be intimidated. His lips brushed against her hair as he whispered, "If I do, will you tell me what color your hair really is?"

Her mouth was open, ready to answer, when she snapped it shut and glared at him. "You're lying."

He leaned back, and this time his look was pure annoyance. "Of course I am. Althea will share information with me because her office is underfunded and understaffed and she knows the value of pooling resources. We've worked together before; *she* trusts me. As for my client with the stupidity not to realize that her cute kitten was going to grow up into a natural predator, I gave her a graphic description of what that animal's talons and instinct to mark its territory would do to her white leather decor. That, and a promise her name would never be mentioned, got a jaguar donation to the zoo and the name of her supplier."

Okay, she'd stepped right into that one, Natalie admitted. Did she really think Ram would be that easy to expose?

"This is going to be a very irritating investigation if you keep scratching at every damn thing I say or do," he said shortly, striding ahead of her.

"Who said this is a joint investigation?" She quickly followed.

The displays turned to re-created scenes of slasher films. Too damn realistic. Whoever had done these knew exactly how blood dripped and flesh tore.

Ram didn't seem to notice. "I have an appointment with Virgil le Blanc."

"The Oddball Ornithologist? That guy knows more about birds than anyone." She stared at Ram. "Nobody sees him except on his Sunday A.M. TV show."

"You've watched it?"

"Charles hooked me on it when we were first married." She covered the moment of awkward memory by hurrying on. "How'd you get an appointment?"

"I helped him out after Katrina." He gave no further explanation, continuing instead with, "Appointment's tomorrow. Want to come?"

"Of course!" It galled her to admit it, but in the time

they'd been apart, Ram had made more progress than she had. She tilted her head to look up at him. "Why are you telling me all this?"

"Connections. Interactions. We're more powerful with joint efforts, and I have no interest in exclusivity." In a subtle motion, his hand brushed her fingertips. "Work with me."

Why was she so tempted? She never worked with a partner, despite Zolton's suggestion. So, why did she lift that glass and smell the temptation of keeping Ram close, seeing him, working together? "Why are you so eager?"

His dark eyes narrowed, and the brush on her hand this time was more deliberate.

She drew back, enough to give him the message: *Not if you're expecting that.* That temptation she wasn't ready to face. If she did, she'd probably give in and she wasn't ready for the complications of bewitching sex. Not yet.

He took the hint, his hands leaving the space between them. "For one, I'm betting you're more skilled at hacking through the Internet to get me a real name, a real place, for 2Wyld. I couldn't find a trace of him."

"You're not a computer person?"

"A necessary tool."

"I bet your cell doesn't take pictures, either."

His easy smile stole her air. "It gets calls."

"So, you think we're yin and yang investigators?"

"I know animals, but you've got underbelly contacts. Note Bennie called you, not me." He lifted his brows, waiting for her response.

Passing a gruesome scene from *The Texas Chainsaw Massacre,* she kept focused on Ram. This section seriously creeped her out. She liked horror flicks, not sadism. At least ahead were the J-horror scenes. "We'll talk after Bennie."

Ram glanced at his watch and frowned. "He's late."

They exchanged a worried glance. Only one more corner, two more panoramas before the exit.

Just then her phone vibrated. Natalie glanced at the number. "It's Bennie." She flicked it open. "Bennie, you—"

No voice. Only the beep of a picture being sent.

The image was the museum's last scene, Jack Nicholson and his axe from *The Shining*. In the center of this one, however, was no wax figure. Bennie sprawled beneath the sharp blade, a thick line of blood around his throat.

She swallowed against a wave of nausea and ran into the next room, tossing Ram her phone.

The room was dark. Before she skidded to a halt, she banged a shin against something hard. She felt Ram arrive behind her, more as a shift in the air and heat, since she couldn't see a damn thing. Thanks to her clunk, he avoided the obstacle.

He grabbed her wrist to put the phone back in her hand. Blindly, uselessly nodding her thanks, she reattached the phone to her belt. Ram's finger against her lips cautioned silence, and she nodded agreement. What'd he think? She'd planned to shout out, "Hello, we're here, come attack us?"

Now that her eyes had adjusted, she realized the overhead lights, dimmed way down, emitted a faint red hue. Ram put his hand on her shoulder. A faint buzzing prickled her skin with a chill, and she appreciated his warmth. Anchored together, they crossed the blood-lit room. Sick at such violent death, Natalie looked for Bennie.

"What the hell?" Her unvoiced prayer had been answered. There was no Bennie in the scene. Only the poor wax sap being hacked. She pulled up the picture on the phone. The scenes matched in every detail but one. The victim.

Ram moved closer as he peered at the picture with her. He didn't touch her, but her senses felt him as acutely as if he'd embraced her.

"Bennie appears to be missing," he commented. Then, to her surprise, he vaulted across the guardrail.

"What are you doing?" she hissed. "Besides leaving fingerprints at a potential crime scene?"

"Making sure the image we're seeing isn't overlaid on Bennie." He crouched, his hands resting on his thighs, his eyes level with the body.

"A hologram?"

"Yeah, like a hologram." He picked up the figure's hand and pressed his fingernail into it. Natalie winced as his nail dug deep into the wax. "Definitely not Bennie." He glanced around. "No blood. Maybe Bennie's faking his own death, with us as witnesses?"

She mulled over that possibility. "If Bennie was in deep-shit trouble, he might go to the effort."

They looked again at the photo. The splay of limbs, the ugly sprawl, the muscle terror on the face. She'd seen unexpected death before. It was never pretty, never neat, never failed to elicit a shudder of dread. That same shudder tightened her spine right now.

"I think this death is real," Ram said quietly.

"Me, too." She snapped the phone shut, feeling queasy, and rubbed her hands down her sweaty arms. Somebody must have turned the AC off, or maybe it just wasn't working.

"Why not just send the photo of Bennie?"

"Because somebody wanted us here? Oh, bloody hell!" Her heartbeat racing to the tune of *I've been so blind,* she took off running. Out of the trap.

Ram, needing no explanation, followed.

Two clangs rang out, the sound of fire doors slamming shut on either side of the room. Natalie pushed at the handle, but the door stubbornly refused to budge. Even their combined efforts failed.

Fire doors weren't supposed to lock. Yet, locked it was. They were sealed in with Jack and the axe.

To hell with stealth. Natalie fished in her bag and pulled out her penlight. Shining it on the door, she looked for a lock to pick or some way to escape.

Ram stepped behind her, and with one corner of her mind she realized he was chivalrously setting himself as a shield. A faint click sounded behind them, and he spun toward the dark room. "Natalie, what did you bump into when you came in here?"

"A bench?"

"No benches."

She twisted and shone her light into the room. Sure enough, not a bench, but a heavy box with screen-covered air holes. A box now open. The click she'd just heard. "What do you suppose that held?"

"Listen."

In the ensuing silence, a droning buzz—low and angry—filled the room, drowning out thought as thoroughly as a siren's blast. Dots swarmed through her beam, flitting like crazed motes.

"Bees," Ram said.

Tiny legs crawled on the bare flesh of her arms, her neck. Stung, stung again with sharp stabs of painful venom. She swatted. Brushed her arms and legs and neck. Swung out, trying to scare them away. They only stung more furiously.

Ram grabbed her hand. "Don't. That'll make them angry. These are Africanized."

"Killer bees?" Horror laced her throat.

"Are you allergic?" he asked desperately.

"Not to a honeybee. These things—could they kill us?"

"If not, their stings are damn painful."

Didn't answer the question. Ah, hell. They were locked in a sauna with a ticked-off swarm of killer bees. She stopped swatting and flipped open her cell phone. "What's the number for animal control?"

"No, we can't let these doors open. We can't let them escape this room."

"How the hell do you propose we prevent that? Let each one get its sting in on us and die?"

"Killer bees don't die after one sting."

"Shit, Ram, I could have done without that piece of information. You're the animal expert—what's the master plan?"

"Here," he said, dragging off his linen shirt and handing it to her.

"What about you?"

"I'll manage." He lifted the collar of his polo shirt beneath, covering his neck. "Wrap that around your head and neck."

She obeyed without question, already feeling the fire of the swelling stings. Fashion for the I-want-to-stay-alive crowd.

"If I handle the bees," he asked, "can you get us out of here?"

"Handle the bees? How—?"

"Can you get us out?" he demanded.

She could handle her end, despite the aching welts. "The plaster in the wall is crumbling. I might be able to get a big enough hole to get my hand through, find out what's blocking the door."

"Do it," he said tightly. He moved away from her, and she caught a whiff of a new smell. Bananas?

Time to work all that out later. More stings, God, the bees were crawling inside, up the sleeves, down her neck. Her breathing harsh, the buzzing jittering her nerves until she felt as edgy as the swarm, Natalie chipped at the plaster. Sweat smarted in her eyes, and she wiped her face, trying to clear her vision. Dust scratched at her throat. Coughing, she kept chipping at the wall.

The repeated stings and rising heat made her dizzy.

At last, she opened a big enough hole. With the beam of her flashlight, she peered through to the other side. A two-by-four piece of wood was wedged against the door handle. If she could reach it . . . She stretched through, straining her arm until the muscles burned, but the wood remained tantalizingly out of reach, an inch away from her fingertips.

She needed an arm extension. Turning around for a tool and to see how Ram was faring, she began, "Ram—" The words died in her mouth, as she took in the scene behind her.

Ram was nearly invisible in the room's red haze. A haze made up of thousands of swarming, stinging killer bees. Dark dots covered his arms—bees that had stung and hadn't fallen off. Others crawled up his shirt and over his head. Her imagination painted them—walking on his eyelids, jabbing stingers into his lips. Dear Lord, how many stings had he taken?

As she'd been working, the bees stinging her had lessened. She'd been so focused, she hadn't registered that astounding fact. Somehow he'd gathered the bees to him.

The scent of banana hung thick in the room, a gaggingly sweet smell. Chanting low, he knelt beside the box. The swarm seemed to speed up, like crazed atoms fired by some unseen energy. His hands stretched out, into the box. The swarm of bees tightened, and then began to stream off him, flowing in an angry river toward captivity.

In a moment, he'd have the bees caged; she'd better have her part finished. From the diorama, she claimed the axe, and then knelt back by her plaster hole. With the hilt of the axe, she shoved the blocking board away.

"Can we get out?" Ram sounded strained. "The bees are contained."

She glanced over her shoulder. He carried the latched box, filled with an angry buzz. "Yes." Matching her words, she shoved open the door. "Let's get out of here before someone comes to view their handiwork."

The hallway was better lit, and empty. Ram headed for the front steps, but she grabbed him back.

"They'll be watching the door. This way." She led him through a second door. "This corridor leads to the building next door, then out into a side alley. Always plan another way out."

They fell silent, the only sounds the buzz of the bees and their own rasping breaths as they sped through the airless corridor, and then out into an alley redolent of old garbage and stale beer. Her skin felt scalded, and the welts began to throb, but she didn't stop. Two turns later, they vanished into the anonymity of the French Quarter.

As if on cue, her phone rang again. A text message. From Bennie's number, the sick bastards. Bracing her hand against a faint tremble, she held it so Ram could read the message, too: *Nowhere safe. 1 warning. Betrayers die.*

A streaming video replaced the text. The ten-o'clock news. An anchorman behind the desk sat beside a picture of a gap-toothed boy. ". . . . Amber alert for ten-year-old Ajani Diako, who disappeared walking to school this morning. Authorities refuse to speculate whether he's the latest victim of the serial killer known as Magic Man." A number flashed to call in information, as the anchor continued, "Now, in other disturbing news, we take you to Maria Maroni."

The scene flashed to a reporter who stood beside the muddy riverbank. Behind her officers toted out a body bag on a stretcher. "Local police need your help tonight in identifying the body of a man found at the Algiers

levee. The man had no identification, and with his fingertips removed, no prints to match." The reporter slid
over the gruesome details. "If you have information
about the identity or death of this man—" The phone
flashed with the news photo of a man's face, slack in
death, his throat bruised with blood.

Then the screen went blank, the connection severed.
The brief view had been enough, though. The murdered man on the riverbank was Bennie.

She exchanged a glance with Ram, her jaw working.
"Bennie didn't deserve that."

"Nobody does." He lifted a comforting hand, reaching toward her, and then dropped it. Respecting the
boundaries she'd set.

In that moment, something indefinable changed inside her. She looked at the gap between them. Only a
few inches, but an abyss of questions unasked, secrets
kept, and doubts unbanished.

This story was undeniably more than one of simple
greed. Bennie killed. The tenuous link to her brother.

Bring me a story, Natalie.

You were pursuing the wrong Montgomery.

Yet, in their shared attack and escape, she and Ram
had worked as one. Their rhythms meshed; their talents
complemented. Like the breeze from an open window
on a spring day, fresh possibilities swept over her dusty
routines.

She didn't want to watch him walk away.

"You should get those stings looked at." He filled the
silence.

"Hydrocortisone will take care of them." Before she
could change her mind, she added, "Except I can't
reach my back."

Stillness, potent and fraught with more meaning
than any gesture, came over him. "What are you saying,
Natalie?"

"I want someone taking care of my back." She took a deep breath, feeling that thrill of the unknown, the dizzy rush of an adrenaline spurt. The gap between them heated. "AX hangs out at a pool hall we should check out."

He lifted his brows. "You looking for an opponent?"

"A partner. You wanted us to work together. I'm willing."

He didn't immediately agree, surprising since he'd been pushing the notion. Instead, he gave her a speculative look. "What changed your mind?"

So many reasons, including something she hadn't even realized was missing: At long last, she was looking forward to tomorrow. She settled for a basic truth, hammered home by gruesome murder. "Seeing Bennie . . . If death's my fate tomorrow, I'd rather regret what I did than what I missed."

"You think I'll be a regret?" Lightly he brushed back a strand of hair that had fallen into her eyes, still without a touch on her tingling, aching skin. "What story are you really working on, Natalie?"

She flushed. How much could she say? For she wouldn't start out with a lie, and wouldn't make a promise she knew she couldn't keep.

"My assignment is to expose those smugglers and find a way to spin the story for NONE readers. I don't know how I'm going to do that just yet . . ."

"Then we'll have to make sure you've got something you *can* write about," he said softly before deliberately tacking on, "*Partner*. Which means, I'm not just watching your back."

"So you'd say we're more of a confederacy?"

"My confederate. I like that."

"Then it's a deal." She held out her hand.

His lips curled into a smile. "My brother-in-law says his people always seal a bargain with a ritual kiss."

Her breath hitched. Then, before she could doubt or

think about regrets, she rose on tiptoe and gave him his kisses. Right cheek. Left. With her lips leaving the barest touch upon his skin. Then she leaned back, waiting for his response.

His, too, were light, a mere brush upon her face. Yet, she was dizzy with a crazy need for more. "The bargain is sealed," he whispered.

Their eyes met above the still air. The buzzing in her ears wasn't just from killer bees. She'd moved forward, ready to taste again the temptation of his lips, when he abruptly jerked back.

He braced his free hand on his thigh, and his breath caught as though arrested by a stab of pain. The skin around his eyes grew flushed.

"What's wrong?" Had he been stung worse than she realized? She checked the jagged pulse at his wrist. "A reaction to the bee stings?"

He didn't answer at first, just gave a quick shake of his head, like a dog throwing off water. Then, he straightened, his breath again coming into control.

"I'm fine, a twinge," he answered.

A man of his health having twinges? "You sure? You're sweating."

"You probably got stung worse than I did."

When he was surrounded by the swarm? She lifted the hem of her shirt, exposing a strip of her abs. "Shall we compare?"

He matched her action, briefly, before dropping the shirt. His abs had barely a pink welt. God, when would she learn? With Ram, do not expect normal.

He lifted her shirt at the back a bare inch, and sucked in his breath. "Those need to be tended."

Feeling cold, she pulled away from him, not admitting how much the stings hurt. "I said I'd take care of them."

"You need me to reach your back." He tossed her words back.

"You need to get rid of those." She nodded to the bee cage.

"Natalie—" He broke off, interrupted by the ringing of his phone. After glancing at the number, he took the call. "Hey, LaMarr."

Whatever this LaMarr was telling him wasn't good. As he listened, Ram's body tensed. With a terse, "I'll be there," he flipped shut the phone, then looked at her. "Something's come up; I have to go." He gave no further explanation, saying only, "I'll see you tomorrow. And we'll play some pool on Friday."

"Why wait half the week?"

"Because Odette Calliope is consulting the spirits to get a rival of AX's to talk to us." With a quick nod, he was off, taking the bee cage and leaving her with unflattering haste.

She watched him go. She might not have much of a life beyond her work and her search for her brother, but Ram did, and he didn't owe her an explanation about it. Yet she couldn't shake the feeling that Ram's sudden business had little to do with the smugglers and nothing to do with being a vet.

For a moment, she flirted with the idea of following him, but the ache in her skin and the lack of sleep finally caught up with her. With one last look at him, his easy path through the milling tourists, she turned and walked to her car.

She had one more place to check for the meaning of that symbol she'd found. Charles's library. Nausea burned in her throat, remembering the last time she'd been in there. The night she had left her husband for good. The night she learned how thoroughly magic could corrupt a man.

Chapter Seven

Ram detoured long enough to dispose of the dangerous cache of bees with animal control, and then sped toward the spot where the Mages gathered. He turned on a CD of chants, humming under his breath and gathering the focus he would need for the work ahead.

Thoughts of Natalie, though, kept breaking through his concentration.

Those nasty stings she'd endured needed tending. Even her lips were swollen. Thank God she wasn't allergic; she could have died from the venom, a thought that sent a scattershot of pain through his chest.

His hands curled tight around the steering wheel. If he ever found the bastard who'd loosed the bees on her . . .

Not helping his focus. Relaxing his fingers, he concentrated on releasing tension. Tighten the muscle, loosen and let the energy flow. Tighten, loosen and let the energy flow.

The magic tonight had been strong and controlled; even the tricky pheromones and the paths of a thousand angry bees were easy to guide. He should be depleted now, but he felt rested, charged, as though he could accomplish single-handedly any spell in the vast Central Library.

Because of Natalie. Working together had felt natural. As if a missing part of him had been restored.

Then, just as her barriers had started to crumble, as she'd smiled with warmth and reached out to touch him, LaMarr's call had come. Ram had wanted to stay and help her with those stings, but the message was one he couldn't ignore. The work of the Mages came first, before his personal desires.

Especially tonight, with the life of a young boy in jeopardy.

That was what was important. The reminder sobered him. He turned up the volume on the chants, channeling his thoughts and desires into preparation. By the time he parked the truck, grabbed his small kit of tools, and found his designated spot near the crumbling warehouses, the power within him glowed as hot as afternoon sunshine.

Ready and anxious to get to work, he leaned one shoulder against a Dumpster and said into his cell phone headset, "I'm ready."

LaMarr answered. "Let me patch in Estrella."

"She's here?" Ram asked. Estrella, an LSU grad student, generally couldn't join them on such short notice.

"Fortunately I was on my way into town to see friends," Estrella answered, sounding breathless, as though she'd run the distance from Baton Rouge. Probably had broken a few speed limits after receiving LaMarr's call. "We have a week break. I was going to attempt to see you two for a Circle."

"Be glad to," Ram told her warmly. Although they'd only worked together a couple of years, he liked Estrella Santiago and her direct approach to the magic she commanded. She'd be welcome help.

"Are you in place, Estrella?" LaMarr asked.

"*Uno momento.* Okay. I'm here and, as usual, I'm on the corner nearest the most foul beer odors."

"Better than the Dumpster I'm next to," said Ram, as he tried not to breathe in the aroma of heat-rotted garbage. "Ready to start?"

"Are you leading, Ram?" Estrella asked in surprise. After all, at their last Circle, he'd been about as powerful as a trout.

"Yes," LaMarr answered, firmly.

From where Ram stood, he couldn't see the others, but he pictured them in his mind's eye. LaMarr—late forties, Black, male and the nattiest dresser of their cell; Estrella—Latina, nanotech grad student, beautiful fall of black hair. Add himself—thirties, Caucasian male, dressed in Yuppie. No one passing would guess the three were known to each other or working in concert.

Using their conferenced cell phones, Ram began the ritual with a low chant and pulled a small vial of cedarwood oil from the bag attached to his belt. He sprinkled oil in an arc behind him, and then, fisting his right hand, he opened the hinged top of the platinum ring on his index finger, revealing the silver pattern beneath. The mark of the Centaur. His fist drew an arc in the air, above the oil. LaMarr and Estrella would match his actions with their chosen tools.

Over the phone, their voices blended, an amplifying resonance of powers. The flow of magic filled Ram. Through the focusing hum of the Mages' voices, the internal glow expanded, became brilliant and tense. The three Mages—Centaur, Merman, Wyvern—were joining.

Their assigned corners formed a triangle. Gradually, he slid the legs of his spell outward, a power spread between the molecules of air. He kept his strength leashed, not wanting to overwhelm the others as their tendrils gently touched and formed a perimeter around the city blocks.

Somewhere inside that thin fence of energy lay a human monster.

They infused their barrier with a seeking spell, and then slowly narrowed the perimeter. Magic advanced, adjusted by the power of the Mages. Energy manipulation, a scientist might call it, if that scientist were to believe in the extraordinary. Energy shaped by ritual and rite, transformed and controlled by the mind and will of the Mage, and created by the interaction between humans.

Ram drew on everything: the voices of the Mages, the reflection of a streetlight off a puddle, the heat and humidity that surrounded him. Power flowed as easily as the slide of oil on polished steel. Ah, it felt so good to once more master and control.

They had to be sure they covered each particle of space. The level of magic they sought would be very faint; they couldn't afford to miss it.

The case had been splashed all over the news. A little boy missing, the fears that the Magic Man—as one reporter had dubbed the serial killer—had struck again.

The moniker was truer than the papers knew. Each time Magic Man struck, the Mages felt the low-level, undisciplined power released. Unfortunately, Magic Man only used that power as he escalated toward a kill, and they couldn't find him before he finished and disappeared.

Tonight, LaMarr had heard talk from the cops. They thought the man and his victim were in this area, but there were too many hidden crannies. They feared they wouldn't find the boy in time.

This time was different, Ram vowed. This time he was at full strength.

The Mages couldn't solve every crime, turn back every atrocity that stained the city. They had neither the strength nor the resources. But, with the abuse of magic, this one they could do something about.

Their seeking spell spread, probing with tiny fingers of power into each small space it encountered. Bit by bit, they tightened the triangle and reduced the unsearched area within.

Ram grew frustrated as they inched their way forward. The spell was taking too much time. Could he overlay it with a second spell? There weren't many children in this industrial area, and a small adjustment might detect the missing boy.

Carefully, he made the necessary changes, nothing that would detract from LaMarr's and Estrella's work. He jerked as a tiny explosion of desperate pain spattered against his skin. Dear God, no. His senses caught the shadow of a child's fading heart.

Ram pushed the dual spell forward faster, in a deep flowing channel. Where was the boy?

"What the hell you doing?" spat LaMarr. "Your edge with me is too fast. It's burning. We'll miss—"

"The child's near me. We don't have time for caution." Where was that pocket of pain? Of misused magic? There! "I've got him!"

At this distance, he couldn't ID an address, couldn't do anything to stop the horror within. Nausea grabbed his throat as Ram ran forward, following the muddied seeking spell. "Tighten in," he ordered. "Near Thalia Street."

Although he couldn't see the others as he plunged into the narrow streets, he felt them move in concert. The perimeter narrowed. His hair rose with the thickening static charge, as energy intensified among the three Mages.

There. To his right, half a block down, was their target. A warehouse amidst many still abandoned to mold and falling beams. "I've got an address."

"I'll call it in," LaMarr said. His talents had gained a measure of respect with some of the more open-minded NOPD officers. His word would dispatch a squad car fastest.

Not fast enough. One life was fading.

"Cover my line, keep the perimeter strong." Without further explanation, Ram detached himself from the triangle and ran to the warehouse, pulling his tourmaline from inside his shirt. He wrapped his fingers around it, warming the healing crystal, absorbing its resonance.

"Fluid as the stream, solid as the rock," he intoned. "Turn aside the dark of day. Be this my shield dagger. Let this, my will, be done."

The power in his tourmaline shot forward, scorching his arm, his palm, his fingers. Thin as a needle, bright as a silver streak, it pierced the night until it found the boy. Rich, thick energy wound off his hand and around the unseen child, bringing oxygen, hope, a few precious moments of safety.

As Ram scrambled up the steps, he heard a faint *whup, whup,* and glanced over his shoulder. Helicopters were closing in, whirling in the distance overhead. The press had gotten wind of the police search and were circling for a story. Damn! If Magic Man saw the choppers, he'd be spooked. At the least, he'd burrow underground and they'd lose his signature. At the worst, he'd take the missing boy with him. Or kill him.

The warehouse stank of mold, excrement, and terror. A warren of rooms spread from the cavernous entrance. Which direction? Ram stopped, probing delicately forward, and then frowned. "I can't get a direction. Something's interfering."

"Does this help?" Estrella asked. From outside, LaMarr and Estrella interlocked their power with his. The triune link grazed forward, ready to pull back as soon as they brushed Magic Man.

Darkness blotted one of the doorways. "Got it." Ram ran silently forward.

"Estrella and I have the perimeter tight," LaMarr said. "He won't escape. We've laid a silence overlay on the warehouse, to muffle the sound of the news copters, but we need to stay outside to maintain it. You okay?"

"Fine, thanks," Ram whispered back, grateful for the ease with which they worked. "I've got his location now."

"Just don't alert him yourself."

Ram grunted, enough of an answer. "Police?"

"Fifteen minutes to converge."

A lot of death could happen in fifteen minutes.

Ram slid through the filthy rooms, his feet moving silently through piles of newspapers. No more words were exchanged between him and the others.

Fingerling probes led him through the maze of rooms, tracing the low level of magic. Muddy and ragged in its execution, but magic nonetheless.

Something else hung in the air, souring each breath, making the power waver. Yes, there was near death, nearer terror, but this was something else. Something outside the magic and death, like an owl hulking in the rafters, waiting to pounce on an unwary mouse. An owl that faintly obscured Ram's target and forced him to work harder.

Not having time to explore the odd sensation, Ram raced up the narrow steps, his heart speeding in rhythm. LaMarr and Estrella thickened the air around him to a shimmering circle.

"Good idea," he murmured. The shadow vision might

give him the seconds he'd need to cast the necessary spell. He pulled out his athame, the band of his ring fitting into the knife's ebony handle. With the other hand, he grabbed his tourmaline. Ideally he would have had the chance to dip the blade into a laurel decoction, but this would have to do; the athame was fed by the combined power of the Mages. The words of the chant rose in his throat as, with a wave of his hand, he eased the door open, and then slid into the room, silent as the pearly fog surrounding him.

Gagging bile rose in his throat. Ajani Daiko, the missing boy, was tied to a metal altar with red cords, still alive enough to whimper. Blood flowed from raw wounds and ran in ugly rivulets down onto black sheets.

Lit only by the fire from black candles, Magic Man cackled as he carved off a strip of skin and held it up. "The power of blood and flesh be mine." Suddenly, his eyes widened in maddened fury. "Begone, demons, or bow down to Moloch. Let die—" He lifted his knife over his victim, plunging it down.

"Malefa alefac lefact!" Ram shoved out his athame, throwing his power behind the spell, and sliced the crude magic circle with precision. The fog streamed from him in an unstoppable torrent. Air spun the obscene magical paraphernalia around the room.

Magic Man froze, immobilized by the cage of pearlescent air. Tarot cards, herbs, and scrolls—the implements of his insane obsession—settled onto the floor. A mirror tipped over and shattered.

"Do you see the source?" LaMarr asked.

"Not—" The words broke as the breath was sucked out of Ram in a forced rush. That lurking power he'd sensed earlier burst, as though it had been waiting for his spell, and scooped up the room's energy. The spell he'd cast on Magic Man wavered, and the killer's hand lowered an inch.

"What the hell?" LaMarr spat.

"The vacuum is too strong." Estrella sounded scared, and her support vanished. "What is it?"

Ram heard LaMarr talking, guiding and calming Estrella; they quickly reestablished the connection, but he could only grunt an answer. His skin was pulled too taut, his attention too divided, for him to speak more. Quickly, his breath coming in short pants, he repaired the weakened spell as the surprising tug on his magic lessened. It did not, however, disappear. As he worked, the parasitic spell hung in the room, more obvious now, dragging in his power. Feeding with a lazy gluttony that forced him to dig deeper.

"Get the source of Magic Man's magic and get out," spat LaMarr. "We're being drained by this thing and the police will be there soon."

Ignoring LaMarr's command, Ram raced to the bound child. The boy's eyes, pain-glazed and unfocused, latched onto him. The light of life held, courageous, but very faint. Too faint to wait for the police?

"You're safe," he murmured. He closed his eyes, blotting out the room, searching for a way to bolster the boy without giving the parasite more power. Opening his eyes, he created a shield around himself and the boy. Was his strength enough? Could he keep the killer frozen, the distorting mist around himself, and the foreign spell at bay?

All three wavered. Too many magics to juggle. An old technique came to mind, one he'd learned many years ago, difficult and rarely used. Separation, not unity. He put the athame and the tourmaline together, then wrapped his hands around them, with the ring touching both and connected the three with the ancient powers of a twelfth-level Mage, a title he could once more claim.

"Aura of blue. Aura of red. Aura of green. Drawn and painted in the wind and the soil and the waters," he whispered, thinking of the night he'd healed Val, of the members of his cell, of Natalie. "Let joined now separate. My command to maintain, to heal, to shield."

The pull of the magic spun through him. Rising heat, rising energy, rising command brought a smile to his face with its beauty. Three braided threads. The Mages. The animals he cared for. Natalie. All one, all separate. He eased the pull of the foreign spell off his skin, then, taking care not to disturb the forces binding the tormenter, he steadied the boy's heart, staunched the worst blood flow, basics for which he didn't need a detailed knowledge of human anatomy.

Last, he dulled the boy's pain. He pulled out the agony, touched the natural endorphins to encourage their own protection. The boy's breathing smoothed.

His hand hovered above the boy's hair. Could he remove the memories of this torment? He ached to do so, to take away the anguish that would bring nightmares and flashbacks.

He swallowed. No. Maybe it was within his power, certainly with the strength that he now felt. He knew a charm for memory shields. But shielding a trauma like this . . . What aftereffects would the psyche create? Best to leave alone the human mind.

Instead, he offered his strength. "You've been brave," he whispered. "Now you're safe. You'll soon be with your mother. Rise above this."

The boy gave a small sigh and the corner of his lips tilted, not really a smile, he wasn't capable of that, but an acknowledgment that hope existed once more. "Angel Gabriel?" His question was but a breath.

"A friend."

As the moment faded, the boy's eyes closed. Not in death, in relief.

"Police five minutes," LaMarr warned in Ram's ear.

"We need that source," Estrella hissed.

With one swipe of his hand, Ram loosened the boy's bindings, then he tightened the cage around the Magic Man. An urge to tighten it to pain, to give back a measure of the monster's depravity swept through Ram.

So strong. He could do it. Could even tighten the lungs, rid society of an evil monster. With the blessing of the Mages, he'd done so before. The sweet temptation ran through him.

His fist clenched against the urge. He was not an executioner. Let justice be dispensed by the courts.

Instead, he sought the talisman Magic Man had unwittingly unleashed. His rippling probe colored the air with a faint shade of purple. There. A jagged-edged black-green circle glowed in the barrier he'd set around Magic Man. The onyx- and ruby-encrusted dagger. How to get it out without releasing the murderer?

Sweat ran down between his shoulder blades. His heightened acuity took in the stench, the ugly taste of blood that lingered in the air, the eye-burning candle smoke. Mundane details returned; his cell phone was beeping a voice mail alert. The extended wielding of power, along with his recent stings, started to make him dizzy.

Still, he had to get that knife. With a slight touch, he spread the cage, attempting to expose the dagger, but keep the killer's feet and arms enclosed so he couldn't move. As soon as the dagger was exposed, Ram grabbed it, then replaced it with a more mundane one that had been lying nearby. Irrefutable evidence for the police and courts.

As he rolled the knife up into the bottom of his shirt, keeping it away from his skin, the pounding of footsteps on the stairs warned him he couldn't get out unseen. Instead, he hurried to the wall next to the door. His muscles shook as they drew on burning anaerobic energy, and the bee stings felt like stabs of fire.

He needed one last spell, but the combined powers of the triune were weakening. To his surprise, he drew not from the charging interaction with the other Mages now, but from memory. Of Natalie. Of how she felt. Of how she might taste. Of how easily she had fitted his movements.

Using a simple spell, he pulled a glamour over himself, shifting the air molecules to reflect the wall behind him. If someone looked intently, he could be seen through the shimmer, but he should be able to fool the police long enough to get out.

Sure enough, the police barging in focused on Magic Man and the boy, giving the room only an initial cursory scan for threats. Ram released the cage holding Magic Man, allowing the police to grab the killer, and then slid out the door. He joined LaMarr and Estrella outside, and they walked a short distance into the deepening night, away from the prying eyes of the press and the gathering crowd; then he released the deceptive spell.

He collapsed against the side of an empty house, only the worn bricks at his back keeping him upright. A disconcerting juxtaposition of exhaustion and awareness took hold of him. His muscles shook with the aftermath, worse than if he'd run a marathon, while sounds—sirens, tires on road, conversations, the roll of distant thunder across the lake—bombarded his ears. He grabbed in deep breaths of the hot air, tasting exhaust and crab-boil spice. At least these breaths weren't tainted with the odors of evil.

Estrella reached a bracing hand toward him.

"No!" he snapped, causing her to jerk back. He grabbed another breath, then said, more softly, "Don't touch me. Don't talk." His skin already burned from the pressure of the humidity. One more touch, one more sound or taste or smell would be unbearable.

The Mages understood, waiting with cautious eyes on the crowd, while his aroused state muted. Moments later, Estrella handed him a packet of trail mix.

He poured the nut and oatmeal mixture into his mouth, washing it down with a bottle of water from LaMarr. "Thanks," Ram said at last, as the calories and hydration worked.

"Were you able to identify the source of the magic?" LaMarr asked.

Ram rolled down the hem of his shirt, and then dumped the object into a cedar box that LaMarr held.

LaMarr's lip curled as he looked at the dormant talisman. "Imbued power and delusion. Still, there may be something deeper to learn." He closed the box with a snap, sealing it in stasis. "Ram, you look beat. We'll cleanse the taint and destroy the dagger at the next Circle. Tomorrow?"

"I can't tomorrow. How about the day after?"

"Fine." LaMarr sounded a bit irritated, but he didn't demand reasons. "In the meantime, I'll see if I can find any reference to that strange vacuum sensation we felt."

An ambulance pulled up as the police led out a shuffling Magic Man.

"That's him!" shouted Magic Man, pointing at Ram. The three Mages slid deep into the shadows and the police saw nothing but the raving killer. "Forgive me for angering you," shouted Magic Man as they shoved him into the squad car. "I will be a better servant next time."

"He thinks you're demon spawn, Ram," LaMarr said drily.

"He might not get an argument from some people," Ram retorted with a matching humor.

Estrella glanced around. "The press is here. We'd better get going."

Ram shifted his shoulders; the edgy currents of the night, the burgeoning crowd, were grating on his nerves. The foreign spell that had dragged at his power was gone, leaving him with only a lingering headache. Yet he couldn't get rid of the unsettling sensation, even as he accepted Estrella's parting kiss. She and LaMarr seemed to have no such unease as they faded into the night.

Ram lingered a moment, scanning the crowd. The drama of the warehouse commanded everyone's attention; three extra gawkers rated nary a glance. Still, he couldn't erase the feeling of being spied upon. He made one more survey of the crowd, but if anyone there had a special interest in him, he couldn't detect the watcher.

EMTs brought out the boy on a stretcher, his sobbing mother clutching his hand. Ram heard the boy tell his mother, "The Angel Gabriel saved me." Press crews shoved forward. Someone scrambling for a photo op bumped Ram, setting his nerves screaming from the touch. Time to get out of here.

Chapter Eight

Natalie pulled into her driveway on edge from the long drive home. Crossing the Lake Pontchartrain Causeway, winds too reminiscent of a hurricane howl had rocked her car. Then, with the wind still playing its post-traumatic-stress tune, the battle against molasses-speed traffic around Mandeville and Covington was followed by a trek on an unlit gravel road, accompanied by the ping of stones ruining her car's paint job. Only when she'd burrowed into the woods surrounding her home had the thick trees cut the wind.

Intruding thoughts of Ram hadn't helped her concentration, but they had been the only pleasant piece of the hour. What was it about him that had her fingers itching to comb through his slightly mussed hair and had her insides in such a twist? Especially since when he'd left her, the man couldn't have been more distracted.

Still, he'd wanted a confederacy. She smiled. The notion shouldn't appeal so much, but it did.

She pulled up beside the porch, turned off the headlights, and was plunged into unrelieved darkness. Not a single neighborly light could be seen. Even the stars and moon were erased by thickening storm clouds.

Normally she cherished the refuge of her home, the few hours to recharge after days in the city, but as she stepped from the car, she was beset by a sudden chill. Rubbing her hands against her arms, she glanced around. A trickle of fog wound about her feet, reminiscent of the best Frankenstein movies, but freaking her out like no movie ever could. Snapping on the flashlight she pulled from her bag, she gave in to a sudden urge to make sure Twig and Twyla, her woodpeckers, were safe.

A thought struck her. Ram might be able to help with the problem they presented.

She skirted the house and headed to the rear of the estate. A stand of massive pines flanked one side, but at the direct back a stand of gnarled old live oaks guarded the Severin family cemetery. Charles once told her that, as a child growing up here, he'd formed a play area beneath the twisted arms of the oaks. Right next to the tilted and crumbling tombstones. To her, it seemed a macabre place to play, but since she'd once forged out a small spot of her own next to a basement furnace, she hadn't commented.

Humidity-spawned perspiration clung to her skin, and her flashlight beam jerked and wavered in a crazy-quilt pattern. Wind sighing through the tops of the trees set the needles and leaves quivering. At last, she reached her destination, a hollowed-out tree, the oldest amidst the woods. Twig, the male, had formed their nest here.

Feeling like a mother checking on her child, she played her light across the rotting wood and caught one woodpecker in her beam. Twig opened an eye and gave her an irritated look.

"Sorry," she whispered, even that small sound a disturbing intrusion in the silence. "Just wanted to make sure . . . You're still safe."

She counted herself fortunate that she'd found the nest. According to everything she'd read since she'd first seen the birds after moving back this year, ivory-billed woodpeckers were notorious for their elusiveness. With the ivory-bill thought to be extinct—a sighting in Arkansas had never been confirmed—it was her responsibility to protect this lone breeding pair.

How best to do that was the problem. Tell DNR? Wildlife and Fisheries? She wasn't convinced they had the manpower or will to do the job properly. She'd read about the species, but she was no bird expert. So far, she'd done what she could, made sure they had food and kept their forest surroundings intact and free from intrusions. With everything else demanding her attention, she hadn't pursued the question.

Now, however, she finally had someone knowledgeable to ask, someone she'd trust with their welfare. Ram.

A gust of hot wind, thick with moisture, moaned across the back of her neck like an unseen demon's breath. Better get inside before the deluge.

"We'll protect you," she promised, turning back to the house.

She pressed her lips together against the memory of small, lifeless parrots. No one had protected them. "I'll stop the smugglers," she promised, uncertain whether she was speaking to the woodpeckers or herself.

She lowered the light and turned toward the house. And she'd get a story with a paycheck good enough to complete her Nepal fund. If the disk didn't provide a lead to her brother, then she would be off to Asia to look for him.

With the flashlight, she picked her way easily through the night. In the first years of their marriage, when she'd lived out here with Charles, she'd explored every inch of the property. Later, when things started getting messy between them, she'd moved into the city, and she hadn't been invited back. But she never forgot. She knew these grounds as well as she knew her name. Even the darkness couldn't erase that bone-deep familiarity.

She'd had offers for this piece of land, offers priced to be irresistible. That was one temptation she'd had no problem staring at and besting. Each offer was from a developer who would tear the house down and uproot the trees without blinking.

Selling was impossible. Even though she owned the estate only because the tragedy of Charles's death happened before she'd finalized the divorce, even though some days and nights she hated this place, even though the taxes were a financial drain she could barely afford, selling never entered the equation.

Now Twig and Twyla gave her one more reason for preserving this land.

Still, she paused as the dark bulk of the house appeared. With its wide balconies, its stilts, its shutters, the structure was as much a part of these uncultivated acres as the Severin family. She'd married into the Severin name, but she'd embraced their heritage as hers. Now, she was the widow of the last of the direct line.

The house had always felt like a home to her. Had she fallen in love with Charles as much for his roots and his home—for his utter assurance that he belonged—as for him? Was that why he'd turned from her? Because they'd both discovered she no longer loved him? Or had love withered in the face of unforeseen cruelty? The questions, the failure of her marriage, bit at her, as she stared at the lacy railings and painted shutters.

How many times had she seen these details? Ten thousand? Tonight, though, she felt as if she had never seen the house from just this angle, possessed by the night and redolent with the sheen of damp and the smell of decay.

Something felt strange. She retrieved the armload of dirty clothes from her car, and then trudged up the steps, the hairs on her arms sensitive to the rising tide of wind.

No, not felt strange, smelled strange. Something lurked above the odor of the fresh pine, old vegetation, and older wood scent. This smell, lingering in the enclosed stoop, burnt her nostrils with a sweet and peppery scent. Like cinnamon.

Or licorice. Nathaniel's favorite treat.

A thud sounded behind her.

"Who's there?" Dropping the clothes, she flung her light around, swinging it in a wild arc over the lawn, letting it be swallowed by the maw of darkness beyond. She listened above the roar of her own blood, strained dry eyes for a flicker of light or shadow.

The night remained a sealed crypt. Not even the bats had been disturbed, and the sound wasn't repeated. The woods held a few apple trees—remnants of a moneymaking scheme by a distant Severin. Maybe an apple dropping?

As she bent to pick up her clothes, the flashlight beam caught on something strange. She picked it up. A feather, like the one she and Ram had found. Purple with a gold tip.

How the hell did another feather from a nonexistent bird get out here?

That ominous feeling—of being watched, being invaded—crept back.

With a knot in her belly, she swung her light around, listened and watched, but again the night gave no answers. Letting out a slow breath, she stood. Balancing the clothes on her hip, she deactivated the alarms and unlocked the door. Once inside, she carefully reset the security, glad that after moving back she'd added the alarm and changed the locks. Tonight she was spooked.

Inside, she dropped her pack and clothes on the floor. It was too dark in here, too filled with gloom and stale, cooled air after the stifling heat of the night outside. She snapped on the lights, filling the house with a warmer glow and revealing the graceful interior. For all the eeriness outside, the interior was genteel charm.

An old house was expected to have antiques, and hers was no exception. However, Nathaniel had the artistic eye and, with Charles's blessing, her brother had put aside his penchant for black leather and studs to help her redecorate. They'd kept the family antique armoires and sideboards, but complemented them with lighter wood accent pieces. In came plants, out went doilies. The flocked wallpaper had been replaced with an airy period floral.

At least she'd gotten this done before Charles spent the remainder of his inheritance in his search for magic and power.

Tonight, however, the home still worked its charm, and she found herself absorbing its peace. Dirty clothes in hand, she headed to the washer and dryer.

From outside, a faint squawk—*kent, kent*—broke the silent peace. What? She froze, listening, head tilted toward the window. *Kent, kent.* The sound was repeated. Innocuous, like a simple child's trumpet, yet it swept through her with the urgency of a siren.

"Twig!" She dropped the clothes and grabbed her flashlight.

Kent. Ke— His distress call was cut off.

Alarms off, locks released, and then she was racing out. Her flashlight beam jerked with the pounding of her heart, cutting the darkness like a wild blade.

The promised storm had arrived. Wind slapped her. She slipped and slid across the wet grass, fat raindrops steaming against her bare arms. Her mind was full of bitter blame.

Stupid, stupid, stupid. I led them right to the nest.

She scrambled into the oaks, ran to the hollowed tree, shone her trembling light up. Sticks, just sticks. The nest was empty.

Barely able to see, her ears filled with rain and moaning branches and the memory of that chopped-off call, she swung the light around. Nothing. Any footprints were washed away by the storm. She shone it through the trees and the beam caught a movement of black shadow against the grey rain.

She took off, running, traction easier beneath the trees. How could the intruders see without lights? Experimentally, she flicked off her flashlight to hide her position.

And promptly stumbled over a root. She caught her balance and flicked the light back on, filing away the fact that whoever had taken the woodpeckers had damn good night vision. She swung her necessary light between the tree trunks. If she was going to announce her position, she'd damn well see what she could.

There. More motion, a thicker bulk. But she couldn't see any specifics.

The storm was muted beneath the pines; another faint *kent, kent* broke through. Her swath of light grazed across a patch of white high in a pine. Twyla! Twyla was free! That patch was the white splotch on her wing. Quickly, Natalie lowered the light, praying that whoever had taken Twig hadn't seen Twyla.

Where was the bird-napper heading? The old logging road?

If so, she was gaining, but she wouldn't close the gap in time. Taking a chance, she veered directly toward the road. The man—if it were a man—was dodging through the trees. If she got to the road first, she might make up more time.

Her lungs burned with pain as she skidded out onto the ruts of the road. Blast! The unrelenting rain was worse in the open. Her sneakers slid, and she fell. Pain shot through her thighs, her knees taking the brunt of the impact. She scrambled up, ignoring the limp hitching her stride.

There was a truck. Her breath rasped harsh into the night. Her attention was diverted by the figure who emerged from the trees, carrying a bulky bag. The bastard had Twig!

Weapon. She needed something to stop him. Damn, damn, damn, she had a gun. Left at the house. Unloaded. She tightened her grip on her only weapon, the flashlight, and sprinted full out. Get there before he got in the truck. One on one, good odds, especially since she had the advantage of furious adrenaline.

Wouldn't have mattered if the odds were a hundred to one.

A slight motion in the corner of her eye alerted her. *She'd miscalculated.* There were two bastards.

She started to spin, to meet the threat, only a fraction of a moment before a kick to her thighs from the unseen second prowler threw her to the mud. Bone-deep agony grabbed her legs. She flailed with her arm, rolled away.

Another powerful blow to the shoulder blades sent her reeling down, followed by a kick to the ribs. Something cracked, and breathing became agony. A vicious boot at the back of her neck held her down.

Blindly, she fumbled for her cell phone, felt the familiar indentations of the keypad. Her fingers, though, instead of going for nine-one-one, hit one-three-six, talk. Speed dial Ram.

Voice mail. What was he doing? Casting a spell? Surgery on a needy turtle? Making love to a beautiful woman who didn't surround him with killer bees?

"Bitch." With a curse, the phone was snatched from

her numbing hand and a gun butt smashed against her temple. On the edge of consciousness, she began to drift. Desperately, she clung to sanity, trying to remember each detail.

Even the hands running a search on her body, the lewd pinch to her breasts, a pinch that would have hurt if the near coma wasn't anesthetizing her. Funny word. An-es-th. An-es-th. Her brain stumbled over the sounds.

"Enough. We have it." A sibilant hiss in the night. From the one who held Twig. "Leave her alone."

Odd voice. Unrecognizable, yet her tripping mind heard an edge of familiarity in it.

The boot pressed her face cruelly deeper into the mud. God, she couldn't breathe! Her lungs heaved in panic, the only part of her able to move. Water filled her nose. Her slack lips and tongue tasted the gritty death.

"No." The strange voice again saved her.

The boot lifted, and she turned her head enough for air. She heard the truck start, one last faint *kent,* then the truck lurched into the rain and she was alone.

How long did she lie there? Long enough to get drenched. Long enough for every particle of her body to find a fresh way to hurt. Long enough to go through a dirty thesaurus's worth of curses.

Long enough for nausea. Her stomach heaved and she vomited into the mud until there was nothing left inside her but the sour taste of failure.

She tilted her pounding head enough to gaze into the night. Right now, she felt as empty, as drained of life as that black sky. She took shallow breaths, forcing herself to keep drawing in oxygen. Her breathing came unevenly; she was pretty sure one of her ribs was cracked.

At last, she let out a long breath, despite the pain. Much as she wanted to shut her eyes, to lose herself to some kind of oblivion, self-preservation began to reassert itself. She wouldn't make any progress finding

Twig by wallowing in pain and despair. Slowly, she shifted her hands beneath her, then stopped with a wince. It hurt to lie like this, but standing upright was going to hurt a hell of a lot more.

Gathering her fading store of courage, she painstakingly lifted herself to her knees. Spears of pain radiated from her abused legs, and she choked on more nausea. With a shove, she stood.

The world spun, then steadied into a relentless throb of pain and an ache in her heart that she'd failed Twig. Pressing her lips together, she retrieved her cell phone, brushed off the mud, surprised that it still seemed to work.

She tried Ram again. Voice mail. She absorbed his deep, steady voice, not examining her inexplicable need to reach him, to share what had happened.

To have him come out and bandage her and hold her. To feel the smooth, clean touch of his skin against her cheek and to be wrapped with the gentle strength of his arms. To give in to temptation.

The greeting ended. She clung to the lifeline until she'd regained a measure of sanity and strength. Until she realized the phone had clicked off without her leaving a message. Redial. Voice mail again. Who kept their phone off that long?

What could she say? He was an hour away. Busy.

Up to her to take care of herself. Always had been, always would be. As she drew strength through the phone, she prided herself that her message was steady.

"This is Natalie. Call me when you get this. Or, when you get a chance. Something happened." Her voice caught as the horror played an instant flashback. Okay, she wasn't as steady as she thought. "I need to talk to you."

She disconnected, too exhausted, too battered to think any more. After dumping the phone in her pocket, she swiped at her muddy cheeks, upset with the tears she couldn't control.

Oh, crap, she'd left the house unprotected, too. What good were alarms if she failed to set them when she left in a panic? She stumbled back to her house as rapidly as her clumsy feet could take her—about the pace of Frankenstein.

Had his stitched-together body parts hurt this much?

The house looked the same. Inside, no sound broke the hushed emptiness; nothing had been moved. The clothes were still in a heap where she'd dropped them. Her purse was still tossed to the side. Antiques and plants and artwork were still in place. She and Twig were the only victims of this thoroughly fucked-up night.

She set the alarms, checked them a second time for good measure, and then leaned back against the door. What to do next? She couldn't think, couldn't plan. Her brain had lost the capacity to think rationally.

The pain in her ribs, and everywhere else, gave her one answer. The clenching in her belly came from hunger as much as dread.

Right now, hold out against the edge of panic. Don't think of Twig, don't think of the pain, don't think about how badly she'd screwed up.

Focus on finding answers.

Clean up and bandage up first, get some food for strength, rest. Dear Lord, she needed sleep.

She stood in the shower, letting the hot-enough-to-boil-crawfish water wash away aches and muck. How long she stood, she didn't know. It wasn't long enough to wash away memory.

When the water turned cold, she finally got out and wiped the steam off the mirror. What a wreck. The lump on her brow was especially fetching. First thing, bandage up that rib. Her skin was already turning a bruised purple. Handling the Ace bandage was a trick, but at last she had a good wrap. She downed two Vicodin, threw on some clothes, and retrieved her phone. The chores exhausted her. She needed food.

In the kitchen, she was munching a tasteless protein bar when a flash of light streaked across the window. Near used-up adrenaline mustered a nervous spurt. Enough to kick-start her fatigued brain. *That wasn't lightning.* She sidled closer to the window, lifting the gauzy curtain enough to see outside.

The rain hid details, leaving only smudges of dark and darker. Yet, unmistakably, a light circled her home, slow and searching. Too steady and low for the strobelike lightning. Someone was out there.

Chapter Nine

When the light disappeared toward the front of the house, she set her jaw against unexpected shaking. If the bird-nappers had come back, they wouldn't find her such an easy mark. Not this time. From the secret cubbyhole installed by some security-minded Severin, she removed her semiautomatic and loaded in the magazine.

Weapon in hand, she wound through the rooms. The alarm system was still engaged. Whoever was out there wouldn't get in unannounced. She edged to a front window. Separating the blinds a scant inch, she peered out. At first she saw nothing out of the ordinary, although the storm gave her limited visibility.

The light had been turned off. Which probably meant the intruder was out of the trees and onto open ground. Damn rain, where was he?

There! A hulk of a shadow appeared from the right, nearly out of sight. She poked the gun through the narrow slats of the blind. Her vision tunneled to that skimpy view. Her brain—the part that wasn't busy shutting down in favor of instinct—recognized her hands were shaking. She braced her shoulder against the wall to steady herself, two hands on the grip.

Her finger slid nearer the trigger. The bastards wouldn't get the drop on her again.

Don't shoot blind, warned the nagging voice of reason. Target in your sights, first. She took her finger off the trigger.

A pair of shadows came into her strip of vision. With the barrel, she traced their motion. Straight to the bottom of her porch steps. Damn, from this angle, she had lost sight of the intruder. As she eased away from the window, a faint whistle sounded from her porch. Calling reinforcements?

She lurched for a better angle, and then skidded to a halt as she crossed the foyer. The bulky shadow filled the frosted glass of her front door. Nausea burned her throat. Run! She twisted, and the motion sent shocks of pain from her ribs.

Suddenly clearheaded, she planted her feet and aimed. Two hands, arms lifted to eye level. No fear, no doubts. Whoever was out there would not invade her home. She took a steadying breath, her fingers ready to squeeze if the door was attacked.

The *Addams Family* theme danced into the silence. Duh, duh, duh, dum. Damn, damn, damn! Her phone. In her pocket and announcing to the shadow that she was waiting right here in the darkness. Calling: come and get me.

"Natalie!" The front door shook under a knock. "Are you all right?"

It was the accompanying barking that broke through her focused deafness. Val. And Ram. She recognized his voice now.

Her tensing fingers relaxed. She set the gun on a

table, and then pulled the ringing phone from her pocket. Ram. She flipped open the phone. "I'm okay."

"Thank God. I called as soon as I saw your message. Don't you answer your phone?"

"I was in the shower." Suddenly she smiled, absurdly warmed by his concern. He'd driven all the way out here through the storm.

"For an hour? Would you open the damn door so we can talk face to face?"

"Oh. Sorry." She closed the phone, and then ran her fingers through her hair, trying to neaten it. A moment later she had the alarms off, the porch light on, and the door open.

Happened every time she first caught sight of him. Her heart did that cha-ching thing, and her blood made a mad rush south.

Damn annoying if it was all one-sided, but from the spot of color on his cheeks and the thorough scan of his eyes she had hope it wasn't. She only had time for an involuntary smile before Val bounded across the threshold into the house. The dog's wagging tail beat a vigorous rhythm, spraying rain as she butted Natalie's legs in welcome.

Natalie scratched Val's head and ruffled her wet fur. "Hello, girl. Did you have a muddy romp in my woods?" She cooed over the dog, getting a rough tongue-lick reward. But her sidelong gaze was all about Ram.

Cha-ching and migratin' south.

He closed the door and studied her, his hands clenched at his hips. A slight frown narrowed his eyes. She figured he was taking in the details: fresh washed hair, green Franklin High gym shorts, oversized Jazz Fest T-shirt, no bra, bruises on her legs, contusions on her face. His gaze flicked to the gun on the foyer table, then back to her.

"What the hell happened tonight, Natalie?" His voice was harsh as he took one long step that closed the distance between them. He stood before her, fists clenched, male anger leashed and ready to battle.

For her? She shook her head, the will to relive the whole story abandoning her. Fatigue crashed her defenses. Instead, she wanted warmth. Wanted him. She took a single step forward, her bare feet butting against his deck shoes. "Hold me."

Without another word, he wrapped his arms around her, and that simply, the barriers between them crumbled.

She leaned her head against his chest, drawing in his steady heartbeat. Her fingers splayed against solid muscle, absorbing his warmth and strength. A faint woodsy scent clung to his soaked shirt. Foreign, yet an indelible part of him.

"Your skin smells nice," he murmured, nuzzling into her hair. "And I probably smell like wet dog."

"You should get out of those clothes."

"Best offer I've had all night." He gave a low chuckle.

One of his hands played over her lower spine in a delicate, soothing caress, while the other splayed across her shoulders in a protective gesture. Despite his wet clothes, she relaxed against him. Her eyes closed, and she slid her arms to his back, drawing him closer. His arms tightened a little, molding her suddenly pliable body.

Smooth as the move was, it still sent a pang across her abused ribs, and she winced. A tiny motion, quickly covered.

Except he caught it. Slowly, taking care not to jostle her, he opened his embrace. One hand brushed delicately against the thin layer of Ace bandage. His gaze, hard with determination, swept across her. "How badly are you hurt?"

"Not so bad that I won't heal in a few days."

He brushed back her mussed hair, exposing the bruise on her temple. "What bastard did this?"

He wouldn't accept evasions or distractions. Yet, she couldn't seem to sort out what to say first.

"Are you safe right now?" he asked, seeming to understand her confusion.

"I think so." She bit down on her lip. "Twig isn't."

"Who's Twig?"

"My woodpecker. They took Twig, but they didn't get Twyla." Words tumbled out like marbles dumped from a bag. "Twyla's his mate. I tried to rescue him, but AX . . . hurt me. They got away. I let them get away." She clamped her jaw tight, shoving back more tears. All her crying had been done in the shower.

"AX was here?"

"I'm pretty sure that I recognized his snarled 'bitch.' "

Ram cursed, his face turning hard again. "Let me look at those injuries."

"You're a vet, not an MD."

"Bleeding's not species-specific. Bedroom or bath?"

A trickle of blood from the cut on her cheek dripped onto her jaw. She hadn't even realized it had opened up again.

"Bath." Despite her doubts, despite her tiredness, the bedroom was dangerous territory.

Suiting actions to words, she led him to the bathroom, showed him where the supplies were, and then perched on the closed commode lid. Val flopped to the floor beside her. Petting the dog, Natalie silently let Ram dab her facial cut with first a peroxide-soaked cotton ball, then Neosporin cream. His fingers worked with deft, impersonal ease.

Natalie stared at his hands and the ring he wore, silvery with a red square in the center, and then at his chest and the raw pink gem stone on his steel neck chain. Anything to avoid his eyes and face, so close she could feel his breath soft against her cheek.

"What's the stone at your neck?" she asked.

"Watermelon tourmaline."

"And in your ring?"

"Ruby in platinum."

"Do they have any special significance?"

"Yes." She thought he wasn't going to explain further when he stopped to examine her face for an injury he'd missed with his peroxide and cream, but he added, "The ring I got in Bhutan. The tourmaline came from a gem store in Maine. For me, it felt like it had healing properties. Take off your shirt," he commanded briskly.

Feeling a tinge of embarrassment that she hadn't put her sports bra back on, she took off the shirt. Ram sucked in a breath.

Natalie looked down. It wasn't the sight of her bare breasts stealing his breath. Since she'd taken her shower, the bruises had deepened, and the Ace bandage she wore had a small stain of blood. The bee stings weren't looking too pretty either.

Their eyes met, and for a moment, she thought he was going to start the questions. Instead, he said, "If it's not better tomorrow, you'll get it X-rayed."

Not a question, but she still nodded.

"Do you have another Ace?"

"In the medicine cabinet."

He retrieved it, and then unwound the used bandage. "Why would AX go after a woodpecker? They're common birds."

"Not these. Twig and Twyla are ivory-bills."

He froze, his hand hovering motionless above her ribs. He fingered the tourmaline at his neck. "The ivory-bill was declared extinct in 1996. There've been supposed sightings in Arkansas and Cuba, but none confirmed. Even fricking NASA was looking for it.

You've got an extinct bird nesting on your property, and you kept that a secret?" He sounded incredulous, horrified.

"I only found them this past year. They've been nesting here for years, but Charles never told anyone. Who should I tell? I called a DNR agent, felt him out a little. His response was indifference. Said he was overwhelmed with important matters like wetlands restoration and I should call animal control to take the peckers to the zoo. Or should I let the local birders know? Let them tromp the habitat and disturb the pair? Who? I'm asking your advice."

"Althea Robinson at Fish and Wildlife is a good agent; she won't be indifferent."

"Then we'll ask her."

In the silence that fell between them, she realized he held the healing tourmaline while his other hand was splayed across her ribs. Heat spread from his palm across her bruised skin, bringing relief from the pain.

Magic.

"Don't," she snapped, jerking away from his hands. Her ribs didn't even protest the move. "What? You deliberately distracted me so I wouldn't notice?"

She started to rise, but he grabbed her wrist, halting her. His jaw was tight. "What is it you think I've done?"

"Magic. Don't deny it. I was in such pain from a cracked rib, I couldn't walk upright. Now all I have is a twinge."

"This is a bad thing?"

Mad not to be hurting? Yeah, she knew she sounded irrational. "I said no magic. I'll stick with Vicodin."

He shrugged. "Maybe you only bruised the rib. Maybe your painkillers are kicking in. I have to rewrap the Ace and take care of those stings."

"No thanks."

"Hydrocortisone only."

She hesitated, then sat back down. She'd see how he

kept his promises. Because, frankly, those stings did itch and hurt.

He rewrapped her ribs with the fresh bandage, a better job than her one-handed effort, then dabbed on the hydrocortisone cream with brisk efficiency and not a single sign of magic. Or desire. It was deflating that he didn't even seem to notice her nipples poking at him.

Finished, he stored the supplies and washed his hands while she put her shirt back on. Natalie rose, brushing her hands against her shorts, unsettled by the intrusive reminder of his powers. Despite his denial, that wasn't any painkiller working magic.

When he turned back to her, her unsettled feeling ripened with the heat of his glance brushing against her now-covered breasts. So, he had noticed. A flicker of some emotion tightened his face. Regret? Longing?

"I should be going," he said.

"It's late." She laid her hand on his arm. "Don't drive away. Stay here."

He stilled, his dark eyes searching her face for answers to questions she'd rather face in the morning.

"There's a guest bed made up," she continued. "I'll dry your clothes, feed you breakfast."

"Protein bars and coffee?" A flicker of a smile crossed his face

Her flicker of a grin matched. "With biscuits and jam."

"Let me get my laptop out of the truck."

She followed him back downstairs. He raced outside, heedless of getting soaked, and Val romped beside him, delighted with the new game, new smells, and a chance to do her business. From the doorway, Natalie watched the two move effortlessly through the dark. The rush of rain-cooled wind dampened her skin and tossed her hair.

Her belly tightened as she let them back in and man and dog gave identical shakes, sending a spray of water over the slate floor. Ram moved like a sleek animal, perfect confidence in his body.

"We're making a mess," Ram apologized.

"Easy to clean. I'll mop up while you change. There might be a robe—"

He held up the gym bag he'd retrieved in addition to the laptop case slung with a strap over his shoulder. "I've got things in here, but maybe you've got a towel for Val."

She retrieved a couple of beach towels and gave him one, then showed him the bath and bedroom. By the time she'd wiped up the water in the hallway, a pile of his wet clothes were outside the bathroom, Val waiting patiently beside them. As Natalie bundled up the damp pile, she heard the shower running and Ram singing— not surprising that he sang on key—too softly to hear the words, only the unfamiliar, appealing melody.

Val followed her to the laundry, winding around her feet and legs as if to say, don't forget me again. Pleased with the company, Natalie found herself smiling and humming a snatch of the tune as she loaded soap into the washer. Since her clothes had gotten wet from hugging Ram and Val, and smelled faintly of wet dog, she stripped and tossed them in too. As she added Ram's clothes, she automatically checked for any stains that might need treating before washing.

Abruptly, the hum caught in her throat. How had he gotten blood spattered on the legs of his pants? And another smear across the hem of his shirt?

No longer singing, no longer feeling the tug that something in this pit of a night had finally turned bright, she braced her hands against the washer and took a deep breath. Just when she'd put past problems and doubts behind her, she got slapped in the face again with the reminder that there was much about Ram she didn't know.

Swallowing the bitter taste of reality, she pulled a change of clothes from the dryer and threw them on.

"C'mon, Val," she called, pleased when the dog needed no second urging. When she got back to the bathroom hall, Ram was just coming out.

Despite her words of caution, she found her body responding once again. He wore gym shorts—definitely going impressively commando there—and a T that displayed equally impressive arms.

A man of magic, yes, but one who had driven here in a torrent to see if she was safe, who kissed like a dream, and who put aside his own desire for her.

"Do you need first aid, too?"

"No. Why do you ask?"

"There was blood on your pants."

"I'm a vet. Blood, piss, and vomit are hazards of the trade." He gave an easy laugh, and the action lit his face.

Yet, he looked drawn and tired, too, she realized suddenly. Worse than when he'd looked after the bees.

She caressed his face, the shadow of a beard scratching her palm. "Where did you go tonight? After the bees? What was so urgent?"

"Emergency at the clinic. A kitten was crashing."

Such a simple explanation, and one she should have anticipated, if she hadn't been so skittish with him. "Did you save it?"

"Yes, I saved him."

"Good." Without further thought to motive or consequence, she closed the gap between them and pulled him into her embrace.

He, too, seemed to need that closeness, that assurance. With a murmur of approval, he laced their hands together, settled deeper against her.

Subtly, the tenor of the embrace changed. His hardening erection stirred against her belly. He turned his head, bestowing a soft kiss on her palm; then his tongue touched between her fingers.

Her breasts tightened, the nipples tingling. He hardened more against her, not bothering to hide his reaction. She pressed him closer, saying, "You fit me. Curve to curve."

His cupped hand crossed her hip, sliding beneath the hem of her shirt, and then he warned, "Playing with fire, Natalie. How far are we taking this?"

Dear Lord, but she wanted him. She wanted that ribbon of desire to explode and consume her. Help her forget. "You're not too tired? From the drive?"

He laughed again. "A man is never that exhausted." His hand traced a delicate path across her cheek, a touch that sent shivers rippling over her shoulders. "I'm making no secret that I want you."

Being in his arms felt deliciously good. Sweeter than beignets and spicier than gumbo. She drifted on sensation. Cedar and dampness and the taste of him. His strong arms and legs. His lips on her hair. His feathery stroke across her neck. Part pressure, part relaxer, pure erotic.

"Oh, my," she moaned. "Where'd you learn that?"

"That?" He repeated the motion, then again with a knee-melting twist. "Or that?" His little finger stroked the soft skin behind her ear and sent a wave of desire so strong that her hips rolled across his erection.

"All of it."

"Germany," he whispered, his lips grazing her hair. Then, the kiss moved south with her blood, as his lips trailed lower. They nibbled the sensitive skin behind her ear. Over the line of her jaw, then to her lips.

She tilted her head, erasing the last inch of doubt, and finally she had what she wanted. Their lips together. Oh, saints, but he knew how to kiss. Expert, just the right pressure, just the right sweet touch of his tongue. She let him take charge, accepting his confident passion.

"I want to make love to you, Natalie." His breathing

rasped into the darkness, and she shivered at the rough edges. She could let him take the decision from her, go with the smooth flow of his hand and the easy persuasion of his voice. Decision by desire and by default.

Except even this potent desire couldn't hide the fact that, except for her repaired rib, every damn inch of her body was hurting. Even her heart, when she thought about Twig.

When she and Ram made love, she wanted a night she could remember, not one blunted by painkillers.

Something in the twitch of her muscles or the tightening of her lips gave her away. Ram pulled back. "I want to make love with you, Natalie," he repeated, "but not if it's Vicodin placing the invitation."

"The Vicodin's the only thing letting me move," she admitted.

He exhaled slowly. "Then we'll sort all this out in the morning. Which one's the guest room?"

Ram stacked his hands beneath his head as he lay in bed and stared at the ceiling. He'd gotten rid of the hard-on, but sleep had proved elusive, even though he was worn out.

Too much to think about: who had prodded Magic Man; the smugglers; Natalie.

Too much still arousing him: the memory of touching the fine grain of Natalie's skin; the thought of her tight, bare nipples begging him to take them in his mouth.

He kicked off the sheet, his skin too sensitive for its slight weight. Since Natalie formed the core of his current discomfort, he focused on her.

Concern over her injuries had stopped him. That, and her stubborn aversion to magic. Damn, she was skittish; her ex must have done a real number on her.

Using magic came so naturally, so joyously, to him. It was as instinctive as breathing and walking. He would have to tread carefully not to spook her and not to fuel her curiousity about the Mages.

He recalled the first time he'd seen her, a moment she didn't even know about. Eight years ago. Well before Katrina, when people spoke of the storm of the century in abstract terms. He'd been exploring his burgeoning powers and preparing to leave in a few days for the trip that had ultimately tested and changed him forever.

First, though, his father had asked him to represent the family at a fund-raiser ball. He couldn't even remember the cause anymore, only that it had been a black-and-white ball. He'd worn the conventional tux, as had most men, while the women wore traditional long gowns, mostly black.

Except Natalie. She'd been in a white suit. All white. From her bleached white hair to her white fitted jacket with nothing beneath but her white-powdered skin, to her white pants and an incredibly sexy pair of snowy stiletto heels.

She'd been laughing, accepting congratulations for an article she'd written about a fake faith healer, an article he'd admired. One look, and he'd been hit with gut-deep twin shots of lust and respect.

Two emotions that still plagued him.

He'd been about to introduce himself, already entertaining notions about how to steer her into his bed and whether to abort his trip, when Charles—a casual acquaintance he'd previously liked well enough—had joined her, embraced her, kissed her. And she'd happily kissed him back.

When he caught sight of the ring on her finger, he'd turned on his heel and left the ball. The next week he'd left New Orleans.

Twice more he saw her. Each time that same stab of admiration and lust. Didn't matter if he stumbled into a bitter argument between her and her husband or if he was mad as hell and blasting her for accusations against his brother's wife. Always, that same combustion.

He flexed his fingers beneath his head. Now added to the mix—power. For a while he thought he'd lost the magic, then when bits had trickled back, he'd thought he would never claw his way back to a level-ten Mage.

Ten? Hell, in two days he'd leaped to at least level twelve.

And Natalie was at the center of it all.

For now, he'd keep close to her by working with her to identify and stop those smugglers. The rest would sort itself out. His eyes drifted shut. He slept.

Until the stabs of agony came.

He bolted upright in the bed, his knuckles pressed against the bridge of his nose. As if mere pressure could relieve the claws of pain that shredded his skull.

A migraine. Except he'd never had a migraine in his life.

The vacuum spell must have tagged him, becoming active in the hours when he'd be most open, most vulnerable. Rolling waves of nausea threatened his stomach. Pressing his lips together, barely able to see, he fumbled for his tourmaline.

Clutching it with his ring hand, he chanted the words to raise camouflage shields. To hide himself from the seeker. The shimmering barrier between him and the attack reflected the spell backward and erased the tag.

Abruptly the pain vanished.

Elbows braced on his upraised knees, he strengthened the shields. Tested them. They were solid. Only then did he allow himself the freedom of curses. He'd gotten lazy in the months without his magic, and let his barriers lower during sleep.

He'd forgotten how much evil could slip in with dreams.

Whoever was behind that spell lurking in Magic

Man's room tonight had set a very clever trap. While Ram was saving the boy, he'd been marked like robbery money, the magical equivalent of a gentian stain.

He'd severed the tendril of connection, but he couldn't erase what had happened. The trap-setter knew something very important now: somewhere in the area was a high-level Mage to destroy.

Ram needed to find him first; the hunt had begun.

Chapter Ten

Mud filled her nose, her ears. Blinded her. She gagged on grit. Until it dissolved and all around her the water rose.

Half walking, half swimming, she tried to reach the airboat bobbing yards away. Each step only kept her treading water, while the muck slid on top of her.

Come get me, *she screamed at the boat, but none of the rescuers heard her.*

Charles struggled beside her, both of them keeping the elderly woman between them afloat, their little Yorkie tucked beneath his arm.

Rescuing hands took their aged burden. Another hand grabbed hers, lifted her up. The rescue boat had moved. She scrambled against the side of the boat. Turned, to see her husband disappear beneath the water. To see her dog drown.

Have to save them! She was face down again, suffocating in the muddy road, past and present mixed. Screaming. The hand again. Not a stranger. Ram. She grasped for life.

Natalie jerked awake, gasping and struggling for air.

Clutching a strong, familiar hand. Her heart raced at marathon speed, the muscles by her ribs throbbing.

"Easy, easy." The hand was real. So was the comforting pat on her shoulder. Ram knelt one leg on her bed. He was dressed in shorts and a T-shirt, his hair mussed, his eyes heavy-lidded with sleep.

He was real. So was Val's damp breath on her feet.

She loosened her death grip. "I'm sorry, I woke you."

"I was awake with my own nightmare," he said enigmatically. "When I heard you shout 'Come get me' I thought the attackers had returned." He settled one hip on the bed. "Want to talk about it?"

Resting her elbows on her knees, she scrubbed her cheeks. God, she hadn't had that nightmare in ages. "Katrina dream."

He nodded in understanding, propping one of her pillows against the headboard and relaxing against it. He stretched his bare feet out on her bed. "I used to dream of dogs, cats, birds lined up outside my clinic. Trying to get in while the waters rose. Like an urban Noah's Ark."

"You didn't evacuate?" she asked, reverting to the where-were-you-during-Katrina conversation that dominated New Orleans society after those August days. She settled beside him, and he wrapped a companionable arm over her shoulder.

He felt so warm, so rooted to the earth. Val joined them on the bed, lying across their outstretched feet.

"My two partners had families. They evacuated with the staff. I stayed at the clinic to care for the animals."

"That was brave of you."

"Bravery had nothing to do with it." His laugh was harsh. "I didn't give a shit about my life right then, but I sure as hell wasn't going to let anyone or anything else die. Not while I had breath to prevent it."

What had shoved him into such a dark place? "You want to talk about that?"

"No."

She laced her fingers through his, offering comfort. When he didn't elaborate, she asked, "How long were you stranded?"

"A week before we saw the first National Guard. A month before I slept somewhere other than the clinic."

He didn't need to detail the particulars of the stresses, losses, and horrors encompassed in those seven days. She heard them in his voice, in the flickering tension of his muscles, in the memory of her own experience.

"How about you?" he asked.

"We were headed out of the city when Charles found out Paulina, his old nanny, had refused to evacuate. We went to her home to persuade her to come with us, stayed with her to ride out the storm, and got trapped when the levee broke."

"How long?"

"Four days before an airboat came by." Four days on a roof in the steaming sun, wondering how high the water would get, not knowing when they'd ever get fresh water or food.

"No wonder you have nightmares."

She dragged a breath around the lump of grief. Charles and Paulina had made it to the boat with her. Burgundy, their Yorkie, had not.

Paulina had passed away two years later; Charles eight months ago. But that day something kind in him had died.

Letting go of Ram's hand, she wiped her face on her sleeve. It didn't take Freud to figure out why the nightmare had resurrected its ugly face. Poor lost Burgundy, now Twig. The suffocating mud, the drowning waters. Too many parallels.

"I was one of the lucky ones." She'd still had a home and resources to rebuild from. Yet even she carried invisible scars of those days. The storm's aftermath had been neither forgotten nor completely overcome. In many ways, large and small, those moments had shaped today.

He wrapped his other arm across her chest, linking his hands together, and laid his head on her hair. With a sigh, she settled deeper against him.

"Being with you strengthens me," he murmured.

She laid a hand across his chest, absorbing his steady heartbeat, even if she didn't fully understand him. Some things were clear. Curls of desire gathered around her, and she had no trouble seeing the stirrings of his arousal.

Was this the moment? The time where the connection between them led to the inevitable lovemaking? Their first time shouldn't be just the scratching of an itch. Or erasing the demons of the past. It should be special.

When did that old-fashioned notion visit and settle in? A strange houseguest, considering neither one of them was a virgin. At least she wasn't. She didn't know much about his history, but those touches hadn't been the fumblings of inexperience. A virile hetero male likely wasn't celibate.

Which led to another, blunter question best gotten out of the way. "Have you had sex recently?"

He laughed, the vibration a tickle against her uninjured cheek. "Was I that clumsy?"

"Oh, the opposite. Protection?"

"Ah, the obligatory health questions. Yes, I use condoms and, yes, my last physical gave me a clean bill of health."

"Me, too," she murmured. "Healthy. No one but Charles while I was married. A couple of I-need-assurance-that-I'm-still-attractive flings when we separated, but no one in six months."

Tension gripped his muscles. *Real smooth, Natalie.* Blathering on about past lovers and a dead husband. "Sorry, I'm out of practice with the sexual small talk."

He leaned back a little, and she gave a grunt of protest at losing the support beneath her cheek. When his thumb traced her cheekbone, she winced a little from the contact against her bruise. Until he leaned over and kissed it.

"You are attractive, Natalie."

"I wasn't angling for platitudes. 'You're beautiful, Natalie, beauty's in the eye, yada, yada.' I've gotten beyond those particular doubts."

He shook his head. "I didn't say you were beautiful. To me that implies glamour, sophistication—"

"When do we get to the compliment part of this compliment?"

Another laugh was her reward.

"You have something better than beauty," he continued. "There's a vibrancy about you, an eclectic style more compelling than any superficial arrangement of features. You crackle with life. That makes you very appealing."

As though he'd revealed too much, he made a move to go, wriggling his feet from beneath Val, who gave a snore of disapproval. "I'd better let you get some sleep."

Natalie put her hand on his arm. "Stay. Let me hold you. Maybe together we can both get some sleep, for the remainder of the night."

The smile he gave her was purely hot sex. "If I spend the night in your bed, my first thoughts aren't going to be about sleep."

A flutter started somewhere deep and spread its wings. Desire dried her mouth, moistened lower. She caressed his shoulder, rubbing against the cotton of his T-shirt in invitation and demand; then her hands moved lower along his belly. She lifted his shirt's hem, wanting him bared for her.

He stopped her. His hand closed around hers, fisting

the material, and his searching gaze took in her face. Then he tilted her face up a little. "Did you know you have charm-fed eyes? When they're not drooping with exhaustion and looking like smudged ash?"

He leaned over and kissed her, sweet and tender. "I don't want you falling asleep right in the middle of making love. My ego wouldn't stand the blow."

"Your ego is healthy as a heavyweight champ."

He laughed. "We'll pause right here. To be continued in the morning."

"You'll stay?"

"I'll stay," he murmured, then gathered her closer, settling lower onto the pillows. The warm, sleepy dog covered their feet.

Charm-fed eyes? She smiled.

Entwined, they slept.

Natalie finished the night without dreams, and when she awoke, a sunbeam had crept across her bed and caught on her exposed feet. Even without opening her eyes, she could feel the sunshine's warmth.

During the remainder of the night she and Ram had gravitated downward, until they were lengthwise on the bed, his front to her back, as tight as life jackets.

His morning erection pressed against her rear. Warmth that had nothing to do with sunshine spread inside her. Giving an experimental swish to her hips, she was gratified when he pulsed against her. His arms tightened, and he began a delicate nibble across the back of her neck. Nothing too demanding, not yet, just a simple, teasing, hello-day greeting.

Lazily, she opened her eyes. Morning had come and the storm had passed. If only the invisible storms could be so easily chased away. A glance at the clock confirmed how late they'd slept. Didn't they have someplace to be today?

A kiss from Ram on the back of her neck confirmed that she did not want to get up. Instead, she rolled away from the clock, twisting in Ram's arms until she faced him. Deprived of the target of his kiss, his lips brushed against her hair.

Then he reared back, looking at her. A moment of stillness and question. Yea or nay?

Her body tightened, zinged to exquisite life, and she smiled. While a gleam of triumph lit his face, she leaned closer, laying him back, and brushed his chest with the aching tips of her breasts. "I think we were *here* last night."

Cradling her hands in his hair, she leaned into his mouth. Gave him the kiss she'd been longing to give.

"Or here." He answered with a smile against her lips, while his hands stroked along her sides and moved up beneath the barrier of her shirt.

When his agile fingers found the sides of her breast, the caress sent a wave of pleasure coursing through her. His other hand began doing delicious, distracting things to her belly. She sprawled more thoroughly atop him, spreading her legs for the thick ridge of his erection.

Something big and blunt bumped up against her butt.

Wrong direction for Ram, at least in this position. She glanced over her shoulder and groaned. Val. Investigating this strange human play.

"We have a chaperone." She nodded at the eager-eyed dog now wedging herself against Ram's legs.

"Let her watch," he growled. His thumbs slid between them, rolling Natalie's nipples.

The tight spiral of desire turned her back to him. "A canine voyeur?"

"Mmmm." He lifted himself upward, pulled by strong abs, to reach her lips.

Behind them, Val whined. Her nails scrabbled against the wood floors as she aimed for the door. An atrocious stink filled the room. Doggie farts. SBD. Silent but deadly.

Natalie waved a hand in front of her face. "I think her need's more urgent, and she can't get out."

"Damn dog," Ram muttered without rancor. "Next time, she's getting a room with water, food, and a doggie door." He rolled off her, then gave her a warm kiss. "She'll expect her morning run."

"The alarm—"

"I saw the code last night." As he left the room she heard him mutter, "Foiled by my dog."

Natalie raked her fingers through her hair. An enduring lesson had come out of the past five years: You are only assured of today, so make every moment count. Whether making love with Ram or facing the work ahead.

She hadn't saved her little Yorkie, Burgundy. She *would* get Twig back.

She *would* find her brother.

And she and Ram had an appointment with an ornithologist.

So, get to work, Natalie. Surprisingly, she felt rested. Her ribs were achy, but not sending stabs of pain to her lungs. Even the bee stings were less itchy and the bruises less sore.

After a quick shower, she threw on clean shorts and a shirt and a pair of flip-flops. The circling ceiling fan was beginning to lose the fight against the gathering humidity. Today, as usual, would be a scorcher.

The dryer was running with last night's wash, but no sign of Ram and Val. Still out on their run. Where did he get the stamina for that long a run in the morning? Morning stamina. Would he also have energy . . . ? Do not go there, Natalie.

Setting a pot of coffee to brew, then turning her attention to the promised breakfast, she turned on the TV for the morning news. Her mind multitasked as she worked, part of it listening for Ram and Val to return, part calculating what she needed to do after they got back from Virgil's.

The news on TV was the same-old: government ineffectuality, worthless celebrity antics, financial and political woes. She stopped making her biscuits when the weather came on. As she watched the track of Hurricane Earl, her stomach twisted into that familiar tiny knot.

Good, Earl was keeping his ass in the Atlantic.

She'd put the biscuits in to bake when the local news portion came on, headlining the capture of Magic Man. Natalie stopped to watch the events unfold. Heard the boy's claim of being saved by an archangel.

"The alleged Magic Man has been identified as Francis Trebonne." The newscaster continued.

Francis Trebonne? Natalie peered closer at the TV. My, God, it *was* Frank. When he and Nathaniel used to drink together, she'd always thought Frank was a wacky—and that was a term she didn't often use—but essentially harmless conspiracy theorist. What had pushed him over the edge to atrocity?

Suddenly, Frank shouted into the air, at . . . nothing. She blinked. Or was it nothing? For a brief second, she thought she'd seen Ram, deep in the shadows, along with two others, right where Frank was pointing.

She had it bad, imagining Ram everywhere, when there was no further sight of him in the remaining seconds of footage.

Yet she couldn't get the idea out of her head. Ram had been there. So what? Nothing mysterious about watching a drama unfold.

Except Ram didn't seem the type for gawking.

He'd told her he was at the clinic.

And there was that blood.

Saved by an archangel.

Nightmares. Not caring if he lived. *Being with you strengthens me.*

Little things that didn't fit. They always nagged at her until she made sense of them. Annoying, but she'd gotten some of her best stories that way.

Ram returned from his run to find Natalie working in a kitchen redolent with the aroma of baking biscuits. His mouth started to water and his belly rumbled. He crossed the tiles to peer over her shoulder, while Val made a beeline to the bowls of water and dog food.

"Did you see Twyla?" Natalie asked, shifting away.

"No." He rescued a precariously perched biscuit from the plate she thrust between them and bit into it. "These are good, Natalie."

"Let's take breakfast outside; I'll show you the nest." She splashed more coffee into her mug. Holding up the pot, she asked. "Want some?"

"Black." He couldn't place her mood, except it sure wasn't the welcoming one he'd hoped to find when he got back. "Something wrong?"

"Just thinking." She passed him a mug, and after Ram slathered their biscuits with peanut butter—protein with every meal—they headed out, breakfast in hand. Val elected to stay with her bowls.

The sun had burned off the morning haze, leaving a cloudless, already sweltering day. Beneath the trees they found a modicum of shade, but little relief from the heat. At this slower pace, Ram found time to study his surroundings. The trees were old, infused with an unsettling aura of patience and indifference.

Given time, he might feel at ease beneath the branches. Not so today.

He finished his first biscuit. "Let's go over what our next steps are."

"I think someone's behind AX, heading the animal smuggling ring."

"Agreed. He's hired AX to do the front work and distributes through the Internet as 2Wyld."

"Which means he's keeping a low profile." She looked over at him. "You do realize we're using 'he' only for convenience. Could be a woman."

"Or a confederacy."

Her lips tilted in a brief smile. "More than one honcho? So noted." Then the moment of humor faded. "Do we know anything about him?"

"He's ruthless, doesn't hesitate to kill," Ram added grimly, thinking of the attacks, of Bennie.

"Why hasn't he killed us? Can't be because he has scruples. Last night—" She took a slug of coffee. "AX was vicious. The other stopped him short of murder. Not that I'm not thrilled, but . . . why?"

Good question. His fists, tensing when she mentioned the attack, relaxed as he pondered the question. "Bennie was a street thug. Our disappearances might cause more scrutiny."

"Or he needs us for some reason. We have something he wants?"

"Information?"

"Why not try to extract it?"

"Not ready to use it? Doesn't want to tip his hand?" He frowned as a thought occurred to him. "How did our thieves know about Twig? You said you didn't tell anyone."

Coffee sloshed from her mug, and he saw the faint tremble in her fingers.

"Did you?" he asked.

"No. Charles must have told someone."

An insidious thought occurred to him. "This may sound strange, but . . . Are you sure Charles is dead?

"What! Of course I'm sure. I identified the body myself and that's not the kind of thing you mistake."

"Identified how? Wasn't he burned?"

"Incinerated," she spat, then added, looking away, "The sight was bad, but what I can't forget is the smell." She gulped down a huge swallow of coffee before she turned back to him. "And yes, I know. Clothes, jewelry could be exchanged, planted on a substitute body. But, despite the burns, enough of his face was untouched. I saw him. I touched him. It *was* Charles."

"I had to ask." He also had to ask the next question. "Wasn't Nathaniel closest to Charles in those last days?"

The color leeched from her cheeks. "Do not bring my brother into this. And before you ask, I sure as hell don't know where he is."

He said nothing as she plunged deeper into the trees with an angry stride.

And you wouldn't tell me if you knew. A line in the sand. Nathaniel, family, came first. He understood the power of that choice, but understanding didn't stop the flick of pain to his heart.

He backed off. "Can you think of anyone else Charles might have told?"

"No. Maybe someone happened to see Twig."

"Coincidence? Doesn't sit right."

She seemed to recover herself and pointed upward. "There's the nest."

They stopped beside the dead hollow tree. The nest was empty. It was too much to hope Twyla would be in her nest; she must be spooked. He began a circuit of the area.

"You looking for Twyla or clues?" Natalie asked.

"Either."

"The logging road is that way." She pointed to her right, and they headed in that direction. "Let's look at another angle. Our honcho seems to target birds. Why?"

"Money. Ease of transport." He finished his breakfast, downing the last swallow of cooled coffee.

Her lips twisted, as though those answers weren't satisfying. "Do we have any leads back to this creep?"

"AX and the animal pipeline." He listed the balls of yarn unwinding in their maze. "Virgil, the ornithologist, may expose more of the pipeline."

"Or maybe I can find out more about 2Wyld. We have a lead to AX, the pool hall where he hangs." She lifted a brow at him. "You really think we should wait for Odette's spirits to nudge this—What was his name?"

"Raoul, and yes, we should wait. We can take my Harley to Palmer's Pool."

"I didn't know you rode a Harley."

"Maybe we both have things to learn about each other." Ram gave in to the temptation to touch her. He brushed the back of his fingers across her shoulder, then down her arm, savoring the intriguing contrasts of Natalie—pampered soft skin, callused fingers, feminine curves with well-formed muscles beneath, utilitarian tank top and painted toes.

When he circled a lazy finger around her wrist, she pulled away from the intimacy. "Still thinking?" he asked.

"Around you, sometimes that's not so easy." Nonetheless, she took his hand and gave him a delicate kiss on the knuckle.

For the moment, he could be patient.

A sudden smile creased her face. She pulled her hand away, raised her finger to her lips, and then pointed up into the trees. He followed her gaze.

His breath caught in awe. Twyla. There she was, staring down at him from the highest limb of the pine. Time halted as he drank in the amazing sight. A two-foot adult female, with all the beautiful coloring of the supposedly extinct ivory-billed woodpecker. Blindly, he took Natalie's hand, knowing unerringly where she stood. Their skin touched, and that thrill of unity washed through him.

After that single moment of exposure, Twyla spread her wings and disappeared into the forest. Ram let out a pent-up breath, somehow knowing she would remain hidden. A tiny feather fluttered down; he captured it and put it in his pocket. "She's magnificent," he breathed.

Natalie smiled, sharing his awe. "Yes, and we're going to get her mate back."

LaMarr might question why Ram went after the smugglers when other Mage business pressed, but LaMarr had never stood in a dappled forest, holding the hand of the woman who made his magic sing, and seeing the mystery of an extinct bird come to life.

Suddenly Natalie gave a pump to her fist. "Oh, my God, I never thought of this. Where does he keep the birds?"

"What?"

She looked at him, excited. "The animals. I was thinking of Twig, hoping he wasn't in a small cage, that he had food and sunshine, and it suddenly occurred to me. *Where* are the animals? They're brought up the back waterways, transferred to the New Orleans gang, and then AX takes them . . . where? Even if they have buyers, even if they ship out ASAP, there has to be a holding place for sorting, getting rid of the ones that don't make it. Wouldn't there be noise? Bird droppings? Pellets of food? Carcasses?"

"It would have to be some place away from people," he speculated.

"You get called on a lot of abandoned exotics. Have you ever plotted out where they were found? Seen if there's a pattern?"

"No. But I will as soon as I get home. I'll e-mail you the results."

They left the trees and emerged into the logging road

and a slap of humid sun. He looked around. "Show me where the truck was."

Natalie pointed. "There."

He bent over to study the patterns in the mud, tracing outward from the truck tires, and returned to their earlier conversation. "At the pool hall, we'll talk to Raoul, but we won't confront AX," he warned. Being that reckless was the short path to a bullet.

"What I'd really like is a peek at his cell phone."

What I'd really like is for AX to feel some of the pain he's caused. Ram stared down at the imprint of a woman's body dug deep in the mud, and his fists clenched. Natalie's body. No way in hell did he want to take her to that pool hall and expose her to that kind of danger. But to suggest she let him handle the bar scene was to assure she'd go off solo. Another moment for patience. Eventually, he would deal with AX.

Fortunately, she didn't guess his thoughts. Instead, she pointed to a smudge in the mud. "That looks like a foot print."

He crouched down to measure with his hand span. "Size ten. Came from that direction. What's down there?"

"Another path to the house; it cuts through the oldest stands of forest on the property." She sounded reluctant, but came with him. The mud, and the footprints, soon disappeared, giving them nothing further to follow. Still, they plunged deeper into the woods, hoping for some clue.

Ancient trunks crowded their path. Dense oak wood—no skinny birch or soft pine here—cut off the sun and surrounded them in green twilight. The only sound was the *thwap* of Natalie's flip-flops.

Uneasy, and not sure why, Ram reached automatically for his athame. Damn, he'd left the dagger at Natalie's.

Just when the path became so overgrown he thought

they might have to turn back, they stepped out of the twilight. A brick building squatted at the forest edge, still buried in the trees, but with a windowed eye on the house.

Whispery slithers crept up his spine. "What's that building?"

"A carriage house until Charles turned it into a library." She turned away from the building, planting her route firmly toward the more distant house.

Had the footprints been coming from here? Instead of following Natalie, he crossed to the library. "Is it locked?"

"It should be." With a scowl, she stopped walking away, but she didn't join him. "I changed the locks when I moved back. The key's at the house."

He heard the impatience in her voice, the desire to be the hell somewhere else, but for the moment he ignored her. The building did look undisturbed. Dust and dried brown leaves from last fall layered the porch, unmarred by any footprints. Yet something about this building was off kilter.

As he neared, he identified what had instinctively drawn him. The building was surrounded by a guard of magic. Not a protective, zap-the-intruder kind of barrier, but one designed to keep the magic inside confined and shielded from other Mages. The guard, however, hadn't been renewed in some time; it was crumbling.

What raised claxons, however, was the barrier's structure. The guard was mostly effective but crude—the magical equivalent of random, ugly concrete chunks. Parts of it showed true elegance, however, as if crafted by one infinitely more skilled. Two Mages or one learning his art?

He drew up at the barrier, and his hand reached to touch it. Abruptly, he jerked back, his fist clenching. He was unable to force himself to pierce the barrier.

Sweat broke out on the back of his neck. Not from this protective spell, but from memory's backlash. The last time he'd touched a barrier not knowing what lurked behind it, he'd almost been destroyed.

Under the stab of remembrance, the sultry day chilled and darkened despite the Louisiana summer sun filling the corners of his vision. He shifted his shoulders, his back burning with the memory of icy lashes. His insides curled in memory of his magic being stripped from him, leaving only soul-deep, madness-inducing emptiness.

The combined power of three Mages had stopped the demonic sorcerer they'd been sent after, but at a terrible cost. One dead, one missing, him left a dry husk.

"Ram?" Natalie touched his arm.

When had she moved so near? He blinked, unable to banish the lingering pain until his skin absorbed the heat of Natalie's fingers. The grip of memory faded as a tingle spread from Natalie's gentle clasp on his arm. The powers stirred inside him, awakened and refreshed by the contact. The longer he was with Natalie, the more intimate their feelings, the stronger the bonds between them. At least for him.

About Natalie, he had no clue. Unfortunately, magic gave him no more insight into the female mind than any other confused male.

"You got so pale. Are you okay?" Natalie asked.

He shifted away from her touch and ran his thumb over his ring. "Sorry. Memory reared its ugly head." He refused to fill the following silence with an explanation, reaching instead for the door handle.

He gave it an experimental twist. Locked.

Before he could examine other entrances, Natalie took his arm and tugged. "We need to get going or we'll be late for our appointment with Virgil."

He allowed himself to be pulled away, not reluctant

to leave the vicinity of those foreboding walls, yet he couldn't help glancing over his shoulder at the building.

Had the person who attacked his dreams last night been the same one who'd constructed the more refined part of the barrier? It seemed unlikely there would be two separate sorcerers working in this city, and neither one detected by the Magi.

So, who was it? Charles Severin was dead, but Charles had had an apprentice. A vanished apprentice.

Natalie's twin brother, Nathaniel DeSalvo.

Chapter Eleven

They never would have found Virgil le Blanc without specific directions and a sturdy truck. Anything lower slung would have caught a dozen bumps ago. Natalie bounced back against the seat as Ram braked beside the unassuming cypress-sided cabin.

Virgil had set the time and allotted them a five-minute meeting. She glanced at her watch. One minute early. Given the discreet alarm system she'd seen on the way in, she suspected their host would have disappeared if they hadn't been expected.

Out in the woods didn't mean low tech.

An enormous man with a Hagrid beard waited on the porch, watching as Natalie, Ram, and Val got out and approached him. "What's your dog's name, Montgomery?" Virgil asked, his voice rough as bark.

"Val," Ram answered. "You said it was okay to bring her."

"Who's the woman?"

"The reporter I mentioned, Natalie Severin."

Virgil looked at her directly for the first time. "This isn't an interview."

"I'm working another story. I'm here for information."

Virgil dismissed her and lowered his bulk into a cane rocker. Apparently they weren't going to be invited in. He turned back to Ram. "You said you had a feather you can't identify."

Ram handed him the odd feather they'd found in her car.

"I found another one on my porch." Natalie rummaged in her bag for it, ignoring Ram's annoyed look that she'd held back that little tidbit. With everything going on, she was entitled to a slip of the mind.

Frowning, Virgil held the feathers up for close examination, and then handed them back to Ram. "No bird alive has this kind of feather."

He stood and turned back to the cabin, indicating their time was up.

"Are you sure?" Natalie called, earning her a glower from Virgil.

"*You're* questioning my expertise?"

"No. I'm questioning why you aren't more curious about a feather from an unknown bird species."

"Because it's a fake. Common game that, fool the notorious ornithologist."

"I examined the feather under a microscope," Ram said. "That gold tipping is an integral part of the structure. It's not dipped or painted on. So is the hue. Purple or red depending upon the light."

"Let me take another look."

Ram gave him back the feathers and from the intent way Virgil examined them, Natalie got the impression he'd been bluffing, maybe seeing if they knew how rare and potentially valuable this find was.

He took a longer look at the feathers, testing the edge against the pad of his thumb, feeling the point of the shaft, flicking at a dark spot with his forefinger.

Finally he looked up at them. "You won't believe me."

"I thought you didn't know what it was," Ram said.

"I didn't say the bird was unknown. I said it wasn't alive. If I'm right, you've got a once-in-anyone's-lifetime find. So, give me a reason I shouldn't pursue it on my own."

"That feather may be a lead to animal smugglers," Ram answered, and Natalie resigned herself to everyone and his dog knowing about her so-not-exclusive story. "Ruthless men. So, unless you approve of stuffing birds into tubes, sedating them so deeply that most of them never wake up, and binding their beaks so they won't chirp," Ram clipped out, clearly fed up with the games, "then I suggest you tell us what you know."

Virgil paled. "I didn't know."

"Anything you can tell us would be helpful." Ram moved closer, and Natalie caught that soothing note in his voice, the one he'd used on Val. And her.

Virgil jerked his head toward the woods. "Your five minutes are up. I've got dead wood to clear out before my show films. You want to talk, you come help. I'm on a deadline."

He slung a crosscut saw over his shoulder, then lumbered off. Natalie caught up to him, with Ram strolling behind, looking around with interest.

"You close to catching these smugglers?" Virgil asked.

"We've got some leads. What's your show about?"

"What do you care?"

"I watch it every week. I planted a butterfly garden because of your instructions last year. Even got a monarch visiting now."

He finally looked at her as more than gnat. "You flattering me?"

"Yes. But it's sincere, so does that count?"

His laugh was a rusty sound. "Do you ever shut up and listen to nature?"

"Rarely, if there are people about. So, what's your program?"

"How to attract songbirds to your yard. Standing dead trees need to be toppled to give new growth a chance. I've got too many trees to cut on one program, so I'm getting a few down first."

They'd reached a dark area of tangled growth and thick trees coated with the ashy bark of decay and death.

"Ever worked a crosscut saw before?" Virgil asked Ram.

"Yes."

"So have I," Natalie added.

Virgil handed Ram the saw. "You two do the cutting. I'll guide the trunk."

Natalie stifled a groan as he pointed to a ginormous live oak surrounded by a tangle of underbrush. Her and her big mouth. The tree had to be three hundred years old and bigger than she could hug. Yet the stripped branches and cracked trunk told a tale of death and decay.

Virgil gazed upward and gave a sigh. "Tree never did come back after Katrina."

Post-traumatic stress syndrome. Even nature suffered. Still . . . "Seems a shame to have to cut it."

"Natural cycle," Ram said.

"Nothing natural about a hurricane," she snapped, then shook her head, joining Ram's laugh as she realized what she'd said. "Well, yeah there is."

"What ain't natural is levee breaks," grunted Virgil.

"A hurricane is a reminder of the existence of great powers," Ram added as he rolled up his sleeves. "Neither bad nor good, simply a fact."

"Yep," agreed Virgil, "and this tree will become a home for bugs."

"I get it," she muttered. "Circle of life. I just wish I'd brought a pair of gloves."

"Are you up for this?" Ram asked her in a low voice, as he took the saw. "After last night?"

"I'm doing OK, but next time I'll ask to see the tree first."

"Aren't you glad you had some peanut butter?"

"You're insufferable when you're right," she said with a laugh. "Let's just get this tree down."

They picked up opposite ends of the saw as Virgil expertly looped a rope around the top of the tree. Natalie caught Ram's dark gaze, then, without further talk, they bent to the work.

Sawing was no intellectual exercise; it was a brute physical experience. Her back and arms soon felt the anaerobic burn. Sweat soaked her as the teeth of the saw bit deeper into the dry wood.

Yet each move became a dance with the man at the end of the saw. She absorbed him through the back-and-forth ripples along the metal, as they joined in the fluid tango of lean and stretch. Ram was strong, but there was a mercurial ease to his motions.

Their gazes met over the tree trunk, and they fused into a single, metal-joined being. Their breathing was in synch, and her chest rose and fell at the same time as his. Even when they lost sight of one another, the joined rhythm never faltered. She was part of him, part of his cycle of breath and motion. A part she felt to the soles of her planted feet and the palms of her aching, blistering hands.

At last Virgil cracked a command to halt. With effort, Natalie stopped, aching from both the effort of exertion and the loss of that beautiful rhythm. Gasping, she braced her hands on her knees as Virgil carefully lowered the tree.

She glanced up at Ram, her view once again unobstructed. Still as stone, sheened with sweat, he was looking at her. His chest still rose in concert with hers. Behind him were only dense trees and the glow of the sun, not a wire of civilization.

Something powerful rose in her. One fact took root, as tenacious as kudzu. She wanted Ram, and not just because when they kissed her hormones outran her common sense.

Sexually she wanted him, oh, yes; Ram was very appealing. But it was more than that, a connection as basic and vital as the need for touch. This ache for him crashed against her, fast and potent, sweeping her into a powerful current. It made her wary.

Because, despite his denials, Ram was also a man of magic. A dangerous, intriguing man of secrets. She needed answers, understanding, and assurances, but life didn't always provide them. The only thing she could do was stay close and touch that tempting flame. And hope she wasn't destroyed.

"Give me the saw." Virgil's order pulled Natalie from her reverie. "Ram and I will break up the trunk, while you clear away that dead brush."

Natalie wiped her face with her sleeve, dragged out a bottle of water from her pack and then shared it with Ram after she handed the saw over to Virgil.

"About the feathers," Ram asked as they started.

"I never saw such coloring on a bird. I'd think it was a crossbreed heron, except for that glittery tipping. Supposedly there's one bird that has that coloring. The Benu."

"The Egyptian Phoenix?" Ram asked.

"The bird that rises from the pyre of ashes?" she asked, making sure she was on the same page and they weren't referring to some rare bird she'd never heard of.

"That's why I said it wasn't a living bird. A lot of breeds have been purported to be the descendants of the phoenix."

"Herons, mostly. Ibis, egret, eagle," Ram added.

The heron hatchlings they'd found—Ram had said they weren't rare enough to interest normal smugglers. She snapped a dead twig in two, startled by the connection. "How could an Egyptian myth be taking form in New Orleans?"

"Birds are also a big part of the Chinese and Southeast Asian culture; talk to some of them Vietnamese shrimpers." Virgil shrugged. "You asked for my expertise. My expertise says those feathers came from a Benu. It's your job to find it, although, if you do, I'd want to be there. You spend enough time in this world and you see some odd things." He tilted his head toward Natalie. "Do you believe in odd things?"

"I report for NONE."

Virgil gave a grunt. "Then I guess odd is kind of your thing. Maybe you can tell me what this is." He nodded for them to follow him and they plunged deeper into the trackless woods. "I spent some time in a hospital a while back. My heart. When I got out, I found this. Not sure why I never disassembled it, maybe wanting proof if anyone started funny business. But, far's I can tell, whoever made it hasn't been back since I returned."

Natalie exchanged a curious glance with Ram, but from his shrug, clearly he had no clue what Virgil was talking about. They scrambled over a fallen log and Virgil pointed to a pile of stones.

"That looks like an altar," Natalie said.

"Like nature worshippers? Or Satanists?" Virgil asked.

"No." Ram circled the boulders—a rarity in this part of Louisiana—looking, not touching them. He crouched down and felt the charred grass, then smelled the ash on his fingers. "Altar's not the right word. This is a place of focus and connection. Where two or more Magi meet to enhance their power."

"What are you talking about?" Natalie asked.

"The most powerful kind of human magic."

"I've never heard of it."

"You wouldn't have." The look he gave her was half amusement, half wary. "Think of this as a dark fairy circle."

Why do I get the impression you're trying to lead me off the track?

"This feels abandoned. I don't think you have to worry about anyone coming back." Ram got to his feet, dusting his hands against his thighs. "Have you found any others?"

"A few."

"Can you give us their locations?"

"I made a list; I'll get you a copy."

As they returned to the cabin, Natalie gave Ram a curious look and whispered, "What connection does all this have to the smugglers?"

"None that I know of, but he seemed eager to help and you never know what information might come in handy."

Satanic altars and dark fairy rings might be suited to a NONE story, but she was after smugglers. Natalie trotted forward and caught up to Virgil. "You wander these areas a lot. Have you ever come across any sign of something that might be related to the smugglers?"

"Like what?"

She shrugged. "A lot of animal waste in one spot? Food pellets dropped in the wood. A collection of feathers. Dead animals."

"I've seen a few things."

"Can you give us those locations, too?"

"Harder to pinpoint."

"Try."

He gave her a long look, then nodded. "Anything to help."

After leaving Virgil and returning to her home, Natalie and Ram agreed they both had information to pursue separately, and planned to meet the next day. She saw Ram and Val off to the city, and then she retrieved her laptop from the front hall where she'd left it. Just last night—seemed an eternity ago.

She'd map the coordinates of those sites Virgil had

given them, ready to cross-reference with Ram's when he sent them on. After that, she'd see if the Internet yielded any clues to 2Wyld. Finally, restock her car with clean clothes and protein bars and head back into the city.

Good to have a plan. Except, when she turned the computer on, it refused to boot, grinding futilely on the diagnostics. Reboot, troubleshooting, damn, nothing worked. What a lousy, stinking time for a hard-drive crash.

At least she'd backed up to a thumb drive. Hours of work with reformatting and reloading lay ahead, but she should be able to run some basics soon enough.

Her insides knotted, however, when she realized the thumb drive was missing from her bag. Impossible. She dumped the contents over the kitchen table, sorting carefully. Definitely gone.

Settling back in the chair, she rubbed her arms against her suddenly clammy skin. A hard-drive crash and missing backup at the same time? When she was very careful with her equipment? Her gaze raked over the strewn contents of her bag. Something else was missing: The printed copies of the photo she'd taken of that odd charm. The one from the smuggler's boat.

Swiftly, she sorted through the miscellany of her bag again, gut churning at the knowledge of what she'd find. Or wouldn't find. The charm. Damn, they'd gotten that, too. Except . . .

Eagerly, she thumbed up the photo file on her phone. She'd taken the original picture with her phone camera, that should still be—

Damn, damn again. Erased.

Every blessed trace of that charm had been obliterated. Her phone erased; the charm stolen; her computer, which she so carefully password-protected so no one could get in and steal her precious files, damaged. The bastards must have used a magnet. And the only time this phone had been out of her possession, except for showering and sleeping, was last night. When AX took it.

She flopped back in her chair, then kicked the solid table leg in frustration, coming to one inescapable conclusion. In addition to Twig, they'd been after the photo of the charm, the photo she'd shown all over New Orleans.

From the mess in front of her, she grabbed a paper and pen and sketched, in words and lines, what she could remember of the charm. The pattern details she could get from a visit to the Dark Phoenix. The attackers wouldn't have realized she'd made that connection; she'd never mentioned it.

Why was that charm so important? No one she'd talked to had recognized it. She'd looked it up on the Web while she was at NONE and came up with nada. Not a single reference to the symbol appeared on the Internet, and nothing was so secret that it didn't make the Internet.

She'd almost given up on it as a clue, thinking the disk symbol was merely an artist's idle design. This theft and tampering added a whole new spin, raising fresh conspiracy and secret cult theories.

Which meant she had to face the one resource left to try. Charles's library.

She leaned back, stretching her hands in front of her, giving a crack to her back and neck. Her muscles protested, and she winced at the pain, adding blisters and muscle strain to her litany of physical complaints. However, the ache in her chest came from none of these, but from dread.

Face the demon, Natalie. Dawdling wouldn't give her courage.

She dug out the key hidden at the back of a drawer, and then marched to the carriage house before she lost her nerve. Too soon, she had the door unlocked and was inside the musty building. The humming air-conditioning and dehumidifier kept the interior dry and cool, but the air tasted stale.

Beyond the tiny foyer, there were two rooms in the carriage house—at least, there were two that she knew about.

The first, Charles had used as a study. Swallowing against a gurgle of nausea, she crossed the leather- and brocade-clad room to a door at the back. Fit into the dark paneling, the door to the library was nearly invisible. Only a swirl on the wall, a pattern that looked like a skull to her, gave a hint of the entrance.

She pressed on the skull mouth and the paneling slid back, as noiseless as a scream in a vacuum.

The room beyond was dark and cold. Not air-conditioned cold. Sucked-out-heat cold. It was a room where nothing of warmth could survive.

The light from the study couldn't penetrate either, and the light switch was beyond reach from the threshold. Shivering, she slid forward, each step pulling her deeper into thick, repelling air.

Before she reached the switch, the door to the study eased close of its own volition and utter darkness dropped on her.

Chapter Twelve

The library hated her.

Did the magic within react to her distrust? Or was her repulsion an inevitable response to evil? Had Charles set it up that way, or had the contents changed him? Chicken or egg? Maybe the sensations were only her imagination, an excuse as to why she'd failed so badly with her marriage. She never knew.

All she knew was each unwilling moment she spent in here, she felt nastiness eating at her like maggots. Nauseating smells turned her stomach, and her skin crawled under the feet of invisible roaches.

She shuffled forward the final inches and, from memory, pulled the chain of the Tiffany table lamp. A cold blue glow spread from beneath the lamp shade, not quite reaching the corners.

Books formed the predominant decor. As she scanned the spines, she couldn't help remembering when she'd been here last. The incident replayed in her mind, causing a fresh wash of nausea. Charles, the cold, clinical look that marred his face, the enchantment he'd cast around her, the unpleasant sex—no, call it right—the rape that followed.

That day, she'd finally admitted defeat and given up on her marriage. They could never recapture what was good about them together. He'd been a talented MD once, specializing in genetic research, but even that had been buried under a compulsion for power. She'd moved to the city, begun divorce proceedings, and hadn't come back until after he was dead.

Ruthlessly, she thrust away the hurtful memory. There'd been early good years; better to remember those instead. Or best, put all of it behind her.

Still, she couldn't help speculate, with an ache too deep for comfort. Ram was also a man of great power. Would he, in time, walk the same path?

Thoughts of the past, thoughts for the future. She had enough problems with today. Her hand fisted on the picture she'd drawn of the charm. Focus on finding the link to Nathaniel.

As she plunged into the stacks for a book of symbols, the sensation of unwelcomeness mushroomed. The air realigned, making her a south pole in a north-pole room. Invisible forces plucked and shoved her toward the exit. She planted her feet and braced herself against the compulsion to leave.

She raced for knowledge before the magic won. Her heart pounded against her chest; she gasped as though the air was being sucked from the room and from her lungs. The titles spun in her narrowing vision. The whispers reminded her that in this world of magic, she was not wanted, not needed, not functional. Her feet scraped across the rug, pulling her toward the door.

The symbols section! She spied the promising titles. Needing oxygen, her heart lurched toward fibrillation. She grabbed four volumes and spun toward the door, escaping as her lungs closed on a final gasp.

The door snapped shut behind her. She ran from the study and out of the carriage house, threw the locks on by instinct, and then raced away. After the black vibrations of the library, nature felt startlingly still, where time held its breath.

Once inside the serenity of her home, she paused in the hall. Leaning against a wall, she swallowed against a mouth dry as crushed gravel—the library always left her with a raging thirst, as though vital moisture had been sucked dry.

Though her chest ached with the motion, she dragged in clean air to dilute the lingering foul odor. Although they exuded none of the library's unpleasantness, the books lay heavy in her arms.

Water first. After downing four glasses, she took an ice-filled pitcher outside and settled on the porch. She needed fresh air to handle the books. With sunlight illuminating the pages, she opened the first of the volumes.

In book three—something ancient and crumbly entitled *Enchiridion Promethean*—she found the symbol. One of a set of twelve. Faded illustrations hinted that the symbols related to magical beasts. She recognized a centaur and a unicorn. The lizard-looking one might be a dragon. Was the bird a phoenix? Hard to tell. She tried to match up symbols and illustrations, but failed.

Unfortunately, the book was written in some ancient language, Latin maybe. She let out an irritated puff of air. Who the hell knew how to read a dead language?

The suspended dagger glowed with an orange light. Streams of muddy brown threaded off the blade and dissolved in the glow, like blood in water.

Ram sat cross-legged on the floor with Estrella and LaMarr, his hands clasped with theirs, their bodies forming a circle around the glow. They held the purification in place until the brown paled to tan, then vanished.

Slowly they lowered their arms, the dagger aping their motion until the instrument rested on the floor, and then they released each other. The glow vanished, leaving only the unimpressive weapon.

Ram stretched, loosening the kinks in his muscles. Val sprawled quietly beside him, and as he leaned over to scratch the dog's head, he caught the scents of coffee and cooking burgers and the hum of conversation from the grill below.

Estrella gave the dagger a puzzled look. "Did I miss something? I didn't learn anything from the purification."

LaMarr let out a disappointed grunt. "No, there were no fingerprints on it, literal or magical."

Estrella got to her feet and stretched. "Well, at least we got the Circle done, and I'm feeling like I could party with the Night Seers. Good to see both of you." She took Ram's hands. "Last night, you were impressive; I see how much I need to learn. I'm sorry I faltered."

"We all have," he assured her. The Mages had no formal training system, only their own skills and the periodic guidance of a mentor. Trial by fire was often a very literal expression. "For your first field experience, you were magnificent." He kissed her cheek. "Enjoy the rest of your minivacation."

She kissed his cheek in return and smiled. "Oh, I will. No more Mage business?"

"None. You're off duty."

"Duly noted." She collected her handbag and left LaMarr's second-floor apartment through the Haven Grill below. Ram and LaMarr followed her out. She gave LaMarr a kiss and then left, her rolling-hip stroll garnering a goodly share of appreciative male attention.

"She's going to be an incredible Mage," LaMarr observed.

"I agree." Ram turned back to LaMarr. "We need to talk."

"I'm famished. Lunch?"

"Thanks." Ram perched on a stool at the counter. The Circle ceremony had left him both refreshed and hungry. Unfortunately the ritual had provided no information about the strange spell they'd encountered last night.

While LaMarr assembled the meal, Ram glanced around the busy grill. The Haven Grill near City Park was a favorite haunt for the city's police. According to the law enforcement network, the Haven was a great place to eat because of fast service, reasonable prices, good muffulettas, the best coffee in the coffee-proud city, and always a friendly smile for the "men and women in blue" and their kin. Firemen, military, FBI, anyone who stood against evil was welcomed.

What they didn't realize was that the owner, LaMarr Washington, had set a charm on the building to repel evil. The Haven was aptly named, a haven away from the daily perils they faced, and they instinctively responded to the cocoon of peace.

The profusion of officers also gave LaMarr an excellent pulse on the city. As Ram waited, he heard two policemen talking in low tones about last night's capture of Magic Man. Two more sat in vigilant silence by the window, watching the comings and goings on the street outside.

LaMarr returned with two plates of burgers and sweet-potato fries. He glanced at Val, sitting at Ram's feet and eagerly eyeing the crowd. "Let's eat back in my apartment. We won't be overheard." Inside the apartment, the men settled at the Formica-topped table. LaMarr set out a bowl of water for Val, then sat and splashed vinegar on his fries. "What you felt last night was more intense than what Estrella and I experienced outside, wasn't it?"

"The more energy I put out, the more the spell absorbed. Fighting only strengthened it." Ram frowned as he cut off a piece of his burger. "The spell was a marker, fully activated only when I cast the words to stop Magic Man, then attacking me last night while I was asleep."

"How'd you escape?"

"Opaque shields and tight focus. No stray magic to pick up on."

"Takes experience to juggle that."

"That's why I'm keeping Estrella out of this. That knife was enhanced to attract Mage attention." Was LaMarr making the same ugly connections that he had?

He was. "The maker wanted you. What better way to identify an unknown? To target and test a Mage?"

"That's sick." Ram's stomach turned. To spawn a killer just to find a Mage?

"Would have been me there," LaMarr said softly, "if your strength hadn't returned."

Ram studied him a moment, not sure if the comment was relief, disappointment, or jealousy. "That a problem for you?"

"Doesn't matter. What matters is, if he wanted our strongest, he found his target. You. So what do we do next?"

"You can help most by researching that spell." LaMarr was a Librarian, a mind Mage empowered by ideas and intellect; experienced in the gathering, exchange, and preservation of knowledge. Those skills were highly useful, but that mind-set meant LaMarr was more theorist than warrior.

"I'll contact the other Librarians, and then we can nose around the underground here for practitioners."

"I'll handle that," Ram said. "The magician is adept; he's dangerous."

"But he's not Mage-trained."

"He is still talented. And evil."

LaMarr finished his lunch, looking resolute. "I'm not afraid of death."

"There are eternal outcomes worse than death," Ram

said quietly, and saw LaMarr turn gray. "I'll set my traps, then wait for the magician to spring them."

"You'll be weaker alone."

Ram lifted one shoulder as he cleared his dishes. "I'll manage. In the meantime, I'll await your information and look for some smugglers."

"Still wasting your time?" LaMarr stared at him.

"They have to be stopped."

"I think your obsession is more about that woman. What is her attraction?"

"Healing Val with her brought back my power," Ram admitted. He laid a hand on Val's head as he used the simplest explanation. There was so much more about Natalie than the strange synergy. All of it vital and fresh and beyond his understanding.

LaMarr shook his head. "You said it yourself, the time was right. You were healed. Can she form a perimeter or a containment with you? Can she enhance a charm?"

Natalie would be horrified at the idea. "No, but—"

"If that spell attaches, harder now because our enemy knows you, and starts sucking you dry, *again,* can she do a damn thing to help you?" LaMarr's voice hardened. "You never told me what drove you back here, but I saw the aftermath. You were crazy. Empty. Alone."

"I wasn't alone. My family—"

"*Alone.* Your family is great, but you didn't give them a fucking clue as to what was going on here." LaMarr tapped a fist against Ram's chest. "Did you? They were happy to have you back, taking up your ordinary vet practice, not disappearing to faraway places. They didn't know how strong you'd gotten, how blessed *good* at magic you were. How losing that power was like having your skin suffocated in plastic and your eyes scoured blind. They didn't know you were *alone.* And that is a slow agony for a Mage." LaMarr shoved his plate away. "Do you want to be stripped to a husk again?"

An involuntary shudder rippled down Ram's spine. "Of course not."

"Then stay focused and stay away from Natalie Severin."

"If I didn't know you better, LaMarr, I'd say that sounded like an ultimatum."

"What it sounded like was me trying to keep you from making a damn, dead fool of yourself. I was there through the worst, helped you find the magic tasks you could handle."

He sounded almost venomous, and Ram noticed Val had grown alert, the hairs on her neck bristling. A nearly inaudible growl rumbled in her throat. For the first time, an uneasy thought crept in. Had LaMarr's support been somehow slowing Ram's return to strength? Nonsense. The notion had no support in fact, but tentacles of doubt, once clinging, were hard to dislodge.

LaMarr sat back, his clenched fists relaxing. "I'm not your enemy, but somebody out there is. Do you have any suspects?"

"The only possibility I'd come up with isn't likely since he's dead."

"Does limit his viability as a suspect. Who?"

"Charles Severin."

"Not that talented."

"Not that we know."

LaMarr rubbed his earring, which held his Mage symbol. "Severin had a protégé. Perhaps the student surpassed the master."

Cold settled on Ram as LaMarr voiced the connection he'd been avoiding. "Nathaniel DeSalvo."

If Nathaniel were involved, he had no question about where Natalie's loyalty would lie. Nathaniel was her only family, her twin—a bond created in the womb. She hadn't stopped looking for him, of that he was sure.

"Think about this, Ram." LaMarr leaned forward. "Natalie's brother was into some deeply unsavory rites before he disappeared. Now we have a rogue practitioner and suddenly Natalie's your left hand. Coincidence?"

"She's not involved," he said fiercely.

"She could be a conduit to you. Promise me you will not rely on Natalie Severin. Not without knowing where her loyalties lie."

A promise Ram could not make. Despite his own doubts.

At his silence, LaMarr gave a disgusted snort. "Ramses Montgomery, a Mage Tracker diverted by a woman. I fear your choices, my friend."

"But they're my choices to make."

"You will at least honor your commitment of silence to the Mages. We work in the shadows that non-Mages do not even know exist. Get close, and she'll expose the Magi. She's a NONE reporter. Our story will be irresistible to her."

"She won't write about the Mages." That promise he would make.

"Then I'll be here when you need me."

They rose, clasped hands and clapped each other on the shoulder, their formerly easy camaraderie tinted with discord. Ram left the cool peace of the Haven Grill for the steamy, chaotic city and knew he had made a choice.

Natalie was lucky. She cornered Jasper Wyoming at his desk in the TV news room before he spied her and escaped.

With a deer-in-the-headlights look, he hefted his camera and tried to scurry away. "Got a shoot. Big doings in the CBD."

She blocked his path, fighting a tinge of guilt. Jasper Wyoming was one of the few legit newshounds who didn't treat her with either pity or scorn. Still, necessity. She threw off the guilt and laid a thin package on his desk.

"What is it?" He eyed the wrapping as though it covered a scorpion.

"Open and see."

"Will it sting, bite, emit poison gases, or cause paralysis?"

"When did I ever?"

"When you conned me into taking photos of those Satanists. They were into sacrifices. With frogs. Frogs with a very nasty poison. A poison one of them threatened to use on my delicate skin."

"Yeah, and you got prize-winning footage, so don't be scamming me. Open it."

He tore open the brown bag, and pulled out the 78 vinyl. Eyeing the simple label, he sucked in a gasp. "A 1955 live recording of Professor Longhair?"

"Playing 'East St. Louis Rag' and 'Baldhead.' Not a scratch on it."

He ran a loving hand over the disk. "Do you know what a treasure this is?"

"Yup, and it should be with someone who can appreciate it." She perched on his desk, sure he wasn't going to flee now, and picked up a ball of Lucite-encased teeth from his desk. She tossed the smooth weight from hand to hand. "I need a favor."

Carefully he set the record down. "What do you want?"

She leaned forward and whispered, "Access to your news footage of the Magic Man capture. All of it, not just what aired."

"I can't do that!"

"The stuff after they brought out the boy."

He shook his head. "It could mean my job."

"I'll owe you."

"You'll take me to bed and fulfill every one of my most debased sexual fantasies?"

She snorted, catching the Lucite ball in her hand, then bargained, "A professional favor for the last fifteen minutes." Dropping the Lucite, she reached for the record.

He slapped his hand on her wrist, then glanced around. "I'll stream it to your cell."

The feed could be downloaded to a computer at work for a bigger screen. "That'll do. I'll be waiting across the street. If I don't have it in ten, I'm coming back for the Professor."

"What's so important?"

"I want to confirm something I saw on the TV footage."

"What?"

She just looked at him, silence her only answer.

He jerked his head to the door. "Get out and let me find it."

"Ten minutes," she warned, and then leaned over again. "And, thanks, Jasper. For everything."

He nodded, catching the subtext. "Next time we've got an alien invasion story, you'll be back on line."

"There are no aliens." With a jaunty wave, she left. Bracing her shoulders on the brick side of the store across the street, soaking in the humidity and the heat, watching a young break dancer collect his tips, she waited.

And wondered why it was so important to chase down the clues to the mystery of Ram. She was wasting time when her focus should be on finding the smugglers and Nathaniel.

Ram was wedging himself too deeply in her psyche.

Still, she waited, and at nine minutes and thirty seconds, the *Addams Family* theme played its ring tone. She answered, and the video streamed onto her screen. When it finished, she fast-forwarded to the end. Using her hand to shield the screen from the sunshine, she squinted. Couldn't get enough details.

With a snap, she closed the phone, hurried to her car,

then impatiently drove across the bridge to NONE. Ignoring the other reporters and Zolton, she headed straight to the computers where they built the Web content. In a few moments, she had the video on the bigger PC screen.

Quickly she went to the point where she thought she'd seen Ram. There! The image was hard to see, but it definitely looked like Ram. He was standing with two other people she didn't recognize. She clicked the images frame by frame. What the hell? One frame he wasn't there, the next frame he was an indistinct blur, and the third frame he was solid. A trick of the camera?

She scrolled back, searching for his two companions. They appeared to have stood on opposite sides of the house, then converged to the point where Ram suddenly appeared. After Magic Man pointed, they all vanished.

She backed up to the single shot that contained all three, framed the small section with them in it, and then enlarged and cleaned up that piece.

Yes, definitely Ram. The son of a bitch had lied.

Of course, she hadn't been entirely truthful with him either.

She touched the screen, right at the point of his heart. Her breath caught, and a tingle ran up her fingers to her palm, as though she were caressing him. As though the connections between them had grown powerful enough to transcend the constraints of distance and digital media.

She didn't recognize the two with him, but her chest gave a pang when she realized Ram was leaning over to give a kiss to the very attractive Latina.

"What are you so intent on?"

Natalie whirled in her seat, then collapsed back. Adam Zolton stood in the shadows behind her, barely lit by the screen. She grimaced at her editor. "Hell, Zolton, you scared me."

"Let me put that one in the record books." He gave her the once-over. "You look fagged. What happened?"

"Bees and someone who didn't like me having that charm I showed you."

He settled in the chair beside her. "Summarize."

She did, adding at the end after his low whistle, "I'm going to need a new laptop."

"So that's why you're here." He nodded to the screen. "What's this got to do with all that?"

"Nothing, maybe, but you were interested in Ram Montgomery." An excuse for her own interest.

He twirled to face the screen and peered closer to the image. "Where was this taken?"

"Outside where Magic Man was captured."

"That's Montgomery. That's LaMarr Washington. I don't know the woman." He patted his immaculately styled dark hair. "Wish I did."

Men. "Who's LaMarr Washington?"

"Owns the Haven Grill over by City Park."

"I've eaten there. Good basic food."

He lifted one shoulder. "I never have. Scroll it back."

She obeyed, then followed his command to forward, even though she couldn't shake the sensation there was something off. He shouldn't be that keenly interested in the minor details of her investigation. Most of the time, he let her fly or crash-and-burn as she would. His concern was the final product.

He swiveled back to face her. "What angle are you taking?"

"I've got nothing to angle." She met him square, not wavering. There were threads she could share, but that earlier protective instinct rose. "All I've got is three gawkers and some insubstantial camera work." She waved at the screen. "There's no story there."

Zolton didn't move, didn't say anything, only sat staring at her in the surrounding, deepening darkness. At last, he broke the tension with a slow nod and rose to his feet. "No story yet," he agreed and left.

Natalie let out a pent-up breath and bent back to the computer. Time to Google 2Wyld.

Thick sweet incense permeated even the distant corner of the "temple" room. Cloaked in a black hooded robe, Ram blinked the stinging smoke from his eyes as he scornfully regarded the faceless magicians circled around a stone altar. So eager for blood. Couldn't they feel the powers eddying from the stones, from their out-stretched hands? Only the merest blip would be generated by the doomed pigeon's sacrifice.

True power lay in the joining. All he'd need was one chant, one minute of synergy, and he could show them. Master them all, bird and human. Hold their lives dependent on his will and whim.

The magic was seductive, so sweetly vicious. Heart feasting on the anticipation, Ram outstretched one finger to beckon its power. Easily, he could command—

Shit! Abruptly, his hand tightened to a fist, and he jerked it down to his side. His teeth gritted in disgust as his shielding snapped into place, scraping off the resident magic. The tourmaline blistered against his skin. He shifted the gem above his shirt and clutched it for focus. Held on until the heat ratcheted down to a familiar glow and he'd cleansed away the vestiges of evil.

Only then did he release a quiet breath and relax his jaw. Tonight he had visited sites where magic, no matter how pure or innocuous or unpleasant, gathered. He'd deliberately left himself vulnerable in order to recognize a likely conduit to Magic Man's puppet master, and this gathering was his prime prospect.

Here, where the chill of the dead mixed with the air's stale dampness. Two practitioners lifted their hands skyward, pigeon blood dripping down their athames as they exhorted the power to come.

Throwing off the temptation to evaporate their robes, to expose them all—not his purpose tonight—Ram circled the room, chanting under his breath and sprinkling his prepared oils upon the walls. None of the ceremony's participants paid him any attention. To them, he was merely a passing whiff of fresh air, quickly swallowed by the heat of frenzy.

When he finished, he paused, making sure he had encased the room, then he whispered the closing chant. The spell sprinkled like a fine, undetectable mist onto each exposed hand, becoming absorbed in their pores. Over the next week they would touch others and spread it throughout the city. Anyone sharing power with them would be marked. The level had been set high, to avoid interference, but when a spell of great power was prepared, Ram would know.

He was finished here. Now to go home and take a long hot shower. Scrub off the incense and the taint of New Orleans' sordid occult underbelly.

And call Natalie. The spell had required two days of careful preparation. His only respite had come at night, when he spoke with Natalie about her progress, or lack thereof, on their leads, before going to sleep. He had cherished those conversations, and from their length, he thought Natalie had, too.

In silence, he slid from the gathering. Now, he could devote himself again to the task of finding the smugglers.

At least until his spell was triggered.

All right! The next afternoon Natalie sat back in her computer chair and gave a jubilant pump of her fist. She had it, the address for 2Wyld. Swiftly, she dialed Ram and rattled off the address in Chalmette. They both made record time getting there and met outside the seemingly empty warehouse.

The sky was darkening in preparation for the daily two to three P.M. shower as they circled the squat building. Not a sign of life anywhere, but beside the Dumpster out back they found an empty bird chow bag. Natalie ran a hand down her arm. "Do you suppose Twig is in there?" she whispered.

"We won't find out standing here," Ram answered, his hands in his jeans pockets. "Front door or loading dock?"

"Loading dock."

Silently, they hefted themselves up onto the concrete platform, where Ram pointed to a small pile of feathers. Natalie's chest squeezed tight. *Be inside, Twig.*

The side door was, amazingly, unlocked. As she pushed it, however, she discovered it wasn't oiled. Fortunately, the nerve-scraping squeal was buried beneath a crack of thunder. They got inside just before the deluge began.

Despite the noise, no one came to investigate; the cavernous building reeked of emptiness. Rain pounded the tin roof in a near-deafening rattle. Natalie took a deep breath—the air smelled like dried feces. Vision limited because of rain-spawned darkness, she pulled out her flashlight and tapped Ram's arm.

He shook his head, and then whispered, "I've got good night vision. Follow me."

No one was here. They found nothing but a dusty office to explore later, until they came upon the only locked door. Pulling out a black knife—where in the hell had he kept that?—Ram knelt and soon had the lock jimmied.

"You have some strange talents for a vet," she observed in a whisper.

"Bet you've got a few skills you haven't shown me, either," he whispered back.

"Maybe." Like her ear for languages and ability to pickpocket.

When they got the heavy door open, they were greeted by a windowless, utterly dark room. Natalie held her breath, but any sounds from within were too subtle to be heard over the storm. She wiped sweat from her eyes and pulled out her flashlight. This time, Ram nodded his agreement.

Her breath caught as the narrow beam flickered across metal bars. Empty cages. Natalie fumbled on the wall beside her, found a light switch, and turned it on. Useless. No power.

She played her flashlight across the room. Ram's curse, pithy and crude, echoed her sentiments. Row upon row of packed-together cages lined the walls. Not all of them were empty, though. One held two tortoises. There was the Lear's macaw. A snake formed a tight coil in another. She located most of the cache they'd tried to rescue, except the heron hatchlings.

The cages were bare metal, what wasn't soiled by feces. Each had only a small bowl of water, no food. At the sudden light, the animals blinked in confusion. A couple still had the energy to ruffle their feathers or scuttle backwards, nails scraping on stainless steel.

"Whoever did this should be folded in thirds, stuffed in a pipe, and have his balls served to him on a plate," Natalie said tightly.

"No arguments here," Ram said. "I'm calling Fish and Wildlife Service."

"No arguments here."

He flipped out his phone, made the call, and then laid a comforting hand at the small of her back as they went from cage to cage. They filled water bowls and poured out food, and at each small square, she shone her light in the shadowy recesses. Every step hardened the clenching in her belly. Only when she got to the last cage did she speak her realized fear aloud.

"Twig's not here." She swallowed hard on the words.

"Let's see if we can find anything in the office."

The files were skimpy, no particulars of sales or business transactions, and she doubted the smuggler bothered with niceties like rent. Not until just before Fish and Wildlife pulled up did she find something that gave her a ray of hope.

"Look at this." She held up a page from the daily desk calendar for Ram to see. Scribbled into one corner were "GC Igu" and 9/02.

He pointed to the letters. "This could be a Grand Cayman iguana."

"Were there any in there?"

"No."

"So if 2Wyld plans to send one out on September second, then he must be getting another shipment in. Soon."

Chapter Thirteen

"Heard you had an altercation at the clinic a few days ago. Everything okay?"

"Yes, Dad." Ram balanced the phone between his ear and shoulder as he maneuvered the mouse. The thermal map on his computer screen zoomed in. "Animal smugglers didn't like their cargo co-opted."

"Were you injured?" Royal Montgomery asked with concern.

"Nothing significant or permanent."

"That's good." There was a moment's pause. "Smugglers? In New Orleans?"

"Birds and exotic animals are big business."

"Birds. Never would have thought. Who's responsible?"

"I'm working on finding out." He heard the unasked questions, the ones his family never voiced because he could never answer them. Is this more of your strange fascination with magic? Will you be leaving again? What can be so compelling that it takes you from home, from us? "Fish and Wildlife Service is, too," he added, offering his father at least the assurance that this fell into Royal's realm of normal. "If you hear any scuttlebutt . . ."

"I'll be sure to pass it on." Another hesitation. "Can you do dinner? Two weeks from Saturday, when I get back in town? You're the only member of the family who hasn't met Angela."

His father's new fiancée. With a rueful smile, Ram shifted the map coordinates. After all these years, his dad still played an effective guilt card. Subtle, but effective. "I'll put it on my calendar."

"Seven. Antoine's."

"I'll be there. Oh, and Dad, make the reservation for four."

"Of course. Who's the lady?"

"I'll let you know after I ask her." He'd just hung up when the doorbell rang. Stretching out the kink in his neck, he opened the door to a biker chick in black leather. Then he caught sight of her hobo bag. "Natalie?"

She pulled off the yellow-tinted wraparound glasses. "Think I'll fool AX?"

"If we stay unobtrusive and in the dark."

Her shaggy hair was slicked-back onyx—the third color he'd seen this week. A small pouch with her cell phone dangled from her waist. Her hands were decorated with a ring on every finger and a skull tattoo, and she wore heavy makeup and bright red lipstick. The makeup, he realized, masked her injuries.

How could she make tough look so sexy?

Then again, she could wear a housedress and brogues, and he'd think she was sexy.

"I'm early, but not that early." She ran a critical eye over his shorts, cross trainers, and sweaty T-shirt. "I don't think you'll fit in."

He wiped a towel across his neck, trying to wipe away his semi-erection. "Sorry, my run lasted longer than normal, and I wanted to check a thermal map I'd downloaded. Do I have time for a quick shower?"

With a smile, she wrinkled her nose. "Please. We don't need to carry the charade so far as the unwashed aroma." Then she gestured. "Can I wait inside?"

He hesitated only a moment—he was careful whom he invited into his home—then motioned her in. Standing in the shadowed foyer, he drew a deep breath. She might be wearing leather, but she smelled like linen. "Will you have dinner with me?"

"Sure. What's the new lead?"

"No lead. No case. I'm asking you to dinner, two weeks from Saturday."

She blinked. "Like a date?"

"Yes." Better get it all out there. "My father and the woman he's making his third wife will be there, too."

"Why are you asking?"

Exasperated, he raked his hand through his hair. "I asked because I wanted time with you that had nothing to do with smuggled animals. I'd like you to meet my family. In small doses. Do you always ask this many questions about a simple date?"

"Questions are a habit." She gave him a dazzling smile, then rose to tiptoe and gave him a cheek kiss. "I'd love to come to dinner. What time and where are we going?"

Women. He had no clue what he'd said right, but he'd accept that he'd said it. "Dinner's at seven. Antoine's."

"I'll meet you here. Now, what's this about a thermal map?" She followed him toward the kitchen.

"I downloaded it off the Internet. Thought maybe a collection of birds would show in the wetlands as a cache of heat." At her surprised look, he added, defensively, "I'm not a complete technophobe."

She lifted her hands. "Sorry. Find anything useful?"

"No. Not enough resolution. Too much interference."

She was looking around, taking in every detail of his home. Best to keep her busy while he changed. The gurgle from her stomach gave him the needed diversion. "You can eat while I shower."

She put a defensive hand to her belly. "It wasn't that loud."

"I have good hearing." He pulled leftover salmon and chorizo from the fridge. "Do you like salmon? This was fresh yesterday; it should still be good."

"Yeah, but you don't have to feed me. I had a protein bar and a cola."

He shrugged as he assembled her plate. "It won't be any good tomorrow. Eat or not. Your choice. But, remember"—He flashed a quick grin and stuck the plate in the microwave—"I'm counting on you to protect me from the bad bikers."

"Wouldn't want to disappoint." She rested a hip against the counter while he pulled out silverware. "You're not a vegetarian? I thought you might be, animal rights and all."

"Eat and be eaten is a natural cycle. What I object to is inhumane treatment."

She was glancing around the kitchen as curiously as she had the entryway. At least if she was eating, she wouldn't be nosing around places he'd prefer she didn't go. She eyed the canisters of whole grains and the basket of apples. "You do a lot of cooking?"

"When I get the chance; it's healthier. Otherwise, takeout from the whole-food grocery. Don't you?"

She shrugged. "I'm not home that much. You're into organic? The body's a temple?"

"This body's the only home I've got. Makes sense to take care of it." He finished setting her place and allowed his gaze to slide across her, slow and caressing, enjoying the way the leather looked on her and the small thrill of desire that tightened his skin. "A temple's too religious. Not enough carnality."

With a final, "Wait here," he strode out of the room, just as the microwave bell chimed.

Natalie snapped shut her gaping mouth as what he'd said penetrated. The veil of heat that rose with his look morphed into a full-body sauna.

Talk about carnal. Well, she'd walked right into that one, she thought with chagrin, and then chuckled. She enjoyed their conversations; Ram was a male who did more than simply grunt.

She pulled the salmon from the microwave and sat down to eat, Val plopping down beside her and resting a warm furry body on her feet.

Two bites, and she decided that if Ram ever tired of the vet business, he'd make a killing as a chef. She also decided she liked his home. Maybe because it wasn't like the digs of any other single male she'd known. Usually those ran to one of two styles: beer-can slob or chrome sterile.

The house had an unfinished aura, as though Ram wasn't quite sure whether he was staying. What was here, though, was eclectic and quality—a Japanese mat on the floor, a piece of artwork that looked African. Not all of it was comfortable or easy—like that dagger with the gem-encrusted hilt—but everything meshed, although she couldn't put her finger on why. She simply knew this was a place she could enjoy.

Finished with her meal, she fed Val the last few bites as a reward for not begging, rinsed off her dishes, and then examined the lineup of crystals on Ram's windowsill, trying to decide if their pattern was significant. Was that red one a real ruby? She was reaching toward it when a leather-clad arm snaked around her and wrapped her hand in heat and power.

"Don't touch that one."

She jerked, her heart taking a leap ahead of her ribs, before her mind caught up. "Ram, I didn't hear you."

"I like the prismatic display on this one," he said, leaning over her shoulder. He surrounded her with his body as he set the clear one rocking.

The resultant rainbow played against his walls, while she absorbed the fresh soap scent of him and the power of his body leaning softly against her back. One of his arms encircled her waist, while the other still encased her fingers. All around her, he was hot and hard, yet she felt cherished more than engulfed. There was gentleness in his sturdy hands.

Pulling her hand from his, she turned in his arms. He stepped a pace away.

Talk about carnal. The man was a walking advertisement for the word. He'd combed his hair back and a pair of mirrored sunglasses hid his eyes. He wore black leather like hers, except his didn't have a stitch of adornment on it. Only the supple leather, so much blackness, with the strange effect that her gaze seemed to slip off him, unable to gain purchase.

Yet her palm itched to run across the smoothness, to feel cool animal skin and the hard muscles beneath. Her breath hitched.

"Will I do?"

She cleared her throat. "You'll do. Can you see out of those glasses?"

His answer was to delicately outline her lips with one finger.

"Good eyesight along with good hearing?" Her voice sounded as if she were speaking on half air.

"Something like that. Ready?"

Yes, yes, yes. She caught herself trying to lean forward into his palm when she realized he was asking to go.

She jerked back. Brought her thoughts into line. Work first, work first.

"The helmets are in the garage. We can get them on the way out." He crouched down and petted Val. "We have to be going; we'll be back soon. Take a good nap while we're gone."

Val gave a woof, then licked his and Natalie's hands, before going to her bowl for a drink.

Ram stopped to buckle a belt with a knife sheath around his waist. Or, at least she thought he had. When she blinked, the belt had vanished against the black leather.

"Wait." Natalie laid her bag on the table. "Before we go, I wanted to show you something."

Heat shot through Ram as his imagination spun quick images of things he'd like her to show. Unfortunately, the thick book she pulled from her bag wasn't one of them.

"I couldn't read the text; it's Latin, I think," she said. "I wondered if you could."

"Let me have a look." Before tackling the text, he examined the book she handed him. The black leather was surprisingly soft, not cracked, considering how old it appeared. He tilted it to let the light catch the red lettering, and his breath sucked in.

Not a title. Four symbols of body, mind, spirit, and cosmos.

The four sources of power.

With the tip of his finger he opened the cover and read the first line: *Artes magicae Prometheus*. The magic of Prometheus. Bringer of fire, according to popular myth. The original true Mage, according to arcana.

Sweat broke out on Ram's palms. Gingerly, he laid the book on the table. Such powerful words needed to be handled with respect, with minimal contact.

Could this really be a copy of the *Grimoire of Prometheus,* the forbidden text of the oral traditions? A book of legend so shrouded in mystery that most doubted it even existed. Faux copies abounded, writers who had taken the name for the sheen of authenticity.

Still something in the touch of this one spoke of truth. "Where did you get this?" he asked.

"The library at home."

"The book is a grimoire." He turned the pages with the barest touch, translating a few of the words as he went. Excitement, awe, caution swirled inside him, a maelstrom.

"Black or white magic?"

"Power doesn't come in categories. Depends upon intent. But the rituals and chants in this book are among the most powerful."

"You know them?"

"I read Latin."

After a pause, she asked, "Why would you study Latin?"

"Si vis pacem, para bellum."

"What does that mean?"

"If you seek peace, prepare for war."

"That's a reason?"

He added a second. "I don't have a good ear for languages. With Latin, who could tell if I pronounced it wrong? Why are you interested in this book?"

Leaning over him, oblivious to the uniqueness of the book, she riffled through it until she found the page she wanted. Then she laid a sketch beside the book. "I want to know what this is."

Oh, bloody hell. His body rocked back, bumping against the chair. How much did Natalie know about these symbols?

"Where did you get that sketch?" He kept his voice even.

"You recognize the design. What can you tell me about it?"

So, no answers until he gave her some. He studied the text, piecing it out until he had a translation, then he straightened, rubbing the ring on his finger. This much he could tell her. "These are the symbols of the twelve sacred beasts."

"What's this one mean?" She pointed to one in the sketch.

"It's the Phoenix." A Mage symbol. He wore his—a Centaur—beneath the ruby in his ring. Symbols were carefully protected, except in the rare book like this grimoire. He gave her a steady look and added steel to his voice. "Why are you asking about this, Natalie?"

"I found something on the boat, the night you fought AX. A charm."

"What does this charm look like?"

"Like a locket. Inside is black stone, etched with that design."

"You told me you found nothing."

"I lied."

He gave a grunt of disgust. "Why tell me now?"

"Because we're a confederacy."

"Right."

At his disbelief, she added, resigned, "And because I couldn't find anyone who knew what it was." Then, after a brief hesitation, she added, "And because the people who took Twig also took the charm and destroyed all my pictures of it."

"Shit, Natalie," he exploded. "You didn't think this was important enough to tell me about?"

"I didn't know until after you left, and I figured I'd see you tonight. Does that charm, that design, mean anything to you?"

"No," he lied.

"Are you sure? You read that book handily."

"I'm sure we need to get going. We can examine the book tomorrow." Get her thinking about something else. As he guided her out the back way, the one with the doggie door, newly installed, he asked, "What's to-night's plan?"

"I found an address where AX crashes during the day. We can go by there first. If he's home, we'll go on to the bar. Pretend to be lovers—"

"That I can handle."

"Not a major part of the plan, Ram."

Maybe not for her. "If AX isn't at home?"

She shrugged. "We have a look around, see what we can see."

"You do realize breaking and entering is illegal."

"Nothing I write has to stand up to a court-of-law test. It just has to pass the test of not getting caught." She was running a hand across his chest, playing at their role of lovers, stirring him. "And being true."

"The test might be keeping you out of jail." He gave a little nip to her ear in retaliation.

In the moonlight, he saw her smile. "So you'd cavil at a little B&E?"

Some of the things he'd done for the Magi flashed across his thoughts. "Not in a good cause. If AX is home, what's plan B at the bar?"

"Talk to Raoul."

"OK." He wheeled out the bike, and held out a helmet to her. "Hop on."

"Sweet ride." She fastened the helmet, got on behind him and then wrapped her arms around his waist. He reached down and shifted her grip slightly, his hand warm and firm upon hers. With the play of his muscles moving against hers, they roared off into the night.

Thoughts, questions, whirled inside him.

Was the person behind the smuggling a rogue Mage? None that he knew wore the Phoenix, none besides himself and LaMarr lived in this area. Why would a Mage bother? Yet someone had desperately wanted that charm.

Foreboding settled on him like a thick clot. Something evil was at work here, something deeper than mere greed.

Chapter Fourteen

Lights were on in AX's home, so they headed farther out, deeper into the Ninth Ward. The pool hall was easy to locate. It sported the only lights in this section of the city. Even the traffic lights out here remained useless tubes, broken by Katrina.

Ram eased the Harley into the parking lot, avoiding the moldy debris and scattered nails, to park in a discreet corner. Absently he held his hand out for Natalie to alight, but she was already off and at his side, looking at the dingy building.

The pleasure of the ride, of having Natalie pressed tight against him, her arms wrapped around him, faded. Being here was sheer folly.

If they got in trouble, they were on their own. No cop bothered to patrol these streets, or would answer a call for help.

Inside, the bar was crowded, although as far as Ram could tell in the smoky interior, AX and his cronies weren't there. He and Natalie slid sideways from the door, close to the wall as they checked out the room and he gathered his wits and his libido after an entire ride with Natalie's curves plastered against him.

Glances located them, shifted away, and then returned to settle on Natalie. He cursed under his breath. That side effect he hadn't foreseen, when he'd enhanced his outfit's natural camouflage traits. He wasn't used to working with a "civilian." He'd be seen, but not noted. Natalie didn't have the same protection. All he'd done was shift attention toward Natalie. Considering there were few women in the bar, that attention was decidedly leering.

As if it wasn't going to be hard enough to keep her safe in here.

His ability to protect her was about to be tested with that bruiser. The one with the missing teeth and the mashed-up face. The one staring at Natalie and running a hand down his crotch.

Unsubtly, Ram wrapped an arm around her shoulders, staking a visible claim. Subtly, taking care not to touch her so she wouldn't notice, he spread the camouflage aura around her in a delicate wrap. As long as they stayed close, he could keep her within this first layer of protection.

The bruiser blinked twice, as though clearing his eyes of an afterimage, and looked away.

"There's a table over there," he whispered against her ear, and she nodded. With his arm draped over her shoulder, he wove them easily through the crowd to the table. It was nicely placed in the rear, so no one sat behind them, and in the shadows.

Once, before they got there, he caught someone else trying to claim the spot. With a softly muttered line, too low to be heard or noticed, he compelled the interloper away. Without further ado, Ram claimed the table, and then caught the bartender's attention. He lifted two fingers.

When the bartender silently delivered two mugs of brew on tap, Ram passed one to Natalie. He took an experimental sip of the beer. Not bad—good head and cold. Too bad he wasn't drinking.

Still, he held it as further camouflage as he and Natalie studied the room. Nothing he saw eased the concern blooming in his chest.

"You know what Raoul looks like?" he asked.

"No, but I should be able to figure it out. Let me study this a bit." She leaned back, lifting her beer to her lips, but not drinking any. One of her hands rested warmly on his thigh, just above the knee.

He laid his arm across the back of her chair, shielding her, and did his own studying—exits, potential threats, mood of the place.

This was a rough crowd—Latino and black predominantly, with a smattering of Caucasian. He suspected they mixed here because there was nowhere else to hang, but each group staked out its turf.

The common denominator wasn't facial color, it was facial expression. Wary and mean, carved by blood and bullets.

Unfortunately, he became growingly aware that Natalie's hand was stroking up and down his thigh, her fingers coming damn close to his balls and her arm brushing against his groin. With predictable results.

He didn't know if the motion was unthinking or a deliberate choice for their charade; the answer didn't really matter since the effect was the same. An effect he couldn't afford.

Bending close, he whispered, "Your hand gets any closer and we'll have to put in plan C, leave here and take care of the erection I'll be sporting."

The heat of her flush scalded him, and her hand jerked back. So, involuntary strokes, and somehow that was more satisfying than a deliberate ploy.

"Don't be crude," she snapped before she put her hand back. On his knee, well away from dangerous territory.

"Not crude, just practical. It's okay for you to admit you were appreciating the feel of my fine leather."

She laughed. "Delusional, too. Quid pro quo since your forefinger's stroking mighty near my breasts."

"Just getting into character, darlin'," he drawled, withdrawing. Okay, so he, too, was making a few involuntary moves.

"Does your character include playing pool?" she asked abruptly, leaning forward, away from his touch.

"It can."

"Are you any good?" She turned to look at him.

"Yes."

"Enough to beat him?" She gave a brief nod toward a Latino man holding court in a far corner.

"Yes. Assuming he isn't hit with a phenomenally lucky streak. That's Raoul?"

"Yeah, and he takes his pool seriously."

"So there's the possibility of a shot in the back if he loses?"

"Just walking in here makes that a possibility. But, he appreciates a good shot. I think it's more likely to earn you respect."

He looked at her, curious. "Do you play? Could you beat him?"

"I know the rules, but I'm not that good. Besides, I don't think he'd be sanguine about losing to a woman. The table next to him just opened. Your updated role is you're indulging me, but I'm boring competition at a pool table." She stood up, then took his hand and tugged him to his feet, speaking a little louder. "It's just a game. I wanna play one game."

"Sure, babe." She almost hid her flinch at his indulgent endearment. "You can even break if you want." He gave her bottom a friendly slap as they claimed the table and cue sticks.

"Oooh." He'd never heard Natalie make that squeal-y sound before, and he'd bet his athame she'd never make it again.

Ram's hand tightened around the cue stick as Natalie, fussing and swaying around the table, racked the balls. She definitely caught the eyes of the men at the table next to them.

Natalie knew the setup. She broke, pocketed the seven ball, and then missed her attempt with the five. "Your turn."

"Stripes. Nine in the corner." He cleanly sank three balls, only one of them giving him any pause on how to set up the shot. Deliberately missing the fourth, not wanting to give away too much, he left Natalie with a straight shot with the five.

She made it, but missed her next. He sank two more, and then left her with another setup.

Glory God, she missed it. He circled the table and whispered, "You don't need to pretend to be that bad."

"I'm not," she snapped. "Stop using your magic."

"Sweetheart, this is pure geometry."

He sank his last two, and then deliberately fluffed on the eight ball. "Here," he said, sounding like a barely patient lover. "Let me show you how to set up the shot."

He propped his cue stick against the table, then stood behind her, wrapping his arms around her, his hands placing hers over her cue stick. She melted seamlessly against him, her curves soft and warm. Together, back and forth, their arms rocked. "Eye on the angle. Stroke gently, smoothly."

She turned her head and muttered for his ears only, "Pool's just one big phallic metaphor."

"Mmm," he answered absently, concentrating on the

hit, trying to ignore the feel of her. "Now hit that sweet spot."

He tapped her cue against the ball, sending it rolling gently into the target pocket.

"I did it!" she cried, then twisted in his arms, startling him by pulling his head down to hers and kissing him, full and sweet.

He wound a hand around her nape, keeping them together for a fraction longer, to the rough interest of their audience. When they'd released each other, he gave her a wolfish grin, touching a finger to the triangle of skin on her chest. He outlined the small area. "Now try a shot on your own."

She missed, and he neatly finished out the game.

"Let's play another," Natalie offered eagerly.

"I think you could use more of a challenge," offered Raoul, the man they'd targeted.

Ram patted Natalie on the cheek. "Another time. A real game calls."

She did a credible pout.

He leaned forward, pretending to give her an apologetic nuzzle, as he whispered. "How do I play this? Lose, win with some difficulty, or clear the table on the first turn?"

She swallowed. "Win, but don't mop up with him."

"Got it. And, Natalie, blend into the background over by the wall." When she hesitated, he added, "I can't afford to have my concentration shot."

He straightened, and then strolled over to the others. "Name's Chris," he offered, shortening one of his middle names.

"Raoul," answered their mark. "Shall we play?"

"Stakes?"

Raoul gave a shrug. "Ten a ball."

Ram nodded his agreement as he chalked up his cue.

"You always wear those glasses?" Raoul asked.

"Genetic condition. Sensitive eyes." He took them off, holding them out for Raoul to inspect that they contained no hidden traps or cheats.

Raoul examined, then handed back the glasses. "Lag for break."

Ram won the lag, his cue ball coming within a hair of the head cushion. Raoul gave a brief whistle. The look he gave Ram was still suspicious, but there was also a measure of respect. So, Natalie's assessment was right. Ram broke the stack, then called "Solids," before sinking the next two balls. The game went back and forth, until Ram sank his final ball and the eight in quick succession, leaving him $20 ahead.

"Another?" Raoul asked, paying with reasonably good humor.

"Sure."

The game took on a tenser aura, however, when Ram won the next by a forty-buck margin. They also began to attract some attention.

Natalie had shifted to chat up the bartender. Ram could feel her restlessness from here, and his odd connection to her startled him a moment before he ruthlessly thrust his unease aside.

His tension, the risk of discovery, multiplied each moment they continued to linger. Smoke thickened in the room, a mix of tobacco and marijuana that distorted the speeding seconds. Time to stop pressing their luck and get what they'd come for.

"One more?" Ram asked with raised brows.

"Up the stakes?" Carefully Raoul chalked his cue tip. "Give me a chance to win back my losses."

"Different stakes."

"Such as?" Raoul gave him a curious look.

"Information."

Instant wariness combined with menace, as Raoul's posse circled closer. "What kind of information?"

"You know a guy named AX?"

"Maybe."

"I want to know what he's working."

Raoul's eyes narrowed. "You don't smell like a cop."

" 'Cause I'm not. Call me . . . a disgruntled employer. One who doesn't like the help getting independent notions."

"I never heard of anyone named Chris brokering deals."

Ram smiled. "You don't know every layer of power in this city. Some of them are very old."

"Me and the boys wondered what you were about when you walked in."

"Now you know. AX is all I'm interested in."

He could see Raoul's mind working, trying to decide if "Chris" was nuts to have come in here alone except for arm candy, or if he had the power not to be afraid.

Caution won out. "I heard some things, and I got no use for that bleached mother."

"One game. Your 'things' against your stake so far, plus another hundred."

"Deal."

Ram had just started racking the balls, when a tingle of warning skittered up his spine. He turned his head slightly for a better look.

Well, shit. AX and crew had just come in.

He paused, taking off his glasses and wiping his supposedly sensitive eyes. With his temporarily bared eyes, he caught Natalie's attention, giving her a slight gesture. It took her only a second to locate AX, and he saw her stiffen. She shifted, as though to leave, but a shake of his head gave his command. *Stay.*

Fortunately, she paid attention. Leaving now would attract too much notice.

Ram bent his head to don the glasses, and used the moment to intone a quick spell. He shifted the molecules of air, the ribbons of energy, the layers of smoke, and when he lifted his head, his features altered subtly with the overlaid glamour. Not enough that Raoul would remark, but enough to disguise himself from AX. Natalie was too far away for the glamour, so he thickened the smoke around her, and spread the camouflage spell into it.

At least his talent with pool didn't require any diversion of the power. That finesse came from an innate gift for geometry, precise body control, and a few hundred hours playing at college.

Without further discussion, Raoul set up for the break. He sank three balls in a row, before missing a complicated shot by a mere centimeter. Clearly, he'd been holding back.

So had Ram. Moving with lazy ease, he cleared his stripes, and then sank the eight ball.

Raoul's eyes narrowed as he realized how thoroughly he'd been suckered.

From the corner of his eye, Ram felt Natalie move closer behind him. Alert, her hands curved in anticipation of action. Protecting his back. He smiled at the image. The other Mages would say he was crazy, considering one of no powers as his backup.

Ah, they didn't know Natalie. Although he wished like hell she weren't in this danger, there was something pleasing about knowing she was so determined to protect him. She would fight as fiercely for him as she had fought for Twig.

Since she was closer now, he could strengthen the camouflage spell, keep AX's searching gaze away. Yet beneath it he could see the vibrant hum of her leashed energy. The woman was spoiling for action and not happy about being cast into the role of decorative but useless.

Time to get out of here before someone exploded. He gave an easy glance at Raoul. "Your information?"

"I heard AX talking on the phone last night. He said, 'Sunday. Midnight, Phoenix. You let me handle it my way. No interference this time.' That's all. He saw me and he turned so I couldn't hear no more, but I got the impression that whoever was on the line was someone he didn't like much."

"How do you know that was his employer?"

"'Cause right after, AX collected his boys and I heard him tell them they had a job to do."

"Where's it going down?"

Raoul shrugged. "Maybe that abandoned voodoo shop on Esplanade."

"Not too helpful, Raoul."

"I said I knew something, not that it would be useful." He licked his lips as his posse moved tighter around Ram and Natalie.

Not good.

Chapter Fifteen

Not good, Natalie thought as she surveyed the six men surrounding her and Ram. Raoul was pissed. He'd made good on the bet, but he was royally pissed at being suckered. Didn't help that the posse was egging him on, telling him to be a man. She shoved her hands into the pockets of her jacket, pretending casual. Not that anyone was looking at her. All eyes were focused on Ram.

Bad time to be reconsidering her decision to leave the gun at home. Except she'd figured Ram would put up a stink and drawing in here would be crazy. She'd bet everyone was packing—everyone but Ram, that is. First sight of a barrel and the bullets would be blazing.

The plan had been to keep things private and retreat when necessary. Except the easy path to the doorway was blocked.

If only she could get close to AX on the way out. His cell dangled at his waist. In a confusing melee, it'd be easy enough to lift.

"Now, I'm thinking," Raoul continued, bringing her attention back, "you owe me some money."

Ram gave an I-don't-care twist to the shoulders and handed back his winnings.

"Mistake," she muttered. "Too easy."

Ram acknowledged the warning with a faint tilt of his head.

Raoul handed the bills to one of his posse. "And a taste of your woman." He looked around, as though hunting for her, despite the fact she stood right next to Ram.

"No." Ram's answer was so quiet and brief that it took Raoul—and Natalie—a moment to register the refusal, despite the not-to-be-messed-with voice.

"No?" Raoul challenged.

Ram didn't bother to repeat himself. Instead he rested that strong hand on her shoulder and pressed her at an angle to the door. The path let them keep an eye on both Raoul and AX, who'd been drawn closer by their unfolding drama. Brow furrowed, AX stared at Ram, as though trying to remember where, and when, they'd met before, but not quite recognizing him.

She and Ram almost made it out before an eddy in the smoke gave warning. Raoul and entourage came crashing after them. Ram shifted her behind him and lashed out in a single move so swift and seamless she barely had time to catch her balance before he stopped.

That fast, two were down. Which left two still charging forward and one coming at their flank. Natalie spun toward the rear threat. Blood thrumming in her throat, she met his charge. Grab, twist, shove with the heel of her hand, and he was on his back, blinking in surprise.

The last two attacked, one going for his gun. Beside her, Ram was a continuous blur, highlighted by a prismatic arc and a whish of cold air.

Then the other two were gasping for air and clutching their guts. A thin line of blood decorated the wrist of the one with the gun, his weapon still shoved into his pocket.

The man at her feet twitched, and her heel landed on his wrist, right at the point to numb the nerves. Just in case he had any ideas about drawing, too.

"I said no," Ram said quietly, not even breathing hard. With a twist of his wrist, the obsidian knife he held vanished. He glanced around at the stunned crowd before hustling her forward with a press to the small of her back.

"I know that fighting style."

Oh, f—Natalie took off running, Ram right behind her. A shot rang out, sending the bar patrons scrambling. Ram's hand convulsed against the small of her back, sending a charge up her spine. He stumbled forward, just as AX plunged in front of them.

Ram moved again, less of a blur, so this time she saw his hand connect with a wrist, his foot connect with a thigh. The bone-chilling instant thud of flesh on flesh, of altered time and space, kicked at her heart. She slipped beneath AX's thrust-up elbow, making a quick grab for his phone as she and Ram shoved past. Damn, it worked. The two of them stumbled out the front door.

Hot slick night slammed her, unrelenting in its steam. They crossed the parking lot, their racing boots crunching on the shells.

"Any good with a Harley?" Ram shouted.

"Damn good."

He tossed her the keys, and she had her helmet on and the bike started almost before he grabbed his helmet and jumped on the seat behind her. Surrounding her, protecting her, she realized as his arm came around her waist. His back was the target.

Not on her watch. Spitting shells, she screamed the bike out of there.

Within seconds, the AX trio was in their low-slung car

and following. A spray of bullets was aimed at the beacon of the Harley headlight. In this dark, lifeless part of
town, she and Ram might as well hang out a sign:
Come. Shoot me.

She reached over and turned off the headlight.

"What are you doing?" he shouted.

She couldn't answer, couldn't turn her head so he
would be able to hear the words. Instead, she prayed
she wouldn't run out of the straight road before her
eyes adjusted. Prayed that the stars and moon would
provide enough light.

Hulks of mold-festooned and abandoned houses
rose on either side of her. Overgrown trees, thick with
summer leaves, hemmed them in and shadowed the
road, leaving only intermittent light to guide them. It
was enough, it had to be.

She risked a quick glance over her shoulder. They
were gaining on her.

With adjusted eyes, she caught sight of a moonlit
street sign and oriented herself. Mental map in place,
she tilted the bike, Ram making the adjustment in
weight without a hitch. They spun down a side street.

She was sweating. The backs of her shirt and jacket
were soaked. Her neck was sticky. She needed to ditch
AX. Headlights swept across the bike, catching them in
a trap of light. The car gunned forward.

AX would expect her to head straight out, so she took
two quick turns deeper into the abandoned neighborhood, shadowed by the ghosts of lives disrupted. The
Harley engine vibrated through her hands. Each jerk
into a turn cascaded more aches across her body. After
one sharp, screaming turn, Ram lost his grip on her
waist, one hand dropping to her thigh. His other hand
hung on tighter. She glanced over her shoulder, silently
asking, *Okay?* and he gave her a quick nod.

Damn and blast; AX had turned onto their street,

more tenacious than kudzu. Two more quick turns. Could he see them? Hear them?

Apparently so. The car spun dirt as it tore around the same corners.

No sense in running in the dark. Headlight back on, she abandoned her zigzag for a sharp turn onto St. Claude. The angling street was her shortest route to the elevated highway and possibly a cop. Full throttle. She abandoned caution as thoroughly as these homes and lives had been abandoned.

If AX caught them, they were dead.

Hot air streamed past her, throwing grit into her mouth. The ends of her hair beneath the helmet stuck to her neck.

Chips spurted off a fallen tree limb in front of her, and she swore. She heard Ram say something, but the words were torn away by the wind. He leaned forward and shouted, "He's losing ground."

The bike was in prime souped condition. Guess the car wasn't.

Another wild shot scattered dust. She might be gaining, but he was shooting.

Still, barring a lucky stray shot, they were going to make it out.

Not. She rounded a corner, and fear roared above the din of engine and wind. What idiot had felled a tree into the road? Throttling down, she barely stopped before reaching the blockade. Six more inches and she'd be ramming trunk. A glance over her shoulder told her she couldn't go back. AX was too close.

Heart hammering against her ears, she looked for a way out. Ram pointed to the side of the tree, and she nodded. There might be enough room for the bike to squeeze through. Turning off the light again, she crawled past the exposed roots.

The car couldn't follow them here. Hope rose again. They were going to make it out.

Not. Again. *Pffat, pffat.* She felt as much as heard the flap of the tire. A fricking flat. The bike shook out of her control.

"Let go," she shouted, and although Ram was behind and shouldn't have heard, he nodded. They leaped away, as the bike crashed into the tree.

Heaving for air, Natalie shoved herself to her knees, then her feet. Her nerves screamed with fire the length of her battered body. Thank God for leather and the fact she'd been going at a crawl.

AX's headlights speared the darkness, slicing the corner like a beacon of death. Frantically, she sought a hiding place. Lots of abandoned houses, none offering more'n a lick of concealment. Trees aplenty, but she wasn't cartoon skinny to be able to disappear behind the trunk of one. Neither was Ram, although he seemed a lot harder to see than she did.

He pointed to one house that was more intact. "There."

They sprinted the short distance and climbed through a shattered window, just as AX's car turned the corner and caught the flat-tired bike in its headlights. Natalie followed Ram up the stairs of the modest house, unable to shake the sense of violation. This had been someone's home. Debris shoved by floodwaters littered the floor, but a neat line of vases on the mantel—untouched in one of the oddities of destruction and looting—indicated someone had once cared for these rooms.

They moved up the staircase, trying for silence. Still, her foot crunched on some shattered glass, and even normally silent Ram bumped against a coat rack. The thud and jingle of loose hooks sounded loud as a doorbell.

He steadied the rack, and they paused to listen. No one came running after them. They passed through a bedroom, then out what had once been a sliding door to a balcony. With cautious steps, they tested the wood. Miracles, it held with only a faint creak.

She saw now why he'd selected this house. As ideal a spot as they could find under very unideal circumstances. A freestanding cabinet stood at the end of the balcony, with a small space between it and the glass doors. She and Ram could squeeze in there, and, with the drapes drawn over the glass, be concealed on three sides. Yet, being outside, they'd hear where AX was. The tree at the opposite end of the balcony might even offer an alternate escape route.

She hoped they wouldn't be forced down the tree. Not with her arms a mass of aches, her legs sore and shaking, and the stings a fierce itch beneath the wet, sticky, stiff leather. Somehow, Natalie found herself wedged first into the cramped space. A deliberate move by Ram, she'd bet; he now filled the opening. Best vantage to see; first one to get shot.

He crowded her, but didn't touch her. His body came within a hairsbreadth of hers.

Her body shook with the effort to keep still. She held her breath, ready to run or fight. Not ready to die.

She blinked sweat-stung eyes, even as she strained to hear above the voice in her head. *Nathaniel, I'm sorry, I couldn't find you.* She touched the tip of Ram's shoulder. Without looking at her, he caressed the top of her fingers. A brief, too-soon-over stroke, but somehow reassuring.

They were in this together. She could feel his heat, smell the faint aroma of sweat and something else she couldn't name right now. Confidence returned.

Ram, I'm sorry I got you into this, but I couldn't ask for a better companion.

Sight was useless. Blackness hemmed her on four sides. Even the square of sky overhead was starless. Instead, she forced herself to concentrate with her ears. Listen and follow the sounds of the night. She and Ram were nearly impossible to see, but if seen they were trapped.

AX sent a spray of bullets, dumb, blind shooting. "You're here. Can't go no place without your wheels."

Never heard of walking?

Another spray of bullets clanged against metal. Probably the bike. Feeling Ram's wince, she laid a sympathetic hand on his shoulder. Connected to him, instead of being distracted, she found it easier to concentrate.

The surrounding night stilled. Distant car sounds, traveling safely along I-10, faded as she followed the sounds of AX and his pals. Searching, giggling, punctuating the night with the occasional bullet. Smart enough to systematically work their way through the surrounding houses.

"That bitch took my cell!" AX called out suddenly. "Kracker, give me yours."

He was going to call his own phone! Frantically, she dug the cell out of her pocket. Where was the volume control? Not that side. There. She thumbed the phone to silent, just as it started vibrating in her hand.

Ram twisted enough to give her a you-didn't look.

Natalie held the phone for him to see and gave him a thumbs-up.

He shook his head, but she could see he was smiling when he turned away.

The sound of breaking pottery broke through the night. Natalie gave a string of mental curses. Kracker and Dawglip destroying the line of vases.

The *asses!*

They were coming up the stairs.

She tapped Ram's shoulder and pointed to the tree,

but he shook his head. With him standing solidly in front of her, she couldn't get out, couldn't leave. Her heart stuttered against her chest.

"Don't make a sound." Ram's voice was barely audible. "Don't move. Cover any exposed skin."

"They'll see us. We're trapped targets."

"No, they won't." He tilted a little to brush his lips against her hair, then against the skin of her forehead and her eyebrows. The light caresses charged through her, and she felt the hitch of his breath in her own throat. "I won't let them."

She stilled, every molecule paralyzed. He was going to do some magic spell, with her in the middle of it.

"Trust me." His voice was compelling. Urgent.

Thick footsteps thudded nearer. She nodded, unable to speak.

He turned away and a chant, low and foreign, glided from his throat.

She bent her head, pulled up her collar over her neck. Her bare hands went behind her back. No skin. No sound, no motion.

Ram stood in front of her, motionless as rock. He mimicked her pose, head bent, arms crossed behind him, one hand cradling the other. Somehow he'd even managed to make his palm look dark.

Their cubbyhole grew darker, although she hadn't thought that possible. A black hole, with light held captive by force. The air became impossibly still, until she became dizzy with the effort to move it into her lungs.

Breathe shallow. Breathe slow. Breathe silent. Her mouth opened to drag in the reluctant air.

Almost silent words drifted and wove around her. The power from Ram, she felt it, faint and caressing as the seductive brush of a lover's lips. An enticing lure to excitement and to danger. Would it turn? Would the lover swirl into a devouring incubus?

The spell wasn't on her skin; it was in her skin. Beneath the layers of cells. *Part of her.* Her muscles twitched, and she felt the answering warning tension in Ram.

No motion. No sound.

Had he been doing this all night? *The bastard!* Using some spell on her at the bar so no one would see her, talk to her. Anger quivered along every nerve, even as her skin recoiled. But Dawglip and Kracker were pushing back the drapes, and she forced herself to remain immobile.

She was blinded by shadows. Caught in a sucking black hole. Devoid of sensation. Buried by the night.

A light beam swung across their balcony, swept inches from their feet.

Force the anger and the repulsion to the side. Deal with the immediate danger. Hold still by necessity, not force.

She was beset by the twin needs to cough and to pee.

The mundane urges broke through her fright. Natalie's lips twitched just the faintest bit; then she froze again as Kracker stepped onto the balcony.

The wood groaned and a sharp crack rent the night. Oh, great. Some piece of their support had given.

"Get back," Dawglip snarled. "That's going to give."

"Not yet. Maybe they left something valuable in there." Kracker headed straight toward them.

The tingle of magic rippled across her, wavering in its strength. Breaking. In all the equations, the one constant she'd never doubted was Ram's strength. How much energy did it take to maintain their camouflage?

In the bayou, he'd taken her hand. I draw strength from you, he'd said once. Risking motion, she slid her hand around to the front and grabbed his sweat-slicked hand, just as the beam from Dawglip's light swung across their niche.

Miraculously, or rather magically, the screen around them tightened. Dawglip's light slid across the edges of the cubbyhole, but the beam vanished at the entrance. Absorbed by a magical black hole.

"Shine that over here," Kracker commanded. "I can't see what's in here worth shit."

Dawglip hesitated, frowning as he peered after the absorbed light. Natalie held her breath.

"Anything?" AX called from below.

"Naw." Dawglip swung away to light Kracker's rummaging. "Hurry up, man."

A moment later they were scrambling downstairs, Kracker swearing about not finding any cash. Once they were back on the street, Natalie sagged a little, and Ram's wet hand slipped from hers. The magic dissolved away, and her skin felt strangely dulled. A glimmer of light returned, along with the moldy aroma.

After a few more attempts at locating Ram and Natalie, the three thugs finally got into their car and back-fired away. Natalie gave a faint cough, and tightened her muscles against that urge to pee. When Ram didn't move, she gave him a small poke in the back.

He shook his head in answer, and then held his finger up in a silent answer.

One minute. Make sure their hunters weren't doubling back. At last, the night sounds buzzed in her ears. Dusty mold incited a sneeze that shattered their watchfulness.

Ram's shoulders relaxed, and he stepped from in front of her. "I think we're safe." His voice was still faint. "Let's get going."

Without looking back, he headed down the stairs.

Natalie clambered after him. "Ram, that magic, you were—"

"Not now!" he snapped.

"I won't—"

"No, Natalie."

They'd reached the bottom, and Ram escaped through the window. When she joined him, he was on the porch, one arm braced on a pillar, his head bowed. His raspy breathing sounded harsh in the night.

Natalie swallowed back her revived anger about the magic. He was pale, and his hand trembled. Single-handedly he'd kept them safe, but the effort had taken a toll. They were stranded. First, get out of here. Later, they could sort out the rest.

"I'm sorry about your bike," she said. "I'll call Zolton to pick us up—"

"No. My partner, Graham Hebert." He fumbled at his pocket. "Number's on my cell."

Something was wrong, seriously wrong. She reached out, then stopped, staring at her hand in horror. Not sweat. The faint, odd smell she'd noticed wasn't mold.

The night wind carried a mix of scents from Ram: sweat—she wasn't so sweet herself—a whiff of freshness, like lime, and something else. A smell that dragged up gagging memory. A smell of clotted nausea and death.

The smell of blood.

Chapter Sixteen

"Why are you bleeding, Ram?" Buzzing with adrenaline, her sleeves stiff with his blood, Natalie unzipped his jacket. He was shaking beneath her hands.

"Was bleeding. One of the bullets got my arm."

"We have to get you bandaged. I'll call an ambulance."

"They have to report a gunshot. Let Graham take care of it."

"A vet's going to sew you up?" she asked scornfully.

"I'll heal once Graham gets the bullet out. Better than spending hours at the ER and answering questions from the cops." With a grim set to his chin, he called and made the arrangements. "We're going to meet him a few blocks over."

As they walked, keeping as deep in the shadows as possible, Ram said, "Take my hand. I need the strength."

"Which side?"

He tilted his head to the left. She joined him, her side brushing against him. He was walking steadier and breathing easier, but beneath the outer quiet, his muscles quivered in exhaustion. So strong outside, such power at his fingertips, yet still a fallible man.

"That's twice you mentioned me giving you strength."

"Can we talk about this another time?"

He didn't deserve her grilling, not at this moment. Still, she had to ask. "One question."

She ignored his muttered, "That'll be the day."

"If you have this power, why not just stop them? Crush their lungs or break all their bones or something?"

"You're bloodthirsty."

"I'm serious."

"Because, up to a point, people have the right to choose their own actions."

"How do you decide that point?"

"That's two questions. Now would you please shut up?"

She decided he had grounds for a little rudeness and shut up.

Graham, waiting for them by the time they reached the rendezvous, turned out to be a fit fifty-something, with blond hair pulled into a ponytail and kind eyes. He wore paisley pajama bottoms, a T-shirt, and sandals. His truck, a late-model Ford, looked as sturdy as its owner.

"H. Christ, Ram, what happened to you?"

"Gunshot. Thanks for coming. Can you stitch me up?"

"Sure. Get in the truck. Where's your bike?"

"Bad place to pick it up."

"If we don't, it'll be stripped by A.M. I got my shotgun and pistol." He stuck out a hand to Natalie. "Graham Hebert."

"Natalie Severin." She shook hands before climbing into the back, while Ram got in front. She leaned over the seat back as Graham put the truck in gear and headed out. "How'd you decide to become a vet?"

"Medic in Kuwait. Decided I liked stitching dogs better."

"You and Ram been partners long?"

"Off and on since he got out of vet school, along with my nephew, Louis. We handle things different from most partners, but the arrangement suits us. And it's profitable," he continued.

"Different? How?"

"Ram travels a fair bit, but his work brings in a slew of business. Louis and I like keeping things going at the clinic, as long as Ram's around for two weeks at fishing season." He caught her eye in the rearview mirror. "You always ask this many questions?"

Getting the feeling not many more answers would be forthcoming, she sat back, letting Graham concentrate on driving while she concentrated on the questions popping inside her.

Natalie sat alone in the clinic waiting area, her feet propped on a plastic chair. Graham and Ram had gone into the back for bullet removal.

She hoped Ram had gotten info from Raoul because she'd gotten zilch. Every time she'd spoken to someone in the bar, they'd acted startled, like she'd been invisible until just that moment. One time, as a kid, she'd wished she could be invisible, but the reality was annoying as hell.

Damn magic.

Maybe she could make better progress now, while she waited. She pulled AX's cell phone from her pocket. The numbers he'd called out were mostly useless. Kracker, Dawglip, some hooker named Candy. The ones not identified by his phone book, she dialed using her phone. One led to an answering machine that picked up immediately with only a synthesized "Speak" as a message. One number gave her pause as she dialed, the sequence vaguely familiar.

"Dark Phoenix." John, her friend the bartender, answered.

Swiftly, she disconnected. Why was AX calling the Dark Phoenix? The bar wasn't his type of hangout.

She pulled up the calls received. Several were from a blocked number, including one he'd received the night they were in the bayou. Interesting, but not useful. She had nowhere to follow on that.

With her phone, she worked her way down the list of unidentified numbers. Telephone company, bar, bar, hooker. One number caught her eye—the call had come in two hours before Twig's abduction. A call from an unblocked number. Stomach knotted, she thumbed in the numbers, then clicked into a voice mail.

"Halo angel, beware the fog demon."

The roar of blood in her ears drowned out all words, all sights. Her ribs clutched painfully around her frantic heartbeat.

Nathaniel? Nathaniel's voice. Nathaniel's greeting.

No, no, it couldn't be.

A beep alerted her that she'd missed the rest of the message. With a hand shaking so badly that she almost missed the button, she disconnected the call and looked at the number. No, she hadn't accidentally dialed Nathaniel's cell, the number she hadn't been able to delete from her auto dial even though it had been disconnected six months ago.

She closed her eyes against the sting of tears. Pictured him in her mind.

Blond hair, hazel eyes, same as hers. People always said they could tell she and Nathaniel were sibs because their eyes changed color the same way. But Nathaniel was the talented one of the DeSalvo twins, the one with the wicked imagination.

She opened her eyes and took a shuddering breath.

Maybe she'd made a mistake. Someone had co-opted Nathaniel's greeting and she'd imagined the voice. There had been a strange quality to it. She Webbed into whitepages.com. The number was registered to a cell serviced by Sprint in New Orleans.

Hands numb, she carefully reentered the number, double-checked the digits before she hit talk. One ring, two rings, three rings, four rings. Voice mail.

"Halo angel, beware the fog demon. Leave your message."

Beep. No mistake.

"Nathaniel? My, God, you're alive. Come back. We've always met every trouble together. I'll help you. I'll—" She heard Ram and his partner coming from the back and swiftly ended with, "Call me. *Call me, dammit.*"

She stowed the phones away and smoothed her sweaty palms down her legs, unwilling to face the implications of her brother calling AX right before the assault on her and Twig. There had to be another explanation, another reason besides the ugly one she was thinking. She had to find Nathaniel, give him a chance to explain.

Chasing away the questions she had no answers for and no reserves to deal with tonight, she looked up. Her poor heart stuttered again as she caught sight of Ram. He looked drawn, the skin on his cheeks pale.

Graham gave them a ride to Ram's home, and as they got out of the truck, he handed Natalie a brown vial. "Pain pills. He can take them every four hours. Try to get at least one down him tonight. The dressing won't need to be changed again until tomorrow evening unless he starts bleeding again." Apparently he'd assumed that she was spending the nights with Ram.

"Are there antibiotics?"

"Penicillin in the butt." He turned to Ram. "Take the

damn pills. You're lucky nothing vital got hit, but you're going to be damn sore for a few days."

Ram gave her another one of those enigmatic looks before he clasped his partner's hand. "Thanks, Graham."

"You'd do the same for me, in the unlikely event." He sounded a little wistful, before he stiffened his spine and left them with a wave.

Natalie stood awkwardly beside the entrance to the house. "Do you want me to stay the night?"

"Yes." There was an odd light in his eyes as he ran his hand along her palm. "It's late. I don't want you driving all that way to your home."

"I'd probably crash at NONE, but Graham said you shouldn't be alone."

"Graham's too cautious, and that's not why I want you to stay." His fingers tickled along her skin. "You can't deny there are sparks between us."

"I'm not that much into denial. But, you're hurt—"

He gave a short laugh. "Not that hurt."

"And we're working together, which could make it messy." *And Zolton wants me to spy on you.* "And . . ."

"And you don't trust me," he said softly.

"You have doubts, too. You don't always trust me."

"Tonight, I'm willing to look past that."

"What you did tonight, Ram. Are you still denying it's magic?"

"What do you think I did?"

"On the balcony. At the bar. Keeping us from being seen." She was trying to understand, to get past her history and stop worrying about what the magic would do to him, but when she kept running into secrets and lies, it was hard.

His fingertips traced a delicate line down her cheek. "Every time I think we're taking steps toward each other, I keep running into your doubts and anger. We don't have to bare our souls to bare our bodies. I'm not asking for eternity. Just tonight."

"I'm not sure if that's reassuring or insulting."

The fever in his eyes had nothing to do with ill health. "Don't you get it? I want you here tonight. What I don't want is Natalie Nurse or Nosy Natalie. I can't deal with either one of them tonight. I want *you*. Natalie. The woman who drives me crazy. No questions, no fussing, just the two of us and uncomplicated sex. But if you're exhausted, if you're not ready, I'll settle for you in the guest room if that's your preference. I simply want you here."

His words wove a powerful picture of need. She traced a line around his strong fingers. They were long and sinewy, suited for delicate work or powerful force. Her answer, she knew, had been decided long ago. "Not that exhausted."

It took him a moment to catch her meaning. When he did, he smiled and captured her hand, then drew it in for a kiss.

She laid her other hand on his chest. "Tonight, you don't want Natalie the reporter. You want Natalie the woman. I'm asking the same thing."

"Not Ram the vet? Trust me, I'll leave the animals out."

She chuckled, amazed that he could make her laugh as well as burn with need. "I want the man alone. Nothing magic in that bed."

His look turned wolfish as he murmured, "Now that would be a disappointment."

She gave him a playful cuff, but they both understood her meaning.

His turn to look away, but when he turned back, there was nothing of doubt or mistrust, nothing of disappointment in the heat of his gaze. "I promise. Will you come in, Natalie?"

A shiver of desire coursed through her. "My pleasure."

"Oh, I hope so." Holding her hand, he drew her slowly across the threshold into the darkened, cool foyer. With a twist of his foot, he slammed shut the door at the same time as he drew her into his arms.

"This is right," he breathed, lowering his lips to hers.

The sound of clicking nails speeding down the hall interrupted them.

"Not again," she groaned and looked down to see Val's sleepy doggy grin. Natalie gave her a scratch behind the ears. "Hi, sweetie, how you doing?"

Val's answer was an uptempo tail wag, which Natalie took to mean "great."

"She's just coming to say hello." Ram crouched down to ruffle the dog's fur. "Romp time's in the morning. Right?"

Val gave an agreeable bark, preened under their petting for a few more seconds, then turned and clicked back to her bed.

"Now, where were we?" Ram cupped Natalie's head with his hands, his thumbs tracing lightly across her cheeks. Then he tilted his head to kiss her.

The touch of his lips sparked such a cascade of heat and longing, she gasped at the unfamiliar ache. Sweet, his deepening kiss was so sweet. Her arms wrapped around the indent of his waist and drew him closer.

He felt *good* in her arms. Felt even better pressed against her. Solid, strong. No hiding his erection. No hiding the tightness in her breasts, the flow of dampness in her groin.

His teeth captured her lower lip. So delicately, they scraped against the sensitive nerves before releasing her with a tiny sucking motion. Her mouth opened, needing more of those touches, and for the moment, he seemed content to take it slow. Exploring her mouth, smiling and repeating a kiss when her moan of pleasure alerted him to its arousing success.

Her hands splayed across the small of his back against the supple heat of his muscles. Her senses were attuned to him. The ripple of muscle, the catch of breath.

With nothing more than a kiss and a hug, the two of them melded. With no more skin exposed except lips and hands, they blended.

"You taste so damn good," he murmured, lifting his head just a little, his breath uneven. He lowered to string kisses across her jaw. "Like fresh spring water."

"I'm afraid there's nothing fresh about me right now."

She should have kept her mouth shut, because he stopped kissing her. Quickly, she lowered her hand, realizing that when he'd released her, she'd absently started scratching her itchy neck.

"Would you like a shower first?" he asked, his hand playing across her nape with a caress as tingling as an electric current.

"I would," she admitted. She didn't want to go to him tonight, for the first time, caked in sweat and blood and calamine.

"Not so fresh here, either. Would you like company?"

She hesitated, then said, "Of course."

Her body tautened at the mere thought of him naked but for soap lather, the wet cascade slicking back his dark hair, a cool mist countering the steam of his touch and his mouth on her. She was halfway to orgasm, and they'd only kissed fully dressed. They could come together in the shower, braced against the wall, within moments of stepping beneath the water.

Normally, she was bold when it came to sex. She had no trouble asking for what she wanted or qualms about experimenting. Yet, tonight, she was an odd mix of bold and shy. Showering together was intimate. Part of her, a strange part of her, wanted to step in more gradually.

And Ram, naturally, caught that hesitation. "Together

can come later," he said, grazing a hand across her belly in a way that made her muscles V together in excitement, the way a fern closed when touched. "I have two bathrooms. You just have to promise me one thing."

"What?"

"While you're in there, alone, rubbing that cake of soap on your breasts and thighs and between your legs, you have to pretend it's my hand."

"I promise," she said huskily, "if you'll think about me kneeling, my mouth around you."

"Oh, God, Natalie." With a feral grin he peeled himself away from her, and grabbed her hand. "Then, come."

"I will," she answered, echoing his cheeky grin.

He laughed. Taking her hand with that same tingle of awareness that danced through her every time they touched, he hastened her down the hall and into what she assumed was his bedroom. The bathroom was attached and he opened the door with a flourish.

"Your shower awaits. Just make it fast." With that, he gave her a swift, potent kiss, then turned on his heel and left.

Inside the bathroom, Natalie peeled off her blood-stained clothes and winced as she glimpsed her reflection in the mirror. The glow of desire faded in the face of reality. Pink bee welts, purpling bruises, a scrape on her cheek, and her hair was a flat mess.

"Not sexy," she moaned. She'd be lucky if Ram could get it up after a sight like that. Maybe they could turn off the lights.

At least she could get rid of the sweat. Stepping into the shower, she groaned again. Together would have been sweet. The shower was pure decadence. Big enough for two, with four showerheads. Pulsating, too.

Swiftly, she turned on the water, keeping it more tepid than warm. Ah, that felt so good. She wore her underwear in, the nylon would clean and dry easily. After she'd rinsed the bra and panties and hung them to dry, she tossed her head back, letting the water sluice down her face. Shampooed out the grime.

The shampoo and soap both smelled like Ram, woodsy, not a hint of flower to be found. As she ran the cake of soap around, she did exactly as he'd commanded. She thought of him. His hand would be rougher than the sleek soap, but also firmer, less slick. Ram wouldn't melt or soften in the steam.

How long she stood there, fantasizing and cleaning, she wasn't sure. Not long, she thought, but apparently longer than Ram, for there was a knock on the door, then it opened a few inches.

"Thought you might want this," he called, though she could see nothing of him, only his hand depositing something on the counter.

"Thanks," she answered as the door closed. "Be out in a sec."

Matching her promise, she turned off the water and quickly dried herself. The something he'd left her turned out to be clothes: a pair of green shorts with a drawstring and a Tulane T-shirt, size large.

"Fetching," she muttered, catching sight of the shorts ending at her knees. She finger combed her hair into place, then sighed. Get that light out fast.

Every light in the bedroom was blazing, she discovered when she came out of the bathroom. Every single light, plus a candle or five.

Wearing shorts and a button-down shirt, Ram reclined on the bed, bathed in shades of light. His dark features and bronze skin glowed like burnished metal.

"Not into mood lighting?" she asked, annoyed that her voice shook.

"You illuminated is sexy. No hiding tonight." His voice was as low and smooth as a cello. His hands were clasped behind his head in a casual pose, but there was nothing casual in the gaze he fixed on her. There was heat and an I-like-what-I-see admiration. The longer he looked, the more his smile grew. A good smile, one that said I'm appreciating and I'm enjoying.

If he could look so thoroughly, so could she. His dark hair was damp and slicked back, just as she had imagined, leaving the stark planes of his face exposed. There was a gash on his forehead, one that had been hidden by his hair. But it was his dark eyes that gave his face so much character. Warm, alert, mysterious.

He sat so still, she couldn't even see him breathing, and his body dominated the space of the bed. Just as he commanded any space he entered.

Natalie's blood heated her cheeks, and the moisture grew between her thighs. Damn, just looking at him, primed by her imaginative shower, and she was one stroke shy of an orgasm. Suddenly she realized why she had been cautious.

This time mattered.

Those very brief affairs she'd had after she'd separated from Charles hadn't engaged her heart or even her emotions. Those had been about sex, nothing more, and she couldn't be hurt. In essence, she hadn't cared.

With Ram, she cared. Ram held a power for her, one she wasn't sure she liked, but undeniable, and she could not resist him.

Because he was more than an irresistible temptation. He brought her back to life, with all its sweetness and danger.

Caring meant you could be hurt.

Ram's smile faded a bit while she stood watching him. She knew she wore her hopes and fears all over her face. Heart on her sleeve, and Ram was too damn good at reading her not to see. Maybe it came from being a vet and reading nonverbal animals. Maybe it came from the utter control he had over his own body.

Whatever, his arms lowered from behind his head, to rest on his thighs.

"Bee stings and bruises are only marks of what make you so very attractive to me," he said.

Damn, how did he do that?

"You don't give up. You demand to know why." A ghost of a smile played across his lips. "You drive a Harley like an exquisite fiend."

"Is that a compliment?"

"Very much so. I love seeing you dressed in my clothes," he added, then stopped, waiting. Waiting for her to make the next move. Giving her one last chance to escape.

Except she didn't want to escape. She was caught and while she was here she would experience every bit of pleasure.

"You are irresistibly tempting to me," she admitted. Temptations didn't work if you thought too far in the future. She knelt on the bed beside him. "Where were you hurt?"

He lifted up the sleeve of his shirt to expose the thick bandage on his shoulder. "It's not that bad, but Graham's into tape and gauze. I'm lucky he didn't try to fit a cone around my neck."

She laughed, and felt something tight in her chest ease. Pointing to the gash on his forehead, she said, "That must have bled a lot."

"More than the bullet wound." He gave a negligent shrug, as though the topic didn't interest him.

Natalie trailed her hands down his arms until she captured his wrists. She leaned forward, a breath away from his lips. "Don't we have better things to do than talk about our boo-boos?"

"Like what?"

"This." She closed the gap between them. Kissed him, eagerly, with want and need. Bracing her hands beside his head to keep her weight off him, she sprawled over him. Cradled him between her thighs. Tilted her hips and grazed against his erection.

Ram grabbed her wrists. He gave a small tug, dislodging her, so she fell with a small "oof" atop him. Her sore muscles protested, and she grimaced.

At once he asked, "Are you all right?"

"Fine." She laid a finger on those kissable lips. "We may have to leave out the acrobatics—"

"Darn." His hand stroked carefully down her ribs.

"Do what you will, and I'll tell you if anything bothers me." She touched the bandage. "Promise me you'll do the same. I don't want to hurt you."

He looked startled, as though no one had ever offered to shield him. Perhaps he was so used to being the protector. *Well, you've got someone now*, she thought fiercely.

The moment passed, replaced by his burgeoning, sexy smile. His hand slid beneath her T-shirt. "Anything until you tell me to stop?"

His palm was warm and slightly roughened against her skin. A man who worked with his hands. He stroked the rounded side of her breast, raising the pitch of her desire.

"The deal works both ways," she whispered, beginning her own passage of discovery beneath the edge of one his shorts, up the length of one hard thigh. Not an ounce of give in the muscle. Beneath hers, his body was taut. Such hardness shouldn't be comfortable, but it was.

No, not comfortable. Right. His body was so right for hers.

Their tongues danced together as their mouths mated. His hands traced a restless pattern across her arms, shoulders, rear, even the backs of her thighs and the so-sensitive area of her neck. He surrounded her in a glow more brilliant than the blaze of lights.

She needed *him*. His touch, his kiss, his body. The

faint woodsy odor of his soap and that masculine "Oh, yeah," as she grazed his sinewy neck with her teeth. Suddenly the thin cotton cloth between them was too much of a barrier.

Lifting her lips from their kisses, she settled back on her heels. His protest broke off, however, when she pulled her shirt over her head.

"Oh," he breathed as his hands cupped her breasts. "Pretty."

He toyed with her nipples, circling them with a single finger, gathering them for a tiny pinch, more erotic than painful. The nip rippled down through her in a rivulet of wildfire. Stroke, press, feather—his hands took command of her breasts and belly, her muscles trembling beneath the unpredictable caresses.

With a sudden move proving his flat abs were all muscle, he sat up, then, without giving her time to think, his arm slid around to brace her shoulder blades, and he bent her back. Just enough to offer her breasts to his mouth.

Oh, she was lost. His mouth was even better than his hands. The tug reached clear between her legs as both breasts in turn received their tender treatment. Her hands dropped to her sides. She'd been enjoying the lean muscle of his back beneath the cotton of his shirt, but she couldn't manage that right now. All she could do was grip the bedsheet, trying to hold back her explosion.

He lifted his head to stare at her breasts, and then he gently blew on them, his breath cooling the moisture from his mouth. When his gaze returned to hers, his look was triumphant. "We could try some toys I brought back from China. Velvet ribbon manacles that go here." He outlined her breasts at the base. "With a charm for here." He pressed against her nipple, the on button for another surge of wanting.

"Rings for you, too?"

"Yeah."

"Would you have to leave the bed to get them?"

"Yeah."

"Later." She tightened her thighs around him. "Right now, I don't want to let you go."

"I can live with that."

"I'm also thinking that you've got way too many clothes on." She undid the top button of his shirt.

To her surprise, he grabbed her wrists and stopped her. He'd done that before, she remembered, in her bed, and she glanced at him in curiosity. Ram? Body self-conscious? Didn't ring true. He moved with supreme confidence and control. Then what?

With a muttered curse, he released her hands and undid the buttons. Granted her silent permission.

Taking care not to dislodge his bandage, she stripped his shirt off his shoulders. She reared back, absorbing the sight of him in a single glance, and her breath caught on a gasp. *My, God.* The words echoed between them, and she realized she'd said them aloud.

Ram's chest was a mass of scars, mostly thin white lines, but some were as wide as an inch. The gouges crisscrossed as though from some frenzied whipping. Even his shoulders carried the brands. She ran a hand across the ridged skin.

What could have inflicted such torture? Who? Why? The questions spun through her, but the one she voiced was, "Back, too?"

He shrugged off the shirt and twisted his torso. The same scars marred his back.

Her throat closed at the thought of the inflicted pain. This had been done by a monster. Done with fury and precise control.

"Who . . . ?" The question died when he looked at her. The deep pain in his eyes warned her not to dig into the past.

"Don't ask, Natalie," he warned, his voice flat. "Not how or where or who. I can't, won't, tell you."

So hard to bite back the curiosity and the empathy. But, if one question was forbidden, there were always more to ask. "Did you succeed?"

"What?" She'd surprised him.

"You're very purpose-driven. I assume you didn't land in a place where this"—she traced one of the broadest lines, a nasty stroke cutting between two ribs—"happened by chance."

"Yes," he answered simply. "I succeeded."

She drew a nail very lightly across his nipple. Were all the nerves irreparably damaged? "Can you feel?"

"Yes. Now."

"This is what gives you those nightmares and ugly memories? What brought you back to New Orleans?"

"Yes." He grabbed her hand, lifting it away from his body.

The reporter wasn't the woman he needed. He'd told her that. Neither was sympathy. He needed tonight, and that's what she would give him. With a slow indrawn breath, she collected herself.

"Am I going to find more of those marks around your penis?" she asked briskly.

"See for yourself," he said, need apparent on his face.

She brushed her hand across the front of his shorts, and he gave a soft "ahhh." The sound of that pleasure speared through her. Giving him a smile, she hooked her forefingers into his shorts and stretched out the elastic. Slowly, she lowered the fabric, freeing him.

No scars. The damage had been confined to his chest and back and psyche. Again, she brushed a hand across him, this time on his bared cock. Long, thick, as well built as the rest of the man. But not ready. She stroked a little more firmly this time, and he stirred beneath her touch, growing hard again.

His hands came up to her waist, tugging at her shorts, but the material caught on her legs as she straddled him. Impatiently, she rolled off, shed the last bit of clothing with absolutely no finesse, and then returned to him.

"Natalie," he breathed, as his hands moved restlessly across her.

Not fancy words, but enough.

They explored one another, learning the feel of skin and muscle, and the pitch of desire rose again. Fueled by caresses. By the flare of nostrils and the musky aroma of desire.

His fingers trailed along her inner thighs. Teasing her as his face grew tight with his own desire. He was ready; his cock filled. She needed to be filled, too, and she tightened with the need to clutch hard on a finger or two, a penis. Her spread legs kept her from relieving the burning ache.

"Inside me," she commanded, lifting her hips, gliding her damp heat across him, ready to join them.

"Not yet." He clamped his hands onto her hips, holding her still, then, like before, he surged to a sitting position. "I want to kiss you again."

The kiss seared through her, burning out thought. The taste of him, the feel of him beneath her mouth joined the sensory cacophony. Finally, he stroked her at the juncture of her thighs. Touched her fiery nub of nerves and sent her spiraling near the peak. He inserted one finger, two. Stroked in and out.

"Yes." She clutched his shoulder with one hand. With the other, she reached down and circled his length. Her fingers forming an O, she, too, mimicked the sex act. Learned that a slow, full stroke made him grunt with pleasure. That he also liked her thumb.

"Yes," he echoed. His breath came harsh and fast, rasping into the silent room.

He was on his own instinctive learning curve as he

flicked a finger to a sweet spot, sending her just shy of an explosion. A shout of longing burst from her. She wrapped her arms around him, pulling him flush against her. Sweat-slick skin to skin. Another flick, with a nip to her shoulder, released the flood. He was watching her, but she was helpless to do anything but meet the command of his fingers. Her orgasm shuddered through her, spasms of such intense pleasure, she could only cling to him and shout her release. He supported her in the boneless aftermath until her breath evened out.

His erection still pressed against her belly. "Your turn," she murmured, and lowered herself along him, sliding body to body, not breaking the threads of contact between them. Pressing against his shoulders, she urged him to lie, to let her have her way. He complied, and she lowered her mouth to him.

"Ah," he sighed.

First just the tip, then inch by inch, she gathered him deeper and reveled in the strength and power she surrounded. When she did her version of the flick, with her tongue, he groaned again. Smiling that she could turn the normally eloquent Ram speechless in bed, she tasted and licked, until he pushed at her shoulders, lifting her away.

"I want to be inside you."

"You are." She licked her lips.

He half groaned, half laughed. "Not there."

Before he finished the word, he'd smoothly shifted positions. Natalie found herself borne to her back against the decadent mattress. He sprawled across the bed, claiming most of the space. Only his chest covered her. He kissed the slope of her shoulder, as his hand stroked along her side. "Unless you'd like to stay on top," he said, teasing her hip.

"No. This is fine." She could get so used to this—the

feel of him in her arms, the slide of his skin on hers. The way she felt so alive.

Her hips moved restlessly against him, and he took the invitation, shifting between her legs without ever breaking contact. His length stroked the outer edges of her damp folds. She needed him inside her. Arching her hips, she pressed him closer. Opened to him.

"Now, Ram," she gasped.

He surged inside her, seating himself to the hilt. "Good," he moaned, bracing his weight on his hands, caging her between his arms. He filled her with flesh and heat and that electric wildfire spark.

She stiffened. *That electricity.*

He began to move inside her. Long, slow strokes that pulled desire through her, each stroke a tug on her heart and mind. The charge resounded between them, amplifying yearning. Bonds of desire forged, feeding each other's passion.

Surrounding her. Taking control.

Magic. The intense, pleasuring sparkle—now a rush of hot demand between them—was *magic.*

She opened her eyes as her pulse jerked into overdrive. This was Ram above her. His were eyes shut, rapt with his need and pleasure. There was light in the room, not darkness.

Yet darkness crept in from the edges of memory. A ball of panic stoppered her throat, and she gasped in a painful gulp of air.

He'd *promised.* Ram had promised her. No magic.

Couldn't be magic. This felt good. Completing.

It was. She recognized the hot champagne effervescence. Her muscles, cells, nerves danced with it, ached with it.

Cowered from it. Her breath came in pants. Her vision faded under the rising thrum of panic.

She grabbed for sanity. Different from last time. Not

forced. No pain. She reached a hand up to touch Ram's face, seeking an anchor.

Without opening his eyes, he grabbed her wrist. His fingers pressed her racing pulse. Stroke faster, harder. The magic spun between them, wrapping around their joined hands.

Shadows swelled from deep in her mind. She yanked her hand. Writhing, she tried to free herself. *Bound by invisible cords*. Unable to move. Memories invaded, memories she couldn't escape.

Betrayal by a man she loved. Magic. Woven into a smoky room and into hurting.

"Let me go," she panted. When her hand wasn't released immediately, she shouted, "No!" She couldn't see the lighted room, couldn't hear any voice above her shout. "No!"

Only anger stemmed that consuming fear. Her free hand shoved at a male shoulder. "Let go of me!"

Chapter Seventeen

Intense pleasure consumed Ram. Lost in the sweet slide of Natalie's skin, he reveled in the strength of her hand in his. He was so near release, only the sound of her voice registered. No words.

"No!"

That registered. Struck through his haze.

"No!"

The word attacked, and Ram's shoulders stiffened, his body still pulsing. What the fuck? No? She's saying no? Now?

Not Natalie, she was no cock tease.

Always respect when a woman says no, son. The rule of conduct had been pounded into him since he'd first admitted he liked that girls had breasts.

No, no, no, Ram groaned. His eyes opened, and the sight of Natalie's face cut through his desire. Her eyes were unfocused, her muscles drawn tight by some over-powering emotion. Which one, he had no clue, except it wasn't desire.

She shoved at his shoulder. "Let go of me!"

The words, the anger were as seductive as a splash of sleet.

"What the hell?" He suddenly realized that he held her wrist and his cramped fingers released her. Had his strength hurt her? "I grabbed too hard?"

"You promised." She shoved at him, this time with both hands.

"What?" His mind was still fuzzed with wanting her. The feel of her clutched around him, the sight of her bared breasts, the lingering taste of her, all pounded into him with arousing messages. He was still hard, but definitely not on the verge of exploding. His skin stimulated by the charge—oh, shit.

"Magic," she said, glaring.

He closed his eyes to erase the tempting sight of her, although he could do nothing about taste or touch or scent. Holding himself very still, he painstakingly stopped his instinctive reaching for her. Shaking inside with the effort, he reined in his desire and power, at last remembering the years of discipline.

Only when the outflow was dammed did he look at her. The wild light was gone from her eyes, although her breath still came in ragged pants. Stiffly, she clutched the bedcovers with both hands.

"I'm sorry," he said. "Did I hurt you?"

She shook her head. "Get off me."

The lady said no.

"I—" What could he say? He *had* broken a promise. Words failed under his still bursting need to come. "I'm sorry."

She shoved herself backward with her elbows, trying to pull her body from beneath him.

"Don't!" he said sharply, that little movement making pleasure spiral again. "On the brink here." Bracing himself on his elbows to take his weight off her, he added, "Give me a moment."

Boring, think of something boring. His brother, Jack, said he recited the periodic table to avoid being premature. Hydrogen, um . . . What the hell was on a periodic table? Bird flu. Symptoms of bird flu. Fever, cough, sore throat, muscle aches. At last, softening a little, he very slowly withdrew and lay down beside her. She immediately rolled away and left the bed.

He didn't want her to leave. He didn't want the night to end this way. Unfulfilled and wrong. If she walked out now, they would irreparably damage something so good.

"Don't go. Please."

At least she stopped before she got to the door. Without looking at him, she yanked on the T-shirt. The cloth covered her breasts and belly, but lower regions were still exposed.

Give me strength. She had such a sweet little butt.

Only with the protection of clothes did she face him. "No ignoring or changing the subject or pretending what happened was my imagination. At the bar you used magic. On the balcony. In this bed. My ribs healed when they should have been too painful to breathe. That was magic. The power of your will. Don't deny it, Ram. Not this time."

Useless to deny, even if he wanted to. With other people, he had no trouble hiding his talents; with Natalie, he had an urge to flaunt them. He couldn't hide from her any longer. "Yes, all that was magic."

She sighed, as though she took no pleasure in the truth.

"Was what I did so bad?" He rolled from bed and strode, naked, to her side. "Healing Val. Relieving your pain. Keeping Dawglip from putting a bullet here." He tapped the bridge of her nose.

"That's not the point. In bed. You promised."

"For that, I am sorry," he said again. "The magic wasn't deliberate. I was mindless; the sensations flowing between us are so enhanced, so pleasurable. To me, using magic can be . . . instinctive."

He tried to find the right words, to sort out what he could and shouldn't say. Impossible when the very texture of her skin tempted him. Impossible when he wasn't entirely sure of the reasons himself. Sure, sex was one of the ways that his magic revitalized itself. But the instinctual seeking, the intensity of the synergy, that was something fresh.

So he settled for basic. "Give me, us, a second chance. I'll know to expect it now; I can control it." At her still doubtful, but calmer, look, he added, "The power won't touch you. I won't promise, because you won't believe me now. Let me show you."

She didn't say anything, but at least she wasn't leaving. From the stand at the bedside, he got out his athame, then wrapped her fingers around the knife's black hilt. "You control the power. Any time you think I'm forgetting, you can stab me with this."

She flung it away, letting it bounce on the mattress. Her hand clenched. "I don't want this."

Still, she didn't move away, didn't leave.

He wanted to be very sure about the emotional minefield he'd stepped into. "What happened just now? In bed."

"I got a little crazy," she said, her cheeks pink.

"Because of my broken promise? Because of the magic?"

"Because I was naked. Vulnerable." She lifted a shoulder. "Magic was once associated with some unpleasant sex."

Two and two made an ugly four.

"Charles raped you, and he used magic to help him," Ram said flatly, a murderous urge rising inside him. If the bastard were in this room now, he'd be feeling the lash of real magic.

She raked back her hair, then crossed over to the window. Bracing her hands on the sill, she gazed out into the night. Her T-shirt rose up above her rear. He pushed back a surge of heat to focus on what she was saying.

"Do you know," she said, her voice a mere whisper, "I didn't mourn my husband when he died. Didn't shed a single tear. That's cold, isn't it?"

"No." Ram slipped on his shorts and joined her at the window. Leaning one shoulder against the frame, he crossed his arms. The need to comfort her with his touch thrummed strong. "You are anything but cold. I think you'd already done your grieving."

She nodded. "He told me to meet him in the library. Even though he knew I didn't like the room. Said he wanted to fix what was wrong between us. I thought I owed us that chance." She gave a bitter laugh.

Lightly he brushed her hair, glad that she didn't flinch from him. "You don't have to say anything more."

"Yes, I do. I need to get this all out. Exposed and done with. I thought I'd gotten past what happened; I've had sex since."

"Not with a Mage."

"Not with a Mage," she agreed. "His idea of fixing our differences was to have sex; I wanted something more. So, he cast a spell. No matter what he did to me, I couldn't move."

"He hurt you." Ram could barely force the words out.

"Some. Worse, however, was the pleasure he mixed in. The responses he forced."

So much worse than he'd imagined. His hand hovered above her hair, then his fist clenched before he could touch her. "I would not hurt you. Force you."

"You're strong, Ram, in so many ways. I've experienced all forms of power in my work, my life, and I know what it can do. What it can become. Do you ever think about that? How that power might change you?"

"Not really. To me, magic isn't something external that pushes me to and fro, it's a part of who I am. I don't always make the right choices, but then magic is neither easy nor casual. It takes discipline, hard work, rite and ritual, but it is beautiful."

"And strong. I thought, even if some of your power . . . leaked out, I could handle it." She raked a hand through her hair. "The intensity—"

"Was not all supernatural."

She looked at him steadily. "I know, and that's new and good. That's why you, we, get a second chance."

He hesitated. "You've got to be real clear for me. Where are we going? Because the last word I heard was no."

"Yes."

Yes as in no longer no? Or yes as in yes, the last words were no? God, a man could go nuts. "Do you want to make love with me, Natalie?"

"Yes."

Clear enough. Straightening, he reached for her, but she stopped him with a hand to his bare chest. Her fingers were cold, but the touch still heated the blood beneath his skin. "No magic," she reminded.

"No magic," he promised. The power within him stirred, reaching to connect with this woman, even as his body stirred with that same arousal. Ruthlessly, he thrust back the yearning connection of the spirit.

Focus on the physical. Focus on Natalie.

He plucked her hand from his chest, and then kissed her fingers, drawing them a little into his mouth. Watching her over their joined hands, he tested her reactions. Let her response lead him.

The aftermath of their aborted joining had left him acutely sensitive. A dusting of pink on her cheeks became a red banner, signaling that she liked the touch. A hitch in her breathing played as loud as a symphony. Slowly, he lifted the shirt off her, caressing the feminine muscles of her back in the move.

She splayed her hands across his chest. "Your skin is always so warm."

"Good metabolism." Resting his hands at her waist, he leaned forward and kissed her lips. With a sigh of pleasure, she ran her hands up and down his arms, kissing him back.

He wanted to carry her to the bed, but his wound wouldn't let him. Instead, he led her back, kicking off his shorts along the way. The athame, tourmaline, and ring he shoved into a drawer before turning back to loving her.

Ram absorbed every vivid sensation. The fine texture of her skin beneath his palms. The taste of salt on her skin and the taste of the cooled night air. Scents of her arousal mingled with the aroma of bergamot candles. He heard the nuances in each breath she took. Took in the whole and stroked her, touched her intimately and in places that especially pleased her.

The power inside him still reached for her, but he kept it contained. Instead, he drowned in the physical. In the exquisite pleasures of their mingling breath and bodies. He absorbed her cries as she climaxed around his fingers and then a second time with his tongue.

At last, when he entered her, it felt so damn good and he was so ready that he nearly came at the first touch of her slick muscles. Instead, he held on long enough for Natalie to come again; then the release crashed over him. Waves of pleasure spasmed through him, and he joined Natalie's ecstatic cries.

He collapsed into a sated afterglow. A moment later, he rolled onto his back, taking Natalie with him. She sprawled atop him.

"That was fantastic," he murmured, his eyes drifting shut.

"Mmmm," she agreed.

"No bad memories?"

"Not a one." She settled closer to him. "Am I too heavy for you?"

"Not at the moment." His hand ran idly along her bare bottom. "I like what I'm feeling."

She pushed up a little, bracing herself on her forearm, so their gazes met. "You didn't miss . . ."

"I meant it when I said it was fantastic," he reassured her, brushing back a strand of her hair that had caught on her cheek.

She stared at him a moment, as if searching for a lie, then with an undecipherable murmur, she lay back down. They settled together, back to front, and sleep rose out of the night.

Ram held Natalie until he was sure she was sound asleep, until her breathing became deep and even, before he reached out his hand. Delicately, making sure he didn't touch her, he extinguished the candles, and then lowered the lights, until only one remained barely lit. Enough to keep Natalie from tripping if she got up in the night.

He settled back beside her, wrapping his arms around her.

What he'd said was true. Tonight had been very good. He couldn't remember ever feeling that he was in such a right place, at least when it came to sex.

He drifted off toward sleep. And if his last thought was *How much better could it have been*? he ignored it.

Morning sex was the best, Natalie decided. Right up there with evening sex. And afternoon. And nighttime. And the noon quickie. She stretched and yawned as she rolled off Ram, both of them sweaty and sated. She propped her head up with her hand to look at him. His eyes were shut, his face somber. He was withdrawing from her, she realized.

"Where are you?" she asked, tracing the line of his chin.

"In bed with you," he answered promptly. Without opening his eyes, he tilted his chin and kissed her lips. "A place I could happily stay."

"But the day starts." Sunlight was streaming in between the cocked slats of the blinds. She moved her hand lower, this time tracing the stripes on his chest. The white lash marks stood in stark relief against the bronze of his skin, now also dappled by the warm sunlight.

Not moving, his eyes still shut, he said, "A seer."

"Come again?"

"I got those scars from a nasty seer with a talent for metallurgy. The titanium alloy whip he designed drew out magic as well as blood."

"You said you succeeded."

"I killed him," he said bluntly. "But I was left completely emptied. Powerless."

"Like most people on this earth." God, what a stupid thing to say.

His eyes opened; then he tilted his head to look at her. "No. Despite a very charmed life, with all the advantages, I always knew something was different inside me. That difference was my magic. For a . . . for someone like me, that power is fused in every cell. For weeks after the confrontation, I was insane with loss, then followed depression even as I picked up the pieces of my ordinary life. Every single day, however, I felt as if I'd had a few limbs chopped off. Until gradually I healed, and the power came back."

She heard the message loud and clear. He'd said it last night, too. He would restrain himself while they were in bed, but the magic was an intimate, indelible part of who he was.

His eyes opened, and he rolled to his side. His hand rested lightly on her bare belly. "I wish I could stay here, close, tasting your skin and stroking you, take an hour so I could slip back inside you."

"But—?"

"That will have to wait until tonight. I have clinic duty today." He kissed her nose. "The shower is yours when you want; I'll take Val for a run after my meditation."

He hustled out of the bed, not looking back, and strode, unselfconsciously naked, across the room. Dear Lord, he had nice buns. When she was alone in the room, she lay back against the soft pillows. No longer sleepy, but thinking.

She had just had the best sex in her life, so what was wrong? A smile played across her lips as she played back portions of the night. The way Ram smiled at her. His gentle touch. The eager way he suckled her nipples. The rougher kisses they'd both needed. The different positions. All good. Ram had seemed pleased, too.

So, what was niggling at her?

Don't force the thought; it will come.

She took a quick shower, then collected her clothes. The underwear she'd washed out, but she frowned at the thought of putting on the blood-stiff pants and shirt.

"Ram?" she called, going into the hall.

Silence answered her, and the house felt strangely empty. Tossing on the clothes he'd given her last night, she went into the kitchen and discovered why Ram had not answered her.

He was in a jungle of a backyard, doing some kind of martial arts routine. He'd put on shorts and a T-shirt, but the clothes didn't at all detract from the masculine power in his body. She realized this was related to the fighting techniques she'd seen him use. She also recognized the magic he was incorporating into the moves. Utter stillness surrounded him. Despite the slight morning breeze, not a single leaf or blade of grass moved near him. A faint sparkling glow surrounded him.

Intent on his task, his face held an intriguing combination of concentration and pleasure. Although their gazes crossed once, and she thought he was aware she watched him, he was disciplined enough not to acknowledge her presence.

A low sound filled the still air, and she realized that he was chanting something foreign under his breath. His hands swept the air and released a shimmering veil of sparks. The sparkle hung in front of him until his forefinger slashed forward, and one of the dots of light shot to a tree at the far side of the lawn.

A ferocious crack rent the morning, and the leafy limb detonated in a white explosion. Sulfur gagged her and smoke irritated her throat as the limb burned.

Beautiful and exquisitely dangerous.

Ram closed his fist and the sound and smell vanished. Most of the flame, too, leaving only the ashy tip. He executed a small bow of his head toward the tree, and said something she couldn't hear. An apology to the tree maybe.

Such deadly power in the command of one man. One man who, by the look on his face, was in complete harmony with this dangerous magic.

Her heart tripped over the answer to what had bothered her this morning. Heavy-limbed, thoughtful, she returned to the house.

Val, finishing breakfast, greeted her with a friendly tail wag. Ram came in and lifted a brow toward Natalie as he slipped on socks and running shoes. "Val and I are going for our run. You want to come? I'm usually gone about an hour."

Run? For an hour? That or a dentist's chair without nitrous oxide. "No thanks."

A few minutes later, man and dog were out the door

and jogging toward the levee, leaving Natalie staring into her coffee.

Ram and magic were inseparable. That fact, driven home by what she'd seen, was what she'd sensed this morning. Oh, yes, he had enjoyed the sex they'd shared as much as she did, of that she was certain.

She had given everything to him, wholeheartedly and without reserve.

He had responded with as much as she had allowed. But an indelible part of him was missing. His magic.

The question of whether they had a future together was moot if she couldn't accept his powers. Her suspicions would eventually tear them apart.

She had two problems, she realized. Connected, but different. One was her could-I-be-more-embarrassing-in-bed panic attack. That absolutely had to go. Face the magic. She was tired of being shadowed by the troubles of her failed marriage. She might have a phobia about fog; she'd be damned if she'd add a fresh one about sex.

The other issue was more subtle, less personal, but ultimately more dangerous. Magic was a powerful force. Her job at NONE was to investigate and expose the underbelly of the more bizarre forms of power. She breathed ink and pixels. Ram was a good man, she believed that, but good men changed. Unless she could come to terms with his power, she and Ram had no future.

And she hadn't even begun to consider the complicating factors of a missing brother who might be involved with the animal smugglers and an editor who wanted answers about Ramses Montgomery.

Well, she needed those answers, too, and she had a closing window of time to get them.

First problem? Accepting his magic during sex. She needed the equivalent of an allergy shot. Exposure to small doses until the stimulus lost its power of harm.

Magical objects often contained residual traces of

the wielder. Last night she'd dropped that knife, startled by the blade's coursing power. She hurried into the bedroom, pulled open the drawer. The obsidian knife, without a gemstone of decoration on it, sat like a black hole, beside his tourmaline and ring.

Gingerly, she picked up the knife and a tingling rivulet wove into her hand, faint but unmistakable. Nothing to fear. She returned the knife to the drawer. The tourmaline and the ring winked back at her. He wore those. Would the emanations be stronger?

A twinge of guilt at her spying was quickly suppressed. Touching always gave her so much more information. In the end, as it always did, curiosity won.

The tourmaline was surprisingly warm and more powerful in its crawly effect on her. Yet the longer she held the pendant, the more accustomed to it she became, and the more the sensation fused with her pleasurable memories of making love to Ram.

Well, she'd probably felt the worst. Ram used the tourmaline in some of his chants, she'd seen that. The ring might be mere decoration. Letting go of the gem, she picked up the ring.

A charge zapped through her, as though she'd grabbed a magical live wire. A painful, powerful current traveled the length of her arm.

"Ouch!" The ring clattered from her hand, spinning across the dresser top before settling. What made the ring so powerful? She shook out her hand, then picked up the ring again, using the tips of her fingers. The jolt grabbed her breath in a vise, but, expecting it, she held on until the shock settled into a steady hum.

She turned the ring over in her hand, pressing and examining it. It gleamed like solidified mercury. Suddenly, in response to her pressing, the ring gave a tiny click, and the top opened.

Natalie stared, and then swallowed hard.

Hidden beneath was a symbol. Nathaniel's symbol. Not the exact same pattern, this one must represent a different beast, but the style was unmistakable.

Ram had pretended he knew nothing about these symbols. Damn him! She dropped the ring into the drawer, then slammed it shut. Damn him! No wonder he'd been so upset when she'd lied to him about finding the charm.

Okay, she didn't deserve righteous anger, not when she still hadn't told him about the symbol's tenuous connection to Nathaniel.

But why had he lied? The book she'd found. Maybe he'd deliberately misinterpreted those pages. Kept her from a lead to Nathaniel. Where had she left it last night? In the kitchen.

The book was nowhere to be found in the kitchen. Natalie fisted her hands at her hips, her heart a frantic tattoo against her ribs. He must have hidden it. Where?

Was there a library? She moved swiftly through the house, opening doors. His home had a Spartan feel, with few possessions and little clutter, except books strewn in every room, each bookmarked. A copy of NONE was folded back to her last article: "Paranormal Investigators in Louisiana: Who's Really Seeing Ghosts." None of the books, however, was the one she wanted. She left the second floor and headed up the narrow stairs to the third story.

A door blocked her way. She turned the knob, but the door stayed shut. After a brief, useless struggle with her conscience, she pressed harder, shoving at it with her foot and hip. The door swung open. Natalie stepped in, bracing herself for an alarm's screech.

The house, however, remained silent. The room she walked into took up the entire third floor and was redolent of spices. She identified clove and sage, but the others eluded her. A throw rug and low table occupied the center, but the only other furniture were the shelves lining every inch of wall, from floor to ceiling. And the shelves were packed. At least a third with books, the rest with braziers, oils, herbs, marble jars—contents unknown—a plethora of magical objects like crystal balls, tarot cards, and some creepy things she couldn't identify. And she'd seen a lot of strange creepy things.

The book was in plain sight on the table. She glanced at her watch; Ram and Val would be returning soon. Hastily, she located the relevant pages and then snapped a copy with her phone. Moments later, the pages were on their way to her e-mail address.

She glanced out the window. Ram was almost back! She shoved the book into her hobo bag, detoured to the bedroom for the ring, and then waited in the kitchen. Ram didn't look at her, busying himself with re-filling Val's water bowl.

Only when the dog was occupied slurping water did he turn to face Natalie.

She recoiled, the anger inside her shriveling. His face was still and cold, as if carved from an iceberg. Eight months ago, when he'd confronted her, he'd been shouting. This was a deeper fury.

"You couldn't resist," he said, his voice falling like chips of frozen cream.

"What are you talking about?"

"Don't play dumb. It doesn't become you." He leaned forward, bracing his arms on the table, invading her space. "You didn't leave a corner of my house unviolated."

She winced at the phrasing. "What? Did you have me tagged?"

"My house has alarms."

"I heard nothing."

"You wouldn't." He straightened, his hands tightening to fists, and asked scornfully, "Did you find what you wanted? Evidence to write about?"

"I found this," she snapped back, letting the ring roll from her fist onto the table. "Did you also lie about what was in that book?"

"I don't owe you every detail about my life. This has nothing to do with the bird smuggling."

"It might have to do with finding my brother!"

He came close. "What the hell are you talking about?"

She started to tell him, then snapped her mouth shut. Val, sensing the anger between her humans, gave a whine, and then planted herself firmly beside Ram. No doubt where her loyalties lay.

"Keeping secrets, too?" Ram pressed the bridge of his nose. "You don't trust me, not when it comes to your brother. I can't keep fighting shadows."

"You're not—"

He cornered her against the counter. "Are you looking for a story?"

"No"—Another lie.

"You want to know what I can do with my magic?"

"Yes." Not really.

His face was drawn so tight, she barely recognized him, but his eyes were what really scared her. They were colder than she'd ever seen. With his forefingers making an O with his thumbs, he held his hands on either side of her head.

"We're not in bed," he purred.

He didn't hold her. She could escape if she wanted, but she didn't move, held helpless as the caress of his magic slid like charged silk across her skin. After last night, her body was already primed to respond with tightness and moisture.

Until the tenor of the magic changed.

His free hand drew in the air; a low sound came from

his throat. Like a massive boa constrictor, the power started squeezing. Her lungs constricted, gasping for air, then as abruptly as it started, the squeezing vanished. It was followed by a single, searing pain across her ribs. If that was the lash that had scarred him, how had he endured? Again, the attack vanished as flame ignited in a fiery aura surrounding her. The heat of it scorched her, only to vanish into cold so bitter that it destroyed flesh.

Again, the spell vanished before it did more than register as deadly. She wasn't hurt except for a stinging aftermath, proving the phenomena had been no illusion.

He leaned forward, his voice barely a whisper. "And to think, you unleashed all of this."

"What—?"

He stepped away. "Just because I can, doesn't mean I will. Now I think you'd better go."

The words weren't spoken in heat. Heat she could fight. These came from some dark, cold abyss deep inside him.

How had he put her on the defensive? She glared at him, although it was hard to glare effectively at someone who wasn't looking at you. Instead, he was looking off into space, rubbing his temple with his thumb and forefinger.

"Are you going to warn me not to write about this?" she asked.

"No."

Because he was confident he could stop her? Because he didn't mind exposure? "Why?"

"You want me to threaten you?"

"It's easier to defy."

"I'm all out of threats. I trust last night meant something to you."

He *would* have to appeal to her sense of fair play, wouldn't he? Or else he had another plan for stopping her, and knew threats were the worst approach to take.

How had they gotten from wonderful sex to mistrust? In silence, she gathered her belongings.

"Leave the book," he commanded. At her mutinous stare, he gave a small sigh. "You'll get it back as soon as I'm sure there's nothing evil attached."

Silently, she yanked the book from her bag and placed it on the table, then stripped off the clothes he'd given her. She'd be damned if she'd take one thing from him. In her underwear—she couldn't stand to put on those bloody clothes—she stalked out to her car.

Ram stood watching her from the porch.

As she pulled clean clothes from the replenished pile in her car, her phone rang. Catching sight of the number, she eagerly picked it up. "Ram—"

"Raoul said that the smugglers had another shipment coming in Sunday. See if you can find out where."

Chapter Eighteen

Ram's clinic shift was nearly over when the text SOS from the Fish and Wildlife agent came over: She'd found a bird; could Ram get there ASAP? Graham willingly agreed to take the last clients, and Ram was soon speeding to the dense pine forest north of Lake Pontchartrain. After parking the truck, he followed the GPS coordinates through the trees.

He scrambled over a fallen water oak and then veered to the left where a gap made the going easier. His gut curled in apprehension. The woods were too quiet. Where were the insect chirps? The rustle of mice? Sunshine filtering through the trees and the scent of fresh pine resin weren't enough to counter his unease.

He reached the coordinates, stepping around the tree to see Althea Robinson crouching in the pine nee-dles. Her back was to him, but she was crooning a soft lullaby to something at her feet. Beyond her was a stone altar, similar to the one Virgil had found.

"Special Agent Robinson." He announced his pres-ence softly, not wanting to disturb whatever she'd found.

The agent jerked around, her hand going to the holster at her hip a second before she let out a puff of air and relaxed. "Dr. Montgomery, you startled me. Can't you rustle some leaves like a normal person?"

"There's mostly pine needles here."

She rolled her eyes at him. "Your humor I don't need."

Althea Robinson was a no-nonsense black woman with a firm grip, a meet-your-eye greeting, and a gun at her hip. She was also the most effective U.S. Fish and Wildlife Service agent Ram knew. They'd worked together in animal rescue groups, and she claimed a lot of his respect. She gave him a brief handshake. "Thanks for coming so fast."

The department often sent to his clinic the injured animals they'd found, especially the more unusual species. Usually the agents brought the animals in, but on occasion they asked him to the rescue site, when the animal needed special expertise in handling or care. Worried about what she'd found, he set his medical bag on the ground and crouched beside her. "What have you got?"

"I was tracking down some illegal traps when I came across . . . Well, I'm not sure what I stumbled onto. Thought you might be able to help. I just hope we're not too late." She brushed aside the pine needles. "It's so weak."

He sucked in a breath at the sight of the half-buried creature—a Galápagos hawk. A magnificent raptor—about two feet in height if it had the strength to stand. Instead, it lay on its side and showed them a wary eye, not even able to snap its beak.

Ram ran a gentle finger along its chest, lifting when the bird flinched. He couldn't see any injuries, felt no broken bones. No blood or malformations, except the glaring one: the bird had no coloring.

"It looks like a hawk," Althea commented, "but I've never seen an albino."

"Neither have I." He didn't correct her mistake.

This bird was not an albino. Normally a Galápagos hawk was a sooty brown-black color, with bands and shadings of white, grey, and buff. Brilliant yellow would tint the legs and base of the beak.

Not this hawk. This one's feathers were pure white. Not only his feathers, but every part of him—beak, flesh, iris, talons. All stark white. It looked as if all the color had been sucked from him.

"A mutant?" Althea suggested. "Maybe it can't hunt successfully, and that's why it's so weak."

"Mmmm." Ram brushed aside the remaining pine needles, taking care not to touch the trembling bird and bring it further anguish. The hawk was fading quickly, and there was only one way to cheat death.

"Special Agent Robinson, can you get me a cage? I'll need it to transport him. I've got one in my car—"

"So do I. It'll be easier to fetch." She scrambled to her feet and was off running, disappearing into the woods.

Not much time before she returned or before he lost the bird. He pulled out his water bottle, and then removed the chain he wore about his neck. The pink and green tourmaline, warm from his skin, gleamed in the shade. He dipped the nugget into the water, shook it over the hawk, sprinkling droplets over the thirsty beak, and then wrapped his fist around the stone. Barely skimming its feather tips, he held that hand above the bird and dug his other fingers into the ground.

"Do you have a name?" Ram asked. "Alatus? Langdon? Vocuer?" The bird returned the question with a stare, the hole of his pupils dark in contrast to the white everywhere else. "Fiero? Feng?" The bird gave a slow blink. "You like Feng?" Another blink. "Feng it is."

"*Aum-hreem. Aum-hraim, Aum-hruh, Feng.*" As he chanted the words of focus, his senses sharpened with acute precision. Just like the night he'd healed Val, except this time he expected it, he used it. The damp warmth of the soil spread through him. Sound returned to the forest—the moan of the wind as it twined around the trees, a bird's single trill. His nose savored the scent of resinous pine.

When the wealth of connections peaked, he braced himself and lowered his personal shields, opening a conduit to the flow of energy surrounding him. The forces of nature, so strong here, slammed against his heart. His breath tripped from the beauty of the power. Trees, insects, birds flying overhead, Althea hurrying through the woods, all filled him.

"Join with me," he murmured. "Flow through me, bend to my will." A knot of heat inside him, right below his breastbone, glowed. The pulsing energy spread like a white heat along sinew and nerve, leaping from cell to cell in an ecstatic, almost painful rush.

Still as rock, he allowed only a trickle of power to escape from the tips of his fingers. Too much at once and the hawk would be overcome, burnt out from the surge. He painted the small flow across the bird.

The hawk's body shook, absorbing the transfer, until at last Ram lifted his hands, slowly raising his shields, dampening the glow within, first to a gleaming light, then to that ember always burning deep within him.

The hawk struggled to his feet and spread his wings.

He was so beautiful. Ram smiled in satisfaction and severed the final bond to the bird. He shook out his cold hands, squeezing them to bring heat to them, bombarded by sensory cues. In that moment of acute awareness, he heard the rustle of a single leaf, moved by a breath, and felt a pulse carried along the ground to his knees. In a heartbeat the sensory overload vanished, but the warning remained.

Someone watched. Someone with sufficient skill to cloak himself against detection.

Feng had been a lure to identify a Mage.

Not letting on that he was aware, Ram rummaged in his med kit. He poured some water into a cup, let the bird drink, and then fed it a food pellet.

"I know. Not as good as a fresh mouse, but it's all I've got for the moment." He put on a leather glove, and then held out his hand. The bird studied him, nipping at the cuff, before hopping onto his fist. Talons dug into the leather. Feng spread his wings, flapping and stretching. "Here's another pellet."

As he fed the bird, he very slowly and delicately spread a seeking spell. The watcher stood behind him. A man and a skilled magician, that much Ram could tell.

"I don't believe it." Althea rejoined them, the cage hanging limply from her fingers. "That bird was about dead."

"Food and water helped."

She gave him a curious look. "You have a strange way with them, Dr. Montgomery."

"I understand them."

"What will you do with him now?"

With that coloring, Feng couldn't be released to the wild. He tilted the hawk into the cage for transport. "I'll take him to the clinic for now, make sure he's healthy. Then, we'll have to see."

He pivoted a few degrees, angling for a view of their unseen watcher, and Althea started coughing. Choking, she slugged down a gulp of water to no effect. Ram turned away from the watcher, as Althea took another gulp, and the coughing subsided.

Message received.

"Do you know what kind of hawk it is?" Althea walked with him back to the cars.

"A Galápagos hawk." And there were less than 150 pairs left, he thought, his jaw tight. A bird near extinction, and somebody did this to one of the remaining breeders.

"Those smugglers must have brought him in." She gave him a sharp look. "Have you found where that shipment's coming in tonight?"

"Not yet. You?"

"No. If you do, you let me know," she warned. "Let me handle the arrests. Make it airtight legal."

"Agreed." Arrests she could have. He was after a bigger, darker power.

The damage to the hawk wasn't the work of punks and smugglers. He'd never seen such an injury, but he knew exactly what had caused it. He could feel the tingle of residual power.

Ram's chest squeezed. Someone had tormented the magnificent, rare creature with a spell that had pulled out every last bit of pigment from the bird. Not a mutation. Magic.

When Althea was gone and Feng safeguarded in his truck, Ram raced back to the coordinates, to where the watcher stood. Gone now, of course. He crouched and laid a hand against the scuffed pine needles. A remnant of the cloaking spell remained, enough to reconstruct the pattern.

Each spell carried the signature of the magician who cast it. He would recognize this one when they met again.

On Mage business, Ram used whatever means necessary to stop evil. He didn't have that same license with civilians, regardless of how nasty. He had to limit his power.

No longer. This affair had gone beyond smuggling and a minor local rogue. No spell he'd ever read bleached every cell. Not even the whip that attacked him had dug out so much. But he'd heard rumors of such a spell. Only one, and the pieces—the Phoenix symbol charm, the odd feathers, the smuggled birds, Feng—all fit.

A prelude to the Phoenix Ritual.

He powered up his computer and glanced down at Val, who was lying at his feet, chewing a rawhide bone. "We're looking for more information," he told her.

She thumped her tail against the floor in agreement.

Time to let the Central Council know what was going on. He composed a summary e-mail and asked for details—rogue Mages who might be using a Phoenix symbol, anything known about the Phoenix Ritual. As an afterthought he asked whether Charles Severin or any known associates had ever come to Mage attention. He cc'd LaMarr and then sent it off. Coded of course. Magic had been brought into the twenty-first century. He supposed the e-mail could be intercepted and eventually decoded—nothing was completely secure—but the code was based on a dead and forgotten symbolic language and would be a challenge. The message was as secure as he could make it.

He'd responded to the rest of his accumulated e-mail when the reply came through. *That was fast.* There were several attachments to the e-mail from Khalil, a Councillor whom Ram knew and admired. He read the body first:

"Welcome back, Ramses. We all celebrate your joy in the return of your Connections. Your Tracker skills—and your pool cue—have been sorely missed, although Tremaine has been grateful to lose no more bets.

"Details are attached, but to summarize—No Mage has used the Phoenix symbol since the traitor Azi was disemboweled. However, if any of his followers still exist, they may have taken the sign for themselves, not knowing its value. Azi stole all known writings on the Phoenix Ritual when he was cast off. The Old Ones disagree whether the ritual's aim was to recreate the Phoenix or to fuse man and beast. If so, this immortal curse cannot be sanctioned. You have the authority of the Council."

Ram leaned back in his chair, his mind circling around possibilities, even as he felt a smile rise. He had missed this, the challenge and kinship of the Mages' work. Oh, he loved New Orleans, loved his vet work, but nothing quite matched the thrill of meeting a chimera under midnight's full moon.

Natalie studied the map spread out on the computer. The big purple point was the warehouse they'd found. The yellow points were where Ram had been called in for injured animals. The red points were where Virgil had said he'd seen evidence of animal caches. She'd even plotted in pink the altars Virgil had mentioned, and overlaid the thermal maps Ram had downloaded. Something should overlap, or at least show proximity, but the pins formed no pattern or association she could see.

She scanned through her notes on the people she'd interviewed when she'd first started investigating the lights in the swamp. She factored in where people had reported seeing the lights. She marked the spots with blue. At last, some correlation, primarily with the yellow, but not enough to pinpoint where the meeting might be.

The meeting going down tonight.

Wait, that one interview . . . The grizzled swamp rat had claimed the aliens followed secret routes through the waters; he'd even drawn a fairly accurate map, considering it was freehand. She located the grease-stained paper towel—they'd been devouring fried catfish at the time—and smoothed it out on her desk.

Where was that tangle of lines? She traced over the map, ignoring the pins, seeking a match. There! Her gaze flitted back and forth between the paper towel and the map. Same pattern of water. Hastily she highlighted the tangle in green, and then stepped back for a bird's-eye view.

That was it! Her fresh eye saw the connections. Tracing the lines, she felt excitement bubble inside her. Here and here, these were their rendezvous areas.

Which one? Virgil knew those waters; he might be able to pinpoint a location. If he'd talk to her.

Hastily she placed the call, surprised when Virgil answered, more surprised when he agreed to look at her map. He was out in St. Charles Parish, setting up a shoot. No fax available; she'd need to come out. She glanced at her watch; she'd still have plenty of time to make the rendezvous, then locate the meeting point and follow AX to his employer.

She dialed Ram, got his voice mail. "I'm e-mailing you a map. The circled area is where I think the action will be. I'm meeting Virgil to see if he can pinpoint more precise coordinates."

"Coloring time?" Zolton's voice startled her.

Natalie turned and gave him a smile. "All for a good cause."

"One that will benefit NONE?" He stood with his arms crossed.

Her smile faded, and she braced one hand on the desk, pointing to the map. "Not yet. So far it's straight smuggling, going down somewhere here."

"No sign of your brother?"

She shook her head.

"Tough," Zolton observed, sounding like he actually meant it. "How about Ram Montgomery? What can you tell me?"

A hell of a story. Ram was definitely a potent worker of magic. And there was that ring symbol. Plenty of threads she could share, but that earlier protective instinct rose.

I trust last night meant something. She was working with Ram, even if he had thrown her out with cause. They were a confederacy. Hopefully not the confederacy of dunces, like the title of the quintessential New Orleans story, but a confederacy nonetheless.

Against all reason and practice, she made her choice. "Nothing to write about."

Zolton's piercing look struck through her. He braced his hand on the desk beside hers, not touching, but the gesture seemed strangely intimate. "There's something different about you, Natalie. You seem more charged."

She swallowed. Was he hitting on her? They liked each other, but there'd never been any hint of sexual interest between her and her boss. "I'm the same as I ever was."

"A very bruised and battered Natalie." His free hand fluttered above the bruise on her cheek, but he didn't touch her. Didn't cross that line. To an observer, the exchange looked like simple concern—employer to employee, friend to friend.

But Natalie was good at subtext, and she read something more. Something curious that she couldn't define.

"What have you learned about Ram?" he crooned. His voice turned seductive, sending a trickle of fear down her spine. She looked at him, dark and shadowed, and wondered if she'd ever truly known him. They'd shared drunken evenings and the joy of breaking open a story. He'd showed faith in her when no one else had. In truth, she had more in common with Adam Zolton than Ram Montgomery.

Except she wasn't in love with Adam.

Oh, shit.

No, she refused to be in love with Ram.

"Nothing," she repeated.

Zolton stepped back. "Drop the smuggling. Work on something I can use."

"Give me until tomorrow," she pleaded. "We have a lead that a shipment's coming in tonight. We can nail the smugglers. Look at this as your pro bono story. You like animals, don't you?"

"Better than I like most humans." He pursed his lips, then leaned back, breaking the odd moment. "Okay, tomorrow, you promise you'll work on something useful?"

He knew she didn't renege on promises, and she owed Zolton. Owed him her best work and her loyalty. She did not owe him Ram. "I promise."

He nodded as if satisfied, and left.

She was waiting for the map to print out before turning off the computer, when a chime told her she had new mail. The translation of those pages from the book! She'd e-mailed them to a woman she'd used before as a resource for ancient texts.

Curious, she opened up the e-mail, tossing a pen from hand to hand as she read. What Ram had translated was accurate, the symbols were of the beasts of magic. Interesting, his symbol was of the centaur. The teacher and the warrior.

He'd just left out a few details. Like: "The beasts are the embodiment of all magic, and the most mighty of talismans. Invoke their power only if your purpose remains in harmony with their will."

The pen stilled in her hand as she continued to read: "The symbols are rich in power if used with sparse flourish and without the braggart's pose. They are kept guarded with the *ars magica,* the flow of mind, body, and soul. Those who dwelt in harmony with the union, within the flowing river of might, the Brethren of the Guardian Mages, masters of the symbols, have vanished into the mists of time."

There was more, about five pages' worth, describing some powerful kind of magic. Too much to absorb right now. With a glance around—no one was watching—

she printed off the e-mail. After sending a thank you for the translation, she deleted the e-mail, making sure also to delete it from the cached files on the shared work PC. She folded up the papers, then carefully stowed them in her hobo bag.

Brethren of the Guardian Mages. She'd heard that term before. The article she'd found in Nathaniel's things, the one that had spurred this whole investigation into the bird smuggling so she could get the money to go to Nepal. That article had mentioned the Brethren of the Guardian Mages. Or, in the original Latin, the Custos Magi.

Maybe the group wasn't as dead as old Prometheus, the author, had claimed.

Chapter Nineteen

Twilight grabbed the sky by the time Natalie pulled into the spot designated by Virgil. The gas station had long ago lost the fight to draw customers off I-10, and had been abandoned to the weeds. A faded green dinosaur sign, riddled with bullet holes, hung limply on a rusty pole.

Her shirt was plastered to her chest the moment she got out of the air-conditioned car. Sweltering humidity left a haze on the day, veiling the red sun with suspended pine dust. Holding the map tucked under her arm, she rubbed her hands together. Too lonesome.

Virgil's dirty truck pulled in behind her, remaining in the growing shadow. He emerged, halting for a glance around before he joined her at her car.

"I appreciate your taking the time to meet me," she greeted him. Before he'd been the relaxed woodsman, but today he looked tense. "Everything okay?"

"The shoot setup didn't go well. A piece of equipment broke, and I'll need to fix it before I can finish."

"Must be difficult to keep everything running smoothly."

"It is. And expensive. Never mind, I'll work it off." He shook his shoulders, and gave her his patented TV smile. "What have you got?"

"The smugglers are moving tonight." She rolled the map onto her car hood, while Virgil watched over her shoulder. Not bothering to explain how she'd come to her conclusions, she pointed to the circled area. "I think they'll meet in this area for the swap, and from the topographical data, these two spots look the most promising. But this is too broad an area. I thought you might be able to pinpoint the meeting place."

Staring at the map, she braced her hands on the hood and waited.

He said nothing.

"What do you—?" As she glanced over her shoulder, the words died a quick death. Sweat broke out again as her stomach churned. She'd misjudged, badly.

Virgil had moved away from her and was holding a gun on her. One he looked very comfortable handling. One he pointed straight between her eyes. The TV smile was erased by hard determination.

"Crap," she muttered, then added, furious, "Where's Twig?"

"Twig?"

"My ivory-billed woodpecker!"

"You have an ivory-bill?" He sounded awed.

"Had. You took him, and I want him back." She stepped forward, fists clenched, then stopped as he raised the gun.

"Don't move, or I will use this."

"Where's Twig?" she asked, keeping still.

"I don't have your woodpecker," he said flatly, and for some reason she believed him. So, who had taken Twig?

She'd puzzle that one out later, when she didn't have a whacked environmentalist holding a gun to her sixth chakra.

He raised the gun slightly. When facing death, the human mind chooses between two paths: panic and clarity. Fortunately, hers chose the latter.

"My guesses were right?" she asked abruptly. Might be a cliché, but if she could keep him talking, connect, he might be reluctant to kill her.

"You're too good. If you'd been off in the coordinates, I would have let you go stake out the wrong spot."

"Too late to change the meet?"

"Unfortunately."

"Where?"

He pointed to a spot on the map, right where she'd designated.

"You're 2Wyld?"

A small incline of his head acknowledged her ID.

"Why? You're about conservation, about preserving—" She gave a disgusted sound. "Money. Right?" These things were always about money.

"My sponsor pulled out of the show. I needed to keep going, to keep getting my message—"

"Your message—" She bit off the accusation. His message was birds stuffed in airless tubes and crushed turtles and endangered species plucked from their homes, but telling him that wouldn't help her stay alive. She shifted her weight slightly for better leverage. "Why birds?"

"Got a particular buyer."

"Who?"

A slight shudder ran across Virgil's big body, and Natalie felt a lick of fear. Nasty sort if he had Virgil scared. Pieces fit together. Virgil was the sap who had the knowledge, the contacts, and needed the money. He made all the arrangements; AX handled the dirty work. But someone else had given him the idea.

"Last shipment," he said with an edge of desperation. "I've got too much to lose."

She'd lost their connection to fear. "I can be leverage," she said hastily. "Insurance in case someone else reaches the same conclusions."

"Like Ramses Montgomery?" Virgil pondered a second, then gestured with the gun. "Lie face down and hold your hands in the air. Slowly."

At least it wasn't mud again. She complied, her mind churning, clearing. He'd taken the out; he wasn't ready to become a murderer. Tie her up, take her with him. Hands clean. Let AX do the deed.

Her mind started edging down that panic path.

No, no, no. She had too much to live for. Nathaniel and Twig were still out there. Ram. Her acknowledged love for him swelled inside her. Yeah, she'd screwed up, and yeah, he had some potent secrets, and yeah, she wasn't sure how the future would unfold, but dammit, she wanted the chance to try. She finally, desperately, wanted to live.

So, think, dammit.

When Virgil fastened her wrists, he'd have to put down the gun. Maybe . . .

Except Virgil didn't put the gun down. He efficiently wrapped a thin rope around her wrists with the gun still in hand. She tensed her muscles and separated her hands slightly, trying for wiggle space, but Virgil knew the trick. With a vicious jerk, he tightened the rope. Natalie gasped from the cutting pain, and by the time she recovered, he had her fastened tight.

As she struggled to her feet, she wriggled her fingers, unable to move her hands apart. No give, and the rope, though thin, was strong. No sawing it with a key, or some such MacGyver moment. She gave an experimental tug. Knot wasn't giving either. She was well and truly trussed.

Dah, dah, dah, dump. The *Addams Family* theme jangled from her belt.

"My phone," she quickly explained.

"Ignore it."

"I'm always connected, and my boss knows I came out here. If I don't answer, it might raise questions."

"Make sure they don't call again."

He held the phone up to her ear while the gun dug into her gut. She caught the ID—Ram.

"Hi, Ram," she answered, breezily, eschewing her usual "Natalie Severin" greeting. "What's up?"

He paused a fraction of a second, then said smoothly, "I got your voice mail. Did you get coordinates from Virgil?"

Her heart squeezing at the sound of Ram's voice, she glanced at her captor, and her brows lifted in question. When Virgil nodded, she answered, "Yes. I was off on my guess. Got a pen?"

"One moment." She heard a rustle, then, "Go ahead."

She recited the coordinates Virgil gave her. They'd place Ram well away from where the meet was going down.

When she finished, Ram asked, "Is everything okay?"

"Right as bees," she answered. "Will you notify your contact at Fish and Wildlife?"

"Yes, she'll be with me."

"Good. I won't be able to talk anymore; don't want to be overheard."

Virgil disconnected them, and then tossed the phone through his open window. "Get in."

Awkwardly, with hands bound, she climbed in and sat on her phone. "What now?"

"You're taking a little nap."

Natalie swore as the syringe needle pricked her arm. The drug was fast-acting, too. Something that gave an airy, floaty, buzz. Just like rum and Coke. Her eyelids sank down despite her best efforts to keep them open.

Vaguely she heard Virgil drive her car behind the station, hiding it from view. Don't go without a fight. The phone pressed against her butt. Slumping sideways against the seat back, pretending she was out—not too much of a stretch there—she pulled the phone into her palm.

Mute it. Don't need to see to dial. She knew that keypad better than she knew her own face; she looked at the keypad more often. Press. Press. Her fingers grew clumsy before she could finish. Muscles disconnected from brain as the drug's hold tightened. One more? No. Just . . . send.

Add one final hope to the list. That Ram's cell was tech-savvy enough for a text message.

Something was terribly wrong. Ram's fingers squeezed around the steering wheel, his body cold despite the day's heat. He leaned against the truck's headrest, trying to control a deep, grinding fear.

Natalie greeting him as though yesterday morning had never happened? Natalie *asking* for W&F? Not gonna happen. Right as bees, which meant she was in deep-shit trouble.

Think beyond the paralyzing worry. She might be a pain in the ass, but she was his pain in the ass.

Throat dry, he plotted her coordinates. He held the map out to Val, sitting obediently in the passenger seat. "As she said, nowhere near her original guesstimate. Either Natalie's logic is wrong, Virgil doesn't know squat, or Virgil's a bastard. What's your opinion?"

Val barked.

"Yeah, mine, too."

And that particular bastard had Natalie. The environmentalist was now up to his ass in alligators.

"Dial Althea," Ram snapped into the Bluetooth wireless, and a moment later he had the agent on the phone. "Got two likely spots. You take one; I'll grab the other." He gave her the coordinates, then savagely threw the truck into gear and tore off.

Dead man walking. The words whispered across his mind, despite the Mage Code forbidding meting justice in a nonmagical cause. If she were hurt, Virgil would be a dead man. Or wish he were.

The night was bitter dark. Clouds and the leafy canopy concealed the stars and sliver of a new moon. Still groggy from the ultra-short-acting sedative, Natalie banged her shin on another cypress knee and cursed. Loud enough for anyone near to hear.

"Be quiet," Virgil ordered.

"You're the one who knows the territory. Shine that flashlight over here so I can see where to put my feet."

He gave a quick swipe over the path ahead.

"That'll last me for five seconds. Are we there yet?" They'd only been on the path about a minute.

"Shut up."

She hitched her shoulder to wipe her sweat-caked neck. Mosquitoes were feasting, and with her hands still tied—at least he'd used her coma time to move them in front—her swatting options were limited. "Got any mosquito repellent?"

"Shut. Up."

"You do know, don't you, that once the smuggling's over, you're expendable."

He whirled on her. "I've got duct tape. One more word, just one, and the tape's over your mouth."

A desperate man and not an idle threat. She'd tried to escape into the dark bayou when they'd first gotten out of his truck. Unfortunately, he'd had the swamp smarts and the flashlight and range of motion. All she'd had was a bloodstream full of faux Valium and desperation.

Not a fair fight; the only thing she'd gained was a more vigilant Virgil and swamp muck on her jeans and boots.

He'd do worse if he had to. She was already gasping in the thick air. Duct tape would suffocate her. Slowly, she nodded her capitulation. Silence from here on out.

At least she'd gotten in her seed-of-doubt bullet point.

As they resumed their trudging, however, she noticed he occasionally swung the flashlight over a cypress knee or vine so she wouldn't fall.

Her phone vibrated against her hip. She ignored it. No sense in calling attention to the fact that she was being paged. Ram? At the wrong coordinates? Wondering where she was?

Ahead of her, Virgil stopped so suddenly that she almost ran into him. He listened a moment, then smiled and moved forward, gesturing for her to follow. Mindful of the duct tape and the muck, she kept silent and obeyed.

They emerged into a small clearing, very similar to the one where she'd first seen AX and the birds. Without the covering of the trees, the few stars that peeked out from the clouds afforded a small measure of visibility.

An airboat waited for them. Virgil strode over, spoke briefly to the single passenger. Within minutes he had the boat's cargo off-loaded. Payment was exchanged, and the boat took off, leaving them in empty silence.

She glanced around. No AX. No hint that Ram was near either. She closed her eyes to concentrate. The air didn't carry a rustle of motion or a molecule of scent. Not even the touch of his magic.

Maybe she'd screwed up the text message. Maybe he'd never gotten it. No matter, she was on her own to get out of this jam. She blinked back stinging sweat. Dammit, but she'd gotten used to being a confederacy.

"We're here," Virgil said into his tiny headset.

A moment later she heard the growl of another approaching airboat. Crook and reporter waiting for AX to land. The airboat pulled up, and AX leaped out, gesturing to Kracker and Dawglip to stay put. He strode over and, with a vicious swipe, backhanded Natalie.

A cry escaped her before she could swallow it, and she staggered back, only to be pulled short by Virgil grabbing the rope around her hands. Blood trickled down her chin from her split lip.

"That's for my phone, bitch."

"No violence," Virgil demanded. "The animals might get hurt."

He didn't care a fig about her, only the risk of a stray shot hitting his cargo. His precious cargo that he stuffed into fricking tubes.

"Just get the damn things loaded," AX ordered.

AX and Virgil soon had the tubes loaded on the boat.

"My money." Virgil held out his hand.

"Got a call from your buyer." AX pulled out his Glock and pointed it at her. In an instant, before her brain could choose between scream and run, AX arced the gun toward Virgil. "Doing away with middle management."

The gun blast deafened her. Virgil's face contorted into stunned pain. Natalie dropped to her back. Her feet lashed out, aiming a solid blow to AX's knee. Damn, he moved and she missed the primary target. He was damaged, but not incapacitated.

She rolled, scrambled to her feet, as covering bullets came from the two in the boat. Fortunately they were more trigger-happy than accurate.

Run. Zig. Zag. Get into the trees before AX recovered.

She heard AX shout. Another shot pierced the night. Zag, not zig.

The world turned black.

Blinded, Natalie ran straight into a tree. Banged her knee and nose against unforgiving wood. Mundane hurts so she knew she wasn't dead unless God had a strange sense of humor about punishment in the afterlife.

She couldn't see anything. Not a blessed thing. Had a bullet blinded her? She blinked. How could a shot blind her and not hurt? Endorphins. Oh, sweet Jesus, she'd been shot and the endorphins were holding back the flood of pain.

Don't be an ass, Natalie. This darkness isn't natural.
Ram!

She slid behind the tree for cover, and then turned toward the clearing. Or where she thought the clearing was. Darkness was as disorienting as fog.

Yes, there was AX, flashlight in hand, but any light more than a yard off was absorbed by the impenetrable blackness. As soon as AX moved on, the strange darkness vanished, leaving only the sticky, cloud-shrouded night. The phenomenon had lasted only seconds, just enough for her to escape.

Definitely not natural.

Apparently realizing he was a visible target, AX snapped off the light and scrambled toward the boat, his pals covering his retreat.

A shadow, a darker black on black, slid through the trees. Ram? Too dark to tell. Another figure, clearer to see, a woman in uniform, skirted the clearing.

"Federal Agent," the woman called. "Alan Xavier, you are under arrest."

"Fuck you!" The thud of AX's feet as he leaped onto the airboat deck carried across the clearing. A moment later the engine roared to life and the airboat reversed into the water.

The woman—must be Althea—swore, and then she spoke into her radio. "Suspects heading up Bayou des Allemands." She lifted her gun.

A streak of fire jetted from the shadowy trees, hitting Althea's chest simultaneously with a spray of shot exploding from the airboat as it disappeared around a curve. With a broken-off cry, Althea slumped to the ground beside Virgil's corpse.

Natalie hurtled from behind the protective tree, scrambling across the uneven ground. She fell to her knees and grabbed the flashlight that had fallen from Althea's hand. Shining it on the agent, Natalie gasped at Althea's blood-soaked face.

Frantically she tore at her T-shirt, swearing when she couldn't get it off over her bound wrists. Her hands fluttered, seeking someplace to put pressure. "Where are you shot?"

Althea didn't answer. Not dead, not dead. Please not dead. Natalie fumbled for a pulse. Thin, erratic, but present. There was no blood on the agent's clothing; her Kevlar vest had protected her. With further examination, Natalie found a bleeding head wound. That explained the blood, but not the lips stretched into an unnatural grimace. Had the conjuror of the blackness attacked the agent?

Natalie fumbled for her phone, praying for an accordion's worth of bars, then froze. The skin between her shoulder blades tightened, as though feeling the prick of a knife in the back. She twisted to look behind her, sensing that something lurked in the night. How, she couldn't say. Eyesight was useless in the blackness of the bayou. No sound, not even a faint whisper of breath, escaped the encompassing darkness.

Yet the hairs on her arms rose as some extra sense detected the disturbance of air. She couldn't distinguish direction or distance. Only presence. Whatever lurked in the bayou was hidden by the night. She stopped her breath, seeking an answer in the cavernous mire behind her.

She sensed something unpleasant, barely detectable, like a few molecules of a foul odor seeped into a sealed room. The back of her throat gagged on the odor of rotten licorice.

Someone—or something—was out there. Hunting.

Silence filtered through the trees. She froze, straining to hear a break in the unnatural silence. Something, anything. A cicada chirp, the plop of a frog, or an owl's hoot. Nothing. Picking up Althea's gun with her bound hands, she rose to her feet and edged toward the threat, weapon at the ready.

Chapter Twenty

Silent as a hunting gator, Ram slid between the trees. Humidity wrapped around him, as comfortable as his own skin. Only a small quantity of light sifted through the trees, but he had no trouble seeing. Beside him, Val moved easily, noiselessly. Perhaps she'd been a wizard in a previous life.

Energy swirled from him, seeking through the dense vegetation. These testing and tracking skills were such a familiar part of him, despite being unused for too many years. He couldn't see Natalie, yet somehow he knew exactly where she stood. Pulse, scent, breath, the eddies of brilliance within his aura, all located her and relayed that she was unharmed. So far.

Others were with her, he guessed, but identifying who or how many wasn't part of this unique connection. Still, he knew the likely prospects. His jaw tightened; he was too far away if the meet went to hell. He gave a soft command to Val. "Let's pick up the pace, girl."

In response, Val loped faster between the vines, her sense of smell as accurate a guide as his magic.

He'd gone through anger and guilt that he'd chosen the wrong site; at least Natalie's text message had turned him around. The distracting fear he felt for her, spawned since her call, he'd also conquered. He'd put emotion aside to get the job done, a skill sorely tried of late.

Sound exploded around him. Gunshot cracked the night with death. A life was extinguished, sending a dark arrow through the energies of the bayou. Natalie! No, still unharmed. Val burst forward, Ram at her side. His hands pistoned forward, then clenched in futility. Still too far to reach Natalie with a protective shield.

Light vanished, slamming Ram to a halt, then a rainbow flare burst behind his eyes. The spell he'd set at the temple had been activated! The evil behind Magic Man was here? The mastermind behind the bird smuggling?

A sweet licorice scent pinched his nose—the trail left by the tracking spell. He inched forward. Damn, he couldn't see a thing, and he didn't dare cast a light to give away his presence. Val whined and stepped on his foot.

Just as abruptly, the light returned and moments later an airboat roared past, carrying AX and crew. They were the lesser of the evils, right now. Ram flicked his fingers toward the motor; it sputtered and slowed, aborting their escape. He'd deal with them later.

Now the hunt began. Angling away from the shore, he followed the currents of air, vibrations of earth, pulses of heat. All clues to where the magician—also using high-level camouflage—moved. Ram would need a direct sighting to attack. Which meant he needed to be close. At least his quarry was working under the same restriction.

The magician had formidable talents. Skilled at concealment, he would have disappeared as the two wove through the maze of green without the added trail of licorice to follow. The uneven soggy ground sucked at

Ram's feet, and the pervasive heat soaked his shirt in sweat. Slowly, he closed the gap.

His hands cupped together. Whispering beneath the sounds of the night to draw reserves of power, he coalesced a glittering ball of bright purple beams, visible only to himself. Concentrate and fortify; when he was in sight of the magician, he would release the spell net.

Footsteps to his right. Muffled and cautious, but unconcealed. Oh, piss. *Natalie*. Abruptly, the night turned cold.

An eddy of air spawned to his left. The magician had also detected her. Thank God, the jungle confused her position, as she sidled around a tree, gun in hand. Aiming at him.

She jerked the barrel skyward. "Ram?" she whispered.

He held a finger to his lips for silence and ran to her side, wrapping the shields that protected him and Val around her. "Hand on my waist," he breathed into her ear. "Move with me. Don't freak at the shield."

Without waiting for her answer, he shifted their positions. Her hand was strong, warm, intimate where her fingers touched him, sending an odd shimmy up his spine. No tremors of fear; even with her wrists tied together, the other hand with the gun was steady.

As she pressed against him, her curvy strength, yin-cool resolve, and feminine pragmatism wove a tantalizing, empowering braid. A waft of her sultry perfume carried to him, and the incongruous scent became an integral part of their shield.

The magician stalked closer as he sought them. Almost in view. Ram's breathing slowed, as each second stretched. Acutely aware of Natalie fitted to his side, he traced the magician's path. Two more steps. One more.

A hooded and robed figure stepped from behind a cypress into a small gap.

Ram struck. The net whistled from his hands like a

bottle rocket and collapsed on the magician. Shocked, the magician spun around, tangling the magical net tighter. He dropped to his knees. With hands hidden by his sleeves, he clawed his chest.

Ram ran closer, working with efficiency to elongate the threads. Finish binding the magician's feet and hands before he could execute his next trap.

The robed magician wrapped one hand in the threads, thrusting his wrist out of the binding at the last second, freeing the steel-link chain at his wrist. *Damn, he wore a Mage charm!* The charm on the bracelet shot a bolt of light into the bindings and cut them enough for the magician to launch his counterattack.

A crude devouring wind sideswiped Ram, and then raced past, sucking oxygen in its wake. The last of the purple net dropped from his hands, its glitter a dull smudge. He doubled over, consumed by agony as cells withered.

Emptied. The echo of loss paralyzed him. Couldn't feel. Couldn't—

Val bit his hand. Not hard enough to break skin, but hard enough for a jolt of pain that broke through the paralysis.

Dammit, he'd frozen. Delayed precious moments. His target had escaped, purple threads drowning in the murky water. The taste of failure sharp in his throat, Ram coalesced new, stronger threads, ready to catapult them at the magician.

Still absorbing all the air in its path, the windfire careened back. Straight toward Natalie. With the dregs of his strength—while one small part of him admired the complexity of the boomerang—Ram flung the knot in the opposite direction. Purple threads wrapped around the vortex. The mass dropped to the ground and, with a sizzle, congealed into a dark clot.

*   *   *

Natalie reeled backward, shoved by some unseen force with a sonic boom wallop. Her ears decompressed with a painful snap, lung tissue collapsed, and her leg muscles abandoned her. The gun dropped from her useless hand.

Then, as abruptly as it started, the attack ended. All that remained was a sizzling sound and a nasty fart stink. With a pop, the sound and smell vanished.

Her muscles snapped back to strength. Ow! Oh holy hell, that hurt!

A movement caught the corner of her eye. Their attacker was aiming another blow at Ram. Grabbing the gun, she pointed and shot. Magic or not, their attacker had a body that could be stopped.

She missed, but the attacker jerked. His power boomed harmlessly over Ram's head. Apparently deciding the fight was getting lopsided, their attacker disappeared into the darkness, and before she, Val, and Ram caught up to him, they heard the sound of an airboat roaring away. She braced her hands on her knees to gasp in air.

Ram swore, his fist cutting an angry arc that left the air sizzling with a shower of sparks.

Even furious, he looked so good, his dark hair disheveled, his body taut. Only twenty-four hours and she missed him. Her body shook, suddenly weak. She croaked out his name.

He heard her. Turning his back on their escaping prey, he was at her side in a single pace. He gripped her shoulders, bent down, and then kissed her.

Oh, dear Lord, how he kissed her. Desperately. Hungrily. Like he was starving for the taste of her. Or imprinting a final memory.

Her lip hurt, but she ignored the pain to return the kiss, measure for measure. She couldn't touch him, not like she wanted with her bound hands holding a gun, so she used what she could.

A nudge and a whine from Val brought them back to reality. Ram gathered Natalie, gun and all, into his arms. The faint quake of his muscles transmitted his tension more than his quiet. "Are you all right?"

"I'd be better if I could use my hands."

Releasing her, he bent to her hands, and the rope soon fell to her feet.

"That's better." She shook out the nerve numbness.

"No injuries?"

"Just a split lip courtesy of AX."

Ram swore, but she silenced him by leaning against his chest, savoring the sensation of someone else being strong for her. His was nice warmth, not the suffocating heat of the airless night. She sagged a little, then jerked upright. "Althea!"

Virgil's body was taken to the morgue; Althea, conscious but strapped to a gurney for the ambulance trip, reported that the airboat had been found with the contraband still aboard. No sign of AX, however. Natalie gave her statement to at least six people before she was in Ram's truck and on the road back to her car.

Silence hung between them, not exactly comfortable. Natalie didn't know what Ram was thinking, but she was remembering the way they'd last parted, and the way they'd clung together. What a tangle of mixed needs.

"Thank you for covering me," she said at last.

"What do you mean?"

"The blackout. I was able to get away from AX."

"I didn't do anything," he said tightly.

Back to denial of his magic and mistrusting the reporter to keep his secrets. She gave a mental sigh. "Is this where you try to convince me that I wasn't attacked by magic?"

He gave her a quick glance of amusement. "Would it work?"

"Not a chance."

Ram tilted his head, an I'm-not-going-to-argue gesture, then pointed. "The gas station's ahead. You'll probably be glad to get home."

"I'm going back to New Orleans."

"Where? You've got no place to sleep there."

She wanted to go back with him, back to his home to drink coffee, and talk about the news, and slip into his arms and take him inside her. But he was sitting next to her all intellectual and withdrawn. Clearly ready to get rid of her.

"Not that it's your problem, but I'll go to NONE. I've got a spot there to crash."

"Natalie, you need rest, and to get that lip tended—"

She leaned against the headrest. "I can take care of what I need."

"I know," he said softly. Silence followed them the rest of the way to the gas station.

Ram parked in the front. As he turned off the truck, a single star caught on the dull platinum of his ring. He spoke without looking at her. "We've broken the smuggling ring. You've got your story."

Was he joking? They had half a story. True, she had a story for the legit papers, a chance to make some real money and put a shine to her rep. Except she didn't care a fig for her rep; she liked what she did at NONE. And now she knew that there was no point in going to Nepal. She wouldn't find Nathaniel there. He was here. Somewhere. "The story's not finished."

"You're going to keep pursuing it?"

"Aren't you?"

He gave a noncommittal shrug.

He was leaving the confederacy; her heart contracted at the thought. She didn't know if she could repair the rift between them, but she had to try. One thing she wanted to clear up first before they parted. "I'm sorry I took advantage of your hospitality, Ram. I was—"

No excuses. "I was wrong."

"But you'd do it again."

"Probably," she admitted. "I have one question."

"What?"

She looked at him then, at his hands gripping the steering wheel, at his gaze steady on her. "Do you have any clue where Nathaniel is? Do you know anything about his disappearance?"

"That's two questions."

She smiled a little. "Can't quite stop. Do you?"

"No." He took a deep breath. "If I had any way to bring your brother back to you, Natalie, I would."

She wasn't entirely sure she'd be able to tell if he were lying or not. But something deep in her soul was convinced he was telling her the truth.

"Thank you." Natalie scooted out of the truck, and a few moments later was in her car, heading the short distance back to NONE, Ram following. She parked, and Ram pulled in behind her. As he opened his door to follow her, she waved a hand. "No need."

"My daddy taught me to always walk a lady to the door."

"Not a date."

"Doesn't matter."

She gave up the argument, didn't even object when he walked her through the empty offices to the sparse corner she'd fashioned as hers. Frankly, she was tired.

He glanced around, but his only comment was, "Do you need a change of clothes? I've started carrying a few sets in the truck."

"I reloaded here at the office." Aching with exhaustion, she yawned. Still, they needed to settle a few things. "Where do we go from here?"

"Write the story you've got, Natalie."

"I'm seeing this to the end. We need the man behind the curtain. Someone was using Virgil, has a purpose for those birds. Someone who attacked us with bees and took Twig."

"Don't you understand?" He turned to her, his face fierce. "You felt that attack tonight. This magician is evil. I have a bird in my clinic, an endangered Galápagos hawk with every bit of color sucked from him, *every bit*. Feng was barely alive from the attack when I saw him. *You* can't fight against true magic. You don't know how. Magic will be used against you, and I can't be distracted trying to protect you."

That stung. "I never asked you to protect me."

"I keep having to step in though."

How could she be so attracted to him at the same time he infuriated her and pointed out some very painful truths?

"I was late tonight, Natalie, and the hunter out there almost killed you."

"Not everything's in your command."

"But being distracted by you is."

"I see." And she did, her heart aching. He was making a choice to pursue the mastermind alone. Because of the magic.

Once more, magic was taking from her a man she loved.

She stepped closer to him. Only eerie lights from PCs left powered lit the room, casting a gleam on him that seemed more menacing than reassuring. Still, she laid her hands against his chest, felt his heart pulse against hers. She lifted slightly on her toes and kissed him.

The pressure on her sore lip hurt, but she ignored it again. Just kissed him with more possession. Laid her claim. When his arms came up to embrace her, she grabbed his wrists and kept their entwined hands sandwiched between them. Kept him from holding her, until she drew away. "Good-bye, Ram."

For once, he looked nonplussed.

She didn't see him out. Only when she heard the door shut did she follow and lock it. Leaning against it, she drew in a shuddering breath and reached deep for the strength to move away.

Would they ever be able to get past the barriers? Was Ram even willing to try? That kiss gave her hope.

First, she had her own monsters to best.

A very long, very hot shower soaked away some of the body aches. The bruises she could do nothing but ignore. Dab on the hydrocortisone cream that was fast becoming her new moisturizer. At least the bee stings were fading. She threw on shorts and a T-shirt, bagged some ice, and then sat on the bed.

Propped against the pillows, she pressed the ice against her lip. Despite a bone-tired body and eyes sandy with fatigue, sleep would be a long time coming. The familiar room, once a comfortable, convenient place to crash, felt barren.

Her life had been reduced to a bag of ice and a cot in the office.

"Pity moment's over." She hit her speed dial.

"Halo angel."

At the end of the voice mail, she said, "Come home. We'll see it through. We always have. Together."

After leaving her message, she hung up. Just as she had done every twelve hours ever since she'd first heard Nathaniel's voice mail.

She stretched out on the bed. She had her story. Ram, even her boss, wanted her going after a new story.

Bull. She was going to see this to the end. She wanted her woodpecker back.

Time to find out who was behind all this. Even if she had to be a confederacy of one. The ache in her chest filled her with a lonely need. She wouldn't give up on Ram, either. "Ramses Montgomery, you're still part of this confederacy, and I'm not letting you secede."

Chapter Twenty-one

Ram waited until he saw Natalie's shadow move away from the door before he started the truck and left. He stopped briefly by his home to take a sleepy Val inside. She gave a perfunctory whine when she saw he was heading out, but soon settled into her bed. Back in his truck, Ram headed east.

The air had spread the tracking spell remnants; he'd lost that lead until the quarry used more high-level magic. Still, he had another thread to follow.

Three times he'd tangled with AX; three times the thug had escaped. This time, Ram was on Mage business and the rules had changed.

This time, he wouldn't have to worry about any threats to Natalie.

He parked the truck on a side street, hiding it in the shadows. He had a small window of opportunity, while the dark still concealed and the authorities had not yet found AX, to get his answers.

He slipped inside AX's house, the locks no barrier to him. One of the nonmagic skills he'd picked up; another Mage would detect magic-picked locks. As he expected, AX hadn't been foolish enough to go to ground at his house. The rooms, however, were steeped with AX's presence; the old notion that a house absorbed the character of its owner was quite true.

The moment he walked in, his tongue curled on a bitter taste infused in the air from the occupant's unholy character. Wasting no time, he found a different location, away from any residual interference. He needed something of AX's. This envelope would do.

Sage oil sprinkled on the carpet formed his circle. He knelt within, spread a New Orleans map on the floor, and then pulled out his athame. Cutting the air, he cleansed the area surrounding him. Next out was a packet of mixed herbs, including patchouli. He rubbed the mass over his hands, leaving the fragrance on his skin, and then sprinkled the herbs atop the map. Last, he crumpled up the empty envelope and set it aflame.

With his hands cupped above the map and the tiny fire, he began to chant. "Plaster, air, wool, and cedar. Release thy spirits. Bring to me the one that I seek. *Quaerere, reperire. Aperire.*"

Concentrating, he beckoned with the magic. Streams of residual energy flowed from the walls and from the personal items spread around him into the fire. The thread of smoke collected in his cupped hands. "*Quaerere, reperire. Aperire.* Form the image."

A wavery holograph of AX was generated in his hands.

"Find your essence," he commanded.

The holograph did nothing. Was AX too far away? Abruptly, the image wavered, dissolved, and then shot, with a single streak of fire, into the map.

Bingo. Rat in the hole.

Ram extinguished the fire, wrapped up the map and sped out, before the cops, watching from outside, even realized he'd been in. AX was close to the French Quarter, in the hardscrabble fringes, hiding amongst a hardened crowd. Not knowing that a Mage sought him.

Twenty minutes later, Ram was parking the truck again, this time around the block from a series of smashed-together shotguns fronted by a cluster of hookers.

As he slipped down a back alley, he kept his shielding thick, hiding his presence, although he detected no other Mage.

The map wasn't detailed enough to pinpoint beyond the middle of the block. He cupped his hands as he slid among the shadows. "Avatar," he whispered, and the image of AX formed from the oils on his hands. As he passed a lilac-shaded home, the image streamed from his hands. In seconds he was inside the house.

Shit! The residual of his marker spell lingered on the stairs. Another Mage had gotten here first. Following the trail, he raced up to the second-story bedroom.

Too late. Nausea burned the edges of his throat as he knelt beside the rigid bodies of AX, Kracker, and Dawglip. Not a mark on them, but they were undeniably dead. Hands frozen into claw shapes. Lips drawn back in rictus.

A flamboyant touch. Someone had, quite literally, scared them to death.

Would they be mourned?

He rocked back on his heels. A quite flamboyant touch, however the bit of grandstanding didn't mean he shouldn't take the killer seriously. One of the most deadly warlocks Ram had ever known had been an outrageous circus clown.

By chance or by design, his quarry, Phoenix, had used a slower death spell, a lesser output of power that hadn't reactivated the marker. Chimes rang at the top of the door, crooking a musical finger and stirring an airborne scent of licorice. *I was here*. Ram smiled as he stood. By using magic instead of a gun, Phoenix had strengthened the previous marker's remnants.

The trail was still too faint to follow more than a few yards, but any use of power would strengthen it, bit by bit. If a cohort joined Phoenix in creating magic, the marker would spread. He had seventy-two hours to find a killer, seventy-two hours before the spell wore off.

Ram left the crime scene, phoned in an anonymous tip, and then followed a trail of licorice down an alleyway. The challenge of the hunt bubbled through his veins; he had missed this thrill.

Rampart Street was eerily empty. Maybe the hour was too near dawn, although not a bit of gray lightened the sky. The way was lit by Dixie beer signs and neon outlines of Barbie-chested women. Following scent and sound, he tracked Phoenix up to a curb. Must have gotten in a car here.

"Where are you heading?" he murmured, but before he'd chosen a direction, rainbow lights flared behind his eyes. The marker! Where . . . ?

His phone vibration interrupted the hunt. He glanced at the number. "Hey, LaMarr."

"Did you feel that?"

"I'm chasing them."

"Want some help?"

"Sure. Just stay a distance—"

"You didn't think I'd come down there?" LaMarr sounded shocked. "Hello. Mind Mage. I can set a better circle here."

Ram attached his earpiece to the phone, tucked the phone into his pocket, and then, while he waited for LaMarr to prepare and call back, he tested outward for the location of the marker.

A tight, potent circle of power burned near the Haven Grill. Ram swore and speed-dialed LaMarr. Pick up, pick up. At LaMarr's greeting, Ram spat. "The rogue magician is coming toward you."

LaMarr bit off a curse. "The Grill's protective spells . . ."

"Strengthen them now!"

"I need to complete the circle."

"There's no time!"

"I can't do it without a circle."

"Do it, then connect with me."

Ram was in the truck and breaking the speed limit when he felt LaMarr ring his wrists with magic. Using the power of cellular, the chants wound through him. LaMarr would be sitting, with the lit candles, the incense, the crystal to focus, sharing power with Ram in a mystically joined ebb and flow. Each strengthened by the Mage-to-Mage connection.

At once, he powered the flow. *Remember, LaMarr works best with words.* "Use a weaving spell. Your current guards, with a protective shield."

"What words?" LaMarr asked, his voice tight, but still controlled.

"*Alii. Alian.* Two strands, four threads each. Use frays at the end. *Avinto.*"

He heard LaMarr chanting the words, imagined him moving through the closed grill. The older man's voice held the tightness of anxiety, but the words still came through clear. LaMarr was good; he'd be safe until Ram could reach him.

If only he were closer, he could set the spells, weave an impenetrable protection. Abruptly LaMarr stopped his chanting and swore.

"What is it?" demanded Ram.

"Screaming. In City Park."

"It's a trick."

"No, it's real. I can feel the spell."

A crude, ugly one, designed to cause pain and suffocation. Ram's stomach clenched. "Phoenix wants you outside."

"I can't stay behind walls if someone's using the power to harm."

"That's what he wants. I'm only ten minutes away."

"Someone will be dead by then."

Damn. LaMarr couldn't ignore abuse. "Do not be foolish."

LaMarr actually chuckled. "I don't intend to be, but, Ram, if something happens, your job is to stop this guy, not to watch over me."

"LaMarr—"

"Your turn to promise."

"I promise."

After a quick call to 911 from the Grill phone, LaMarr fell silent while Ram tore down Canal.

"I'm coming up on the Grill," Ram announced into his headset, worried that he hadn't heard anything from LaMarr. The flow of magic between them hadn't stopped, but . . . "Where are you?"

"Near the old Tulane stadium."

Ram heard LaMarr's sharp breathing. In the background, too close, he could hear a woman sobbing, begging.

"Ram, he's torturing her."

Ram's heart leaped in pain, and then settled into a steady rhythm of cold calculation. "Build your personal shields, LaMarr," he said steadily, trying to import calm.

"I have."

"Not strong enough; remember the encounter with Magic Man."

LaMarr made a noncommittal sound. The woman's voice gave a single shout, then died over the phone. Ram pulled up beside City Park. The overhanging oaks blackened the night, leaving him emerging into darkness and suffocating heat. He stood listening, sensing.

Ripples of magic eddied through the park, some very ugly and painful. Stinging the lungs, burning the nostrils.

"I found her, Ram. She's alive, unconscious, no physical damage, as best I can tell. Probably attacked her mentally. I wonder what spells? I'll strengthen her until—"

LaMarr was getting sidetracked. "Get out of there!"

"I can't leave—"

"I'm almost there. I'll take care of her."

LaMarr swore. "He wants you alone. No network. No meshing. Only way to beat you."

The brief rainbow flare behind Ram's eyes colored LaMarr's strangled gasp. Phoenix's magic leeched into the bond between LaMarr and Ram. The leech drew in power from Ram. A light, easy flow became a sucking, draining torrent. Ram tried to weave the churning power into a shield around LaMarr, but his friend couldn't block the outflow.

"Don't let him take you," Ram spat. If he could just touch LaMarr, he could fashion the shield. "I'm almost there."

"He's growing stronger. Using me to tap you. Breaking contact."

Abruptly, the drain ended as the magical connection between them was severed. Not so the phone. The speaker carried every nuance of LaMarr's keening wail.

Pressing his lips together, Ram raced through the darkened park to the nidus of the vanishing magic, a vortex that slowly erased all the lingering ripples, all trace of licorice, until the park was left with just the scent of trees and magnolias, fresh-turned wet earth, and humidity.

Phoenix, as Ram now thought of the rogue, knew he was marked. He wouldn't use such powerful magic again until he was ready to attack.

At last Ram found LaMarr: ashen-faced, grimacing,

breathing shallowly, comatose. Not a single mark on him. The shields had kept him from death, but the vacuum had stripped away his reason.

Furiously, Ram punched nine-one-one into his cell, got the ambulance on its way. He did a quick check on the woman, a jogger with more stamina than sense to be out so late. As LaMarr had said, she seemed okay. No blood or bruises and breathing steadily. Gripped with guilt and anger, he grasped his tourmaline and held LaMarr's hand. He spun words to heal, to repair whatever rift had sliced mind from body, but nothing worked.

Dammit, nothing worked.

The ambulance and police came in record time. More statements to the police, more staring at the flashing red light of the ambulance. When he tried to go with LaMarr, they stopped him. "No civilians in the ambulance."

More assurances by the police. "He's always been a friend, Dr. Montgomery. We'll watch him. We'll find who did this."

No, you won't. Not if Phoenix didn't want to be found. Still, he let them take LaMarr, waited behind.

Your job is to stop this guy; not watch over me.

"I'll find him," Ram promised, watching as the ambulance sped away. There would be no other Mages. No other innocents. No Natalie.

Just him and the vanished Phoenix and the magic.

He swallowed hard, feeling the gaping loneliness. A right and necessary choice that felt so utterly wrong. His body aching with fatigue, he found his way back to the truck, but instead of going home right away, he drove to the offices of NONE.

He slipped in the side gate, sliding through the small side yard until he stood outside the room where Natalie slept.

He laid his hand on the siding, and then closed his

eyes. He could almost see her, smell the clean scent of her shampoo. Taste the freshness of her lips. Careful not to touch her with his magic, he drew in a long breath, filling his soul with her nearness.

"Good-bye," he whispered.

Natalie opened her groggy eyes, confused from being pulled out of deep REM sleep. The sound of a truck pulling into the NONE driveway was a quiet break in the night.

"Ram," she whispered, though how she knew it was him, she wasn't sure. He was here, he needed her. She held her breath. No, he was leaving.

She buried her face against the pillow, holding back the tears, and then abruptly threw the pillow away. No more denying.

Ram turned, ready to go, but made the mistake of looking back at temptation. Natalie stood in the open doorway, dressed in a T-shirt and unzipped jeans.

"Come in," she said simply. "I don't want you to leave."

Of their own volition, his feet took him where he needed to be. At her side. He brushed a hand across her blond hair, her natural color, smoothing the locks caught by a tendril of wind. He'd tried to sever their bonds, to go his separate way, but she'd refused to be left.

They'd gained one more night.

"You look tired," she said. "Is something wrong?"

"Nothing I want to talk about." He tucked the hair behind her ear. "This isn't a sensible choice."

She caught his hand and brought it to her lips to kiss his knuckle. "I don't think the word 'sensible' will ever characterize us."

She was probably right. His hand stroked her scalp, raking through the strands of hair. "You know you're as beautiful half asleep as you are awake."

Lame, Montgomery. But his brain didn't seem to work around her.

Still, she smiled. "Where's Val?"

"At home. Snoring until dawn."

"There's no one else here. Stay with me. Tonight." Natalie took his hand and pulled him inside. Not a plea or a command. A statement of fact.

Tonight. No promises for the future; he wasn't capable of giving her that.

She didn't need them. Natalie made plans, but she never expected the future to fall into place with them.

"I'll leave before anyone comes," he said as he crossed the threshold.

Immediately, she bracketed his face with her hands and kissed him. Immediately the wildfire between them blazed out of control.

Basic needs started giving the commands. Gather Natalie into his arms. Kiss her. Keep the magic carefully leashed. Release only the hunger of desire.

But she was having none of slowness. Not now. The blaze was stoked by their kiss in the bayou, by loneliness and danger.

She tore at his shirt, popping the buttons. "Sorry," she muttered.

"I'm not." Not when her hands stroked his now bare chest, leaving streaks of fire in their wake. With a muttered oath, he got rid of the shirt, giving her free rein to touch, even as he turned her face up to his.

"Kiss me," he demanded.

She obeyed, grabbing him with a fierce need, their lips melding. Her hands roved his tight skin, then lowered to his pants, undid them, slid pants and shorts to the ground. He kicked them away, then turned back.

"Get rid of these," he muttered, tugging at her jeans, and in short order she was blessedly naked. One kiss to her breast, one stroke of her hand on his erection, and he was near explosion. "I need to be inside you."

Another demand she obeyed with a smile, backing up to the hallway wall. Spreading her legs. Lifting her hands for him to capture.

"Are you sure?" he asked, stalking after her and nodding at her wrists.

"Yes."

He gripped her wrists, tightly, not to hurt, but so that she couldn't free herself. She'd have to ask for her freedom. He held her firmly against the wall as he kissed her, taking command of their loving.

Then he raised his gaze, drinking in the sight of her. Eyes half-lidded and glazed. Skin beautifully flushed. Battle scarred. Not a hint of fear or reluctance. "Now?"

"Now," she echoed.

He let go of one hand to guide himself, using his thighs to spread her more, then with one thrust, he was seated inside her. Deep and wet.

"Don't stop," she pleaded.

"Not going to," he replied with a grunt and began to move.

Stroke, thrust, one arm still pinning her wrist, the other wrapping her waist to draw her up, keep her close. Her breath, her scent, all heady elixirs. Thrusts claiming. So sweet, so wet and hot.

"Mine!" she shouted, spasming around him, her body drawing taut. Her hand dug tight into his butt muscles, forcing him deeper.

"Mine!" He erupted. Shattered in bliss.

Power rose in eager joy as he swiftly withdrew. He grabbed for a remnant of sanity. He shuddered from the release and from the disciplines of control. At last he opened his eyes.

Natalie was watching him, her face buried in shadows. She lifted a hand to his cheek. "We've got a couple more hours, and I have a bed."

He kissed her palm. "Then let's make the most of them."

Natalie jerked awake. What had roused her? No one coming in; the building remained silent. Not the linger-ing scent of bayberry from the extinguished candle. She worked saliva back into her dry mouth. Sleeping with her mouth open? That must have been attractive. She opened one eye to darkness, saw Ram deeply asleep beside her, his breathing slow and even. At least if she'd been unattractively snoring, he hadn't heard it.

A faint beep crossed the silence. Too familiar for her to have any doubts as to the source. Her phone. Voice mail or text message? The beep sounded again. Text.

Maybe Zolton with a reminder she'd promised a new story. He had a habit of working in the wee hours and forgetting other people considered that a time for sleep. Screw you, Zolton. She snuggled deeper into Ram's strong body. Screw Ram instead. After all, they'd come to bed, curled against one another, and promptly fallen asleep.

Beep. Natalie gave a small sigh. Who was she trying to fool?

Carefully she extracted herself from beneath Ram's arm, checking to see that she hadn't awoken him. She stood at the side of the bed a moment, scratching the back of her head, messing up her already mussed hair, trying to remember where she'd put her phone. It had been attached to her clothes . . . ah, yes, ripped off and thrown in the hall.

She retrieved the phone from the pile, and then flicked on the screen light, absently noting the time. Still a couple of hours to sunrise. No wonder the room was so dark, so sultry.

She hit the buttons to retrieve her message. And froze. Stared at the screen.

Blood dropped from her brain faster than the Tower of Terror. Dizzily, she plunked down, sitting on the floor amidst her discarded clothes.

She reread, word by word, the message she'd absorbed in one glance: *Nat, ciao. Library ASAP. TELL NO ONE.*

The phone dropped from her numb hand. She braced her palms on the floor, drawing in deep gasps of air. Oh, please, please, please, if there is a God in heaven, do not let this be some cheap, ugly prank.

No. Impossible. Tears streaming down her cheeks, gulping silent air, she sprang up, haphazardly threw on her clothes. Stuffing the phone in her pocket, she skidded back to the bed.

Tell no one. Not even Ram? How could she not tell the man she loved?

Tell no one. How could she break Nathaniel's trust?

She knelt by the bed, her hand stroking through the soft thickness of Ram's hair. He needed a haircut; the ends brushed against his collar. Gently, she leaned over and gave him a delicate kiss, her heart breaking into two separate pieces.

"Time to rise."

His hand groped for hers, ringing her wrist when he found her. Then, with a small sigh, he settled back into sleep. He must be exhausted.

The phone and message hung heavy at her waist. "Time to go," she said, a bit louder, giving him a little shake.

He murmured a protest, and then barely opened one eye. "Not that late," he mumbled.

"Yes, it is. Please, Ram." Her throat closed. She felt like such a traitor, a fraud to the loving they'd just shared.

Accompanied by a few more protests, Ram eventually rolled out of the bed and donned his clothes.

"I'm sorry you have to leave," she said, with one bit of honesty in this whole rotten, deceptive ending, her fists clinging to his shirt.

He cupped her neck and gave her a lazy kiss. "Get some more sleep."

"I will. You, too."

One more kiss, then the other half of her heart left.

As soon as his truck was out of sight, she shoved on shoes and was out the door, her Mustang purring into the birthing morn. The words of the text message burned deep: *Nat, ciao.* Only one person in this world knew that code, developed by two kids in foster care. Knew those words held a significance she would understand, couldn't ignore.

Nathaniel. Her brother was back. And he needed her.

Chapter Twenty-two

"Nathaniel?" Natalie called softly. On her own property, with her brother near, she should be shouting and running. Yet something about the graying night held her in check. Kept her voice to a whisper, her footsteps muffled. She approached the library with caution, mindful that text messages could be faked.

She wished Ram were with her.

The faint hoot of an owl sent her flashlight beam jerking from ground to sky to tree canopy. Nothing. Nothing moved except her. Even the wind had died and taken the cricket chirps and June-bug buzz. Too still. Outdoors was never this quiet and motionless, unless a disaster was in the offing.

Reaching the library, she swung her beam across the vacant porch. She risked a louder call, her free hand resting on the gun at her side. She wouldn't be taken unaware this time. "Where are you?"

"Here."

Heart leaping, she swung around to the voice. It came from the corner deepest within the woods. She

could see nothing of him, only hear that one odd sylla-
ble. A single word that did—and did not—sound like
her twin.

Caution be damned. She hurried toward him.

"Stop! Don't come any closer."

The command drew her up. The voice held a faint
lisp, but she recognized it. Her hands trembled. It was
really her brother. Yet something was terribly wrong.

"Nathaniel," she breathed. Blood racing, tears—of
joy and dread—wetting her cheeks, she shone her light
on the corner.

"Put that away!"

With a pop, the bulb was extinguished. Natalie swallowed on a lump of fear and edged forward. "What's
wrong?"

"Unlock the library, then leave."

"I'll unlock the library, if that's what you need, but
you know damn well I'm not going to leave. Not after all
these months." Her outstretched hands pleaded with
him. Afraid he would disappear before she'd even
touched him, she continued her cautious pace.

"This isn't something you can fix." His voice slipped
away.

"Don't! Do not disappear again." She swallowed back
a sob. "Whatever you do, don't leave."

"Oh, Natalie." The words were a regretful recognition
of her pain.

Insides quivering, she rounded the corner of the carriage house. She still couldn't see him. The light seemed
to be sucked from the patch of ground where his voice
had retreated. Blindly, she reached for him.

Touched him. Sweat trickled down her spine, as she
interlaced their hands. His fingers were thin, his grip
weak. Slowly, she stepped backward, drawing him with
her into the pale light.

My, God, no. Acid burned her throat as she pushed back the urge to throw up. She turned her head away, unable to face the creature he'd become.

"Unlock the library, then leave," Nathaniel said gently, trying to tug his hand from hers, but his effort was weak.

Natalie refused to let him go. With her initial nausea controlled, she steeled herself and faced him again. The awful changes struck her so powerfully, she nearly doubled over, but she forced herself not to look away.

The arm she held was human. The other arm was not.

Purple-red feathers had replaced skin. Long at the shoulder, they tapered and shrank until his hand was covered in mere down. Not quite a hand anymore, the little finger fused to its neighbor like the tip of a wing.

Bad as that was, his face was worse, especially the eyes. For as the features changed, his humanity was being lost.

His lips had begun to stiffen and draw forward, like a beak. That accounted for the strange sound of his voice. His eyes—she could look at him, but she couldn't force herself to meet his eyes. No longer hazel, they were round and black like an eagle's.

"I can see better in the dark," he said with a touch of laughter. "Or catch the movement of a mouse in grass."

His ability to share her thoughts had not changed. Unfortunately, she no longer had that insight. With her free hand, she dashed the tears from her cheeks. "You have the weirdest sense of humor." Then, with a strangled cry, she wrapped her arms around him and hugged him. Hard. Feathers or not, he was her twin and he was home. "I missed you."

World-class understatement.

"I've missed you, too." His good arm returned her hug, and they shared a silent, blessed reunion.

"I've made you cry," he said at last.

"Of course, you idiot." She did look at him then, at his eyes. "I've been frantic. Lost."

His turn to look away. "I guess I would have been too."

She gave him a punch on the arm, and not all in play. "You couldn't have called? Texted? Sent an e-mail? 'Hey, Natalie, I'm still fricking alive.' "

"I'm sorry. I was preoccupied."

Her anger died, useless in the face of immediate problems. "What happened, Nat?"

"It's complicated."

"I've got time." She gestured toward the main house. "Are you thirsty? Hungry?"

He nodded. "Recently, food's been hard to come by. Got any licorice?"

"I'll get some tomorrow." She drew him back with her, into the house, into the light. Questions hummed inside her, but for once she dammed them. Focus on the immediate needs, savor his return before the real problems intruded.

When they got in the kitchen, she had to force herself to release his hand. Not completely irrational fear whispered he might vanish if she let go.

While she heated vegetable beef soup, he drank a glass of water. Slowly, spilling some because his mouth no longer worked right. She tried not to let her horror show, but she couldn't hide it from her twin. When the soup was ready, she set a bowlful in front of him, added crackers and an apple she'd cut into small pieces to the plate, refilled his water glass, and then sat across from him. She waited in silence as he struggled with the food. To offer to feed him would be more than he would allow. She walked a thin line; his pride could overtake his need at any moment.

He looked thin, translucent. The changes were like a parasite, absorbing his life and humanity. She allowed him to slake his hunger before she said, "Talk. Start at the beginning. What happened the night you disappeared? What went so terribly wrong? Where have you been?"

Why have you returned? How deeply are you into this? Are you still practicing magic? Doubts she couldn't voice.

He crumbled a cracker, not looking at her. "We were trying to do a Phoenix Ritual."

"What's that?"

"In simple terms, regeneration. Charles had been studying avian DNA markers, and he thought he found one that harkened back to the phoenix."

"I thought the phoenix was mere myth."

"So did I. Charles didn't. He was obsessed with the idea of recreating the bird."

"Especially after Katrina."

Nathaniel nodded. "His concepts were beyond anything I'd ever heard, but the way he presented them seemed real and possible. He wanted to meld science and magic."

"What went wrong?"

"I don't know. The ritual is tricky—it requires a lot of preparation, fire, precise control—any number of elements could have gone wrong. When the fire exploded, it took out almost the whole grove." He broke off, swallowing hard, then looked at her. "I am so sorry, Natalie. I couldn't save him."

Laying a hand on his winged arm, she swallowed back more tears. "Neither could I."

"Standing there, alone in the scorch and the stink, I knew I'd be accused of his murder. So, I ran."

"It was an accident."

"Maybe not," he returned slowly. "The original ritual needed three Mages. We modified it for two, but Charles worried the changes wouldn't be potent enough. Then, when we started, I got the impression a third Mage had joined us."

"Who?"

"I don't know. We were robed; only Charles spoke. I saw a shadow. Hell, with the smoke and incense and my intense focus, I may have hallucinated the whole thing. If a third man was there, he vanished after the explosion."

"Maybe your third man is my bird smuggler." She sat back, her mind churning. The magician in the bayou, the Phoenix charm, Dark Phoenix—birds and magic intertwining.

How did Nathaniel fit in? She couldn't look at him when she asked, "Were you here the night they took my woodpecker?"

"No. What are you talking about? What woodpecker?"

"You placed a call to AX."

"I don't have a phone. Tonight I paid a guy on the street ten bucks to use his cell."

"What about the missing charm with the Phoenix symbol? You used that symbol when you designed the bar." To avoid looking at the damning steel links he wore at his wrist, she pulled out her sketch. "What's the significance?"

"Nothing. Just some random design I saw."

Not true, Nat, I can still read you for that lie.

"What's going on, Natalie? Why the accusations?"

She folded up the sketch. "I think your unknown third Mage is resurrecting the Phoenix Ritual."

"That ritual is dangerous," Nathaniel warned.

"So, you finally agree with me. Soon as we get you better, you're going to stop mucking about in this magic nonsense."

"No," he said slowly, but with a determination she hadn't heard before tonight. "If I survive this, I'm going to study harder."

"What? No! After all the pain it's caused?" Her fingers bit into his arm. "Don't. Promise me you won't get drawn back into that morass."

"That's one of the reasons I stayed away," he said softly. "I couldn't face your demand that I give up studying magic."

"Dammit, Nathaniel." She jerked to her feet, stung by the criticism. Angrily, she cleared the table. "I have a right to be concerned."

"You do, but not the right to order my life." He sounded more sad than angry.

"Then help me understand." She threw dishes into the sink, heedless of the shattering china, and rounded on him. "Is it the thrill? Like a coke addict? The secret satisfaction of being able to do what others can't? The power? What?"

"All that, to a degree. Don't you experience those same things in your reporting? The addictive thrill of breaking something big? The ability to spin words like no one else? The power you hold over others by what you expose?"

Her jaw snapped shut. "It's not the same."

"No?" He raised his brows, a gesture so Nathaniel on a face that held so little of him that her heart shattered. "Those things don't have to be bad," he added, exposing wounds Ram had also tried to get her to heal. "There will always be people who abuse their power. You don't trust them, Natalie. That's good. We need watchdogs like you. But I've done some changing these past months."

"That's the truth, Birdman," she said tartly, then clapped her hand over her mouth. How could she have said that?

Nathaniel made a faint sound, like a strange, rusty laugh, softening a measure of her anger. "Unflinching as always. And here I thought you'd forgotten that story I told you."

"The Birdmen who flew out of the fog to steal away little children? Not bloody likely. I slept with a table knife for months, ready to stab the first one that tried to get me."

"I didn't, because I thought they would take me to a better place."

"The difference between you and me."

"Yes, but what Birdman realized is that to stand against evil you need more than knowledge and courage. You need to be strong, powerful to win."

He had changed. She began to pick out the broken china.

"I was wrong to put you through these past months." He pushed to his feet, looking stiff as an arthritic octogenarian. Turning her from the sink, he wrapped his one good arm around her. "I love you, Nat."

"I love you, too, Nat," she said with a sniff. Leaning her face against his chest, she let the tears flow again, one last time. She heard his heartbeat, a rhythm she had known since the womb. A little faster, maybe, but still familiar, and gradually the tears eased.

Oh, it felt good to hold him again. Except, she was surprised to recognize that something had changed irrevocably between them. He was a vital, important part of her life, she would do anything to make sure he was healed, but he was no longer the only man who mattered.

She pushed back from him, scrubbing at her face. "Look at me. Ms. Weakling Tears, when we should be helping you."

"You're entitled to sixty seconds of weakness in this life," he teased. He pulled a garbage can closer. "I'll pick out the broken pieces, while you rinse and load the dishwasher."

The task he'd chosen was easier to do one-handed, she realized, but asked only, "How did you end up like the star of one of your horror tales?"

"I wasn't this . . . freak at first. I fled because of panic. Only later did I slowly begin to change. The faux beak is quite new."

"How—?"

"Somehow, the fire seared the ritual into my flesh. I've tried to find a way to reverse it, but I can't. I'm hoping the library might have an answer." His face twisted. "It's consuming me, Nat. Molecule by molecule, I'm losing my humanity."

He was scared. Hell, who wouldn't be? She loaded the last dish, then turned and braced her hands on the counter behind her. "We need help; we can't do this alone."

"Right," he said with sarcasm. "Who are you going to approach? 'Sir, my twin is turning into a heron. Can you help me?'"

"You know who I mean; you've been watching me."

"Ramses Montgomery." At least he didn't bother with a denial. Nathaniel shook his head. "I've heard whispers. I've been racking my brain about who could have been our third. And the only one I'm coming up with is Ram Montgomery."

"Funny, he keeps saying the same thing about you."

"I don't trust him."

"I do," she said simply, knowing it was the truth. She had questions about Ram, mysteries she couldn't answer, but on a primary level, she trusted him.

On the other hand, as overjoyed as she was at having Nathaniel back, she also had questions about her brother—the charm, the pieces of the story he was keeping from her.

At last Nathaniel nodded. "Let's get some sleep. You can call him in the morning."

Ram and Nathaniel. She trusted them both; she just hoped she wouldn't be forced to decide which one she trusted more.

Noon had passed, and the day was sweltering by the time Ram turned off the truck in Natalie's drive. He and

Val got out, and the dog took off after a sparrow with a gleeful bark. "Come back when you're tuckered out," he called after her.

"Woof!"

Ram shoved his hands in his shorts pockets, and his sandals slapped against the thick grass as he went around the main house. Natalie's cryptic call had asked that he meet her in the carriage house.

Anger warred with concern and curiosity, three sharp talons in his gut. She'd thrown him out last night not because she was worried about being found screwing at work, but because something more important had driven her back here.

Whoever had called her—he'd heard the beep, just hadn't registered at the time what it meant—could be setting a trap. Phoenix was close to making his move, and Ram would bet a hog in a haystack this wasn't coincidence, that plans had been set in motion.

Warily, he paused on the porch, testing. The odd, stitched-together vibrations he'd sensed the first time he'd come here were just as strong today. This time, however, he didn't allow them to mess with him. He shoved open the door and strode into the darkened building.

A study of some kind, judging by the large desk. Cool and dark. Natalie, pacing the floor, spun at his entrance. In a heartbeat, she raced across the length of the floor and pulled him into her arms. Rising on tiptoe, she kissed him.

Synergetic power flared between them, electrifying as ever, but he didn't return the kiss. Not with someone unknown waiting and watching in the blackest corner.

With a sigh she lowered to her feet. "Thank you for coming."

"What do you want?" he asked, coolly.

Paling, she retreated. "I want you to help Nathaniel."

"What's wrong?" He didn't ask her; he asked the figure in the back.

"This." The man reached out and snapped on the desk lamp.

Ram's throat closed on a wash of bitter acid, and he couldn't stop the involuntary flinch.

The blond man's beak-mouth twisted in a gruesome parody of a smile. "Repulsive, isn't it?"

"Nathaniel?"

"In the feather."

Natalie joined her brother, putting her arm protectively over his shoulders in a gesture that spoke louder than any words. "You're under no obligation, Ram. You can say no without even a reason. But I don't know who else to ask."

His brows lifted. "I'm a last resort?"

"You're the only person I trust," she snapped. "Can you help him?"

Why was he trying to hurt her? When they both managed that task without even trying. Maybe because he was surprised by how much it hurt to see her and to know he was losing her to a rival he couldn't fight.

Nathaniel gave him a steady return stare, impassive. Him, Ram didn't trust further than he could spit. Despite the fusing of man and bird, Nathaniel was still atop Ram's list as the best candidate for Phoenix, especially wearing that steel-link bracelet.

Reversing the spell's effects was aiding the enemy, and even if Nathaniel weren't Phoenix, or Ram knew a reversal, he couldn't afford the energy to heal Nathaniel, not now.

"I can't—" The refusal stopped as he looked at Natalie, at the glisten of moisture in her eyes, at the hand running nervously down her arm, and his chest contracted, making breathing and cool rationality difficult. He couldn't refuse Natalie, regardless of the cost. "I can't without knowing what happened."

Natalie closed her eyes, briefly, her hands still fluttering along her arms, and breathed, "Thank you."

Her agitation, he realized, was more than worry over her brother. This room, this building . . . what had happened to her here. "Let's sit on the porch," he suggested. "My dog will be looking for me, and we're too deep in the country for anyone to see Nathaniel."

Outside, Natalie took a deep breath and sat on the steps. Nathaniel sat beside her.

"What happened?" Ram asked, leaning against a porch post.

"A Phoenix Ritual." Nathaniel gave a brief summary of that night.

So, the legend was true. "Do you have a copy of the ritual?"

"Only my part." Nathaniel pulled a scorched and worn paper from his pocket. Obviously, he'd studied it many times.

"You don't have a reversal." Not a question; Nathaniel would have used it.

"We thought you might," Natalie said.

"Depends on what I read here." As he sat cross-legged on the grass to study the paper, Val trotted out of the woods and made a beeline for them. She paused at the foot of the stairs, a low growl coming from her throat as she stared at Nathaniel.

"Don't think she knows quite what to make of me." Nathaniel seemed visibly nervous.

Ram petted Val to keep her calm, mentally complimenting the dog on her good sense, while he read. Cold washed across him, as the sense of the ritual became clear, and his fingers tightened on her fur. Val gave him a warning growl, and he let go, his jaw tight. "What was your purpose?" he asked levelly.

"To recreate the phoenix, using modern avian DNA. I was so thrilled; I thought Charles would use the bird's healing powers for genetic diseases." Nathaniel gave a bitter laugh. "I was mistaken. He wanted the bird for himself."

Ram shifted his tight shoulders, the scars aching. He had only half the ritual, but what he was reading wasn't about creating a phoenix. The ritual was twisted to create the essence of the phoenix within the Mage. It was about regeneration and eternal life for evil. At the cost of untold birds and the powers, or life, of the fellow Mage.

Either Nathaniel was quite naive, or he was concealing the real purpose of the ritual.

Question was, which? Painstakingly, Ram folded the paper. Only when his anger subsided enough so he could speak calmly did he nod to the carriage house. "I don't have a reversal. Maybe there's something in there."

Natalie, reaching to pet Val, froze, her hands suddenly cold. "You're going to look in the library?"

"If we all look—" Nathaniel began.

Natalie shook her head, fast and definite. She'd known, even though she'd tried to ignore the fact, that they'd have to go into the library. She'd also known she could not. She couldn't force herself to help with this. "I think I'll stay out here in the sunshine."

"We could use an extra pair of eyes."

Ram clapped Nathaniel on the shoulder, moving him toward the library. "She won't know what to look for; let her relax. You start looking; I'll be there in a moment."

When Nathaniel was out of earshot, Ram crouched beside her. "You think I'm going to turn evil by going in?"

"Don't laugh at me. That room is *wrong.*"

"And I've got shields against that sort of thing."

"Don't stay too long." She grabbed his hand, stopping him before he left. She lowered her voice, taking no chance Nathaniel could hear her. "What was it about the ritual that made you angry?"

"It's not about creating a phoenix, it's about becoming a phoenix. Resurrection founded upon the death of the companion Mages."

A shudder ran along her bones. "Someone like that would be unstoppable."

"Yes."

"My God," she breathed. Her hands tightened. "Be careful. I don't know what he plans to do in there."

"You're finally thinking he's Phoenix, our man behind the curtain?"

"I think he knows more than he's telling. I don't want you caught unaware."

He kissed her knuckles. "A possibility I've considered from the moment he turned on the light."

Ram and Nathaniel were in the library an hour—Natalie knew because she looked at her watch seventy-five times. Even Val had tired of the limp game of fetch, and had sprawled under a tree to paw at the dirt.

"Did you find anything?" Natalie scrambled to her feet.

"No," Nathaniel said, flatly.

"Yes." When Ram took her hands, his fingers were bloodless, cold. "I told you I would do anything within my power to help. This is in my power."

"No, I'll find another way." Nathaniel pivoted, ready to storm away.

"What is this spell?" Natalie asked impatiently.

"Ritual blood transfer." Ram gave the book to her.

"Except in magic, blood means life," Nathaniel added as she skimmed the ritual, obviously afraid that she was understanding very clearly the terrible details.

"Then there's only one answer." Her hand shook as she handed back the book. "I'll be the donor."

Chapter Twenty-three

Ram, with Val at his heels, entered the old grove before sunset, reluctant as hell. Natalie had ignored all of his objections, and the damnable fact was, she was right. If anything went wrong, Ram could fix a misarrayed spell; she couldn't. Nathaniel had to control the connection—she just had to sit there—and her twin was growing weaker. To wait would increase the risk.

At last she'd pulled Ram aside and given him the one argument he couldn't resist. Her fingers were cold as she took his hand. "I know he may be Phoenix, and I know this is a horrible thing to ask of you, to let him grow strong."

"He manipulated you into this position."

"Maybe. Probably. But don't you see? He's the only family I've got. I can't give up on him. I have to believe that, in the end, he won't hurt me."

He did see, and seeing sucked. She'd been betrayed once by a man who'd sworn to be faithful. If her twin also failed her, then a mouse would have a better chance of escaping a viper pit than Ram would have of convincing her to trust him. Or to believe that magic was only a reflection of the man within.

On that one shred of hope, he agreed to help.

She complied with all the preparations, including the twelve-hour fast, without hesitation. The only time he saw her quail was when he asked Nathaniel about some necessary ingredients.

"There's a workroom in the library," Nathaniel said.

"What?" she said. "I've never seen anything but books and arcana."

Nathaniel looked at her with a measure of pity and sympathy. "There are rooms attached, Natalie, that you know nothing about."

They used the same grove as for the original ritual, and Ram chose the time of the next day's sunset. Everything was prepared with as many safeguards as he could manage, but he couldn't get rid of the nagging sense that this whole gamble was a royal screwup.

Natalie and Nathaniel were waiting in the stand of ancient trees. Natalie wore a red shirt and shorts, as instructed, and Nathaniel had put on the requisite white. They were holding hands, with a closeness that defied months of separation and magic.

"You don't have to do this, Nat," Nathaniel said.

"Yes, I do." She kissed his cheek. "See you on the other side, Birdman."

Then, she spied Ram. Coming close, she wrapped her arms around him and laid her head on his chest. "Thank you," she whispered.

"I'll protect you," he said in a voice for her ears alone.

"I know, but what you don't realize is I'd protect you, too, if you ever needed it."

Ram gave in to a different need, then, not caring that Nathaniel watched, not caring that he was supposed to be keeping his distance for both their sakes, and kissed her. Just at the small swelling of her lip. Gently, so as not to hurt her.

When he lifted, she gave him a tremulous smile. "I'm ready."

Val stretched out beneath a tree while Ram took his place. The twins sat cross-legged on straw mats, facing each other, Nathaniel's athame between them. Nathaniel picked up the knife. His jaw set, he drew the knife without hesitation across Natalie's palm until blood oozed from the slice. She flinched at the first pierce, then held steady. He made a twin cut into his own palm.

She joined their hands, blood commingling. Ram tied a black cloth around their palms, and Nathaniel started the necessary chant. Ram cast the circle guarding them from the curiosity of a stray entity, then drew back, alert for an ambush.

Natalie's eyes closed, but Nathaniel's stayed open as the spell was initiated.

Exchange energy; remove the nonhuman invader. The spell was simple in concept, a mere taste of the connections that formed the basis of his power, but it would be a straining beast to control.

Despite being separate from them, Ram also felt the flowing transfer whisper across his skin like mint on a spring breeze. No, not mint. Licorice. The barely perceptible scent slid across his nose.

Cold rage spun through him; if Nathaniel wasn't Phoenix, then he was but a step away. And Ram couldn't do a damn thing about it, not now, not without endangering Natalie. Ruthlessly he reined in his emotions. He could do nothing but make sure she remained safe.

The setting sun cast a red glow on the twins, as crimson

as the blood flowing between them. So far the transfer was going smoothly. Some energy would be drained from Natalie, but not so much that she couldn't replenish it within a few days, just as a blood donor replenished plasma. Yet Ram couldn't stop the gnawing tension as the feathers dropped off Nathaniel, as down became flesh again, and lips reformed.

Natalie stirred restlessly on the mat, sweat beading on her forehead. A knot of dread curled tighter; one of his concerns had been Natalie's reaction. He couldn't break the circle and touch her as he wanted, so he crooned to her, calming her. She stopped fidgeting, but gulped in air.

The last bit of down dropped to the ground. Completion, but Nathaniel didn't end the ritual.

"Nathaniel, break it off," Ram ordered.

In panic, Natalie jerked her bound hand. The flow of energy surged from Natalie to Nathaniel. Stronger. Faster. Not stopping.

Dammit, for Natalie's sake, I gave the bastard the benefit of doubt. Grimly, he chanted out the words he'd already prepared, piercing through the circle. He yanked the knot and pulled their hands apart. Dripping blood stained the straw mats. Their connection was too deep, too powerful. The rush of life became an arctic wind, swift and achingly cold. Natalie sagged, her skin pale and her lips blue. Nathaniel gazed straight ahead, unflinching, the magic swirling around him in an elaborate dance.

Ram lifted his athame. "Be done!" he shouted, cutting through their connection. The vicious flow died. Nathaniel, completely healed, jerked backward. Natalie collapsed, limp and drained. Ram scooped her into his arms.

Nathaniel lifted his hand. "Sweet saints, it worked."

"You drained her," Ram snarled.

Nathaniel's gaze jerked upward, and then he, too, sprang to his feet. "I didn't know."

"The hell you didn't. You did something in those preps. Something so I couldn't break the bond, and don't bother with a protest." Ram, with an unconscious Natalie in his arms, strode off into the night, Val beside him.

"Where are you taking her?" Nathaniel caught up, grabbed his arm.

Val growled at him. Ram swung around and shoved out a hand. Nathaniel flew backward and slammed to the ground. "Somewhere you can't reach her."

"She's my sister, my twin. You can't separate us. She'll be back."

"At least she'll be prepared the next time you try to kill her."

"I would never," Nathaniel shot back. "I'm trying to protect her."

Ram stopped at his truck. His hand clenched against the urge to slam Nathaniel into a new version of hell. "Well, you did a piss-poor job of it."

With that, he laid Natalie on the passenger seat, and Val jumped in to guard her while Ram ran to the driver's side. Nathaniel reached in the open window to touch Natalie's face.

"*Don't touch her.*"

The metal turned white hot and Nathaniel jerked back. His fists clenched in impotent fury. "We both know she amplifies power. You're using her."

"You don't know a damn thing."

"Yeah, but how will Natalie look at it?" he shouted. "She asked me to give up the magic. First thing. She hates it, and that won't change."

Ram didn't bother to answer what he knew was the truth. Angrily, he shoved the truck into gear and turned it in the road, heedless of Nathaniel jumping out of the way of his tires. Without a backward glance he sped off.

Natalie awoke groggy with a throbbing headache and a raging thirst. Unable to find the energy to move, she nestled deeper beneath the heavy quilt and tried to dredge up some memory of what had happened.

Nathaniel. Something had gone wrong.

Yet even the spurt of terror couldn't spur her to move more than to slit open her eyes. Daylight. Ram sprawled in a chair beside her, asleep and looking as beat up as she felt. A shadow of beard colored his cheeks and chin.

As if sensing her awakening, his eyes opened. "How do you feel?"

"Thirsty," she managed. "Nathaniel?"

"Healed. Not a feather or a beak." His face was shuttered as, from the bedside, he picked up a lidded Barney cup, complete with a plastic straw, and then held the straw to her mouth. She took a grateful sip, then another. He'd done this before during the night, she recalled, although she hadn't been able to talk.

"Got any drug allergies?" he asked.

"No."

"Then take these aspirin." He held out a couple of white tablets.

She swallowed the bitter-tasting medicine before saying, "Thank you, Ram. For everything. You could have walked away—"

"No. I couldn't."

With an ineffective murmur, she gave in to exhaustion and slept.

The next time Natalie awoke, she was still thirsty, the headache was manageable, night had fallen, and she now had the strength of a neonate.

She turned her head from being buried in the pillow.

Ram slept beside her, atop the covers and taking up more than his half of the bed. His hand rested on her nape, and she realized that she had bent her arm so their fingers brushed.

In sleep, they wouldn't be separated.

She realized something else. She had to pee really, really bad. As she struggled to free herself from the covers, Ram awoke.

"Where are you going?" he asked sleepily.

"Bathroom."

"Let me help you."

"I think I can manage the task alone." She slid to the side of the bed and got her feet onto the floor, but when she tried to stand, the spinning room dropped her to her knees. She clutched the bedside. "Whoa."

Ram helped her stand, and then he held the cup to her mouth. "Drink."

"Not gonna help the immediate problem."

"You're dehydrated."

She took an obedient sip; then he gathered her into his arms and carried her into the bathroom. Fortunately, the trip in his embrace seemed to give her strength. He left her alone to complete the rest of the business, which she managed by clutching the nearby sink. When she finished, she leaned against the marble and splashed her face. Her palm was bandaged, she saw, and she was wearing another T-shirt and shorts from Ram. She gathered her wisps of strength, and, using fixtures and walls and doors, managed to get back to the hall.

Ram was waiting, back braced against the wall, arms crossed, no emotion on his face. Her heart did a thump-y thing. Despite the bloodshot eyes, the beard stubble, and the mussed-up hair, the sight of him was a shot of pure arousal.

He straightened when she appeared. "Are you hungry?"

"A little." He started to pick her up, but she shook her head. "Let me walk."

They made slow progress to the kitchen. Natalie clutched his arm, and with each step her energy returned. Still, she took his offer of a chair, while he nuked a couple of frozen meals. "Where are we?"

"Near Amite. A hunting cabin of my Dad's, although all the family uses it." He set a glass of water on the table.

"Hence last night's Barney cup." She took a sip, then shuddered. "I ache worse than if I'd been bungee jumping and the rope broke. I hope to God I never experience a gut kick like that again. I didn't realize it would be so bad."

"It wasn't supposed to be."

"What do you mean?"

He didn't look at her, seemed intent on watching the microwave count down. "I know you won't believe me, I know you'll try to defend him, but Nathaniel tried to kill you."

She scraped a hand through her messy hair, trying to remember details. "Why do you think that?"

The microwave dinged. He put the meals on the table with silverware and took a bite before he answered. "When Nathaniel was healed, he wouldn't stop the exchange. You tried to let go, and the spell became a drain. He almost killed you. He says it was an accident, but I know magic, Natalie. He had to do something ahead of time to prevent me from intervening."

Churning over what he'd said, she nodded and bent to her meal.

"What, no argument?" he asked at last.

"No."

"Do you believe me?"

"Yes."

"It's not coincidence he returned now."

"I agree."

"So you'll stay away from Nathaniel?"

"No."

"Dammit, Natalie—"

"Look, Ram." She pointed her fork at him. "You know that Nathaniel altered that spell. I know that no way on God's green earth he would intend to murder me. So, what I'm trying to do, if you would stop asking so many questions, is reconcile those two facts."

Natalie bent back to her meal, a little ashamed at her outburst. After all, Ram had done nothing but go against his better instincts to help her. "I'm sorry. It's not you I'm mad at." She was angry at Nathaniel. What the hell was her brother up to? Despite what had happened, she had an ugly feeling she wasn't the ultimate target.

Ram was. A dreadful, icy shiver ran through her. Her hand shook a little as she forked the last of her food.

Ram was pulling away from her; she felt the wary distance in him as keenly as she'd felt the knife blade on her palm. She was losing him.

But, dammit, she would not lose him to the machinations of her brother. If Nathaniel intended to harm Ram, she would have to find a way to stop her twin.

When they finished their silent meal, Ram leaned his chair back. At least Natalie had some color back. When he'd brought her here, she'd been as white as Feng. "Do you believe now that you brother is Phoenix?"

"No." She tapped her unused spoon against the table. "We do have an alternative." She told him about Nathaniel's far-fetched version of a shadowy third Mage.

"Nathaniel could have lied."

"Maybe but I don't think so." She smiled slightly. "Where's Val?"

"Outside."

Taking two steps to his side, she bent over and, to his surprise, kissed him.

Hard. Demanding. As needy as he had been after finding her caught by Virgil. Her fingers threaded through his hair, her thumbs stroked behind his ears, and the pressure on his scalp was unbearably erotic.

"Do not turn me away," she whispered against his lips. "I need this. We need this, and before you ask, I'm feeling much, much better."

One kiss, one touch, one demand and he was hard. His hands locked onto her curvy waist. The play of feminine muscle danced across his palms, and he tugged her closer. Without breaking the kiss, without stopping her teasing, wet tongue, she shoved off her shorts, yanked off her shirt, and straddled his lap.

She was already wet for him. He could feel the dampness through his thin nylon shorts. She lifted his shirt and stroked across his engorged cock.

"Are you sure?" he gasped. Why was he protesting?

Because her hands shook as they ran across his aching chest, across the tape and gauze and scars. Because her face was still wan, with only the flush of desire on her cheeks. Because he was afraid, very soon, he was going to use very unpleasant methods to stop a dangerous magician. Skills she had no idea he possessed. And because he feared that magician was her twin brother.

"You feel so good," she whispered, her teeth scraping his neck. "How can I not be sure?"

"Natalie." The word was a strangled cry. He gripped her wrists, pushing her back a little. "This won't stop me, what I have to do."

She swallowed. "I know. But, maybe, this will give us a reminder that, at a very basic level, we are so much better together."

"A confederacy." He brought her hands to his lips and kissed her knuckles, then released her.

"Aren't you the one that's been spouting all the advantages of mutual cooperation?"

"You're cute when you're smug."

She lifted herself off his lap and stood beside him, naked, fists at her hips, a frown between her brows. "Do you want to make love to me?"

With a swift motion, he lifted his hips and stripped off his shorts. Gripping her hips, he pulled her back down and slid inside her slick, wet channel.

"I'll take that as a yes," she said with a cheeky grin.

"I prefer actions to words." And he began to suit his actions to his needs, sliding deeper, then back.

For once, she preferred actions, too, and soon they were mindless. Endless moments later he exploded inside her and she surrounded him with her release.

Limply, she clung to him, her arms draped over his shoulders. A few minutes later, when she hadn't moved, he realized she'd fallen asleep.

He yawned and got up stiffly, with Natalie in his arms. It wasn't getting easier to keep his magic from touching her. But after her experience with Nathaniel, it was more necessary.

He yawned again, settling Natalie on her feet so she woke just enough to stumble with his aid to the bedroom. He didn't have the strength to carry her, not tonight. The past days had taken a toll on him, too.

She slid beneath the bedcovers and went instantly back to sleep. He stared at her a moment, longing to hold her, and then slipped into bed with her. He wrapped an arm around her, settling comfortably against her warm, pliant body. His other hand circled his tourmaline.

The next morning, Natalie woke and stretched. She felt pretty darn good after an uninterrupted night's sleep. More rested than she had in days.

Except the last thing she remembered was sitting on Ram's lap in the throes of a glorious orgasm. Oh, how humiliating that she'd fallen asleep. She glanced at the empty bed, at the mussed covers, and the indented pillow. The sheets were still warm, too. At least Ram was not long gone.

She threw on the closest shirt and scrambled through the cabin, looking for him. The small cabin was empty, so she went outside. Val was lolling in the sunshine and a call to Ram died in her throat.

A shallow feeder stream of the Tchefuncte River meandered in front of the cabin. Ram sprawled in the stream, his arms braced behind him, his face turned to the hot sunshine. The water reached barely an inch on his butt. He wore only his tourmaline and ring. Otherwise, he was gloriously and freely naked.

Pagan masculine beauty and power. Something primitively feminine rose inside her, recognizing the elemental connection between them. Last night, she'd tried so desperately to grasp it; this morning he made it clear by skinny-dipping.

He turned and a lazy, contented smile crossed his face. "Join me." She chose to sit on a sun-warmed rock beside the stream, and stick her toes in the rocky water. His glance licked over her. "You look rested."

"I am. You too."

His answer was to turn back to the sun with a smile. "I think we needed this interlude."

For a short time, she basked in the sunshine and the heat, before saying quietly, "Nathaniel used the phoenix design of that charm at Dark Phoenix. That's really why I kept it secret. AX got calls from a number with Nat's voice mail too, although Nat denies it was him. One call came right before they took Twig."

Full disclosure. They needed to pool all their information. Going blind against Phoenix was dangerous, but Ram seemed to think that holding information back was a way of protecting her. She wouldn't make that mistake.

She sighed. "In the bayou, we only saw the one good hand."

"With a steel-link bracelet the same as Nathaniel wears," he said, then added quietly, "The attacker killed AX."

"And that's why I think you're wrong about Nathaniel."

"You don't think he's mixed up in this?"

"I didn't say that. I said he's not a murderer, and he wouldn't kill me."

"Then maybe you'll be able to point out another suspect." He got up, the water sluicing down his thighs. Hungrily, her gaze followed him.

"Sweet saints, you look good nude," she muttered. He preened good, too, she realized with a grin.

After drying his hands, he pulled a photograph from his pile of clothes and handed it to her. "Five years ago a man who called himself Phoenix—and used that symbol you found—began to collect followers. Phoenix was a strong, but evil Mage."

"So he could be working here?" she asked eagerly.

Ram shook his head. "No. He's most definitely dead. But that's a picture of him with his adherents. Do you recognize anyone?"

She squinted at the grainy photo as she smoothed it out on her knees. After a moment's study, she sucked in a breath. "That's Nathaniel and Charles."

"That's what I thought."

No wonder he was so convinced Nathaniel was Phoenix. She shook her head, refusing to take that final step. There had to be another explanation, and she found one. "Adam Zolton, my boss, took the photograph. His credit's in tiny print on the bottom. He's been insistent I find out more about you. Any idea why?"

"No. What have you told him?" he asked casually.

"Nothing." She rubbed a finger across the telltale name. "He saw the television footage of you after that serial killer was caught, though."

"What television footage?" His voice was definitely getting sterner.

Full disclosure sucked. "The one where you suddenly appear in the crowd. I thought I saw you in the crowd and downloaded the footage to be sure." She looked at him. "You lied to me, Ram. You said you weren't there."

"My life is not an open book, Natalie, but I haven't lied about anything regarding us. I think our Phoenix fueled Magic Man's madness, but at the time I didn't know his connection to the smugglers. What did Zolton see?"

Not much of an apology. She put the hurt aside. "You were with a man by the name of LaMarr, but he didn't know the woman."

"Zolton saw LaMarr with me?"

"Is that important?"

"Only because LaMarr's unconscious in the ICU after being attacked."

"Oh, I'm sorry." Natalie sucked in a breath. "Could Zolton be Phoenix?"

"It's a possibility."

"Let me have another look at that photograph." She held it out, studying it in the sunshine, then squinting closer to the photo. The image was so faint. "That looks like John Smythe. He's a bartender at Dark Phoenix and a friend of Nathaniel's." A curl of excitement unfurled in her belly. "AX was calling Dark Phoenix, too."

"Are you sure it's him?"

Honesty forced her to shake her head. "As far as I know, John's never been into magic."

Thoughtfully, she handed him back the photo. Nathaniel, Zolton, John—all men she thought she knew. How could she consider one of them a cold killer? Whereas Ram, whom she wondered if she knew at all, had never been a suspect, despite being the most powerful Mage she knew.

She tilted her head to look at him, now stretched out on the towel, his eyes closed. "You're going after Phoenix soon."

"You can't come with me," he said, not opening his eyes.

"I know you think I'd be a liability."

"You are very smart and very talented, but you don't have the necessary skills to battle a Mage."

"Then why not call one of your brethren Magi?" she asked, feeling hurt.

That got his attention. He sat up, and she was unhappy to see that tension had returned to his shoulders and his half-filled erection had withered. "What are you talking about?"

Full disclosure really sucked. She nodded toward his ring. "I had the text with those symbols translated." She didn't have to tell him what she'd read; he'd seen the pages.

"Sorry to disappoint, but there's no organized magic union. No brethren. We Magi are just a few people, some good, some bad, mostly in between." He lay back on the towel, facing skyward. "I did ask a fellow Mage to come. Khalil will be here tomorrow on a flight from Prague."

She wasn't losing him; she'd lost him. Natalie bit back the pain. Lost him to a mistress she couldn't fight, one she barely understood. "Tell me about your magic," she softly asked. "About these connections."

"Humans are, in essence, social creatures. Babies deprived of touch wither; recluses grow ill. Strength comes from connecting to the energies around us."

"Like Nathaniel did?"

"No! That's magic vampirism, sucking out energy." Not looking, he took her hand, playing a little with her fingers. "Have you ever been in a meeting where ideas start coming fast? Where each thought builds and becomes better? That's synergy. For a Mage that kind of charge can be transformed into the power of magic. The stronger the bonds—mental stimulation, spiritual communion, shared purpose, sex—the stronger the power."

"When you said I give you strength, you meant that quite literally." She looked at their hands. "Does that happen with any woman?"

"Not with so much power." He got up from the towel. "I don't understand why, with you, it's so strong. Maybe because you can feel the magic. Maybe you have a touch of talent?"

She shook her head. "I report. I don't practice. But if you're stronger when you work with someone, why not use me, too? You will need every advantage in going against Phoenix."

His face was covered by the shadow of a pine. "You'd do that for me? You're that determined?"

"Yes."

For a moment she thought he would agree, but then he shook his head. "Khalil and I will handle this."

"Do you know where to go after Phoenix?"

He hesitated.

"I have to know where to stay away from," she snapped.

"Stay at NONE tonight."

"When are we leaving?"

He didn't bother to look at a watch. "We have to leave in an hour."

Sometime tonight he would face Phoenix without her. The worst of it was, she understood why. Only took one lesson. She'd been smacked in the bayou with the fact that she could be used as leverage against him.

Yet, a harping instinct kept replaying the notion that leaving her out was wrong. She'd told him the truth—much as it went against her nature, she would have stayed as backup. But she should be there, some-where.

"After you fight Phoenix, assuming you survive even though you're not using all the resources available, then what?"

For a moment she thought he wouldn't answer. Then he said, "I don't know."

Oh, God, that was bleak. She hugged her knees to her chest, staring at the water. Refusing to believe they were simply a moment out of time.

"What are you thinking?" Ram asked.

Thinking that by logic you're right, but by my heart you are wrong. Natalie took a breath and stood, then tugged Ram to his feet. The damn, stubborn man needed an-other reminder. She backed toward the water. "I was thinking of what we might do in the meantime."

"What?" He shadowed her steps.

"This." She scooped both hands in the water and splashed him, then laughed. Oh, the look on his face was priceless.

He stalked over to her, picked her up in his arms, and smiled. She grinned back. Until he took her, not back to his bed, but down the stream, where the water deep-ened, and dunked them both.

She came up sputtering and splashing. He splashed her back, and the water fight began. They were adding something new to their connection. Laughter.

When the hour ended, when their river-cooled skin had warmed and dried, when they hesitated on the threshold before leaving, Ram traced a line at her temple, brushing back a strand of hair. "I was wrong earlier, Natalie. I do know one thing. When this is all over, I will come find you."

Chapter Twenty-four

The ride back to New Orleans was empty of conversation. Ram, all warrior-jawed and somber, played a CD of chants and hummed quietly to himself. Natalie scoured her memory for every scrap of detail about Phoenix, trying to find some advantage, some lead left to exploit. They stopped at her home on the way into New Orleans for a change of clothes and for her car. She wasn't surprised, though she was a little disappointed, that Nathaniel had disappeared again. At least he'd left her a note, promising to call her soon.

Just before they separated, Ram fastened a chain of intricately woven wire about her neck. Hanging from the center was a pendant divided into two liquids. "In case something goes wrong," he said. "When you shake it, the liquids combine to purple, and you'll be protected—camouflaged, impervious to magic—until they separate. You'll have about ten minutes to get away. But it can only be used once."

"Thank you." Carefully she tucked the pendant beneath her shirt. She drove the final miles into New Orleans alone in her Mustang, losing sight of Ram's truck on the Causeway, as a trickster fog played peekaboo with the elevated road.

When Natalie got to NONE, however, she couldn't force herself to go in. Closing out the chilling night, retiring to her dull cot, smacked too much of turning her back on Ram. Of failure. Of scared-to-face-the-magic failure.

Instead, she smacked a hand on the steering wheel and drove to the French Quarter and Dark Phoenix. Fog wrapped around her ankles as she strode through the narrow streets. The air felt as damp and thick as Cool Whip.

So many threads webbed around the bar. Maybe the fog was lousing up her judgment, but she'd come up with a question she couldn't shake. What if someone had loosed those bees on them not just to scare them off the case, but to keep them from finding . . . something?

Dark Phoenix was a couple of hours from opening, but the back was unlocked for the employees and office staff. From Nathaniel's days of ownership, she knew the warren of rooms as well as she knew the inside of her car.

Strange to be here when it felt so abandoned. There was something forlorn about a bar exposed by harsh incandescent light and hung over with the stale aroma of smoke and liquor.

She crept along the halls, listening for footsteps and voices. Only a radio played somewhere with the weather report: Heat and rain tomorrow, big surprise there. Bad fog tonight. Great. At least she'd missed the traffic on the Causeway, but the airport had closed.

Tiptoe up the stairs, pass the second-floor wax museum, and on up to the third. At the door, she put her ear to the wood, listening. No sounds penetrated from the other side. Empty or well-insulated? She couldn't tell. Cautiously, she opened the door and flinched as the old wood creaked and moaned.

Wouldn't have mattered if the door had splintered into a hundred pieces. The room was empty except for dust bunnies. Not a Mage, not a bird, not a vial of oil. She slapped a hand against the door jamb. No way someone was doing a major league, end-of-the-world-as-we-know-it ritual in here tonight.

A purple feather drifted down from the light fixture. She captured it and ran a finger across the wispy edge, her stomach churning. Same color as Nathaniel's. He had come to John first. Was John the one who had betrayed him?

As she snuck back down the stairs, the sounds of men talking carried to her. She moved cautiously, catching sight of John and one of the other bartenders, before she ducked to stay hidden on the stairwell.

"Thanks for covering me tonight," John was saying.

"No problem. I can use the cash." A door closing indicated they'd separated.

From the scent of his cologne, John was still in the hall. Whew, he wore it strong tonight. Natalie held her breath as he passed, oblivious to her, humming.

Humming? When had John learned to carry a tune?

Her insides curled up, dry as dead June bugs, when she recognized the melody: Beethoven's Fifth. *One of Charles's favorites.* With a trembling hand, she grabbed hold of the pendant on her neck, feeling anchored to its warmth, to Ram, as she peered over the banister. Even from the side, the man was definitely John. The tattoo pattern was distinctive. Then he passed through a haze of smoke, and she pressed a fist against her mouth as a veil of Charles's features appeared over John's.

Oh, my God. Dizzy, she dropped to the stairs and bent her head between her knees. Breathe deep, breathe slow, stop hyperventilating. Swallow the nausea. She was going nuts. Post-trauma stress, eight months delay. Had to be why she was seeing her dead almost ex-husband.

Unless . . . Unless John really was Charles. Charles had lived, John's body buried in his place. Impossible. Unless you believed in magic. Then, a lot of odd pieces came together for a nasty picture.

Ram thought he was going up against her brother. Oh, God, and the airport was closed because of the fog. His friend Khalil couldn't get in. Galvanized, she shoved back her weakness. After making sure "John" had vanished, she raced out of Dark Phoenix. Hurrying to her car, she texted the message: John is Charles.

Sent it again and again and again. Ram wouldn't answer his phone, wouldn't pick up his voice mail, but he might get annoyed enough at the persistent TM for a look. If he had his phone. Maybe phones weren't allowed at rituals. She had to get to him, and she knew, now, where the ritual was going down.

The library.

Deep beyond the carriage house lay a jungle of rampant weeds, impenetrable brush, and misshapen trees. Abandoned to an unforgiving Mother Nature, the uninhabited mix of marsh and overgrown park was an unpleasant place to walk, but Ram preferred the hidden approach.

He'd delved deeper than he'd ever gone to track the last dregs of the searching spell he'd laid last week. The elements of ritual were collected together in the library.

Ram untangled a vine that had wrapped his ankle, scratching his hand on a line of thorns. From the traces of magic, he suspected Phoenix had enhanced the discouraging barriers. Add swarms of mosquitoes, a cottonmouth or three, and near unbreathable humidity, and you had the makings of a thoroughly lousy night.

Don't forget the fog, hanging opaquely between the

trees. Fog thick enough to close the airport and delay Khalil. Ram had decided to go on alone. One more day, and Phoenix might be too strong to stop.

At least Natalie wasn't enduring this miserable trek.

Beside him, Val gave a quiet bark for his attention. The same vine had tangled around her paws.

"Sorry, girl," he whispered, bending to release her, "but you insisted." His spine tightened as he ruffled her burr-crusted fur. He wasn't superstitious, but there was a peril in ignoring omens.

He'd tried to leave Val at home, but she'd refused to leave the truck, even with coaxing and the temptation of a treat. She'd even growled and nipped when he'd tried to carry her inside. In the end, he'd let her come along.

Mage and dog struggled through the final yards. The underbrush, nearly obscured by the thick fog, wove branches and twigs into an impassible barrier. Ram frowned; he wasn't ready to use magic and alert Phoenix, but he needed a touch of power to pass.

As he and Val stepped into a small opening, a faint breeze caught the fog, separating it. His heart gave a lurch. Empty cages. The birds had already been sacrificed. Twig, too?

Hurriedly, Ram closed the last yards to the library. He stopped at the foot of the stairs and knelt to Val. "You stay out here," he warned.

She whined and put a paw on the bottom step, looking rebellious.

"No," he said firmly, in a tone he'd never used with her. "You can't come in." He covered her with a reflective shield. "Stay there," he whispered, pointing to a tree; he waited until she obediently trotted over.

Haze also permeated the interior, leaving its contents only partially visible. Remembering the time he'd been in here before, he crossed the study and went into the library.

Bone-cold fog wrapped around him, as the door swung shut. His shields tight against the plucking evil, he lifted his hand. "Light," he murmured, and a silvery glow from his palm spread out through the room, chasing back the fog, revealing the books. No one here, but he could feel the coalescing powers beyond. He used the light to cross the room in silence, and stopped in front of the two doors hidden at the back. The one on the right led to the workroom; the left he'd not been in.

He closed his fist, and the light vanished. Noiselessly, he opened the left door to a maw of blackness.

A lightning attack from a hidden Mage shot from the utter dark. Gold-shimmering magic whipped around him like a noose. Ram grunted against the pressure slam. His shields held, dissolving the strangling power and freeing him.

He spun, sending a lashing retaliation of paralysis. A glancing hit, if the bit-off curse was any indication. With both of them visually and magically shielded, luck entered into the hunt more than he liked. He held out his hands and muttered, "Clear vision."

The darkness thinned, then on wavering wisps of smoke, light spread out, clearing the cavernous room. One second to see a cage with Twig and two pyres, before he twisted his knife, reinforcing the protections around him, as he cut toward the man revealed. Acid scoured his belly. Dammit, he'd hoped he was wrong.

Exposed, Nathaniel DeSalvo swung around to face Ram.

Fog, why did it always have to be fricking fog? Sheer cussedness drove Natalie into the shrouded woods. Her flashlight beam penetrated the edges of the thick mist—just enough to lead her by inches—before being devoured.

As she eased her way forward, her foot disturbed a

mat of decomposed leaves, releasing an aroma of mold and death. Yet even that faded against the vacuum of the fog. No thin tendrils tonight; the fog hung damp and suffocating, even among the trees. A blank slate that erased all senses but clammy touch.

Fog swirled around her like a mummy's wrappings. A single splash sounded somewhere ahead. Heart racing as if she'd downed a pot of espresso, she searched the night. Something was moving. To the right or ahead, she couldn't be sure, but it was definitely out there. She swung her light, trying futilely to catch some hint of who or what it was.

Nothing. No smell, no sound, no sight escaped.

She trudged forward with a sharpening edge of fear. After what seemed like hours and miles—but was probably only minutes and feet—she pulled near her destination: the library. She turned off her flashlight and stopped, unable to force herself to enter the library from hell.

Nothing here, either. No sound, no light, no tingle of magic. Had she judged wrong? She jumped at the possibility, pivoting, grateful that she wouldn't have to go inside.

Again, she stopped. No, this was the place, she was sure. But she didn't need to go inside. She could wait, concealed, until she saw Ram. But what if he were inside already? Hurt?

Face the demon, Natalie. Jaw set, she forced herself up the first step, then another. The already-steamy night turned suffocating, the fog blinding her as if a thick quilt had been flung over her head. Shuffling forward, she entered the study, then, drawing a breath for courage, she pressed open the library door.

The fog followed her. People went nuts without external stimuli and now she understood why. They imagined things. Like that shadow.

Not imagination. Not imagination that her skin tingled in warning, in recognition of magic seeping through the dampness. Not imagination that a shadow stalked her.

She reached for the gun at her waist, and then strangled back a cry as a burning pain raced up her arm. Damn, damn, damn, it felt as if she'd dipped her arm into molten lead. She jerked her hand off the gun, and the pain lessened. She tried again, and the agony shot through her again, worse.

"Got the point," she muttered. "No guns."

No sooner had the words escaped than a hand, holding a knife as dark as old blood, snaked around her neck. Circling the wrist was a steel-link chain holding the phoenix charm. She froze.

"Put your hands behind you." The command wasn't distorted by the fog.

Slowly, she complied, not wanting to give that knife pricking her neck a reason to slip. Full circle. Fog and a knife to her neck, except the person holding this weapon was far more dangerous than Bennie.

A sinuous rope bound her hands and held them immobile at her back. She tugged experimentally at the bonds.

"Don't bother," he said. "I'm the only person who can undo the spell."

She swallowed. "What now?"

"We go inside. Always too curious. You should have stayed away. Now your weakness will be used against you."

"Don't call me Nat. My brother trusted you. John." She tacked the last on deliberately. Maybe knowing he was Charles would give her an advantage at some point; no sense in revealing knowledge until she had to.

"John" laughed softly as he tied a gag around her mouth. "The DeSalvo twins aren't noted for their perception. Now, walk."

*   *   *

Ram thrust out his hands, sending rivers of pain to De-Salvo.

"I knew you'd come," DeSalvo snarled, doubling over and raising his hands. His face twisted in anger, as he threw out spells of stabbing confusion. "Stay away from my sister."

"Or what?" Concentrating and countering, Ram deflected the attack. Too easily. Where was the strength, the showboating, the calculated cruelty? Where was the marker? Abruptly changing his original plans, he wove the ingredients of a confinement spell.

"Or this."

Ram grunted as his breath caught on the noxious smell of sulfur. The air-stealing spell sucked at his lungs. He lifted his tourmaline and touched his throat, breaking the hold. Now that had been a clever twist on the standard fare.

But not the signature of the magician in the bayou.

Even as the question arose, with a very disturbing answer, the last threads of his confinement spell knit into place. Behind him, the pyre beneath Twig's cage burst into a tower of flames. Twig screeched in raucous panic and flapped futilely against his bars. Ram raced for the bird and thrust his hand into the fire. Agony seared his arm as magic-enhanced flames tore through his shields. Grabbing the cage, he pulled it from the fire and dropped it—sorry, Twig—clear of the danger. In the same motion he flung his confinement spell toward DeSalvo.

The seconds of delay cost him. DeSalvo's magic-steeled cord wrapped Ram's ankles, halting his movement, just as a multi-razored attack from behind shredded his shields.

DeSalvo wasn't Phoenix—a conclusion he'd reached about three seconds ago—but DeSalvo sure as hell was helping the bastard. Whether he knew it or not.

An invisible lash slashed across Ram's shoulders, followed by another. He shuddered under the twin blows. With quick swipes of his athame, he cut through the ankle cords, then the magic whip. Shoving himself to his feet, breath hissing, he yanked a small green crystal from his belt. The original trap he'd prepared, the one doubts had kept him from releasing on DeSalvo.

The tip of his athame grazed the crystal, ready to stab inside.

"Don't," came a lazy command from the darkness. "Or she dies."

Ram froze, his athame a second away from releasing death. His hand curled protectively around the crystal, but he kept the knife ready, his muscles quivering with power. His heart contracted as Natalie stumbled into the room.

"Dammit, Natalie," he said in unison with DeSalvo. "You were supposed to be at NONE."

"You were supposed to be laid up," echoed her twin.

She gave them both an "I'm sorry" look above the gag, as John Smythe, their true Phoenix, stepped into the clearing close beside her. He was dressed all in red, pants and shirt, even boots, a red so deep it was only a shade off black. The Mage color of life and death.

"Put down the crystal and the athame," John ordered. "Slide them toward me."

Ram obeyed, keeping his attention on Natalie.

"John?" DeSalvo, held impotent by Ram's confinement spell, looked puzzled. "I said I'd stop Ram from reactivating the Phoenix Ritual."

"Well, obviously, you couldn't."

"What are you doing with Natalie? Your power is limited, you never studied . . ." DeSalvo's voice trailed off, as he comprehended, and he added drily, "Apparently you acquired some knowledge while I was gone. God, I've been such a fool."

John tilted his head. "In your defense, you were near death. Hard to see how I reinforced your misconceptions."

"So, you set us battling, knowing we'd weaken each other."

"Knowing Ramses would contain, or kill, you. You have enough power to be dangerous. For him, I found a different leverage." He gave Natalie a little shove, and she glared at him over her gag.

Suddenly Val leaped out of the shadows. Snarling, she latched onto John's arm, and Natalie jerked, her eyes wide with shock. John flung off Val, and then his arm shot out, sending the dog crashing against a table. She fell, whimpering, and scuttled backward into the dark.

Ram spied the wound on John's arm. There was a matching injury on Natalie. Blood oozed from her fresh wound, one that matched Val's teeth marks.

"I'm sure you can see her predicament, Ramses."

"She's tied to you. You get hurt; she gets hurt."

"And if I'm unconscious, she dies."

Hastily, Ram bit back the words that would have put John in a coma. Though his chest heaved with pain for Val and for Natalie, he didn't dare make another move. Not while the other magician held Natalie bound. More than the spell of paralysis, that threat kept him immobile.

"You bastard!" DeSalvo pounded against his confinement, then settled back with a seething glare as he realized he was well and truly hamstrung.

"Ramses does good work," John commented before returning his attention to Ram. "I would guess you've about used up your ready power. No circle to replenish you. You can't even touch Natalie to draw from her. I expect you've taken advatange of the fact she's a Resonant."

"Able to amplify any power? That's a myth."

"Like the phoenix."

Ram didn't bother to answer, and Natalie just rolled her eyes in annoyance.

John's lips tightened when they didn't respond. With an impatient gesture he looped one end of Natalie's bonds around a steel pole, effectively anchoring her. Pacing back, he spread his hands, and fire poured from the burning pyre. Two twined lines of flames—the black to burn away magic, the yellow to burn away flesh—licked across the floor, enclosing the three men in a circle of hell.

From his pocket, John removed a sealed glass flask, nearly filled with a thick, milky fluid. The liquid undulated with a pearly glow as he poured it on Twig and repositioned the cage atop the pyre, ignoring Twig's panicked screech. Ram studied the placement—Twig's cage formed one point of a triangle, DeSalvo made the second, and Ram made the third. John stepped into the center—a point within a triangle within a circle. A wall of cold, blue fire lifted around him.

Ram studied each move, each chant, each juncture, and his mouth dried with the knowledge of what was to come. The anchor—DeSalvo. The flesh—Twig. The magic—him.

Three to give; one to emerge.

Inexorably, the black flame snaked from the circle. He stared, mesmerized. When it touched him, it would sear away all power, every last molecule. Leave him empty. Again. Leave him with the madness. He couldn't overcome this loss. Not a second time.

The flames reached his feet. His back shrank from the spreading pain, and nausea rose in his throat. He couldn't do it. With a burst of light, he freed himself of the paralysis spell and leaped from the flames.

A crook of his thumb, and the green crystal jumped back into his hand. The athame was now outside the circle, but he'd crush the crystal with his bare hand, if necessary. He tensed, beginning a silent chant, ready for one last blast.

"Shall I hurt her?" John asked softly.

"She'll be dead if you succeed."

"No, she won't. She's outside the circle. I've always protected her."

Ram looked at Natalie. She was watching him, not her brother or John, and shaking her head. Then, she looked down at her belt, her arms straining at the bonds. He suddenly became aware that his cell was vibrating with a text message. From Natalie? With a fingerling of power, he touched the buttons.

John is Charles. His gaze flew to Natalie's and she nodded.

A big change in the equation. Charles was a high-level talent, but one who wanted Natalie alive. The walls of this room would be attuned to protect him as well. If Ram shattered the crystal, he might not kill Charles, but everyone else in the room would be gone.

Throat tight, he lowered his gaze to the athame, then back to Natalie. Could she free herself? Swallowing hard, feeling as scoured as sand-bleached bones, he locked his gaze with her. He dropped the crystal and stepped backward into a flame of boiling ink.

Pain screeched through him as the flames devoured the magic in his skin. He heard the screams of DeSalvo and Twig as similar wildfires burst around them.

His tourmaline shriveled, scarring his chest. Vials of oils and herbs popped, filling the hot black room with lavender, sage, patchouli, lemon. The aromas of his craft stung his eyes. Crackling energy coalesced above him, a shimmering, vibrating layer with the essence of his power.

The flames reached deeper, flaying him layer by thin layer. He clenched his fists against the hell, fighting the

loss with every particle, fighting to keep the power collected in a thick cloud over his head.

Natalie watched Ram step backward into the flame and
a scalding hurt consumed her skin. If only she could
shout how much she loved him, how much she'd been
a fool. Her eyes watered with the strain of trying to see
him through the acrid smoke. The crackling fire and
scorching heat consumed the stifling air.

A nudge at her hand snapped her gaze downward.
Val! The dog began to chew at the ropes. *No! You'll kill
me or yourself!* Natalie tried to stop her, but the gag muffled her shouts and the tight bonds kept her from moving away.

To her shock, she realized Val was slowly, patiently,
making progress.

No person can undo these bonds. Val wasn't a person.

She stared at Ram. That flame was consuming his
magic, and he'd willingly stepped into it. To give her a
chance to live.

Damn Charles and damn the obsession that drove him.

With a snap, the rope tightened back against her
arms, and Val whined. *Your fear will be used against
you.* The bonds strengthened on her fear.

Time she quit puppet-jerking to the touch of magic.
The man she loved was in agony, being drained of all
that mattered to him because of her, because he was an
honorable man who had tried to protect a rare bird and
a bothersome woman. That was all she needed to know.

She didn't know what changes the future would create in him, or her. Five years ago, she hadn't realized a
brewing hurricane named Katrina would take her city,
her dog, and ultimately, in a roundabout way, her husband. You couldn't tell the future. You could only make
your plans and then grasp the joys of today.

For her, that meant Ram. And his magic.

A wet tongue lapped at her palm, drawing her attention back. Val had unleashed her. Carefully, making sure she wasn't seen, she let the rope fall to the ground, away from her skin.

Val collapsed on the floor. The dog had been hurt by John's—no Charles's—attack. She swallowed back the tears in her throat. "You hang in there. I'll get Ram out of this. He'll heal you."

If Charles hadn't taken her gun . . . Ah, hell, shooting him probably wouldn't work. Gonna have to rethink that gun-as-protection strategy. If only she understood better how some of this magic stuff worked.

Break the triangle, break the spell. Free Ram and hope he knew what to do next.

As Charles turned his back, she silently ran forward. Scooping up the athame and hoping it had some miraculous power, she dashed through the wall of flame. God! That hurt! Fire flayed her skin, scorched her hair, even her brows and lashes. She stumbled to the other side.

Charles was reaching high into the storm coursing between him and Ram, the true fuel of the spell. The phoenix charm glowed. The black flames around Ram soared, hungry and consuming.

Catching sight of her, Charles roared, "Do not interfere," and sent a streak of flame toward her.

She twisted the pendant, frantically shaking the liquids to purple. The flame bounced off her. Ten minutes.

Without thinking, she leaped into the black inferno.

Ram had collapsed. His skin was as gray as ashes. Sweat and smoke and tears burning her eyes, she knelt. Oh, my God, he wasn't breathing. He had no pulse. She thrust the athame into Ram's hand, wrapped his fingers around it, laid his other hand atop his ring. He didn't stir. Not even the power of his ring could cheat death.

Ram was dead.

No, no, no. She grabbed his shoulders, pulled him up into her arms, and then kissed him. *Take desire from me, take life from me.* She kissed him hard, urgently.

Charles threw flame and pain and madness against her, but the pendant protected her and the man she embraced. Drop by drop, red and blue separated themselves and still Ram did not stir.

"Take my magic," she demanded as the last red drop settled.

Suddenly, Ram shuddered and the black flames around him sucked downward, consumed by an unseen, roaring vacuum, accompanied by the flames around Nat and Twig. Ram's arms snaked around her, plastering her against him, kissing her back, just as hard, just as urgent.

Kent, kent.

Warned by Twig, Natalie jerked around. Charles, his face contorted beyond reason, had pulled her gun.

Before she could think, before she could even register the sound of the firing, Ram's athame flew past her cheek and buried itself into Charles's wrist. The gun dropped from his hand.

Ram shoved himself to his feet, dragging her up with him. "Strip away glamour, strip away deception," he chanted, his voice low and icy.

Charles's face reappeared behind the guise of John.

"The wheel turns, the wheel returns, bring forward, bring back, so mote it be," Ram said, his voice commanding. In a quick motion, his hands jerked down. "*Esrevere!*" The flames roared up from below, a spinning torrent of energy that shot forward, passed over Charles, then snapped back.

Magic boomerang.

Natalie scrambled over and retrieved her gun as Ram

stalked over to Charles. Gun in hand, she hurried to Nathaniel.

Blessed be, he was alive. Joy pirouetted in her chest, as she bent to touch him.

His eyes fluttered open. "Damn, body-slammed, but I'll live."

"Damn right you will, Nat."

He nodded behind her. "Ram needs you."

She glanced over her shoulder. With Ram's sweat-slicked face cast into relief by the burning pyres, he appeared akin to the very demons he fought, as he stood, hand outstretched, over Charles. The flames in the room spread, consuming everything in crackling haste. Not magic, just the destruction of fire.

Natalie lifted her brother. "Ram," she shouted. "Get Val."

Startled, he glanced around, as if seeing the flames for the first time. She grabbed Twig's cage and, bracing her brother, stumbled toward the door. "Come on," she shouted.

Ram scooped up Val, her weight seemingly of no notice, and followed Natalie out. Charles stumbled along behind them, through the library and study, and outside to the dense foggy night. Behind them the library collapsed into a conflagration of oils and herbs and ancient linen, filling the air with thick acrid smoke. Outside, Ram stalked over to Charles, still holding Val, his athame outstretched as he chanted, low and compelling. "This is for Natalie," he growled, and Charles screamed.

Racing back to Ram, Natalie grabbed his iron-hard, unyielding arm. "You're killing him."

"He won't attempt to resurrect the Phoenix then," Ram answered coldly.

"This is his way, not yours."

"You know nothing about my way."

"Yeah, well, we'll rectify that later. I sure as hell don't want to watch you tried as his murderer." She pointed her gun toward Charles. "Can he cast any spells against me?"

"No."

"Then go." The sound of a distant siren cut through the night. "Hear that? The police will be here soon. I texted Zolton our coordinates with the proviso that if I didn't text every thirty minutes he should call the police." She shoved at him. "Get going. Take Twig and Val. They need your healing and you can't do that with the police milling about." She planted her feet and turned her weapon on her husband. "I'll deal with the police. Go! Get Val, you're wasting time."

She glanced over to make sure Charles was behaving, and when she turned to look at Ram he'd vanished.

Chapter Twenty-five

Ten days later, Ram stretched out his feet, sprawling in a chair as LaMarr devoured a Bud's Broiler chili dog.

LaMarr regained consciousness four days after the arrest of Charles Severin. LaMarr had insisted on returning to the Grill, but remained bed-bound for a week. Ram stayed near, giving the strength that only another Mage could share. He'd left to get some sleep and spend time with Val only when Estrella came from Baton Rouge to replace him.

He hadn't seen Natalie.

Now that LaMarr was well on his way to recovery, it was time for good-byes.

"You boomeranged the Phoenix spell so that Charles was the one stripped of magic?" LaMarr asked enthusiastically. "I never heard of a Mage doing that."

"Nothing else would have worked in a room built by Severin." And he couldn't have done it without Natalie's kiss.

"It's good to have you back to full strength. I'm not sure anyone else could have stopped him."

"The Mages would have found a way."

"Heard you've been talking to the brother."

"Just some advice, where to go, who to see if he wants more training. In the end, he came through. He started with the wrong mentor, but I think his heart knows the right path."

"Was Charles working alone?"

"With the animal smuggling." Ram paused, recalling the "temple," calculating the resources Charles would have needed to stay concealed for months. "There may be others."

"How will you track them?"

"I won't." He owed LaMarr the courtesy of truth. "I'm through."

LaMarr paused to wipe chili grease. "You're quitting the Mages?"

"You don't quit the Mages, you just stop working on their business. I told the Council I was retiring."

"Because of Natalie? Because of what she'll write about you?"

He and Natalie might have been lovers, but he feared her loyalties lay in many other places besides his bed. Once, the prospect of exposure would have meant serious preventive measures, but with Natalie . . . He would let her write whatever story she must and then deal with the aftermath.

The secrecy of the Custos Magi was another matter. He couldn't regret the lie he'd told her, claiming he knew nothing of the brethren of magic. He might be revealed as a lone wizard, but the Magi would remain hidden, free to pursue their necessary work.

And so, he'd stayed away from her. Knowing he couldn't come back to her unless he'd made his own peace with his choices.

"Because I love her," Ram said simply, admitting it aloud for the first time, amazed at how good and right it sounded. He loved her, not just because of the sex or synergy, but because the whole of her was a mirror of his soul.

"You'll miss the work you did for us," LaMarr warned.

"I will," Ram admitted, his chest tightening.

"The world will be a more dangerous place."

"What can we hope for, if I'm lying to her every day?"

"What can you hope for if you're denying your talents?"

Ram gave him a man-to-man grin. "There are compensations."

Ram's grin faded a little. Question was, would the lady have him?

She had come into the library for him. That gave him hope.

LaMarr was studying him, seeing more than the words. "Go to her," he said quietly. "You, and she, will always be welcome at the Haven Grill."

"Your story isn't what I expected." Adam Zolton threw the copy on Natalie's desk.

She leaned back in her chair. "I know, but it's damn good, so you're going to buy it anyway, aren't you?"

"Magicians, fog, a phoenix spell gone awry. Our readers will love it." He perched at the corner of her desk. "What did you leave out?"

"For a while, I pegged you for Phoenix."

"Me? A megalomaniac?"

She shrugged. "You do have a certain arrogance, and you did take that photo of the original magician called Phoenix."

"I've taken photos of a Gay Pride parade. Doesn't mean I started swinging a new direction." He gave her a steady look and changed the subject. "You were open about your personal involvement in the story."

Natalie squelched the imp of curiosity, the one that wanted to start digging into the mysteries of Adam

Zolton. This was neither the time nor the place. "I screwed myself once before by not being honest, and Nathaniel wanted his story told."

"Your brother's working at the Dark Phoenix?"

"At least until Charles's trial is over." Then, she suspected Nat would be off again, his wanderlust always stronger than hers. Saints, she would miss him. She stretched and glanced around the emptied office. "I hadn't realized it was so late. Will you excuse me? I have to get ready for an appointment."

"Next assignment—we got reports of an alien abduction over in Biloxi."

She groaned. "How about a professor with conspiracy Armageddon theories?"

"Go for it." He got to his feet but paused in the doorway on his way out. "By the way, you're welcome to roost in the office as long as you need."

"Now that the story's done, I'll start looking for my own place."

When he left, she turned off her desk lamp and went through the shadowed building to her small room. It was more crowded now, and her chest tightened at the sight. All she owned, right there.

A useful motto: Never own more than you can carry in two suitcases and a backpack.

With Charles alive, even though he was in prison, she no longer had the rights to her—no, his—home. He had told her to get off the property. She'd packed her two suitcases and backpack and left, just her, her private tears, and her newly activated divorce papers.

At least Althea had made sure Twig and Twyla were protected, but there was no place for Feng. No place for her. Not there. Not in Ram's life. He'd made that abundantly clear, disappearing the past couple of weeks.

He wouldn't give up the magic, he couldn't. So, it was past time for her to show him that she loved him, magic or not. She trusted him, even with his magic. Trouble was, he hadn't given her the chance. She braced her hands on her knees and stood. Well, that was about to change.

Ram's doorbell rang just after he finished a strenuous tai chi workout. He knew who was at the door before he opened it, and not because of Val's happy barks. From the way the power within him sparked. From the sudden lightness in his heart.

He opened the door. "Natalie."

"Ram."

She looked so good. Her hair was blond, and she was dressed more elegantly than he'd seen her. Beaded black top, narrow skirt, and high heels that showed off painted toes and did very sexy things to her legs.

He swallowed against a mouth gone impossibly dry, and stirred against the nylon of his shorts. Gripping the doorjamb, he fought the urge to pull her into his arms and mess up that perfect red lipstick and find out what kind of underwear a woman could wear beneath such a sleek, tight skirt.

Instead, he managed, "You look good."

Natalie ran a critical eye over his shorts and sweat-soaked T-shirt. "Is that the new attire for dinner at Antoine's?"

Damn, he'd forgotten. "Dinner with my father."

"The invitation was never rescinded, so I considered myself still invited."

Her smile sent his breath into a dizzying spin. "Give me ten minutes—"

She laughed softly.

"What?" he asked.

"Difference between men and women. We cream, shave, shampoo, exfoliate. Ten minutes wouldn't even get the shower done for a woman." She gestured to the porch swing. "I'll wait here for you."

His chest squeezed around the realization that she wasn't expecting him to ask her in. To come here must have taken tremendous courage, and a belief that together they had something rare.

He took her hand, and then stepped back into the house, opening the door for her, drawing her after him. "Come in."

The pulse in her wrist played an erratic rhythm as she nodded and accepted the invitation. Leaning over, he breathed deep her powder and perfume scent. "You're wearing Magic. My sister, Isis, developed that scent."

"I know."

She couldn't have sent a clearer message. He kissed her cheek, then the corner of her mouth, leaving him heady with needing her. Rising, he nodded toward the living room. "Make yourself comfortable. Would you like something to drink? Wine?"

"No thanks. Go shower, I'll be fine." He was halfway to his bedroom, so he might have imagined her last words. "I have all the temptation I need."

Natalie glanced around the black and white elegance of Antoine's as Ram greeted the maître d' with the familiarity of an old New Orleanian. She couldn't remember the last time she'd eaten here. Maybe some society dinner, but those times were faded, washed away. Tonight was a fresh slate and she was looking forward to meeting Ram's father, Royal, and the woman he'd asked to be his third wife. Curious whether the bride-to-be was older than she was, she laced her hand through Ram's crooked arm as they followed the maître d'.

"Is Langdon our waiter tonight?" Ram asked.

"Of course. When Royal Montgomery reserved the private room, he would have no other."

A private dining room for four? Natalie felt Ram's arm tense as they walked into the private room. The *crowded* private room. Her courage collapsed. Was any adult member of Ram's family missing?

He stopped at the entrance before anyone noticed them. "I'm sorry, Natalie. I didn't know they'd all be here."

"Why are you sorry? Wanted to ease them into the idea you're with the nosy fringe reporter who flings belligerent accusations when she's drunk?"

"What?" He scowled, as he laid a hand atop her hip. Definitely masculine you're-mine-we're-together body language. "I want you to like them. I thought that would be easier if you met them more slowly. Not en masse."

He wanted *her* to like *them?* She wasn't the one on trial? The one having to make nice in the desperate hope she wouldn't be thrown on the streets? She grinned at him. "I'm ready for 'em."

His confused look told her he didn't have a clue how he'd made her happy.

"We've been spotted." His arm slid around her waist, snugging her close.

An older man detached himself from the group and crossed the room to join them. The four men were Ram's father and brothers, she decided. There was a strong family resemblance among those four, one Ram did not really share.

His father clapped him on the shoulder, shook hands. "Isis and Darius came for a visit, and she insisted on joining us, and when the others heard . . ." He shrugged. "We haven't seen much of you."

"I know." Ram offered no excuses or apologies.

"But you're here; that's what counts. You didn't say who you were—" Royal turned to her, gave a visible start.

Apparently Ram had decided advance notice wasn't the smartest policy.

He skimmed through the introductions. After a hesitation almost too brief to notice, and a glance at Ram's protective hovering, Royal took her hand, too well bred to give in to either curiosity or unhappy recognition. Instead, he welcomed Natalie with cordiality if not warmth and introduced his fiancée. Natalie offered him a mental apology for her earlier uncharitable trophy-wife assumption. Royal's fiancée was a gracious woman in her midfifties.

Not looking nearly as gracious as Royal was the clump of testosterone known as Ram's three older brothers: Thomas, Beau, and Jack. Thomas and Beau looked at her with mistrust; Jack's expression was more active dislike. Well, it had been his wife, Leila, she'd accused of witchcraft and dealings with the occult.

A waiter took Natalie's order for club soda with lime, and then there was nothing left but to become a Christian to the lions. Ram kept his hand planted at her waist as they strolled toward the cluster.

A lot of solid New Orleans here. Thomas ran the family construction business, the Montgomery logo a familiar, respected sign as the city rebuilt. Beau was an assistant DA with a stellar record of conviction and a swirl of political-office buzz. Jack was a university professor with a reputation for brilliance.

All watching them with wary eyes. All gathered around Leila as a shield.

Natalie's stomach curled on a spurt of acid. *Outsider*. She lifted her chin and met their eyes directly. Ram's family was important to him, she knew that, and she didn't want to be the cause of a rift. He might want her to like them, but it was as vital that they like her.

Ram nodded at his brothers, as his fingers curled tighter on her waist. "You all know Natalie Severin."

"DeSalvo," she corrected.

"Yes, we know her," Jack said bluntly as he shifted

close to his wife. Leila would set the tone of the night. Gracious or vengeful?

With a penetrating glance at Ram, Leila stepped away from the Montgomery males. She took Natalie's hands, and gave her an air kiss above each cheek. "Forgive us. We were all so thrilled that Ram planned to bring a woman to a family dinner that we intruded. Of late, he has been much the recluse."

"Nothing to forgive," Natalie murmured.

Leila looked over her shoulder, spoke to the Montgomerys. "Natalie and I made our peace some time ago," she said softly. "Irrationality in the wake of sorrow can be forgiven."

Then she turned back, her hands tightening just a little. "Natalie promised not to pursue a story on her ill-founded notions about me. Isn't that right?"

Natalie bit back a smile. Oh, the woman was good, considering Natalie had never promised not to pursue the odd links she'd found. She'd apologized for her behavior and her accusations and admitted that she didn't think Leila had any connection to Nathaniel's disappearance. Consigning Leila's story—but not the questions—to a back burner now labeled off-limits, Natalie returned the smile. "That's right," she promised.

The exchange broke some of the awkwardness. The waiter brought her drink and the conversation drifted to a variety of topics, some easy, some generating heated discussion until a dark-haired couple breezed into the room. "Sorry we're late," the woman called out.

During greetings, Natalie studied the couple. Here was the family resemblance; Ram could be twin to the woman. They were very close in age. No doubt this was his younger sister, Isis. Surprisingly, the one sibling she'd never seen. Hadn't someone once said that Isis lived overseas? Morocco maybe?

As Ram greeted his sister, she saw a bond that was missing between Ram and his brothers. Acceptance? The brothers' attitude held loyalty, but also a touch of wariness, as though they weren't quite sure of Ram. Because of his magic?

Isis's husband caught Natalie's eye. Woo-hoo, now there was a sexy man.

Ram's grip on her shoulder tightened just the slightest, and she caught him frowning at her. "I can look," she whispered. "He is gorgeous."

"As long as you're just looking," he growled back.

"I never poach. Besides"—she leaned closer and ran her fingers up his spine—"of all the fine specimens in this room, you're the only one powering my lustful thoughts."

"Keep those thoughts simmering. For later."

"You didn't think I came for the crème brûlée?"

He threw her a startled glance, and then smiled.

Heat going south again. Still, she couldn't contain her curiosity. There was a resemblance between Darius and Ram. Not in looks; their features were quite different, although they were both tall and dark-haired. No, it was something indefinable. When Darius took her hands in greeting, gave her the same dual cheek kiss as Leila had, she had her answer. The tingling of power bubbled up her arms. Magic. Yes, magic, yet somehow different.

Isis joined them. "Ram, Darius wants to talk to you. About a . . . lion. Been terrorizing some people he knows. He thought you might have some suggestions." When Ram hesitated, Isis waved her hands at him. "Go. Natalie and I can girl-talk."

Ram raised his brows at Natalie. She'd seen through Isis's flimsy excuse, too, but nodded her okay. "Your sister and I need to get to know each other."

Of all the members of Ram's family, Natalie suspected it was Isis's approval she needed.

Ram leaned over and gave Natalie a kiss. "She's a tiger, but you're a match for her," he whispered. With that, he straightened and strolled to Darius.

"I like your taste in perfume," Isis said with a grin. "A perfumer shouldn't have favorites, but Magic was always special to me."

"It's an elegant scent."

Isis ran an approving eye over Natalie. "Classy outfit. I like the blend of brocade and beads."

"Thanks. I got it at The Attic." She named an uptown consignment shop.

"I thought it looked vintage. Clothes aren't made with such care to detail anymore."

"I like to shop there; you can find some unusual pieces and it's affordable."

"How long have you known my brother?" Isis asked, their chitchat completed.

Natalie took a chance. "Long enough to realize he's a man of considerable talents."

Isis sucked in a breath. "The . . . talent. It's back? Strong?"

"Yes."

"Solomon be praised." She glanced over at Ram, in close discussion with Darius. "I thought we'd lost him. The rest of the family was just glad he was back. They couldn't see; he was further from us than he'd ever been. His spark wasn't there. Now, it is." Abruptly she rounded back to Natalie. "You write for NONE, don't you?"

Tired of veiled and not-so-veiled suspicion, Natalie crossed her arms. "Is this where I get the warning not to expose him or I'll have you to deal with?"

"Yes," Isis returned boldly.

"You *and* your husband?"

Isis sucked in a breath, her cheeks turning a little pale. "What do you mean?"

"I mean he, Leila, and Ram aren't like the rest of us." She leaned closer. "I'm a reporter for NONE. That's not going away. I notice things and I pry. That's not going away either, and nothing I say will assure you of my intentions."

"So what are your intentions when you walk out of this room?"

Hopefully making passionate love with your brother was the first answer, but she didn't think that reply was too politic. "That's between me and Ram."

Something of Natalie's love must have leeched into her voice and expression for, after a long moment, Isis nodded and Natalie knew she'd passed the test.

Isis glanced briefly at her husband before she returned to Natalie. "I'll give you one piece of advice. Embrace the power within him and accept that, at times, the siren call will come above all else, even you. If you can't, the struggle and doubts will tear you apart."

The rest of the night passed muster as an impromptu family gathering. Natalie seemed to settle into his family, but Ram didn't feel the tension leave him until at last he and Natalie were alone inside his home. Well, not quite alone, as they went through what was becoming a pleasurable ritual. Greet Val, play with her, while the edge of desire grew acute between the humans, until at last Val returned, contented, to her warm bed.

Then, he turned to Natalie, a hunger for her blazing through him.

Afraid she would disappear if he stopped touching her, he drew her fully into his embrace. God, she felt so good, and he had ached so to hold her. He kissed her, slowly and deeply. His palm stroking up and down her spine, he tried to show her his heart. But he knew Natalie needed words

"I love you," he said, unable to manage anything fancy. Just the raw truth.

She held him tighter, and broke into a huge smile. "I love you, too."

Joy blossomed in his chest. Deep and sustaining, it fired the magic that flowed through his blood and bones with a description-defying richness. The wind whispering outside, Val's snores, the scent of oregano and thyme from dinner, the pressure of Natalie's hands on his chest—every connection deepened and bloomed. At the center was Natalie. The fine texture of her breath caressed him. Her perfume combined with her skin for a uniquely beautiful scent that left him dizzy.

"I'm a man of magic," he warned. "I can't deny that, or be anything else."

"You can be my lover, a vet, a brother and son, a pool shark."

"Are you asking me to give it up?"

"Ask you to cut out the fiber of your nerves and the membrane of your cells? Never. I only meant . . ." She paused, as if searching for words. "You were willing to step into your worst nightmare, to be stripped of all you cherish—"

"I cherish you."

"—stripped of your magic in order to protect me."

"I had no choice."

She scowled at him. "Will you stop interrupting me when I'm trying to tell you something important?"

He grinned at her. "Something like you trust me."

"Oh, yeah, summarize it in three words."

"It works. I love you. I trust you."

"I have something for you." She handed him a manila envelope.

"What is it?" He moved down the hallway, slinging his jacket on a coat rack and loosening his tie.

"Open it."

They reached his bedroom. He sat on the edge of the bed to open the envelope. She knelt behind him, her slim skirt hitching up to her hips, and started working the buttons on his shirt. Trying to remember to breathe, he slid out the contents. Her article, "Phoenix Unrisen."

"So am I going to have the anti-magic crowd picketing my sidewalk in the morning?" he asked, trying to lighten the moment.

"Read it." Her hands slid beneath the buttons, stroking lightly over his chest.

Made it damn difficult to read the article, but he managed to skim through, then he turned to her in wonder. "You didn't mention me?"

"That's why I told you to leave the library. Too many people would know."

He sucked in a breath as she undid the button on his pants, and she delved down. His world realigned.

"I'm a reporter for NONE, and I've just buried a huge piece of a name-making story. If that doesn't prove I love you, that I trust my future to you, then I don't know what will."

"Oh, Natalie." He turned and cradled her face in his hands. He had been given a precious gift. "You don't have to prove your love to me. I feel it in every breath I take, because I feel how much I love you." It had taken him long enough to recognize the emotion, even though his magic had kept smacking him upside the head with the evidence. "And not because of any resonance theory."

"I know," she interrupted. "Make love to me, Ram."

To hell with explanations. With spare motions, he rid himself of the rest of his clothes, then helped her with hers. "Your body is so incredibly arousing," he murmured, stroking her belly. "Curves and muscles and a cute rear end."

She seemed to crave the feel of him, too. Soon, they tumbled onto the bed. She reached out and pulled him over her, spreading her legs for him to settle intimately against her.

He covered her with his body, the tip of his penis finding her hot and wet and ready. "I love being inside you," he murmured as he slid into her, giving her every part of him, except the one part she didn't want.

"Let me feel your magic. It's part of you, and it will be part of our lives."

"Are you sure?" He stroked a hand across the soft jagged strands of her hair. "In bed, too?"

"I'm positive. I finally learned: It's not the magic that determines the man, but the man that shapes the magic."

Softly he began a musical chant, as he rolled over and positioned her on top of him. His hips moved in control, in and out, each stroke filling, then emptying her.

Natalie looked down at him, her hands a restless slide along his chest. His black hair was loose and soft against his neck. The planes of his face now looked a little harsh. His dark eyes were not focused on her, but on an inner compulsion.

"Take my hands," he said, his voice musical.

Embrace the power within him.

She laid her hands over his, and Ram resumed the chanting.

Around them, the darkness thickened, until she could see nothing of the room. Only the green glow that surrounded them, pale at the edges, but where their hands joined a brilliant emerald.

At first she felt nothing but the strength and warmth of his palms beneath hers. Then, the tingling started, ri ing from the contact of his hands on hers, from the slide of his penis in and out. It lingered like an airy caress inside her, even as the desire for him rose like a sharp tide.

Wait a minute. Where was the passion in that magic touch? Where was the fury and the life? She glared down at him as he carefully watched her. As if she was some injured turtle.

She reared back and slapped the mattress. "Don't!"

Immediately he started pulling back.

"No, I mean don't do it half-assed. I'm baring myself, giving you all of me. I want all of you in bed with me. Don't hold back a thing, not passion or fury or power. I need to know what that feels like."

"You should take it slow."

"I don't do slow." She pulled herself off him, cringing at the wrenching loss. But she couldn't stand to be the only one losing herself. She couldn't be waiting to find out if memory would rear its ugly head. "I'm going to take a shower while you figure out where the energy went."

She was halfway to the bathroom when he caught up with her. The waves of fury bounced off her.

"How can you be so desirable and so infuriating? Is this what you want?" H grabbed her hips and kissed her, his lips crushing hers. His body was hard, hot, engulfing her as he backed her up.

No tingling power, this crashed against her and dove inside her with waves of pleasure so intense that she could barely breathe from the onslaught. Desire spiraled until she was dizzy with need.

"Yeah, this is what I want." She grabbed him closer. Color sparked around them like fireworks. Emerald and ruby and topaz.

They were in the bathroom, and he was still backing ᵤₚ, into the shower, where, with a flick of his hand, d on all four pulsing shower heads.

ᵣ from all directions, his hands, his tongue, his

magic, his desire all pulsed against her, filling her with brilliant steam. Not a particle of skin was left untouched, not a piece of her mind or her heart left without a caress. Despite his anger, she felt his tender cherishing.

She gave back to him, kissing and holding him with frantic effort.

"Turn around," he growled. "Put your hands against the wall."

With a thrill riding in her throat, she complied. The feel of his soapy hands was slick along her sides, her breasts. He teased her nipples with one hand, while the other stroked in her curls below. One finger, two fingers slicked inside her already ready sex. She couldn't see him, she could only feel him and the spiraling magic.

"Spread your legs." He nipped at her ear.

She spread them, and his cock surged inside her from behind. His flesh, his magic, filled her and pumped until she shouted and clawed at the slick walls. He shouted his release, too.

Then, heedless of their soaking wet bodies, he carried her back to bed. As soon as they were on the bed, he came inside her again.

The magic was less frenzied, but deeper. Strengthening, growing more powerful with each word of the chant he spoke. The emerald color took on a milky cast and began to swirl, like fog. Binding their hands together in magic. Moving up her arms, her elbows, her biceps. She started to pull back, but Ram's fingers tightened around hers.

"Stay." More request than command.

Certainly she could handle this, the embrace of her lover's magic. The sensation of his hands, his tongue, his lips, stroked every part of her, even though physically only his cock and his hands touched her. Color soaked inside her, blurring the edges of their separate bodies as the smooth-flowing river became a torrent.

Their hips moved and joined, harder, faster, until turbulence exploded inside and around them. They fell silent, and the desire was reduced to a tingle inside her, fading and releasing her body.

"Fantastic." Natalie stretched atop Ram in his bed. She gave him a tiny kiss on the corner of his mouth.

"My pleasure. Literally." His lazy hand down her back sent an echoing shiver of need skittering through her spine. "No reluctance?"

She smiled against his sweaty chin. "Not a lick."

"No licks?"

She chuckled softly, then stuck out her tongue and stroked his neck.

His arms tightened around her. "Keep that up and you'll be in trouble again. Just give me a few minutes. Like twenty."

"Didn't take that long the first time."

"Yeah, well that was two recoveries ago."

"With all that synergy flowing?"

"Magic, not Viagra."

"Try this." She started kissing him again, their lips melding into sweet accord.

He traced the curves of her sides, the indentation at her waist, her hips, reigniting the fire. He rolled her over, so she sank deep into the bed. He shifted to her side, never breaking the nipping, sucking, exploring kiss between them.

"Ten minutes," he murmured.

The power grew between them, a flow of energy so rich her body purred with desire. Not one-sided, not a flow born of fear and domination, this came from two in harmony.

Yet it wasn't the magic she craved. That was lagniappe. She wanted him. The taste of his tongue on hers. The so-right pressure of his lips. She wanted the way he groaned when she used her mouth around him, and she wanted the heat of his skin on hers and the hard embrace of his fit body.

He stroked into her, rejoined their bodies, and for those moments nothing else mattered.

"I could never have written a story about you," she murmured, "titled 'Phoenix *Unrisen*.'"

When he broke into delighted laughter, she knew the real power between them. Love.